TO: Lynn

Thank you!

All my best,

~ Oma xo

MW01592850

THE
RING

GINA MARECKI

Halo
PUBLISHING
INTERNATIONAL

ISBN: 978-1-63765-009-7
LCCN: 2021906958

Halo Publishing International, LLC
www.halopublishing.com

Printed and bound in the United States of America

To those fighting silent battles. Stay strong.
Use your voice. You've got this.

PROLOGUE

I *was darkness. I was hate. I was fear, anger, and pain…*
There was no hope in my life.
I could not breathe or settle myself, always living in fear…
Until I ran.

Then, I found a refuge from the pain. I could live again, breathe a little bit, even if I was always looking over my shoulder. But then…

I became numb. There was nothing that brought joy or the spark that made me feel alive. Good thing was, there was nothing that brought the fear or the darkness anymore either.

Time passed in a predictable routine: wake, eat, work, eat, sleep, repeat. Mundane, numb, predictable, and that was good. I was not looking for more; I was happy in my safety net. Then, there was a small spark; I found a light. A brief feeling that brought me back to the land of the living. I was not sure I wanted that, but once there is a spark, a flame spreads.

I began to feel, to experience emotions that had lain dormant. But there were still some things I wanted to avoid…

Then…then, I met him. He brought a new light, a bigger flame, blinding at times, not threatening to burn, but making me feel so high that I never wanted to come down. Preventing me from catching my breath, but not in fear—this was the kind of breathless you read about. When we were together, all felt right in the universe, as if this was supposed to happen.

It was normal. I was relaxing into him; there was a feeling of light, calm, love, freedom…peace. Drunk on love, drinking it in, I dared to say I was happy. I found me, the me that I had lost. I began to like myself again.

Honestly, I liked me better when I was with him because I escaped the darkness. Once there is that kind of flame, a fire blazes.

CHAPTER 1

Ashley had to get out of there. The need to escape was overwhelming; it filled her entire being. She anticipated the feel of the frigid air against her skin, craved the sharp intake of air into her lungs, even if it burned.

She needed to feel alive, to experience something other than the hell of being stuck in this prison. The shut-in feeling was making her crazy, and she needed a break from her torturous thoughts.

She'd been trapped in that house for way too long. On top of that, the entire town had been without electricity for three days, which felt like weeks. She laced up her Nike trail runners, pulled her merino wool hat down over her ears, slipped on her North Face running gloves, and headed out for a run, not caring where she ended up. The sky was a clear, brilliant blue, the air crisp as it touched her skin, her breath forming white clouds in front of her.

The roads were covered with snow and chunks of ice, littered with pine branches. Downed power lines lay across several of the side streets. Large trees and branches were strewn across lawns and roadways. Neighbors would think she was crazy to be out in this mess. They would think she was crazy to stay indoors in that mess, too, if they only knew what was going on in that perfect little house…

What else is new? Ashley had stopped caring what others thought. The neighbors heard enough from her house to know something wasn't right. Her world was caving in, and she'd had enough. This life was suffocating her, closing in on her every day she stayed, always a black storm cloud hanging over her head, even when the most glorious blue sky and golden sun shone bright over the horizon.

Ashley started a slow jog to warm her tight muscles. The rhythm of her movements calmed the tension in her shoulders and neck. She breathed in the cold air deeply, filling her lungs with life.

Her outlook was bleak; she didn't foresee any escape from the hell she was living in. She was a prisoner in her home, as well as in her mind.

Breathing difficult.
Pulse quickened.
Push the thoughts away, keep running, and push harder.

No matter how hard she pushed, it was difficult to keep the grim thoughts at bay. She had bigger problems than her intrusive thoughts. She needed a plan to leave. To finally be free.

Sweat streaming down my face.
Every muscle straining to go farther.

It would be wonderful to be free, but she would have to be on the run.

Heart beating fast.
Muscles screaming.
Hold on; do it.
Fight through it.

Once that happens, nothing will ever be the same, she thought as she maneuvered around a fallen pine in the road. She dodged a downed telephone pole and wire.

Don't think.
Push harder.
Bring it. You've got this. Do not break.
Feel the rush.
The road was wide open ahead of her.
She thought, *There is nothing left to do but run.*

CHAPTER 2

Ashley tried to match her roommates' stride, but she was always the one who fell behind. All night, she had practiced breathing exercises to calm her nerves, but they hadn't helped.

Tamara twisted her hair into a ponytail. "Oh my God, this weather has ruined my hair."

"It's so humid!" Eliza whined.

"We have to talk to some of the hot frat guys tonight." Jodi let out her devilish chuckle.

Giggling, Ashley tried to fit in and join in the excitement. It was senior year, and she'd never been to a frat party. Ashley had accepted the invitation, begrudgingly, at her roommates' insistence. She spent most afternoons engulfed in research projects for her classes, as well as working at her part-time job at the art-supply store.

Ashley's roommates had drawn her out of her shell, slowly at first, and now she did everything with them. She decided leaving her hometown and dysfunctional family and attending Maryland College for Art in Baltimore was the best choice she'd ever made. This life was free of her family's stifling criticism, her parents' incessant fighting, and her constant walking on eggshells to avoid conflict with them.

"Here we are." Jodi's voice brought Ashley back to the evening. Jodi turned to the group. "Are we ready?" She paused for effect before entering the party.

"Ready," Tamara affirmed.

"Yes! Let's do this," Eliza exclaimed.

"Ready." Ashley adjusted her shirt and fidgeted with her bracelet.

It took Ashley a few weeks at school to realize she didn't have to walk on eggshells anymore. No one cared if she left something out of place, or if she liked to draw and listen to music while she studied. It was freeing not being criticized. Her roommates eventually became her best friends and new family.

Jodi pushed open the door as a steady beat of music grew louder, inviting them into the dimly lit room. Bodies moved to the rhythm of the music. Their group made their way through the line of college girls awaiting entry into the party. Ashley lifted onto her tiptoes, peering over the heads of the other girls and eyeing the group of undulating bodies and unlimited access to alcohol. She was excited to venture out and meet new people, but Ashley was still leery of some of the college fraternity guys, having heard rumors of them partying way too much and using girls then dumping them.

Bouncers were checking IDs at the door even though any girl was allowed in. Guys, on the other hand, were turned away unless they were in the frat. Jodi flashed her grin to the bouncer as Ashley stayed toward the back of the group and held her student ID tightly.

Her shock of blonde hair caught the eye of everyone she passed. Her slightly curvy figure, long, sleek hair, and bright green-blue eyes made her stand out in a crowd. She remembered her roommates giving her a look-over when she first arrived at school; they told her later that they'd thought she was a snob since she was so quiet. They soon became fast friends, however, especially after Ashley let her guard down and began to enjoy having a circle of friends she could rely on.

Jodi tossed her hands up toward the ceiling and let out a "Whoo-hoo!" signaling her entry into their destination. Ashley approached the tall bouncer with sandy-blond hair and handed her ID to him. He smiled, revealing dimples that made her weak in the knees.

"Hello, Ashley Ragan." He handed her ID back to her, not breaking eye contact. "Have a nice time, but be careful in there." He held on to the card a moment longer, still holding her gaze.

He had taken her by surprise when he said her name, but then she realized he had read her name off her ID. "Thank you." She couldn't break away from his dancing ice-blue eyes. He was tall and lean, had a fade hairstyle, and apparently skipped a shave that day.

"Ash! Come on!" Jodi called to Ashley, waving her on.

Eliza tugged on her arm and teased, "Earth to Ashley."

"Yeah, coming." She smiled at the bouncer then followed her friends.

He waved as she walked past. "See you later."

"Wow." Eliza hooked arms with Ashley. "Um, I hope there are more here that look like him."

Ashley laughed as they pushed their way through the crowd, bumping into another group of friends Tamara knew. They continued making a path toward the small kitchen where a group were gathered around a makeshift bar. Cases of beer were piled on the kitchen counter along with an array of spiked seltzers, a large cooler of a red punch, and a keg by the back door.

"Ashley, want a spiked seltzer?" Jodi held up two cans of a strawberry-flavored drink.

"Yeah, sure." Ashley gladly took a can, happy for the distraction.

They stood off to the side of the main room, surveying the crowd for any guys worth talking to.

Two guys from the beer line approached them, swaying and slurring their speech. "How's it going, ladies?" The tall one with way too much swagger leaned against the wall next to them.

Tamara nudged Ashley and rolled her eyes. Eliza sipped her beer and turned away.

"We're doing all right. Hey, there's Samantha!" Eliza hooked arms with Ashley, maneuvering her away from the beer guys.

"What are you doing?" Ashley held on to her can, preventing it from spilling.

"Those guys were creeps! Did you see him checking you out? He couldn't even make eye contact; he was too busy staring at your chest."

"Oh my God." Ashley laughed as she rushed forward, coming up short as she bumped into a guy with his back to her. "Oh, I'm sorry." She held up her hands, avoiding contact, then glared at Eliza.

He turned slowly, smiling wryly. "Hello, again."

Her breath caught as she realized it was the bouncer from the door.

"Running out of here already?"

Eliza giggled. "Hi, no, we were getting a change of scenery." She stood taller.

"I didn't get a chance to introduce myself before. I'm Stephen." He held his hand out to Ashley.

She swallowed hard then shook his hand, feeling an instant spark.

His eyes were alight as he watched her.

"Nice to meet you." Their hands maintained contact a moment longer.

"Where are you running off to?" He kept his attention on Ashley as Eliza attempted to move into his line of sight.

"We're trying to get away from a couple of drunk guys that were hanging around us." Eliza flung her hair off her shoulder and smiled.

"I'm sure you'll have a lot of guys following you around tonight."

Ashley wasn't sure to whom he was directing the comment, but he kept his attention on her. Ashley chuckled. "Yeah, right." She tried to keep the conversation going.

"Well, the wrong guys, anyway!" Eliza guffawed and fluttered her lashes as she leaned in toward Stephen.

He glanced sideways at Eliza then turned back to Ashley. "Well, stick by me. I'll help keep the unwanted guys away." He gave Ashley a smirky grin as she fidgeted and giggled.

"Awesome." Eliza rolled her eyes at Ashley, turning away to win the attention of the older frat guys.

"So, do you go to school here?" Ashley twisted the can and bit the inside of her cheek.

"No, no, I'm actually the hired help." He laughed.

"Um…" Ashley furrowed her brow.

"I'm their bouncer. The guys hire me to work the doors so they don't have to do it." He put his hands behind his back and leaned against the wall.

"Oh, that's cool. How did you get that gig?" Ashley took a sip of her drink.

"I'm a police officer, graduated from the academy. I'm waiting to hear back from a couple of potential jobs. In the meantime, I take side jobs for extra money." He looked down sheepishly, his face blushing slightly. "It's not glamorous, but bouncing pays well."

"I bet. Do you get in a lot of fights?" Ashley nodded toward the two guys they'd escaped from across the room, who were now starting to shove one another.

"No, I try to avoid that part."

"That's got to be challenging, especially with crowds like this."

Right at that moment, one of the two guys shoving dropped his beer on the floor.

Stephen sighed and nodded. "Yeah, Danny can handle that." He pushed off the wall and waved across the room to another bouncer. "They hire a couple guys to man their parties. Idiots." He clenched his jaw then turned his attention back to Ashley. "So, what are you going to school for?"

"I'm an art major." She held up her hand, heading off the questions. "I know—what will I do with that? My minor is graphic design, to use in the real world."

"That's great. No judgment here. Sounds like you have a good backup plan if your art isn't hanging in every gallery in the state. Are you a painter, a sculptor…ah…"

Her cheeks lit up, turning pink from his attention to her. "I draw and paint mostly." She settled against the wall next to him.

"Nice." He grabbed a water bottle from a nearby table and unscrewed the cap, taking a long sip. "Tell me more; where are you from?"

"I grew up in Easton, Pennsylvania. Moved here for school." Her insides twisted, searching for something more exciting to share about herself.

Stephen nodded, smiling. "Do you miss home?"

"Ah, no. My friends are here now. No real desire to go back."

Ashley took a long drink. There was no way she would go back there, recalling her last two disastrous trips home. Thanksgiving break started out great; then the shine of her family wore off quickly. All the unwanted feelings of being back in that house resurfaced.

When she returned home for the longer winter break, she was run-down and sick, sleeping the first two weeks home. Her mother wrote that off as stress from school and exams. However, Ashley knew that wasn't the case. She was happy at school; that was where she flourished and had amazing friends. It was a noticeable difference when she returned to school; those feelings of stress and anxiety melted away, and she was happy again.

Her stomach churned. She decided to redirect the conversation to avoid questions about her family. "What about you?" She finished her seltzer.

"I grew up outside of Richmond, Virginia. Lots of crime, I needed to get out of there. So, I hear you with not wanting to return home. I always wanted to be a cop, but not there."

Ashley's shoulders relaxed, tension fading, happy that someone else shared her sentiment of not loving their hometown. Her friends never quite understood her feelings, always returning from vacation with stories of their cool families and friends back home. "Are you looking to be a cop in Maryland?"

"That's the plan. Or near Alexandria, Virginia. Playing the waiting game. Perfect world, I'd like to work in Maryland and buy a nice house with lots of property in Virginia."

"That sounds great."

"What are your plans after school? Graduation this year, right?" Stephen turned to face her.

Ashley sighed. "Yeah, done in May. I can't believe it. I have a couple interviews lined up with graphic design companies here in Baltimore. It'll be good exposure to get out there, even if they aren't in the exact location I want to be in. But I'm not sure what I'm doing." She fiddled with her empty can, knowing she needed to line up other job prospects and start apartment hunting, again reflecting that she would never return home after graduation.

"Hey, want another drink?" He motioned to the kitchen.

"Sure." She pushed off the wall, happy for the change of subject.

"Come on; I'll get you through this motley crew."

He walked beside her and cleared a path. Sorority girls stopped and admired him, trying to get his attention. The frat guys stepped aside, not uttering a comment to Ashley as she passed.

"Wow, you have quite a presence here." She reached for a different flavored seltzer this time.

"I've worked a lot of their parties this year. They're familiar with me." He glanced down at his water then around the room.

Ashley nodded and stifled a smile, flattered that this popular, gorgeous guy was talking to her. She was attracted to his laid-back attitude and his killer looks. Stephen was a charmer, impressing her with his stories of his time in the police academy, while continuing to be a gentleman.

Time passed in a flurry of new faces, more drinks, and people watching. Ashley saw the time on her phone read 3:00 a.m. "I can't believe what time it is." She scanned the room for her friends. Jodi and Eliza were talking with a group of guys; her other friends were playing a drinking game with a larger group.

Tamara waved and approached Ashley. "We've been trying to get your attention. Looking a little busy," she whispered under her breath.

Ashley shushed her friend.

"We're thinking of heading back. You ready?"

"Yes, sure." Ashley turned to Stephen. "We're gonna head out in a bit."

"Yeah, figured, everyone's winding down. Want a ride back to your dorms?" He looked between Ashley and Tamara. "Probably shouldn't walk back this late. Ya know, a lot of creeps out there."

"Yeah, um, let me check with my friends." Ashley turned to Tamara.

"I'm sure we'd all like a ride. I'll check." Excitedly, Tamara rushed to the girls. Ashley saw her pointing to her and Stephen and the girls nodding.

"That's kind of you, but you don't have to leave the party."

"No, I want to. I can drop you off wherever you'd like."

Tamara, Jodi, and Eliza walked back to them. "Okay, we're in if the offer still stands."

"Yeah, let's go. Give me a minute to check out with John." Stephen touched Ashley's arm lightly. "Be right back."

"Oh my God, seriously, Ash. He is gorgeous." Eliza held on to Ashley's arm.

"Nice, Ash. Walks in and scoops up the hottest guy here." Tamara shook her head.

"And probably the oldest guy here. How old is he?" Jodi peered around, looking after Stephen.

"Okay, I saw you all talking to a bunch of guys. Did you meet your dream frat guy?" Ashley nodded across the room, toward the guys shotgunning beers.

"Yeah, not so much. Some of them were cool. We're invited back Sunday for flag football." Jodi shrugged, smiling at her roommates.

"Cool." Ashley saw Stephen across the room, shaking hands with someone she assumed was John.

"He is hot. I sure hope he'll be here for touch football. I'd let him tackle me." Eliza nodded her head, looking Stephen up and down.

"Yeah, Ash. Watch out; you are gonna have to fight girls off for him."

They saw three of the sorority girls flocking Stephen, tilting their heads, trying to get him to stay. He smiled and touched one of the girl's shoulder, then walked toward Ashley and her friends.

"Seriously, hot," Jodi agreed.

"Ash, you hit the jackpot with this guy." Tamara twirled a strand of hair.

At that moment, Stephen strode up to them, smiling a dreamy heartbreak smile, glancing from one of them to the next, then settling on Ashley. "What'd I miss?"

"Nothing. Just saying how lucky we are to get a ride." Eliza stifled a giggle.

Ashley took a deep breath and shrugged.

"Perfect, then let's go." He placed his arm around the small of Ashley's back and led them outside to his pickup truck.

***

"Can I see you again?"

Ashley felt her friends watching as Stephen stood close to her in the parking lot of her dorm. Her friends were trying to steal his attention, dancing on the bed of his truck.

"Stephen, want a drink? Come on." Eliza popped open another beer.

He didn't pay any attention to her. "Tomorrow?"

Ashley blushed as he took hold of her hand. "Yeah, okay."

"Is this okay?" He referred to their hands clasped together.

"Yes." She laughed nervously as he moved closer to her. She could feel his breath on her cheek.

"Good." He motioned toward her, his lips so close. "Is this okay?"

Her heart raced as she pictured him kissing her. "Yes," she breathed.

Slowly, he touched his lips to hers. The warmth of his mouth made her melt against him. He placed his hand on her cheek, drawing her closer; every move was slow and primal, making her want more.

She placed her hand on his chest, wanting to touch him, loving the taste of his kiss.

"Mmmm." He placed his hands around her waist, biting his lip. "Wow, Miss Ashley. You're hard to resist."

Ashley drew closer to him.

He kissed her cheek, then trailed his lips down her throat. "Want to come home with me? Then, we won't have to wait until tomorrow to see each other. We could have breakfast."

"I c-can't…" Ashley stammered.

"Why not?" he whispered, kissing her lightly.

Pulling back, she felt she could be convinced to do anything when he looked at her like that. She had to talk herself back to reality. There was no way she could go home with him.

"I can't. Tomorrow, we're heading to DC. We've had this planned…" Her resolve was melting as he brought his hand up to cradle her face.

"You're so beautiful. How can I let you go?" He sighed, kissing her again. "Well, I guess I'll have to wait until Sunday, then."

"Yes, Sunday," she repeated, hypnotized.

"Okay." He held her hands and stood back from her. "I hope I can survive."

"Stephen, stop." She nudged him, and he pulled her toward him again.

"For real. Last kiss, then I promise I'll let you go back to your friends."

"I had a great time. Glad I went to the party." She realized her face hurt from smiling so much.

"Me, too." He kissed her lightly.

"Oh, I should give you my cell number." She reached for her phone in her back pocket.

"That would be helpful. Even though I could probably find you if we forgot." He pulled his phone out of his jean pocket. "I'll text you my number."

She gave him her cell and received the text with his number, saving the contact information. *Stephen Keene.*

The girls hopped off the truck and called to Ashley, "We're heading in! See you up there!" They cackled and stumbled toward the front door of the building.

Stephen watched them go then closed the back of his pickup truck. "All right, Ashley. Sunday it is." He kissed her one last time.

As he drove away, she thought that Sunday couldn't come soon enough.

CHAPTER 3

Ashley woke up and stretched, smiling to herself. Her mind wandered to Stephen and his kiss, how she felt next to him, how he might be the one… She needed to calm down. She just met him, yet she could picture them together beyond their one moment. She rolled onto her stomach and stacked her chin on her fists, dreaming of their day together on Sunday, wondering what they would do.

She reached for her phone and checked messages. There was a new text alert. She sat up smiling, hoping it was from Stephen. Tapping on the icon, she saw it was. Her stomach had butterflies as she clicked on the message.

Stephen: *Morning, sunshine.*

Oh God. Those two words sent her reeling; she grinned from ear to ear as she lay back down. *How the heck am I supposed to answer that?*

She started to type, *Good morning.* She thought she had to say more than that, so she added, *Last night was fun.* She backspaced to delete what she'd entered and tried again. *Great time last night.* She stopped and deleted again; then she typed, *Can't stop thinking of you.*

She typed and erased a few more times, then settled on keeping it simple.

Ashley: *Good morning. I had a great time last night. Thanks again for the ride back.*

She hit Send and cringed. Maybe he wouldn't even respond; he was probably busy. That was something she couldn't worry about at the moment. She needed to get herself ready for their day trip to DC. She put her phone aside and shuffled over to the bathroom she shared with Eliza, deciding to shower first.

As the water streamed over her, she thought about how much she and Stephen had in common, especially not wanting to return to their hometowns. He didn't talk about his family, and she was relieved he didn't ask about her family. Her jaw tightened.

***

At a young age, Ashley wanted to escape her homelife. Running away wasn't an option, although the thought had crossed her mind. She discovered drawing as an escape from the stress. She began to daydream, fantasize of a different life, one with a lot of siblings and parents who never yelled. She had a sister, Elizabeth, who was two years younger. They grew up in middle-class America with a dad who worked a white-collar job at a big corporation in town and a mom who stayed home.

Elizabeth and Ashley looked alike, but Ashley had a unique beauty from the day she was born. Her mother bragged about her beauty in one breath, and then was disgusted with it in the next. People would compliment Ashley or comment on her exquisite eyes, and her mother would tell them she "would need more than her looks to make it in this world." Then, she would proceed to brag about all of Elizabeth's academic achievements.

As Ashley approached her teenage years, friends would comment that boys must be lining up at the door for Ashley, but her mother would snidely comment something to the contrary, leaving Ashley feeling as if she were at fault.

***

Ashley stepped out of the shower and towel-dried her hair. She wiped the steam away from the mirror, staring at her reflection. She was happy despite the bad childhood she'd had. She liked her life away from home. Dressing in jeans and a T-shirt, she wrapped her hair in a towel and returned to her bed. She pulled out her sketchbook and pencil.

***

As a child, Ashley began to sketch the images and colors she dreamt of; soon, drawing became her escape. She would spend hours drawing

22

a scene that played in her mind, at times filling half of her sketchbook with images full of brilliant colors. The feelings and emotions she felt inside flowed onto the page. She began with colored pencils and then turned to oil paints and pastels. Over the years, she invested in brushes, easels, sketch pads, and large paper for painting. This helped her escape the dysfunction of her childhood and carried on as she entered high school.

Taking an interest in art classes, she dove into all things related to drawing and painting. She eventually became part of the art club, winning awards and art contests. In high school, she was inducted into the National Art Honor Society, which earned her a hefty scholarship to college.

There were moments of calm in her childhood home, a cycle of normalcy, and Ashley remembered occasionally being happy. Then, things would explode. From up in her room at night, she would hear her parents yelling and bury her head under the pillow to block them out as the arguments escalated. She never remembered what the arguments were about, never wanted to hear the details. She always felt as if she were the cause of the stress because, the next day, her parents would yell at her if she didn't do things exactly as they wanted.

She never knew if it was going to be a good day or a series of bad days at home. There were whole blocks of time that she could not recall from her childhood; she always had a feeling of being unsettled and was haunted by memories in which things weren't quite right. Ashley pushed the uneasy feelings away by dreaming of an alternate reality.

***

She finished drawing a house with a wide-open field surrounded by flowers and a sky outlined with clouds. She could hear banging around in the kitchen as she walked out to the common room of their apartment. They had two bedrooms and two bathrooms; each bedroom was shared by two girls. The common room had one large sofa, a love seat, and two chairs and led to a galley kitchen with a small table and chairs as well as a breakfast counter.

"Hey." Ashley sat at the counter.

"Hey. How are you feeling today?" Tamara glanced at her sideways as she poured a cup of coffee.

"Pretty good. I drank a ton of water last night." Ashley flipped through a magazine that was on the counter.

"That's not what I meant." Tamara smirked and leaned on the counter. "The hottie bouncer? What's his name?"

Ashley pushed away from the counter and walked into the kitchen to grab some coffee. "Um, you mean Stephen?"

Jodi came waltzing in smiling.

"Yeah, we couldn't pry you two apart!" Eliza called out from their bedroom.

"Okay, guys. Funny." Ashley turned and leaned against the counter, stirring her coffee.

"Seriously, Ash. How'd you guys leave it?" Tamara asked kindly.

"We're getting together tomorrow." Ashley couldn't suppress her grin.

"Nice." Tamara drank her coffee and nodded.

Ashley sat back down at the counter.

"No flag football at the frat party, I'm guessing." Tamara smirked.

"I don't think so." Ashley smiled.

"Come on, ladies; we should head out soon." Jodi filled her to-go coffee cup and stood by the door.

"Jodi's ready; we all better hurry up." Tamara strolled to her room to finish applying her makeup.

"I still have to dry my hair!" Eliza peeked out of the bedroom in her towel, hair dryer blaring.

Every outing began this way, and Ashley grinned, loving the predictable personalities of her friends.

***

"Want to check out a party tonight?" Stephen sat on the couch in Ashley's apartment. It was Sunday, and her roommates had left for the touch-football frat party.

24

"Yeah. Where?" Ashley busied herself in the kitchen, looking in the fridge for a beer or something she could offer to Stephen.

"At my buddy Patrick's house. He throws great parties." Stephen scanned the apartment.

Ashley found two Bud Lights in the bottom drawer and joined Stephen on the couch. She handed him a beer.

He took both bottles and twisted off the caps, handing one back to her.

"Thank you. Cheers." She took a sip, contemplating the party. "Party sounds like fun." She would go if she could spend time with Stephen.

"You'll have a good time. Great group of friends. You'll see how a real party is thrown. None of the frat-guy BS." He took a long drink from his beer then put his arm around the top of the couch. "You okay? You seem quiet."

Ashley shifted in her seat and laughed. "No, I'm great."

"Okay." He chuckled. "Do I make you nervous?" Stephen leaned closer.

Ashley felt her pulse quicken. "No," she lied, fidgeting in her seat.

"Good." Stephen edged closer to her. "Can I kiss you?"

His voice pulled her in. Ashley nodded, unsure she could speak. He lowered his lips, softly touching hers. She closed her eyes and returned the kiss.

He peeked at her. "If we keep this up, we may not end up going anywhere."

***

The party was located thirty minutes from campus in a small close-knit neighborhood of cape-style houses. His friend's house was a modest cape on a square lot, with a fenced-in, lush backyard. There were several cars lined up on the street in front of the house.

Ashley rubbed her hands together as she surveyed the house and the people stepping out of their cars. She saw two couples walking in with cases of beer and platters of food. She bit her cheek. "I feel bad; I didn't bring anything." She sat on her hands to stop from shaking.

"No worries, I brought the drinks, spiked seltzers that you like, and I have some food for the grill." He put his hand on her leg. "Hey, don't worry. You'll have a good time."

She released her hands from under her legs and held his hand. "Okay."

"Great." Quickly, he kissed her on the lips and jumped out of the truck to retrieve the food and drinks from the back seat.

Ashley tentatively climbed out of the truck, checked her reflection in the window, and tugged on her shirt.

Stephen stood beside her. "Wow, you look gorgeous. Maybe we shouldn't go in." He kissed her again, making her legs weak. "Would you mind carrying this?" He handed her a small cooler.

She took it, happy to occupy her hands and feeling as if she were contributing something to the party.

They walked toward the side of the house, and Stephen opened the white picket fence to the backyard, letting Ashley enter, then followed close behind her.

"Hey, Stephen!" A tall man—she'd call him a guy, but he was definitely older than the boys she hung out with in college—approached and gave Stephen a backslap.

"Hey, man. Thanks for having us." He turned to Ashley. "Patrick, this is Ashley. Ashley, this is Patrick." Stephen grinned widely as he placed his hand along Ashley's back.

"So nice to meet you, Ashley. Please come on back; make yourselves at home." He gestured to the backyard where picnic tables and lawn chairs were set up in groups. Music was blaring from the house; there was a table set up with a bar and coolers of beer, ciders, and waters.

Ashley noticed everyone there was paired up. She tucked her hair behind her ear and shifted the weight of the cooler.

Stephen handed the large cooler and bags of food to Patrick and took the small drink cooler from Ashley, motioning toward the minibar table. "Let's get a drink."

"Definitely." Ashley followed Stephen, stopping when he introduced her to his friends.

"Hey, Bobby. How's it going, man?" Stephen fist-bumped Bobby.

"Sup, Stephen. Been a while." He pulled Stephen into a hug.

"Bobby, this is Ashley. Ashley, Bobby. We grew up together." He threw his arm around Bobby's shoulder.

"Nice to meet you, Ashley." He shook her hand then turned to Stephen. "What, now you're dating beauty queens? Where did you meet this guy?" Bobby moved away from Stephen and closer to Ashley.

She chuckled as Bobby held on to her hand.

"We met at her college. She's an artist," Stephen boasted, grinning.

"Oh, smart, too. Well, I'm honored to meet you." Bobby bowed slightly then whispered, "Hey, if he bores you, let me know. He might have the looks, but I've got the personality."

"All right, all right." Stephen patted Bobby on the shoulder. "I think she's figured out I have a personality."

Ashley laughed out loud, enjoying the banter. Stephen reached for her hand and grinned sheepishly.

"Yeah, yeah." Bobby waved them off. "Get yourselves some drinks; then come back over."

"Hey, Stephen!" another friend called, waving from over by the bar.

"You ready to meet the rest of these guys?" Stephen leaned close, his warmth calming her.

Ashley took a breath. "Yes, ready." She pulled his hand closer as they made their way to the bar and into the thick of the party.

CHAPTER 4

"**C**an you stay? Come on; hang out."

His ice-blue eyes drew her in. The right thing to do would be to leave. She hesitated, glancing around his apartment.

He leaned back on the couch, nodding to the seat next to him. "Stay for one."

She shrugged; staying for one couldn't hurt. "Sure, why not."

"Great." He hopped out of his seat and strode to the kitchen. "Spiked seltzer okay?" he called from the other room. "Or a beer?" He peeked his head back around the corner, holding on to the wall.

"Seltzer would be great," she called out then sat on the couch, sitting on her hands. Her insides felt like fluttering butterflies as he returned with his swagger and smile.

He popped open the can. "For you. Cheers." They touched the cans as he sat down next to her then took a long drink. "Ah, perfect." Settling back, he placed his arm around the top of the couch. "So, how you doin'?" He raised a brow, nodding and using a New York accent.

She covered her mouth, almost choking on her drink. "Oh my God, stop."

"I know, right?" He laughed out loud and took a drink from his beer. "Tonight was fun."

"I had a great time." She looked down at the can, tracing the design with her finger.

"See? I told you my friends were cool." He nodded and took a drink.

"They are super cool, for sure." She smiled, remembering the night.

"I think you're super cool." He moved a strand of her hair away from her shoulder, tilting his head toward her.

She laughed. "Well, I don't know about that."

"Yeah, I do. You are fine. Best-looking girl there. Not that I was looking around." He held his hands up.

She pushed his chest lightly. "Stop."

"I'm serious. I couldn't take my eyes off you. Neither could the guys there. I had to tell them you were off-limits." He looked down at his hands and tilted his head. "Maybe I shouldn't have spoken for you. Maybe you wanted to talk to the other guys."

"No, I wanted to be with you." She reached for his hand, remembering how he held hers at the party, how he would place his arm around her shoulders when they walked through the crowd. Her pulse raced.

"Really?" He looked at her sheepishly.

"Really."

His eyes searched hers. "Can I kiss you now?"

"Yes." She looked away, her cheeks pinkening.

He leaned toward her, his lips lightly brushing hers. Her breath caught in her throat as he placed his hand on her cheek, drawing her toward him and kissing her deeper. She was lost in his touch, his mouth warm on hers, his tongue moving against hers seductively. She placed her hand on his chest as she drew closer to him.

He broke from their kiss and breathed, "Ashley," trailing kisses down her cheek and along her neck.

She almost spilled her drink, so she placed it on the table next to her. He, too, placed his beer on the table and turned toward her with a smirk.

Ashley wrapped her arms around him, feeling his strong back and shoulders. His hands roamed lower toward her waist, one resting on her thigh as he resumed kissing her mouth, building the tension. His hand moved under her shirt, resting on her waist, the heat of his touch sending a thrill through her. Her excitement increased as she realized he'd mentioned his roommates were away for the weekend; they had the apartment to themselves.

"Ashley, I want you so much." Stephen's voice was hypnotic.

Before she knew it, Ashley was standing, he was lifting her shirt over her head, and she was pulling his shirt loose from his pants. He took her hand and led her to his room. They removed each other's clothes hastily, Stephen almost tripping in an attempt to take off his jeans, laughing as they tumbled into his bed. His hand moved down her waist and rested on her hip.

The streetlight outside, the only light in the room, shone through the window, revealing Stephen's sultry expression. His breath deepened, and he paused, watching her, looking at her body. Then, he moved over her, placing his mouth on hers.

She felt dizzy from the alcohol and from being so close to him as she pressed her body against his, arching her back, straining to be closer, feeling his heat. He removed her underwear, placing his hand on her skin, warming her entire body with his fingers. She didn't want to wait to have him inside of her.

He tugged his boxers down his legs and off, kicking them aside. She placed her hand on him as he sighed. He positioned himself above her and pushed against her. Her breath caught in her throat as he moved, pressing harder, deeper.

She'd never felt this way with other guys. She didn't have that much experience, but nothing before had ever been like this. The silkiness of his skin on hers, his breath as he moved faster, his lean body straining against her, her hands pulling on his back, digging her nails into him. The rush, the silence, the calm enveloping her as he lay on top of her, the sweat of their bodies mixing together. His heart beat loudly against her as he calmed his breathing until he fell asleep. She lay still until she, too, slowly drifted off, not wanting to ever move from his arms.

They had fallen asleep tangled up in each other and Stephen's sheets. She woke early, remembering she had a class in the morning. Stephen tried convincing her to stay and blow off class, but she knew she couldn't miss it since her final was coming up. Stephen insisted on driving her back to her dorm.

The clock on the microwave read 7:00 a.m. when she stumbled through the door of her apartment. Tossing her things aside, she crawled into bed and set her alarm for 9:30 a.m. so she could catch up on sleep. She fell asleep remembering details of their night together and dreamt of Stephen and their bodies entwined.

***

Her alarm sounded, bringing her out of her blissful state. Ashley had to drag herself out of bed since she'd not gotten much sleep after being with Stephen the previous night.

She blindly dressed, walked to the small café located in the building next to hers, and grabbed a coffee and a bagel. As she walked across the parking lot toward the Art Building, in her morning-after haze, she thought she saw a truck that looked like Stephen's parked next to the tennis courts. She smiled; maybe he came to surprise her. Or maybe he was visiting one of his friends from the frat.

She stood at the crosswalk, waiting for a bus to pass by, sipping her coffee and sneaking a bite of her bagel. After the bus pulled away from the sidewalk, she continued walking across the street with a group of other students who had exited the bus. Looking toward the courts, she saw the truck was gone. *Maybe I imagined it was him, wishful thinking.* She smiled to herself and continued on to class, smiling at the memory of him and how he'd held her all night.

***

"Why can't I see you tonight?" Stephen tapped his pen on the dashboard of his truck.

"I have to study. I'll be at the library all night." Ashley rummaged through her backpack, looking for her textbook.

Stephen sat back in his seat, tossing the pen aside. "Mm-hmm, yeah, what about after?"

"I'm going to be there all night. This is for my final. Sucks." She looked around the room, wondering where her textbook was. "I can't find my freakin' book." She knelt to look under her bed.

Stephen peered out the windshield. "Yeah?" He turned the key in the ignition, firing up the engine. "Who else will be there?"

She stood, looking again at her desk. "Jodi, Tamara, and some others from our group. We have one group final; then I have to study for—"

"Right. Well, let me know when you're done. Maybe you'll have time for me." He ran his hand through his hair.

"Stop, you know I would rather hang out with you. Finals are almost done." She turned off the light on her desk.

Stephen was silent. He put his truck in Drive and pulled away from the curb.

"Are you still there?" Ashley stood at her desk and glanced out the window.

"Yeah, yeah, I'm still here." His voice was clipped.

She leaned toward the window as she saw a truck that resembled his pulling out of a parking spot across the street.

"Hey, Ash, we're leaving. Ready?" Jodi pulled her backpack onto her shoulder, calling Ashley.

Ashley glanced away from the window. "Oh yeah, one sec." She turned back to the window, and there were no cars outside, no sign of the truck. "Um, I have to go. I'll text you later?"

Stephen rounded the corner onto the main road. "Yeah, sure."

"Okay." Ashley bit her fingernail. "Don't be mad. Are you around Thursday night? I'll be done with my final around four. We can grab dinner."

"Yeah, sounds good." He huffed.

"All right, talk to you later? I miss you." She sank into her desk chair.

Stephen's grip loosened on the steering wheel, and he took a deep breath. "I miss you, Ash. I feel like I haven't seen you in a while. Sorry for gettin' on to you."

"It's okay, Stephen." Her shoulders relaxed.

"Come on!" Jodi called out to her.

Ashley stood quickly and whispered into the phone, "I miss you."

"I can't wait to see you." He couldn't stop thinking of her body against his; he was craving her touch. "Thursday," he breathed.

"Yes." She smiled at the thought. "Bye." She pressed End and shoved the phone in her backpack. "Coming!" She hurried out, closing the door behind her.

Stephen thought of turning his truck around and driving back to her dorm. He'd been sitting outside of her dorm for forty-five minutes. He thought she was telling the truth. If he didn't have to be at work, he would have waited until she left. He didn't trust her friends, but he was trying to trust her.

***

"I can't go. I'm meeting Stephen tonight." Ashley checked her phone then shoved it in her back pocket.

Tamara gave Jodi a look, and Jodi shrugged. "All right, you're gonna miss a great party."

Tamara fixed her hair in the mirror. "More frat guys for us." She turned to Ashley and smiled broadly. "See you later." She turned toward the door.

"Bye." Ashley waved as they left, their giggling and singing echoing down the hall.

Ashley checked her phone again. Stephen was supposed to text when he was off work, which should have been around eight. Her phone read 9:15 p.m. and still no word. Huffing, she sat back in her chair, spinning her phone on the desk.

She should have gone to the party and met him afterward, or had him pick her up there, but he didn't want her to go. He said the last party of the year was the worst one. *"Cops always break them up and bust everyone there if there are drugs, which it is guaranteed there will be."*

She didn't want to get in trouble the last week of school. She'd warned her roommates, but they laughed.

"He doesn't want you meeting anyone new," Jodi teased.

"Why would you want to go? I'd go with Stephen over this party if he was my guy." Tamara smirked.

Ashley had to agree; she'd much rather be with him than be pawed by the frat boys. Yet, he wasn't here or calling, and she was stuck in her dorm, waiting, while everybody else was at the big party.

Ashley was left with the silence of the room. She checked her hair, touched up her makeup, and paced.

About half an hour later, her phone buzzed.

Stephen: *Hey, sorry, running behind. I'll be there in 30.*

"Seriously?" She tossed her phone on the desk, shaking her head. She saw the textbooks in a pile, remembering she had a final on Monday, so she thought it wouldn't hurt to check her notes. Distracted, she checked her phone as the time crawled.

True to his word, thirty minutes passed, and a text came through saying he was parked out front.

Ashley stood up from her desk and peered out the window. His truck was parked on the side of the road. Quickly, she put her things aside, grabbed her key and her phone, and turned off the lights, leaving the dorm.

She jogged down the staircase then slowed. She shouldn't hurry for him; he'd made her wait. She pushed open the stairwell door that led to the entry hall and saw Stephen standing outside the glass door, hands in his pockets, looking at the ground, shuffling his feet.

He looked up and smiled sheepishly.

Ashley slowed and pushed the door open. "Hey."

"Hey, Ashley. I'm so sorry." He took his hands out of his pockets, looking remorseful. "I didn't mean to keep you waiting. Are you mad?"

"No, I…" Ashley hesitated.

"I know; I'm an idiot." He held his hands out. "I'll make it up to you. I promise." His blue eyes danced, and he smiled broadly.

"It's okay. I'm glad you're here." She couldn't resist him.

He moved toward her and hugged her close. "I couldn't stand it if you were mad at me. Forgive me?" He hovered, his face close to hers, his lips inches away.

"Of course," she breathed, and he kissed her, one hand on her cheek, the other wrapped around the small of her back.

"Excuse us." Two girls moved to open the door Stephen and Ashley were blocking.

"Oh, sorry." Ashley held on to Stephen as they stepped aside, letting the girls by. Ashley covered her mouth, giggling after they passed.

"Oops. You ready to get outa here? Go have some fun?" Stephen took hold of her hand.

"Yes, definitely." She held his hand tightly, ready for the night ahead.

CHAPTER 5

A s they rounded the corner, she saw it. It was the most perfect Victorian-style house in historic Alexandria, with a white picket fence and a plush green lawn.

Stephen slowed the car.

"Well, here it is." He pushed the gearshift into Park and leaned across the dashboard. "What do you think?"

"Stephen, oh my God." Ashley looked from him to the quaint house in disbelief. "It's so cute!"

"Want to check it out?" He smiled, pleased that he knew what she liked.

"Yes!" Ashley exclaimed and grabbed her handbag.

Stephen stepped out and jogged around to her side of the car.

Having only graduated two weeks prior, Ashley couldn't believe they were at this turning point in their relationship. Ashley's graduation was a celebration her family barely acknowledged, let alone attended.

***

Stephen was there the entire ceremony, with a bouquet of flowers and a huge grin. He took her out to dinner at the most upscale restaurant she'd ever been to, ordering filet mignon and lobster tails. At dinner, he'd surprised her with the news of his job offer as a cop in Fort Washington, Maryland. His plan was to move to Alexandria, Virginia, just as he had told her at that first party when they met. Stephen asked her to come with him. They could find a house together; she could get a job, and they would start a new life.

That was exactly what she wanted. A readymade life far away from her hometown. She had no need to explain any of this to her family since they didn't care to participate in her life. She took his hand and said yes.

Stephen stood up from the table and pulled her into a hug, then lifted her off her feet, kissing her. "Woooo!" he exclaimed and looked around, basking in the attention from the other diners.

"Stephen." She grabbed his hand, her face turning crimson as she held him close.

He kissed her again and sat across from her smiling. "We are going to have the perfect life together."

That weekend, Stephen helped her pack up her belongings from her dorm and moved her stuff into his place, which had room since one of his roommates had moved out after graduation from the academy. They began to look for houses in Alexandria and the surrounding towns, which led them to this home.

***

Ashley stepped out of the car, taking in the picture-perfect house before her. Around the front of the house, there were flower gardens filled with daffodils and roses. The taupe exterior was accented with white and black trim and a black front door. There was a small front porch with railing that matched the picket fence. As Ashley walked up the brick staircase leading to the porch, she noticed it was worn, but had character. The tower—or round room, as Ashley called it—was adorned with wide windows.

"The agent is here, so we can go right in. Ready?"

"Ready." She steadied herself.

Stephen opened the door and stood aside, bowing slightly. "After you."

"Why, thank you." She smiled and scooted into the entryway, stopping to admire the tall ceilings, the bright light coming in through the transom window and windows along each side of the door. The foyer was a soft light grey with gleaming hardwood floors.

The real estate agent strode through the foyer toward Ashley and Stephen. "Hello, you must be Stephen. Catherine, nice to meet you in person." She shook his hand then turned to Ashley. "And you must be Ashley. I've heard everything about you from your husband."

Ashley shook the realtor's hand and looked at Stephen stiffly. "Uh, yes, nice to meet you."

Stephen hurriedly chimed in. "Thank you for seeing us so quickly. I couldn't wait to show Ashley." Stephen held Ashley's hand, beaming.

"Let's show you around, then, yes?" Catherine led them from the foyer to the round room on the right.

Ashley nudged Stephen's side. He smirked, giving her hand a squeeze.

"Ooooh, I love this room. The light is beautiful." Ashley moved toward the turret windows, where there was bench seating. Light streamed in, filling the room with a warm glow. The walls were a pale Victorian blue. The room was furnished with a love seat, a simple, whitewashed wooden coffee table, and matching end tables. The cushions of the love seat matched the cushions on the window seats, a pale blue-and-white print.

Across the foyer was a larger rectangular-shaped family room with a large couch, love seat, and chair with maple end tables. There was a television on a stand in the corner. The room was lined with windows that faced the front yard.

"This is great, isn't it?" Stephen turned to Ashley.

"Yes, perfect." She caught his gaze.

"Let's move on to the kitchen." Catherine walked down the hallway that led to an eat-in kitchen.

There was a small half bath off the hallway. The kitchen was spacious, with maple cabinets and granite countertops. An oak-stained and white-painted country-style table and six white wooden chairs were to the right in a nook. There was a window above the sink and a large bay window in the nook. To the left was a door that led to the backside of the house.

Retreating down the hall toward the front of the house, Catherine mentioned that the stairs led to two bedrooms—a master and a guest room, which could be used as an office. Between the two bedrooms, there was a bathroom in the hallway. Overall, the house was in good condition. Some of the wood floors had normal wear and tear, some creaking spots, but it added to the charm of the house.

Catherine led them back downstairs and told them the house was for rent, fully furnished, except for the beds in each room.

"Would you give us a moment?" Stephen smiled at Catherine.

"Yes, of course. Take your time. I'll be in the kitchen." Catherine retreated to the kitchen, and Stephen and Ashley walked outside to the front porch.

"Well, what do you think? It will be available in two weeks." Stephen inhaled deeply, looking around.

"I like it. The rent seems affordable. Once I get a job, I'll be able to split it."

"We don't have to worry about the rent. We can make this work." He held his breath.

Ashley thought about it. The space had everything they wanted. An option for an office, a small backyard on a nice street, and it was far away from Ashley's hometown. It was perfect.

"I'm in"—she smiled, holding his hand—"husband." She giggled.

Stephen looked over her shoulder toward where Catherine had retreated. "Shh, I had to. Looks better." He took another breath and placed his hands on her shoulders. "All right." He pulled her close and kissed her on the lips. "This is going to be perfect. Let's go tell her."

Stephen took Ashley's hand and led her through the front door. Her stomach flipped with excitement at the visions she had of their perfect life together in their own little corner of the world.

***

Ashley found a job as a design assistant to the lead graphic designer at Arlington Heights Design. Her role was to design the layout of the magazine, getting content from the writers and editors.

"This is a big deal. I can grow in this job." Ashley sat next to Stephen on the couch, with her legs curled under her.

"That's great, Ashley. You sure this is the best job offer?"

"The money is great and the opportunity even better. It is the best of all worlds. I can buy a used car and drive to work."

Stephen was silent a moment, then smiled and hugged her close. "I'm happy for you. For us." He kissed her.

"Thank you. I'm so happy for us, too." She circled her arm around his waist and tucked her head into his shoulder, smiling at their perfect little world.

***

That weekend, they shopped around for a car, finding a used Maxima with low mileage. To celebrate the house, the job, and the car, they attended a fund-raising event for a local animal shelter. There were dogs of all sizes available for adoption. The minute Ashley saw Sammy, they both fell in love. He was a mutt with brown fur and the deepest brown eyes that drew Ashley in.

"Can we get him?" she pleaded with Stephen.

He looked around the room. "Oh, all right." Stephen laughed at how excited Ashley was. Deep down, he'd wanted a dog, but preferred Ashley find one she liked. He petted Sammy on the head. "Sammy is perfect."

***

Ashley filled Sammy's bowl with food and topped off his water bowl, then walked down the hall to the family room. "Ready?" She eyed Stephen, who was sitting on the couch with his feet up.

"We're not going tonight." Stephen set his jaw.

"What? But I told—" Ashley held up her hands.

"It doesn't matter. We're not going." Stephen picked up his magazine.

"I told them we'd meet them. It's been planned." Ashley dropped her arms to her sides in disbelief.

Stephen placed the magazine aside and glared at her. "You planned it. I didn't. You know I can't stand those phony friends of yours."

"What?" Ashley stood motionless. "You and Rob got along."

"No, I tolerated him. You are clueless." He returned his attention to thumbing through his reading material. "And you need new friends."

Ashley's hands trembled; her heart thudded loudly as she stood by the door. *Why would he talk to me like that?* "Well, I'll go. I'm not going to cancel on them."

Stephen placed his magazine on the side table then stood to face her. "You're not going to meet them."

"Yeah, I am, Stephen; this isn't right." Hand on hip, she shook her head.

He moved within inches of her face. "Why would you go out with them without me there? Looking for a new guy already?" His voice was cold.

"Wh-What are you talking about? K-Kim and N-Nancy a-and—" Ashley stammered.

"Save it." He turned away from her.

"Stephen?" She moved toward him.

"You don't care about me. You'd rather hang out with those random people than be with me." He stood looking out the front window.

"Stop, that is not true. I wanted us to go out together." Ashley hovered behind him, her voice small. "We never go anywhere anymore."

Stephen shook his head and stepped aside. "I like being with you here. Obviously, you need more."

"Don't say that. I love you." She reached for his hand.

He hesitated, looking down, then placed his hand in hers. "Sometimes, I can't tell." His shoulders slumped.

"Stephen, I only want to be with you." She pulled him close and hugged him. "You have to know that."

He pulled her tight against him. "I want us to spend the night at home. Work has been stressful lately." He stepped back and brushed his hand over his face.

"I didn't realize…" She reached for him.

"It's okay. I didn't mean to snap." He placed his hand on her back and kissed her cheek. "I should have told you. I'm dealing with a lot of shit at work. Fucking dirtbags, they have no respect for us." He pulled her close, searching her eyes.

"We'll stay home, then." She smiled warmly.

He kissed her gently. "Thank you. Thank you for understanding." He trailed his lips down to her neck, pressing his body into hers.

She felt the thrill of his hands and mouth on her, disarming her. "I need to text them to cancel. What should I say?" she whispered.

"You'll think of something." His kisses intensified; his hand moved under her shirt.

She broke the moment, reaching for her phone. "I better do this." She laughed as her shaky hands texted Nancy, saying she had been nauseous all day and fighting a migraine. When she finished, Stephen took the phone from her and tossed it on the couch, pulling her toward the stairs leading to their bedroom.

His arms were immediately around her, surrounding her with his aura, roaming, pressing, removing her shirt, her bra. Then, he quickly removed his own clothes as she sat back on the bed, shivering. He leaned across, pulling her underneath him, pressing hard into her. She lost herself in him, in being overpowered by his raw emotions.

Later in bed, as he held her, their naked bodies entwined, he whispered in her ear as she drifted off to sleep, "Don't leave me, Ashley. Ever."

***

"I have a surprise for us today." Stephen beamed as Ashley shuffled into the kitchen.

She stretched and smiled, remembering their night. She caught her mind drifting to earlier in the night when Stephen refused to go out with her friends. Her brow furrowed slightly.

"We're going on a picnic by the ocean." Stephen gestured toward a cooler on the floor by the counter. "I promised I'd make up for making us stay in last night."

"Good morning." Ashley walked over to Stephen and leaned in to kiss him. "That sounds lovely."

He wrapped his arms around her. "You're lovely. And last night was awesome." He growled low and kissed her neck.

She squeezed him in her arms, laughing. "Stephen!"

"You slept okay?" Stephen's cool blue eyes searched hers.

"Yes, like a rock." She kissed his nose.

"We can head out whenever you like." He stepped back to the counter, placing the cutting board and knife in the sink.

"Sounds good." Ashley stifled a yawn. "I need coffee." She opened the glass cabinet, reached for a large sage-colored mug, then poured the steaming coffee. She topped it off with Half and Half and a small spoon of sugar. "Perfect." She sat on the bench in the breakfast nook, tucking her feet under her, settling into a lazy Saturday morning. "Where are we heading exactly?"

"It's a surprise. But you'll love it. I'll go get changed." Stephen gave her a quick peck on the cheek and hurried off down the hall.

Ashley leaned back on the bench and watched the white, fluffy clouds moving their way across the blue sky, savoring the moment and sipping her coffee. The steam from her coffee swirled by her lips, and she wished her sketch pad were nearby. She'd grab her pad in a moment and spend the morning drawing. She closed her eyes, enjoying the warmth of the sun on her face.

"Let's leave in a little bit," he called from down the hall.

Stephen's voice snapped Ashley out of her reverie, and she whispered, "What?"

She'd been looking forward to lounging. She sighed loudly; knowing Stephen's high-energy moods, he wouldn't want to wait around. She stood, taking another sip from her mug before begrudgingly leaving her happy place.

***

"Isn't this great?" Stephen reclined on his towel. The boardwalk and beach in Ocean City bustled with people walking, jogging, and skateboarding.

Ashley smiled, admittedly having a good time. "Yes, it is." She reached for a strawberry. "This picnic is amazing." She gestured to the fruit, the sandwiches, and the bottles of Blue Moons.

"Glad you like everything." Stephen took the last bite of his sandwich and wiped his hands together. "Want to take a walk around?"

"Mmm, yes," Ashley said in between chews. She packed up the remnants of their picnic.

"We can leave everything here. Should be fine." Stephen stood, brushing crumbs and sand off himself. He stretched his arms overhead, his shirt lifting and revealing a pistol strapped around his torso.

Ashley's breath caught, and she turned away quickly. *Why would he pack that on his day off?* The gun made her uncomfortable, no matter how many times she saw it left out on the dresser at home or when he had it holstered in his uniform.

She stood, and he reached for her hand. "Let's go, pretty lady."

They walked onto the boardwalk, stopping at the T-shirt shops, surveying the various food stands with the smells of candy apples and fried dough. They passed the amusement rides, watching the roller coaster as it raced down the big hill.

Stephen pulled her close as they passed the Ferris wheel. "Having fun?" His arms held her near.

"Yes, so much." She searched his eyes. "How about you?" She could tell by his smile he was enjoying the day.

"This is perfect." He kissed her then held her at arm's length. Slowly he began to turn in a circle, holding her hands.

Ashley giggled and held on tighter as he sped up, the world a blur behind him. All she saw was him at that moment, happy and relaxed, and she wished they could stay like this forever.

***

As time passed, Ashley wasn't sure how to read Stephen when he returned from work; his moods were erratic, silently brooding one moment, exploding with anger the next.

One day, she was silently working in the kitchen, assembling dinner, and she heard Stephen swear in the family room. She took a deep breath, not ready for one of his rants. *Please let him get over it. Please, not tonight,* she silently prayed.

Stephen's heavy footfalls approached.

She closed her eyes, calling on her patience.

"I have to leave." He grabbed his keys off the counter.

"What?" Ashley turned to face him, holding the spatula. "Dinner is almost ready."

"Eat without me. I got a call." He adjusted his holster. "Don't look at me like that. I gotta go."

"Okay, I wasn't… I'm disappointed; that's all." She looked away then glanced back as Stephen leaned toward her.

"Well, I didn't plan for this—son of a bitch calling me in." He tightened his jaw then slammed a fist on the counter.

Ashley jumped. "Is everything okay?"

"Yeah, fucking fantastic," he muttered then shook his head. "I gotta deal with fucking dirtbags that want to nail everything on the police. Their goddamned lot in life is my fault."

Ashley nodded, although she had no idea what he was talking about. She'd heard this rant before and tried talking it over with him, but the result was always Stephen erupting and yelling that she had no idea what he had to go through every day.

"Can you have dinner? I made your favorite." Ashley turned and smiled, but it was too late.

He pushed off the counter and stormed past her and out the door.

***

Work had been good for Ashley, keeping her days busy. It became one of her only social outlets as time went on with Stephen.

She developed a friendship with Faith, not only on work-related items but outside of work, taking lunch breaks together and meeting for a jog after work on nights Stephen worked late. Spending time with Faith was a calm respite for Ashley before her trek home to the unknown.

After a while, Stephen began to drink. Then, he began to yell, and then yell some more.

Ashley sometimes thought, *Why the hell am I sticking around?* She thought she could leave anytime. Yet, when he was so remorseful and told her he would never act like that again, she thought she loved him. When things were good, they were great. She was everything to him, his life, he told her.

Stephen would take Ashley to the gym with him occasionally. Ashley preferred working out on her own—running, hiking, or meeting friends for a group-exercise class—but he insisted he could get her in better shape with his workouts.

Ashley told him that she needed to be around friends, that she missed her girlfriends from school. She suggested Stephen should start spending time with his friends, too. That way, when they were alone, it would make it even more special. But when she met friends for lunch or went to a fitness class with them, he would constantly text and call, then ask her a lot of questions about what they did and where they went, needing specific details.

Stephen did take Ashley's advice, and he started planning time out with his friends. Then, he took it to another level, staying out until all hours of the morning. When she questioned with whom he was hanging out, he would laugh, telling her she was being jealous. He told her it was her fault because she drove him to hang out with his friends. Secretly, Stephen loved the feeling that he was making her jealous.

Ashley couldn't believe he had turned the situation around on her. The head games were making her second-guess herself. *Am I to blame for him being out all night? Am I not giving him enough of my time?*

She tried hard to balance out his moods, making sure she was home straight from work and soon eliminating any social time away altogether.

***

Ashley made her rounds at the Arlington Heights Design outing, ensuring sure all the guests were getting their photos taken. This was their annual meeting, and every year they updated the employees' photos. Faith had met her there early to help with the logistics of the meeting. Ashley was thankful to have her help. Once Faith got everything set up, she turned the reins back over to Ashley.

"Hey, Ashley. How's it going?" Ashley's boss, Scott, came over to get his photo taken. He was nice enough, attractive. He always took time to talk to Ashley; he was polite, friendly, but not flirty. He sat for his photo shoot then stayed to talk to Ashley before heading back to dinner. "I should head back. Looks like dinner is served. Coming to eat?"

"Yeah, in a bit. I have to finish here first."

"All right, make sure you eat." He smiled and pointed at Ashley.

"Thanks, Scott." Watching him, she could understand how all the girls craved his attention at the office, hanging on his every word. His easy-going attitude and quick smile were attractive, but he was not her type.

Chad, the photographer for the evening, put his camera down since there was a lull in the action. "Hey, want to grab dinner?"

"Yeah, I might. Seems like there's a little break in the action." Ashley saw movement behind him that caught her eye. Her breath caught in her throat. "Oh my God," she whispered as she stood frozen while Stephen appeared.

"Ashley, you okay?" Concerned, Chad looked at her.

"My boyfriend is here," she heard herself say as she stared at Stephen walking toward her with his eyes locked on hers.

"Uh, that's a good thing, right?" Chad looked over at Stephen and then back to Ashley.

No, he is fucking crazy, and he showed up uninvited, Ashley thought about saying to Chad. Her heart raced. Stephen kept his eyes on hers, smiling that knowing smirk that said, *"You won't say anything. You wouldn't want to make a scene, would you?"*

It took Ashley a second before she answered Chad, "Yes, uh, yeah, it's a good thing." She laughed and smiled.

As Stephen approached, his expression softened, reminding her of a time when they were happy. Maybe she'd imagined that initial mocking expression. Maybe not.

***

Stephen waited patiently for her, wanting to watch her in her element at work. He spotted her in the group. *She looks happy and relaxed,* he thought. Stephen knew this was a big deal for her; she'd worked hard on the plans for the annual company outing for the employees. Stephen was there to make sure she wasn't sidetracked by any of the guys who worked with her. She'd said that she didn't want him to feel left out, that she wouldn't be able to spend much time with him since she had to work most of the event.

It's perfect. She has no idea that I am here, he thought, pleased with himself for finding out exactly where the dinner was being held and for catching a ride with Robbie from work. He'd wait a little longer before he made his entrance. Stephen thought to himself, *She will be pleased that I came here to rescue her from the scum that are following her around like rabid dogs.*

***

"Hey," he smiled sheepishly, looking down, his cheeks lightly flushed.

"Stephen, what a surprise!"

He stood tentatively before approaching. *She's so pretty,* he thought, and all his anger disappeared. *She is doing her job,* he told himself. He hoped he didn't look like a fool in front of her and her coworkers. He waited for her to make the next move, not wanting to seem aggressive.

She reached out her hand, and he took it gently. "I can't believe you came all the way here." She seemed genuinely happy, which made him feel at ease.

"I wanted to surprise you," he said softly.

"You did!" She smiled at him, pulling him closer. "Chad, this is my boyfriend, Stephen."

Chad looked from Ashley to Stephen, taking Ashley's word that this surprise visit was all right. "Nice to meet you, Stephen."

They shook hands.

"That Nikon is an excellent camera. The shutter speed must catch the lights in the sky tonight," Stephen said while pointing toward Chad's camera.

Chad nodded, impressed that Stephen knew about cameras; he took any opportunity to talk photography with a willing subject. They compared experiences with different lighting and lenses. Stephen asked to see Chad's work, and Chad showed him some of the shots from that evening.

"Well, it was a pleasure. I'm off to grab some dinner before I have to get back to work. Nice meeting you." Chad walked off, proud of being told how good his photography was. He was glad Ashley had a great boyfriend who'd come to surprise her.

"I hope you aren't angry I showed up." Stephen shoved his hands in his pockets, looking at the floor. "I wanted to surprise you."

"You did. I didn't think—"

Stephen smiled sheepishly. "Robbie dropped me off. He said, if you were mad, he would swing back around and get me."

"Wait, you didn't drive here?" Ashley questioned.

"No, my truck is in the shop."

Stephen pulled something out of his pocket. "I wanted to see you because it's our anniversary this weekend. Nine months. Three months since we moved into the house." He handed her a small box wrapped in silver paper and a navy-blue ribbon.

"Stephen…" Ashley took the box and held it in her hands.

"Surprise." He smiled.

"I can't believe you had Robbie drive you…and this…" She gestured to the tiny box.

"Open it." He looked around. "I mean, if you have time. I know you're working."

Ashley smiled and carefully removed the paper and ribbon, her hands shaking slightly. Stephen took them from her. She lifted the lid to the heavy hinged leather box.

"Oh my God, Stephen." She brought her hand to her chest. The ring shimmered brightly. The gold ring intertwined and twinkled with small diamonds around the top quarter.

"Happy anniversary. I thought this was symbolic of us, how our lives came together."

"Stephen, I love it." She smiled and took the ring out of the box carefully, for a moment wondering, *Is he proposing? Is he going to get down on one knee?*

"Let me put it on." Stephen placed the ring on her right ring finger. "Looks perfect on you."

"It's perfect." Ashley hugged Stephen and breathed a little easier. "Thank you. I'm glad you're here."

"Me, too." He kissed her cheek.

Ashley noticed that everyone was taking their seats. "We should get seated. Dinner will be served soon. Perfect timing."

"It's okay that I join in?"

"Yes. We have extra seats; a couple people couldn't make it. Let's go over near Chad and some of the people from marketing. I think you'll like them."

She made introductions, and Stephen charmed his way through every conversation. The night flowed easily. Stephen made small talk with her coworkers; he held her hand, glancing at the ring every so often and winking at her.

After a decadent dinner of filet and rock lobster, a beyond-rich chocolate dessert was served. Ashley's job of hosting the event was almost finished. *Time to close the tab.*

"I'll be right back."

Ashley met with the event coordinator to go over final details. The manager came in to make sure everyone had enjoyed their evening. As Ashley spoke with the manager, she saw Stephen talking with Scott. They seemed to hit it off, Stephen seemingly ever attentive to Scott's end of the conversation. She turned back to the coordinator, signed off on the bill for the evening, and said her good-byes.

The last group left the party, telling Ashley what a wonderful evening they had, thanking her for her hard work. Scott turned to Ashley after saying his good-byes to everyone. "Thank you, Ashley. This was a great event."

"You're welcome. Everything went smooth, and the food was delicious."

"I appreciate the time you put in on this. You did a great job keeping everyone in line." Scott laughed.

"Yeah, everyone behaved." She laughed out loud.

Scott reached out to shake her hand and put his other hand on her arm in a friendly gesture. "You throw a great party. Have a good rest of the night." He nodded toward Stephen, who had been talking to the bartender, but glanced in their direction and waved. "Stephen's a great guy. Enjoyed talking to him."

"Thank you. Yes, he is. Thanks for letting him attend tonight." She smiled and waved back to Stephen, twisting the ring on her finger.

"Of course, of course. You two have a great night."

"See you Monday." Ashley grabbed her handbag and sweater from the table and made her way over to Stephen.

"Ready to go?" He was leaning against the bar.

"Yes, I'm done. Good night." Ashley waved to the bartender.

"Let's go." Stephen put his arm around Ashley's waist as they walked out to the parking lot.

"I guess I'm driving you home since you got dropped off here," Ashley joked, nudging his side.

"Yeah. Ha. I'll drive." He extended his hand for the keys.

"Great. I'm exhausted." She tossed the keys to him and slid into the car, resting her head against the seat. "That was a great night, but I'm beat." She kicked off her shoes. "I hope you had fun." She turned, curling in her seat to look at Stephen.

Stephen kept his gaze forward as he drove. "Yes, it was a good night. I was able to talk to some of the people you work with." He glanced sideways at her. "They're okay."

Ashley laughed. "Only okay? Who do you mean?"

"Well, Chad was nice but a total dork. Your marketing friends are a little stiff."

"No, Faith and Bill are great! I like them, anyway." She jutted her chin forward.

Stephen was quiet for a moment, keeping his eyes on the road. "Scott's a piece of work. I don't like that guy."

"What? You're kidding, right?" Ashley sat up in her seat and turned to him, brow furrowed.

"I don't know; he rubs me the wrong way." He gripped the steering wheel.

"Oh my God, I don't understand that at all. He gets along with everyone." She giggled and turned to face forward in her seat.

"He hangs around you too much." Clenching his jaw, he pressed harder on the car's accelerator.

"Scott?" She slapped her hand on her leg and turned to him again, incredulous. "He's my boss! Stephen, seriously?!"

"Ashley"—he was shaking his head, laughing—"you're so naive sometimes. You don't even see it. This is why you need me." His condescending tone further annoyed her.

"Give me a break, Stephen. You have no idea what you are talking about." She sat rigidly facing ahead, a small knot forming in her stomach.

"Don't I, though?" He shook his head. "This night would have been perfect, but you're different when you're around your so-called friends."

Ashley's jaw dropped open. "Um, this was a work event. I told you I had to work. I spent as much time with you as I could. I mean, you did show up unexpectedly."

Stephen huffed. "I should have known you didn't want me there." He snickered.

"I did; remember when I mentioned it? You said you would be bored. Then, I agreed you would hate being around those people. And, guess what? I was right!" Her voice had risen to a higher pitch; her insides shook.

"You didn't want me there so you could have all of those guys' attention. Guess I'm not enough." He drove faster.

"Stephen, you have to calm down. Everything was going fine until you started picking everyone apart. It's like you are looking for a fight." She tried to calm his anger. "I was glad you came."

"I'm not looking for a fight, Ashley. I want you to admit that something else is going on. You looked so worried when I showed up. Caught in the act? Huh?" He glared sideways. "You and that loser, Chad?"

He veered off the main road suddenly. Ashley's heart sped up; her stomach lurched and churned. He drove down the dark road, passing a marina on the left of them. He suddenly turned the car into the parking lot.

"What are you doing?" She grabbed on to the seat, her hands sweating.

Gripping the steering wheel, wearing a manic expression on his face, he didn't answer.

Oh my God, she thought, *he's going to knock me out and throw me over the pier with cement blocks. This is it.* She thought of jumping out of the car while he was driving. *Then, what?* He would get out and drag her back. *No one is here to stop him.*

Everything was dark except for the small lights along the dock. Some of the boats were covered for the season, gently swaying with the current. There wasn't a soul in sight.

Stephen parked the car and left it idling; he sat and just stared at the boats.

The silence was deafening; Ashley didn't dare break it. She was sure he could hear her thundering heartbeat. *What if he has his gun?* She shuddered at the thought.

He opened his mouth to speak, but no words formed. He looked as if he were waiting for an answer to a question he had long been waiting to hear. Quietly, he began to utter words, although Ashley could not make out what he was saying.

Finally, he spoke up, "Where did it go?" Still staring off toward the darkness, he asked, "Where did it go wrong?" He turned to Ashley suddenly. "Where, Ashley?"

She didn't know what to say. *Where? How about everywhere. How about it's been going wrong for a while?* She kept those thoughts to herself, not wanting to say anything that would push him closer to his breaking point.

He turned to her, grabbing her arm. "I'm not stupid, Ashley. I know what I saw tonight." He gritted his teeth.

"You saw nothing. You're delusional." She tried pulling her arm away, immediately regretting that remark, wishing she could take it back.

Stephen grabbed Ashley's shoulder, pressing his fingers into her skin. "I know what I saw." He clenched his jaw, looking through her, his eyes void of emotion.

"Let go, Stephen. You're hurting me!" Her shoulder tensed as she tried pulling away, but his grip tightened. She twisted her arm free as he pushed her, knocking her head against the passenger window. She felt tears spring into her eyes.

Stephen reached toward her, this time not in anger. His expression changed as drastically as it had at the start of his outburst. "Ashley, are you okay?"

She cringed away from him, leaning against the door. "Don't."

He looked at her face, then at her arm, and turned away, putting his head in his hands. "I'm so sorry."

Ashley didn't dare move or say a word, half in shock, half not knowing what she should do next.

His breathing calmed, and he turned to her. "I don't know what to say. I thought... It doesn't matter what I thought. I'm an idiot. You're all I have." He sat quietly for a moment. "There's so much going on at work. I'm under so much pressure; you don't even know." He grew silent again, putting his head in his hands again. "I took it out on you."

She eyed him suspiciously as she rubbed her arm.

Stephen looked out the window. "I was put on probation."

"What?" Ashley was taken aback.

"It's a lot...there's a lot going on. I'm dealing with a ton of stress." His voice shook.

"Why didn't you tell me?" Ashley thought about running. She moved her hand closer to the car-door handle. She again wondered if he had his gun.

"I didn't want to burden you with my stuff. You have so much going on. You've been busy with work lately and planning this event. You didn't have time to worry about my shit." He rubbed his hands down his legs.

"But acting like this toward me is okay?" Her voice rose in anger.

"No, no, Ashley. It isn't." He turned to her, making himself small and humble. "How I behaved? It's unacceptable. I'll never act like that again. I understand if you don't believe me. I know I'm not good enough for you."

For a moment, Ashley thought maybe she'd been neglecting him, not paying attention to the signs. She questioned herself, *Did I ignore Stephen when he talked about work?* She thought she'd asked him about work, and he'd dismissed her, but maybe she'd been preoccupied with the deadlines and the planning of this event. "Stephen, you can tell me anything; you know that, right?"

"I know. I know. I didn't want to burden you." He leaned his head against the seat.

"You need to open up so you don't keep blowing up. You've been like a time bomb lately," she said calmly.

He looked up and nodded in agreement. "I should have been able to handle all of this, but... You don't understand the pressures of being a cop. People put words in your mouth; they love to blame us when something goes wrong. The criminals have the rights, and we don't." He turned to her, fire in his eyes, heated about the topic.

She could only imagine his stressors, dealing with the people he dealt with all day, keeping it all in line, all the time. "Maybe you could talk to someone that could help?"

His look turned hopeless, broken. Part of her softened, realizing he needed serious help. She wanted to ask about the probation, but didn't want to push him over the edge.

"You can drop me off. I can get an Uber or find some way to get back." He looked down at his hands in his lap.

She was leery of him driving and of being with him, but didn't want to leave him alone, either. "No, it's fine."

Stephen held his hands out. "Ashley, I'm sorry."

"I know." She inwardly cringed.

"I will do anything to make this up to you. I'll give you space. Whatever you need." He hesitated then placed his hand on Ashley's hand. "Anything. Forgive me."

Ashley didn't want to fight. Maybe they needed space; maybe he needed to straighten out whatever was happening at work. She didn't know; she only knew this relationship had to change.

"Okay. I want to go home now." Her shoulders dropped; she was exhausted from the stress.

"You got it. I promise to make this right." He put the car in Reverse and slowly drove out of the marina and onto the highway.

Ashley stared out the window as tears filled her eyes. She wanted to believe Stephen. She wanted to believe that things would work out for them.

Stephen drove calmly and asked questions about her work, expressing true interest, apologizing for criticizing her coworkers. He shared that he knew he had to deal with his work stress better. He told her the probation was all a big misunderstanding that needed to be worked out. Everything would be fine once he met with the heads of his department.

For a moment, she saw it. Ashley imagined Stephen changing his ways, getting the help he needed, and getting his job back on track. She saw them carefree, as they once were. She fiddled with the ring on her finger.

As they drove back toward their life together, Ashley tried to maintain the fairy-tale vision of their life, but it quickly faded to black. No matter how hard she tried to conjure up the happy times they once shared, she couldn't picture anything past what had just happened… and the darkness and hate she'd seen in his eyes.

CHAPTER 6

The week passed without Stephen having any other episodes. The quiet was welcoming to Ashley. He had left black-and-blue marks on her shoulder from where he'd grabbed her and held on like a vise. He was remorseful and couldn't do enough to try to "make up" for it. Stephen made sure to give her attention, gifts, and to do pretty much anything he could to make it all right again.

Stephen told Ashley the misunderstanding at work was "taken care of," but he was taking some time off from work. He was upbeat and agreed with whatever Ashley wanted to do. His truck was back from the shop. He hopped at the chance to go to the store for her if she needed anything.

For a time, things seemed lighter, easier.

Then, things became dark quickly.

The following week, Stephen told Ashley he was suspended indefinitely from work, which sent him spiraling into a major depression. His moods were manic. Ashley wasn't sure what state he would be in day-to-day, or even morning to evening.

As things were getting stressful with Stephen, running became more and more of an outlet for Ashley. She packed her running gear and went for her run straight after work so as not to get sidelined by Stephen.

On Friday, Ashley finished a huge project and went for a long run after work. She was elated, feeling she could handle anything that came at her.

"About time you were home," Stephen said under his breath as she walked through the door. He was sitting on the couch, watching Sports Center, which he had done since he lost all enthusiasm about proactively searching for a side job. His erratic emotions deflated

Ashley's hopes that things could get better between them without an intervention.

Sammy stood from his dog bed and greeted her at the door, tail wagging, tongue out.

At least he's happy to see me. "Sammy, hello, my boy." She bent over, petted his head, and kissed him. She walked over to the couch where Stephen sat and leaned over to give him a kiss.

He didn't look at her but offered his cheek.

"How was your day?" She put her hand on his shoulder.

"Great." He sat stone-faced.

Ashley waited a beat then walked down the hall to the kitchen to put her things down, Sammy following closely at her feet. She kicked off her shoes and sighed loudly.

"My day was great," he yelled to her from the other room.

Her stomach churned as she ran her hands along Sammy's back. *He knows Sammy gets upset when the yelling starts. Why? Why is he doing this?* She couldn't take another night of his yelling or punching the counter or slamming doors all night. She had to say something.

Ashley returned to the family room and crossed her arms, bracing herself. "We cannot spend all our time fighting." She was at a loss for what to do. She'd tried everything—from leaving want ads out on the counter, to e-mailing friends at work, asking if they had any connections for Stephen to get a side job.

The first couple of days, he was optimistic about the thought of working again, saying he could do construction or even some side security jobs. He lost his motivation by the week's end and dropped deeper into his depressed state and angry moods.

"Seriously, Ashley? What am I supposed to do?" He looked as if he honestly was at a loss.

"Um, you could try to get another job." Ashley turned and left the room, tired of the endless argument. As Stephen got up to follow her, she cringed.

"Ash, wait. Listen, I'll try. Give me another day," he pleaded, hands out.

She turned to face him, surprised at his change of tone, but again defeated in this fight.

"Tomorrow, Ash, I promise." He reached for her hand.

"Okay. Tomorrow."

***

Stephen woke up early with Ashley, happy and smiling, bringing her coffee while she was in the shower. As she left for work, he had a smile. Her mood was so much better because of it.

Later in the day, her phone buzzed.

Stephen: *It is going great!*

She was looking forward to the possibility of a good night with Stephen. As she pulled her car into the driveway, she noticed his truck was not there. *No truck. Maybe he will surprise me with dinner.* She smiled at the thought as she opened the door to their house.

Ashley opened the mail, fed Sammy, changed out of her work clothes, and threw in a load of laundry, occasionally glancing at the clock then the driveway. There was no sign of Stephen. She texted him and stared at her phone, willing a response. There was no word.

***

The sun set; the hours passed—still no call or message. She grabbed some snacks to nibble on while she folded the dried laundry, holding out hope. She went from disappointed, to nervous, to angry, to a sense of dread that settled low in her gut.

What if something happened? An accident? A disappearance? What if he took off?

Her mind raced with all the possibilities, none of them taking root since she would have gotten a call if there had been an accident or if his truck had been found abandoned. She wanted to call around, but didn't want to seem desperate. The digital clock in the kitchen read 10:00 p.m. Finally, she decided to text his friend.

Ashley: *Hi, Robbie. Have you heard from Stephen?* Ashley chewed her fingernails.

60

He responded a few minutes later.

Robbie: *Hey. No, last I heard he was in the city this morning. Probably met up with some of the guys.*

She sat staring at the phone, not sure how to answer that, when her phone buzzed again.

Robbie: *He'll show.*

Ashley: *Thanks.*

Stupid, Ashley thought. She didn't want to appear to be a desperate girlfriend chasing him down. Ashley felt tired. All the stress had been eating at her, and she hit a wall. Pulling a blanket off the couch, she placed the phone by the pillow and laid her head down. She just wanted to close her eyes for a little bit.

***

Stephen drove down the dark road with his headlights off, looking for a parking spot. He found the apartment, number 53, on the right side of the road. He parked his truck, as usual, in a space past the building. He pulled his baseball cap down low to cover his face, shoved his hands in his pockets, put his head down, and made his way to the front steps. He rang the buzzer.

"Come on; come on." He fidgeted on the front stoop, looking around.

Finally, the door opened. "Hey, you made it." Wearing next to nothing, she leaned against the doorframe.

He walked in without saying a word and closed the door.

"You look like you need a drink or something stronger."

He took off his hat and tossed it on the chair. "Yeah, I could use a little something."

She smiled a knowing smile, sauntered to the kitchen, and retrieved a bag out of the back of the pantry.

He wished he could use the stuff, get his fix, and be left alone. But that wasn't how she worked. She knew why he was there, but she wished he were there for her, so he played along.

He took her in his arms. "You cut your hair." He touched the strands that hung loosely to her shoulders.

"Yeah, you noticed. Is it too short?" She self-consciously brought her hand up to the side of her face.

"No, no, I like it." He kissed her neck as she closed her eyes and smiled. He knew she wanted him to come around more; she'd told him countless times she wished he would move in with her. He held her gaze and smiled.

"Let's get high." She waved the bag in front of him.

"All right. Then, a little more of this." He kissed her again, good at the game when he wanted something. And she had what he was looking for.

***

Ashley slept and had busy, vivid dreams. She was running through a yard; she didn't recognize where she was, but it was a backyard in a neighborhood of close-knit houses. Looking up, she saw a military plane flying low, at the tree line, coming at her, and she couldn't outrun it. The motor whirred loudly in her ears, and the faster she pumped her legs, the slower she moved. The trees were being taken out by the plane flying lower, until it eventually touched down with a crash. She fell to the ground, silently screaming as she saw the underbelly of the plane falling toward her.

***

Stephen woke in a haze, his mouth as dry as the desert. Taking a second to let his eyes adjust to the dark, he remembered. He was at Danny's place.

He realized he was in her bed, her naked body lying across his. Squinting, he tried to read the clock. An ashtray was teetering on the edge of bedside table; some needles, his lighter, and his cell phone lay strewn near it.

The clock read 5:30 a.m. He inwardly groaned. He'd hoped he could slink out of there and slip home while Ashley was asleep. Now, that wouldn't happen. She'd be getting up for work soon, but he had an excuse ready.

He rolled out from under Danny, found his clothes, and crept out of her room so as not to wake her. Dressing as he stumbled toward the door, he pulled his hat down low then left quietly, closing the door behind him.

***

Ashley bolted awake. Her heart was beating fast; her breathing was rapid. Sammy sat up at her feet and whimpered. "It's okay, Sammy. Only a dream…"

She looked around the dim room, rubbing her eyes; light was beginning to filter in through the windows. Hearing a *click* in the kitchen, she remembered that her phone was near the pillow and that Stephen had never come home. Another noise came from the hallway, then footsteps, and Stephen was there in front of her. Checking her phone, it read 6:04 a.m.

First, a wave of relief washed over Ashley. *Thank God he isn't hurt*, she thought. Then, it sank in. *Where the hell has he been all night?*

"Ashley, hey. Sorry to wake you up. You should be in bed." He tried to cover the slur in his speech.

"Where were you? I texted you." She stood up to face him, wrapping herself in the blanket.

"My phone died. I met up with some of the guys, and we had a few beers. I was in no shape to drive." He swayed slightly.

"You couldn't have used someone's phone to let me know?" Ashley pulled the blanket tighter around herself.

"We were at the bar; you know, time got away from me, Ash. Don't be mad." He waved his hand.

"Yeah. Where did you stay?" She eyed him warily and folded her arms across her chest.

"Ash, I expect a little freedom to go out. I've been stuck doing nothing. You could be sympathetic." He let out a laugh and leaned against the side table.

"You're kidding, right?" She dropped the blanket onto the couch.

Stephen swayed a bit; then he began to pace the worn hardwood floor. "Seriously, Ashley, it's all about you and your work, while I'm struggling."

She tried to bite her tongue; her patience was running thin. "Stephen, I've been trying to help you find work, and you never followed up with any of the people I contacted. And, yes, I'm working a lot of hours because we need the money and—" She stopped. *Why am I explaining myself?* "Wait, were you even out looking for a job yesterday?"

"Give it a rest, Ashley," he hissed.

She picked up her cell phone from the couch and put it in her sweat pants pocket.

"I don't need to look for a job. I'm a cop!" he yelled. "A cop, damn it. They're lucky to have me on the force." He shook his head and swore.

"This is unbelievable." She dismissively threw her hands in the air and walked past him toward the bathroom.

"I'm unbelievable," he muttered. "I'm unbelievable." His voice was rising. He turned abruptly, following her down the hall, and slammed his hand against the wall. "You, bitch!"

Ashley froze.

"Damn it, Ashley! You're always pushing me!" He seethed with anger.

She backed up toward the kitchen, hoping to be able to use her phone to call someone. *But who?*

Stephen lunged toward her. Ashley panicked and turned to run, but he caught her arm, spinning her around, slamming her against the wall, and holding her there by the throat. His grip got tighter, cutting off her air, as he raged about her selfishness. He punched the wall again, this time within inches of her head, smashing a hole through it, flecks of drywall spraying her face.

Ashley grabbed at Stephen's hand around her throat, not able to tell him that he was holding on too tight. Thrashing and desperate for air, she tried frantically to find a way to make him let go. The only thing she could think of was kneeing him in the groin. *If only I can reach...* He was standing so close she wasn't sure how much force she could generate, but she jerked her knee up with all the strength she could muster. It was enough to throw him off-center; doubling over, he loosened his grip. Ashley slipped free and ran toward the kitchen.

"Son of a bitch," Stephen yelled. He bent over, stunned momentarily. Taking a breath, he sprang forward. His reach was long, and again he grabbed her, this time catching her by the shoulder and shoving her hard.

Ashley lost her footing, falling forward; her head barely missed the granite counter. She fell to the floor, slamming her shoulder on the hard wood and knocking her head into the cabinets. As she lay there stunned, she couldn't catch her breath. Dazed from the impact, she slowly attempted to stand, using the cabinets for balance.

Stephen approached as she gripped the edge of the counter with both hands to steady herself. She thought, *This is the last time he will do this to me.*

The. Last. Time.

Turning to face him, she was ready to fight back. Quickly, she swung her arm and caught him with her open palm, smashing it into the side of his face.

Stunned, Stephen fell back from the impact. Anger filled his eyes, and his jaw clenched as he lunged toward her.

Ashley couldn't move fast enough to avoid him. He caught her by the arm, jerking her toward him. She froze under his glare. He kicked her legs out from under her, dropping her to the floor. There was a loud *thud*, and it took her a moment to grasp what it was—her head hitting the floor.

A white light began to cloud her vision. She heard crying and realized it was her own. The pain hovered around the back of her skull, and darkness edged the corners of her vision, but she knew she needed to stay present. Freezing was not an option. Fighting him did not work.

Her primal instincts told her to run.

The light from the rising sun was shining through the screen door. Taking a visual scan of the space, Ashley saw that the only things between her and freedom were about six feet of space and a flimsy screen door. Car keys were on the counter on the left side of the door, but the car was parked at the end of the driveway. Stephen would block her attempt at a fast getaway if she attempted to get in the car.

Best bet is to run. And run fast.

This all took a matter of seconds, although everything seemed to be moving in slow motion.

Stephen was pacing, yelling at Ashley to stop crying because he needed to think, that this was her fault.

Ashley pressed up and launched toward the door. She grabbed her keys, pushed open the door, ran down the steps, down the short driveway, and out toward the road. She heard the door push open again behind her and Stephen's steps approaching.

She ran.

"Ashley!"

Her heart racing out of her chest, adrenaline fueling her pace, she veered out of the driveway and fled toward Main Street. There would be people, traffic, rush hour—he would be seen. As cars sped by, she hoped someone would stop and say something. But no one did.

What the hell is wrong with everyone? she thought. *Don't they see this psycho chasing a girl down the road?* Then, she thought, *Maybe I'm the one who looks crazy.* Running in her bare feet, sweat pants, and hoodie, her wild blonde hair trailing behind her. She checked her pocket, making sure her phone was still there.

"Ashley, wait up."

Sounds like he's calling to one of his buddies, she thought. She rounded a corner, slowing her pace, catching her jagged breath.

Stephen caught up. "Ashley, wait a second."

She turned briefly to look at him. "Leave me alone." She was seething. "You wouldn't want me to make a scene, would you?"

Stephen looked past Ashley and put his hands in his pockets.

Ashley turned, almost bumping into a man who seemed to appear out of nowhere. The concerned look on his face led her to believe he had seen why Ashley was running.

"Are you okay?" He nodded toward Stephen. "Is he bothering you?"

Finally, someone with some sense, she thought.

Out of breath, Ashley stopped. "I'm okay. He was leaving." She glared at Stephen.

Stephen knew to back off. He wouldn't want anyone to witness him losing it, drawing more bad attention to himself or from the police. Holding his hands up, he backed away and nodded his head. "It's all good. We're fine; she needs time to cool down."

Ashley was disgusted. "Unbelievable," she muttered.

Stephen turned and walked away, hands still in his pockets.

The young man watched him go and then turned to Ashley. "Sure you're okay? Want me to call someone?"

Ashley took another jagged breath and thought about it, her heart sinking. *There's no one I can call.*

"No, thank you. I'm fine now." She attempted a smile.

He looked skeptical. "Are you sure?"

"Seriously, I'm okay. I'll be fine. Thanks, again." She did her best to calm her trembling voice.

"Okay, I'll take your word for it." He didn't look convinced.

Quickly, Ashley turned and walked in the opposite direction, making sure Stephen wasn't around. She glanced behind her and noticed the man was gone as well. She walked on, keeping her head down.

Ashley steadied her breath and silently thanked God. Her hands shook, and she didn't notice where she was headed until she came to the end of the walkway. Looking up, in front of her stood the beautiful, old stone church with large stained-glass windows that she'd always admired; it was beckoning her to safety.

Ashley was drawn to the old church and up the steep stone steps. The large, dark wooden doors were closed, but the music from within flooded her ears. She leaned her ear toward the door and heard the echoing voices of the choir and the piano. The sign above the wooden door read, "All are welcome in this place."

Ashley looked down at her bare feet and her sweat pants. She sighed and ran a shaky hand through her hair. Slowly, Ashley reached up and pushed lightly on the door. It gave way, opening with a *creak*.

Stepping inside, she shut the door quietly behind her and stood with her arms wrapped around herself as she trembled. Her skin felt cold, although the air was warm. She hoped none of the morning Massgoers would notice her.

There was a small bench tucked in an alcove to the right of the door. She slipped in without being noticed, reveling in the fact that it was dark and hidden from view. There was a small window in the alcove that looked out onto the main road and the walkway. The bird's-eye view gave her the advantage of being hidden while watching to see if Stephen came back that way looking for her.

Suddenly feeling a sense of safety, Ashley settled into the bench, pulling her knees up to her chest and taking a deep yet unsteady breath. She felt for the phone in her pocket and positioned herself so she could look out of the window. He would either try to find her, or he would take off if he thought she'd called someone.

So, she waited and prayed.

Fifteen minutes passed, and as predicted, she saw Stephen's truck drive by the church slowly. She held her breath as he passed. Ashley waited another ten minutes, making sure Stephen didn't return.

Her fear had dissipated and turned to anger. *How dare he do this to me?* she thought. Ashley knew she needed to leave Stephen, for good, before it was too late.

Ashley quietly left the church before the Mass ended. She began her walk home, keeping her head down. She was self-conscious about how she must look, walking down the street with no shoes on and appearing as if she'd just rolled out of bed. She hurriedly made her way the two blocks, then turned down her street on high alert as she approached the house.

Ashley thought of calling the police, but Stephen had so many connections and friends. Even with him on probation, he continued to keep in touch with many of the officers from his department. She felt trapped with no way out. This time, though, Stephen had pushed her too far. It was time for her to act.

Ashley noticed the lights were on at their house, and the door was open, but there was no sign of Stephen's truck. She slowly walked up the stairs to the door. Behind her, a car pulled into the driveway.

Ashley froze with fear.

The car retreated, turning around and leaving in the opposite direction.

"Dear Jesus," she breathed, her heart hammering out of her chest. Then, her phone vibrated, making her jump. She pulled the phone from her pocket, her hands trembling, and tapped the text icon.

Stephen: *Ash, I'm so sorry. I don't know what's happening with me. Please call.*

Ashley shook her head in disbelief. *No fucking way, not this time,* she thought.

She walked through the kitchen door, that flimsy screen door she'd bolted through what seemed like only moments before. She shut the door, locked it, and looked around, not knowing where to begin. Down the hall, the mess from the hole in the wall loomed.

Wanting to call someone, but afraid, embarrassed, and angry with herself, she leaned against the counter. Exasperated, she let out a sigh. "Get a grip," she told herself.

Ashley walked from the kitchen, down the hall, and up the creaky staircase to her bedroom. Sammy was sitting up in his bed. *He looks worried,* she thought, *if a dog can look worried.*

"It's okay, Sammy."

Looking at herself in the mirror, she sighed again. She pushed her sleeves up then moved her tangled blonde hair away from her neck. There were black-and-blue spots across her arm and more spots around her neck. His finger marks had left their imprints on her pale skin.

Ashley rubbed her shaky hand around her neck, realizing that the longer she stayed in that house, the more of a chance there was that Stephen would be back. If that happened, she'd lose any chance of getting some help.

She reached for her phone and stared at it. She knew Faith was the only one she could trust, so she texted her.

Ashley: *Can I come stay with you for a day or two?*

Faith's response was almost immediate.

Faith: *Hey! Yes! Come over. Is everything okay?*

She stared at her phone and let out a small laugh. *How do I even answer that?*

Ashley: *I'm okay. But I need your help.* She stared at her screen, hesitating with her finger hovering over Send.

This changes everything, she thought.

She hit Send.

CHAPTER 7

Ashley frantically thought about what she needed to pack. Her stomach clenched; she worried that Stephen would show up at any moment.

Her phone buzzed again.

Stephen: *Ash, I'll give you space. I can stay at Robbie's for a few days. I'll give you all the time you need. Don't call anybody.*

Ha, she thought. *That's what this is all about.* He wasn't sorry, and this had nothing to do with letting her have space. Stephen didn't want her to call the police because of the bad attention that would bring, causing even more damage to his career.

Ashley: *It's best if you stay at Robbie's. I need time. Please don't come home.*

She waited. *What if that makes him angry and he comes back?* Her stomach churned with dread.

Her phone vibrated.

Stephen: *I promise to never do anything like that again. I'm sorry.*

She shoved her phone into her pocket, rushed to the closet, pulled out her duffel bag, and filled it with anything she could find. Sweat shirt, pj's, jeans, T-shirts… She tossed in her boots. Ashley changed quickly into a pair of jeans. Next, she went to the dresser and grabbed handfuls of socks, underwear, and bras. She ran her hands through her hair again. *Toiletries.*

She grabbed the duffel and rushed out of the bedroom, into the hall, and into the bathroom to pack her bag of toiletries: hairbrush, comb, mini shampoos, and anything else she could grab quickly. Sammy followed closely and sat alert. She realized she hadn't even brushed her teeth yet. Her anxiety was at an all-time high; her hands shook as she squeezed toothpaste onto her toothbrush. She brushed her teeth, rinsed her mouth, packed her toothbrush in the toiletry bag, and stuffed that into her duffel, pulling it over her shoulder.

"Come on, boy," Ashley said to Sammy. She needed to pack up his things and take him with her. There was no way she could leave him behind. She went downstairs, found a tote bag hanging on the hooks by the door, and threw his food and leash into it.

Before Ashley left, she bolted and chain-locked the two doors to the house from the inside. Her plan was to climb out a first-floor window in the family room that looked out to the front porch. She would close the window and leave it unlocked, just in case she needed to come back. She had no idea how long Faith would let her stay.

What if she asks me to leave after I tell her what happened?

Ashley thought Faith may not want to be anywhere near her, in case Stephen found out where Ashley was and showed up. Ordinarily, Ashley would never have taken this leap of faith and trusted someone with her life, but she was desperate and had no one, except Faith, to turn to now.

Ashley thought locking the doors from the inside might buy her some time. If Stephen came back without calling and saw the chain across the door, maybe he would leave. If he decided to break the chain, maybe Ashley could use that against him if she called the police, especially if she saved his texts. She wasn't sure this would work, but she had to do something to safeguard her space.

Ashley dropped her pocketbook in the duffel and her keys in her pocket. After grabbing her duffel, Sammy's bag, and Sammy, she climbed out the front window onto the deck. She glanced around; no one was on the street. She closed the window, walked to her car in the driveway with Sammy, and left for Faith's house.

***

On the drive to Faith's house, her mind raced. *Is this the right move? What other choice do I have?* She didn't know anyone else; going back to her family wasn't an option. She tried to quiet her mind and concentrate on her breathing. She arrived at Faith's door, pale and afraid, with her bags and her dog.

"Ashley! Sammy! Come in." Faith stepped aside and gestured for Ashley to enter. Faith held her hand out to Sammy and patted his head.

"Are you sure? I'm sorry, but I couldn't leave him there…" Ashley held on to Sammy's leash.

"Absolutely. Charlie will be thrilled to see him! They haven't seen each other since the park."

"Thank you, Faith. This means so much." Ashley stood awkwardly, clinging to her bag and Sammy's leash, in the bright entryway of Faith's cape-style home.

Faith hugged Ashley as she remained stiff and unsure. Sammy held the same posture.

"Come on; come in." Faith led Ashley and Sammy into her bright-yellow kitchen. The cabinets were a rich walnut, and the yellow-and-blue pattern on the curtains and seat cushions was warm and welcoming. "You can put your bag down wherever you like." Faith gestured for Ashley to sit in one of the chairs at the island counter.

"Charlie's outside. Come on, Sammy." Sammy looked at Ashley.

"Go ahead, Sammy."

Faith opened the slider, and Sammy made his way over to Charlie. When the dogs saw each other, they circled and ran out to the backyard.

Ashley stood watching Sammy jump around and play. *To be free,* she thought.

"Sit. Tell me what happened." Faith sat in one of the chairs and pulled one out for Ashley.

Ashley placed her bag by one of the tall chairs at the island and sat. "I don't even know where to begin."

"That's okay. Would you like some tea? I already have the water on." Faith stood and moved toward the stove.

"Yes, that'd be wonderful." Ashley sighed, relieved by the distraction.

Faith busied herself getting mugs out of the glass cabinets next to the stovetop. She opened the corner cabinet and took out tea bags and honey. Steam spouted from the teapot. Faith dropped a calming herbal tea bag into each of the oversized periwinkle-blue mugs and poured boiling water into each as the television aired a midmorning weather update.

There was an unseasonable cold front heading their way with a threat of snow and ice—rare for Virginia, even rarer this time of year. The weathermen were having their spotlight, showing every possible scenario.

While the tea bags steeped, Faith kept busy getting spoons for the honey.

Ashley absently watched the news. She fretted about what to say, nervously rubbing her hands on her legs. "Stephen pushed me…and choked me." Her mouth was dry, her voice cracking on that admission.

Faith didn't miss a beat. She kept preparing the tea, silently waiting for more details.

"I ran and, well, he left."

Faith handed Ashley a mug, finally making eye contact with her.

Ashley sat wide-eyed. "I had to get away from there."

"I'm glad you contacted me." She put her hand on Ashley's.

Ashley smiled, feeling Faith's genuine concern. She breathed easier for the first time. "Me, too." They sat in silence at the island in Faith's warm kitchen, drinking their tea and watching the dogs through the slider. "He's on probation from work. He was involved in something bad. I don't even know who he is anymore."

The sun shone in through the garden window above the sink; there was no threat of a looming storm. From the outside, this would all look routine, two girlfriends hanging out with their dogs and talking about everyday things…yet this was nothing like an average day.

"What are you going to do?" Faith broke the silence.

The loaded question, Ashley thought. She nervously rubbed her hands together. "I need to leave."

Faith sipped her tea. "Will he let you?"

Ashley held her mug close, letting the steam warm her face. "No."

Faith sat silently gauging what she should say next. She'd watched Ashley's demeanor change over the time they'd worked together. One day, Faith noticed bruises on Ashley's arm, even though Ashley thought she was doing a good job of covering them up. Faith knew that she needed to speak up.

"This situation isn't going to get any better." Faith held her breath, nervous, not wanting Ashley to shut down, but she thought Ashley was ready to face the truth. "This is your choice now. You can continue living your life under his control and in constant fear. Or you can realize you are someone who matters and take back control."

Whoa. The realization hit Ashley—she wasn't living her own life. She was covering up for someone who had serious problems. Ashley wanted to be someone who mattered, someone who made a difference. She had lost her hold on the life she once imagined.

"Do you want to leave Stephen for good?" Faith locked eyes with Ashley.

Ashley didn't waver. That was why she was there. "Yes, but where will I go? I have no one…" She felt the anxiety climbing up inside, overwhelming her with the prospect of leaving and not knowing where to go.

"I know someone who can help you." Faith smiled gently.

Ashley furrowed her brow, surprised at this revelation. *Who does Faith know that can help me escape?*

Faith smiled. "My brother. My brother can help you escape."

***

Faith explained that her brother, Matthew, owned a farm that had been in their family for three generations. Unlike Matthew, Faith didn't have the patience or the money to maintain a life on the farm. But Matthew was different.

He and his wife, Anna Marie, had married young and worked in finance in New York City. They invested and made their own small fortune. Matt's clients were also wealthy, and he'd earned a trusted reputation in the industry. He'd managed portfolios for diverse clients ranging from CEOs of major companies, to actors, to agents in the FBI and Secret Service.

However, farm life was in his blood. He loved the laid-back, noncorporate mind-set of the farm. Matthew and Anna Marie had planned to work at their jobs in the city with the hope of making enough money to start a family and live on the farm, but fate intervened when Anna Marie was diagnosed with late-stage brain cancer, the tumor located in an inoperable part of the brain.

To help get through that unexpected nightmare, Anna Marie and Matt immediately quit their jobs, took out the money they'd saved, and moved to the peace and serenity of the farm, far away from the craziness of the city. That time was bittersweet for Matt; he'd finally fulfilled his dream of a life on the farm, but at a severe price.

Anna's sickness progressed. By their third month on the farm, she spent most days in bed, slowly deteriorating. The day Anna Marie passed away was one of the most brilliant sunny days; the sky couldn't have been bluer. The breeze blew through the open windows of the master bedroom where Anna Marie had been living her last days. Matt made sure that the room held her favorite things: music, photos, books, and fresh flowers.

The nurse had ended her shift, and Matt was sitting in his favorite chair by his wife's bedside. He set aside different times each day to sit with Anna, either reading or talking to her, mostly while she slept. That day, she was alert and spoke with Matt, sharing memories of the farmhouse. What seemed like only moments later, she breathed her last breath while Matt held her hand.

The moment his wife died, Matt made a promise that he would dedicate his life to helping others battling cancer. He planned to use the farm as a refuge for people visiting sick family members in the area. Or if someone had a spouse who was ill, they could come and stay in the farm's guesthouse. They could experience the peace and tranquility that existed there.

As years passed, Matt helped many people who had been affected by brain cancer. Word spread quickly through friends and friends of friends. If people were struggling financially, Matt offered them jobs on the farm to help them save money for medical costs. Matt occasionally helped people who were not fighting cancer, but who were in tough situations and needed a place to stay. Matt was careful about whom he took in or allowed to work on the farm. He used some of his old contacts in New York City to do background checks on who was coming to his home. Faith was confident she could count on Matthew to help Ashley with her situation.

Ashley was hesitant at first, but the more Faith shared with her, the more it sounded like the only way out. Ashley agreed to let Faith call her brother.

Faith showed Ashley to the guest room and told her to make herself at home; then, she went to call her brother while sitting in her study. Faith didn't tell Matt all of the details of Ashley's ordeal because the situation was sensitive. She explained that Ashley needed his help to stay alive, that she was trustworthy and willing to work while she planned her next steps.

Matthew told Faith he would help her friend. He ensured her the farm would be a safe place for her to stay. Faith then told Matthew Stephen's name, knowing he could find out information about him. That would help to keep Ashley safe if he came looking for her.

After the call, Faith gave Ashley the address to the farm. She assured her it would be a safe place for Ashley to hide and map out where she would go next.

Ashley pulled Faith into a hug, fighting off the tears. She would be forever grateful. Now, she had a safe haven, a place to go when she escaped.

With her pocketknife tucked under the mattress, Ashley spent the night in a restless sleep. She berated herself for sticking with Stephen for so long, questioning endlessly, *How did I let it get this bad?*

There was no answer.

Finally, Ashley passed out from sheer exhaustion, resolving to leave Stephen as she drifted off.

***

When Ashley woke, she realized that she needed to return to her house. All of her personal information and paperwork was still there. She hadn't even thought of packing any of that.

As she drove back to the house, Ashley had a moment of clarity. Her life had been irrevocably changed the moment she started putting together the plan to leave Stephen and the circumstances in which she'd been trapped. Everything she thought she knew was forgotten. There was a new world waiting for her, and she was ready for this new chapter to begin. That gave her a new sense of empowerment and the confidence to move forward.

But, first, she would have to make sure Stephen was not at home. It was a risk, but she needed to get her things and get out quickly.

Ashley noted how quiet the street was as she approached the house. Neighbors were either at work or out and about in their normal routines. She parked her car across the street from the house and looked down the driveway. No sign of Stephen or a strange car. Ashley thought she could go up the front steps, and it would look as if she were going in the front door.

Get in. Get out.

Checking for cars again and with Sammy in tow, she ventured across the street toward the front entry. Ascending the steps, she didn't hesitate as she continued toward the farthest window from the front door. Nothing looked disturbed.

She nudged the window, and it went up without a hitch. Quickly, she peeked inside as she lifted one leg over the sill and into the house, swiftly entering the family room. She helped Sammy over the sill. Instantly, she closed the window and glanced around the room. Everything looked in place, just as she had left it.

It's all right, she told herself. *No one is here.* She wanted to get the rest of her things and get out of there as quickly as possible.

As she stood in front of the window, she thought she heard another set of footsteps. She stood motionless to ensure that her mind wasn't playing tricks on her. Then, she smelled cigarette smoke.

"Ashley." It was Stephen.

Ashley looked to the door and saw the lock had been broken. *How could I have missed that?*

Footsteps were approaching, echoing off the walls. Stephen would block her attempt if she tried running out the front door. Her mind whirred.

As swiftly as she'd come in through the window, she raised the window, grabbed Sammy, and climbed back out again. Sammy barked as Ashley retreated and told him to run.

Stephen threw open the front door. "Ashley!" Stephen's booming voice called out.

Ashley knew Stephen would head her off at the steps, so she jumped the railing and landed wrong on her ankle. "Damn it," she hissed, trying to gain a lead on Stephen, her ankle throbbing and slowing her down.

The space between them closed, and before she reached her car, Stephen was by her side, grabbing a firm hold on her arm. "Ashley," he pleaded with her in case any eyes were watching, "are you okay?"

Sammy ran to Ashley's side and growled low, fixing his eyes on Stephen.

Stephen looked at Sammy. "Get outa here, stupid dog."

A tow truck rounded the corner. Ashley thought this could go down in one of two ways. She could put up a fight and look like a crazy person, while Stephen remained stoic and made sympathetic eyes toward the driver of the truck. Or she could go along with him until the tow truck was out of sight. *That could be risky.*

The truck passed by them quickly, before she even had a chance to decide and react. Then, she noticed a police car turning down their street, driving slowly. Ashley's heart soared. This was what she needed to save her. Stephen would see the police and let her go. Or, better yet, the officer would stop to talk to them and notice Ashley's distress. He would ask if everything was all right, and she could tell him, *No, no, it is not all right.* Then, she could explain what happened…

It was a patrol car from the neighboring town, and it slowed to a stop on the side of the road.

"What the fuck? Did you call someone?" Stephen hissed as he released Ashley's arm.

Ashley felt relief and elation wash over her. *This is it. Prayers answered. Amen!*

The officer parked his car beside the curb, then leaned across the seat, and removed his sunglasses. "Excuse me, sir, I'm going to need to see some ID."

Ashley thanked God, almost giddy at the fact that she could now bust Stephen.

Stephen squinted then approached the vehicle.

Ashley tensed a moment. *What is he going to do?*

Stephen stopped, then threw his head back, and laughed. "Well, look who it is."

The officer laughed, put his sunglasses on the dash, and then climbed out of the vehicle. "Stephen, how the hell are you?"

Ashley, motionless, looked between the officer and Stephen. They knew each other and began talking and laughing as she stood dazed, mindlessly patting Sammy's back. *This cannot be happening.*

"Guess they let anyone be an officer around here!" Stephen shook his head at the good-looking officer who smiled and laughed. "What are you doing out here, man?"

The officer shook Stephen's hand. "I heard you were a cop out here, so I looked up your address."

Stephen shook his head and walked toward Ashley, motioning for her to come over.

"Forgive me, Ashley. Come here. Come meet my buddy." Stephen was in full charmer mode and smiled genuinely at Ashley.

She wanted to tell him to fuck off. Then, she had the vision again that she would somehow look like the crazy one.

"Tim, this is Ashley." Stephen beamed.

He is good at this, she thought.

Tim extended his hand toward Ashley and flashed his grin. "My pleasure." He bowed slightly then looked at Stephen sideways. "How did you end up with a beautiful girl like her?"

"I know. I'm such a lucky guy. I don't know how she puts up with me." Stephen looked at Ashley with a love-sick grin.

Ashley felt nauseous, and her heart raced.

"Well, Ashley, if you ever need anything or get rid of this clown, feel free to call me." He looked down at Sammy at Ashley's side. "Hey, who's this?" He glanced at Ashley. "Okay if I pet him?"

Ashley stood stunned then snapped back to reality. "Oh, this is Sammy." She petted his head. "He's friendly." She glanced at Stephen out of the corner of her eye and saw him snickering.

Tim petted Sammy, and the dog panted and rubbed against him. "Sammy. Great dog."

"So, what are you doing out here?" Stephen nodded to Tim.

"We're patrolling neighborhoods around the county, ya know, for the big storm. It's like a ghost town; everyone's hunkering down. I heard you were a cop in town, so I went by the station. They said you were on leave. Injured?" Tim nodded toward Stephen.

Ashley looked at Stephen, waiting for his response.

"Yeah, I'm on medical leave. Had a back injury. I'll be back soon. How about you? When did you move to Virginia?" Stephen redirected the conversation. They continued to joke with each other and reminisce.

She gauged the distance to her car, wondering if she could possibly go inside, gather what she needed, and leave. *Unlikely.*

Ashley tuned them out and thought about the incoming storm, how that would mess up her plans of escape. She looked again at the house.

"Hey, man, I've got to get going, but let's catch up soon. Now I know where you live, so you better stay in line." They shook hands.

Ashley panicked as Tim was getting ready to leave.

Tim turned to her. "Hope to see you again. You're with a great guy here. I owe him a lot."

Ashley couldn't believe this was happening and found it difficult to speak, but managed to say a quick good-bye.

Stephen placed his arm around Ashley's shoulders as she cringed away from his touch. He waved erratically at Tim, calling out, "See you soon!"

Ashley stiffly watched the police car as it pulled away, the last of her hopes dashed as their conversation replayed in her mind. *They are longtime friends. He owes him a lot.*

Her hands began to sweat. She realized that this brotherhood went deep, each of them looking out for one another. She also came to the realization that Stephen's friends would never turn on him. He was protected by this invisible ring and could get away with anything. If she didn't leave him soon, her fate would be sealed, and she would be trapped in this hell forever.

***

Stephen's hand came down hard on the table beside her, making her jump.

"You shouldn't have done that. Chain-locking the doors after you left?" His eyes turned dark; then he brushed past her.

Now that they were back in the house, Ashley needed to diffuse the situation so she could devise a plan. As she stared out the window, she saw the first snowflakes begin to fall. *No, no, no,* her mind screamed. This storm would throw off her timing.

Ashley knew it was imperative for her to escape. Stephen had the entire police department on his side even while he was on probation. The longer she stayed, the deeper and deeper Ashley would fall into this hole with no way to climb out.

***

A winter storm was rare in Virginia. Snow, especially late March, was even rarer. But, true to the weatherman's word, the storm hit hard with fast accumulation and iced-over roads and trees. Trees and power lines were downed from the weight of the ice, causing the town to lose power.

Stephen calmed after his outburst and seemed happy to be sidetracked by the storm, keeping busy with chipping away ice on the driveway, getting the generator working, and helping neighbors with downed trees. He and another neighbor had a chainsaw and offered to help clear trees on their street.

The roads were littered with debris from the storm, so Ashley stayed inside. She busied herself with cooking what was in the freezer, making soup and a heavy casserole. Comfort food. Food that was filling. While Stephen was still out, she gathered her social security card, her personal bank account information, and her passport; she stashed them in her workbag. She packed clothes in her duffel bag and stored it in the trunk of her car in hopes of leaving.

Ashley shredded documents and personal information that she no longer needed. She would freeze when she heard a sound. Then, after realizing it wasn't Stephen, she would gather more necessities, pack them away, and count down the time until she would be free.

CHAPTER 8

*T*here were days I did not feel anything. I was numb. Thoughts of driving off the side of the road, ending it all, were appealing. The darkness settled over me, dragging me down. I fought to get through each day. My breath was shallow, but my heart raced. Emotions raged in my mind and coursed through me, keeping me unsettled. I needed to break free of this life. Break free of his hold on me. His hold—like a vise around my throat, constricting my air—was slowly squeezing the life out of me.

***

The creak in the floorboards, the click of the door, the thundering of my heartbeat echoing through the night…

Stephen's voice cut through the darkness, "Where are you going?"

Frozen midstep, she glanced at the clock—3:05 a.m. Ashley stuttered, "T-To th-the ba-bathroom…" She sounded groggy, half asleep, not wired like her insides. Ashley tiptoed to the bathroom and took deep breaths to calm her frayed nerves and to stop the shaking that had taken over her entire body. *I'll never fall back asleep.*

Grabbing a drink of water with a trembling hand and taking a small pill from her stash that was tucked away in her toiletry bag (hidden behind the box of tampons—a place he would never touch), Ashley steadied herself and hurried back before she was missed.

As she crept back into their darkened bedroom, her stomach clenched; her hands were ice-cold. Fear of being smothered by Stephen's anger and disappearing altogether consumed her. Pulling the covers back, she slowly crawled into bed, deep into the dark. His arm

84

circled her waist, and he pulled her in, trapping her, intent on never loosening his hold.

***

Ashley woke to another day without power. Stephen busied himself with more storm cleanup; he walked down the road to a friend's house to help with their generator.

The roads were clear around their neighborhood, so Ashley decided to go for a run to clear her mind. She opted to drive to her favorite trail in Chestnut Ridge. She chose that popular area because from there she could also survey the condition of the roads in town.

There were other cars at the trail, so she felt comfortable running on one of the easier paths. There was no sound, only her breath and the steady beat of her footfalls. As she ran, her thoughts whirred; she wondered, *When did this all go wrong?*

In hindsight, she could pinpoint the warning signs—the ones that screamed and the ones that whispered. They were moments that didn't stand out when she was going through them, but when she began to trace it back and follow the map of the turning points, the little bumps, and the major roadblocks, it all became clear. A harsh comment, a pattern of behavior that started small, just as a tiny crack in the foundation that goes unnoticed until the entire tower crumbles and crashes down.

Ashley had that moment of clarity. Things weren't always this bad. The relationship between her and Stephen began with an instant spark, a flurry of emotion. It was a fairy tale—boy meets unhappy girl, takes her away from her troubled past, and sweeps her off her feet. He wanted to spend a lot of time with her, but that seemed normal. She wanted to be with him, too. *That's how it is in new relationships,* she thought. But his jealousy had mounted, and his anger and rage had exploded like a dormant volcano, spilling over and threatening to trap her forever under his molten manic behavior.

As she arrived at one of the overlooks, Ashley looked across the expanse of valley. She knew there was freedom out there, and it was within her reach.

***

That evening, the deadly silence jolted her awake. She glanced at her bedside clock. Again, it read 3:05 a.m. She quietly climbed out of bed...

The creak in the floorboards, the click of the door, the thump of my thundering heartbeat...and...

Something is different.

Heavy breathing and snoring from Stephen as he slept soundly— the heavy dinner and abundance of red wine, along with an Ativan that Ashley crushed and sprinkled in it, induced his sleep.

Stepping out into the hallway... Still no change. Heart hammering in her ears, Ashley couldn't decipher sounds as she walked toward the bathroom. Then, still hearing steady snores, she changed her route and veered toward the stairs. Silently, she made her way down, avoiding the squeaky spot on the second step and not daring to turn around.

Keep moving. Do not stop now.

As she headed toward the front door, Sammy looked up at her with sad eyes. Ashley would never leave him behind. *Stephen will probably kill him or let him loose to starve in the woods,* she thought.

In a single sweep, she scooped Sammy up in one arm, grabbed her workbag, and snatched her keys off the hook. Swiftly, Ashley opened the front door.

Keep moving. Do not look back.

Waiting to hear a loud, booming voice and footsteps in the hallway...waiting for a hand to grab her arm...or her hair...

Keep moving. Breathe.

The car was gassed and ready to go, as it had been...waiting. She was ready, too, but her legs were like lead as she crept down the walkway toward the driveway. She opened the car door and dropped

Sammy into the front seat. Ashley had a bag of treats ready in the glove compartment just in case she had to keep Sammy quiet.

Sammy whimpered and sat upright in the front seat, obediently waiting. He knew to be as silent as he could—bad things happened when he barked at night.

Ashley started the car, praying for a safe escape and not looking back, but envisioning the front door of the house flying open and then being stormed by rage.

Keep moving. Lock the doors. Put the car in Drive. Breathe.

She was waiting for a fist to come crashing through the window. It never came. Her foot pressed on the gas…

Move ahead, and never look back.

***

With the full tank of gas, Ashley knew she could keep driving without a pit stop. She had stowed away in the trunk enough money and clothes for her and a bag with Sammy's leash, food, and water bowl. She couldn't afford to lose any ground. At the police departments, Stephen had contacts who owed him favors.

The pit in Ashley's stomach lasted for most of the ride. Sammy sat up straight in the passenger seat, reflecting Ashley's posture. His senses were on high alert. The farther away they drove from Stephen, the more the stress seemed to lessen.

Eventually, Ashley eased back in her seat, lowered her shoulders from around her ears, and exhaled loudly. At the same moment, Sammy whined, circled around his seat, and then lay down, his head on his paws. He looked up at Ashley for reassurance.

"Good boy, Sammy." Those were the first words she'd uttered since saying good night to Stephen, since running in fear. Her breath caught as she petted Sammy's head. "Settle down now. It's all going to be okay."

She felt the weight of him sink into the seat as he let out a sigh and closed his eyes. Somehow, he understood what was happening.

"We'll finally be free."

***

The drive should have taken six hours, but it took closer to seven since she stopped at a few roadside truck stops for breaks for her and Sammy. She made sure to stop at busy roadside rest areas loaded with cars, semis, and tractor trailers of all sizes. She wanted to be lost in the crowd, not stand out.

What if Stephen is here? That is crazy, but what if he followed me? Or what if he notified the police, and they are here to drag me back? Her irrational thoughts were taking over.

She needed coffee and a break from driving. Baseball hat on and in an oversized sweat shirt, she prayed not to stand out.

***

The clock on the dashboard read 10:00 a.m. as Ashley drove up the long gravel, tree-lined driveway of Matthew's sprawling farm. Sammy sat up at attention, taking in the new sights and smells. The house was a spacious yellow, colonial-style home. There was a welcoming farmer's porch, and the estate was surrounded by tall oak trees and fields of green. It was picturesque and had a red barn to the right side of the house at the end of the driveway.

Two yellow Labrador retrievers ran around the lush front yard, while two men loaded hay into the back of a black pickup truck. With a worker, a tall man with dark hair peppered with grey was unloading wood from another pickup truck. The tall man with strong features stopped what he was doing, removed his gloves, and watched Ashley's car as it slowly approached. She guessed he was Matthew. She drove her car behind his truck and then immediately confirmed her assumption as he approached her car. His expression was so much like Faith's. His cerulean-blue eyes were similar but a much deeper color.

Ashley took a deep breath as she put the car in Park. Sammy's tail was wagging. He was ready to be free. *Am I?* she asked herself.

CHAPTER 9

Ashley climbed out of the car, cautiously looking at her surroundings. The weather had improved—warm and sunshiny—as she drove north. Here, there was no sign of the early spring storm. Matthew approached smiling warmly.

"Hi, you must be Ashley." He put his gloves in his back pocket then extended his hand.

She smiled and walked around the open car door. "You must be Matthew." Tentatively, she shook his hand then withdrew and put her hands in her pockets.

"You found it okay? I know it's a long ride." He squinted in the sunlight.

Ashley nodded. "Yeah, it was long, but the directions were perfect."

Sammy barked from the front seat.

"Oh, Sammy." She leaned into the car. "Come on, boy. It's okay."

Sammy climbed across the seat, as cautious of his new surroundings as Ashley.

She took the leash from the seat, hooked it to his collar, and then led him out of the car. "It's okay, Sam." She looked up at Matthew. "This is Sammy. He's a little nervous…" She didn't finish, unsure of what else to say.

"Hey, Sammy." Matt leaned down to pet him. "Hey, little guy. It's okay. I have two dogs that'll love to play with you."

Sammy warmed up to him quickly, loving the attention and Matt's calm demeanor.

"Sammy was watching the dogs as we drove in." Right on cue, the two dogs ran toward them.

"They are friendly." Matt reached his hands out to calm the dogs.

"Oh, hi!" Ashley petted them as they sniffed her hands and play-fully moved around Sammy.

"This is Tanner and Scout. Tanner has the blue bandanna. Scout wears the camo collar. He's not a bandanna fan."

Ashley laughed as Sammy circled the dogs, ready to play. It was a good distraction from why she was there.

"Let's get your bags, and I can show you to the house."

Ashley opened the back door of her car to get her bags; then she retrieved the small tote she had stashed in the trunk.

"You travel light." He reached for the larger duffel. "May I?"

Ashley stood awkwardly clutching her bags; then she released the duffel. "Yes, sure. Thanks."

"All right. Let's get you settled. The dogs seem to be having fun."

She smiled as she watched Sammy running free around the yard with the dogs.

As they approached the house, Matthew introduced Ashley to Jake, Cody, and a woman named Jess; each of them worked on the farm. Matthew told her they had dairy cows and chickens for eggs, and they baled hay for sale to horse farms. He mentioned something about horses and that there were crops? She tried to keep everything straight. There was something about sunflowers, too.

Her mind whirred. She was exhausted from the trip, and all the stress was taking a toll on her. She tried to be polite, but her attention was waning.

Matthew led her up the wide wooden-plank steps leading to a farmer's porch adorned with four classic antique-white rocking chairs and large pots of bright-colored dahlias flanking the main doorway. He held the door open to an expansive entryway filled with light.

A woman walked toward them.

"This is Leanne. She's been with my family for twenty years. She knows everything there is to know about the farm."

"Nice to meet you, Ashley. I'll take her from here. Go back to work."

Leanne looked to be in her fifties, was tall, and had ashy-blonde hair pulled into a ponytail. She was dressed in a flannel shirt and jeans and had an apron tied around her waist.

Matthew smiled. "Yes, ma'am." He looked at Ashley. "She keeps me in line and on schedule. We'll keep Sammy busy out here. Do you have food for him?"

With shaky hands, Ashley ruffled through her tote bag for his food and leash and handed them to Matthew. "He should be good running around out there, but I can take him if he gets to be too much, or if he gets tired."

"Great. He'll be fine. See you later." He smiled and walked off.

Leanne showed Ashley around the first floor, the meticulous country-style kitchen with antique-white cabinets and grey counter-tops. There was a wall of windows that let in the sunlight and views of the fields. She told Ashley how she cooked the meals for the workers and guests.

She led her into the main family room, which was lined with built-in shelves that were full of books and photos; there were comfortable couches and two large chairs with oversized ottomans in warm tones. There was a massive stone fireplace with a dark-wood mantel. The two-sided fireplace opened into the family room on one side, as well as the kitchen on the other.

Leanne took her to the guest room upstairs, toward the back of the house. She would be next to the room where Leanne stayed when she slept at the house a few nights a week, particularly when guests stayed at the farm. That made Ashley feel at ease. Having another woman present while she was staying there was comforting.

The guest room was full of sunlight. Large windows were open, letting in a cool breeze; the smell of grass and lilacs filled the room. There was a vase with sunflowers in one corner and a small glass jar with lilacs on a desk by the windows. The windows overlooked a mas-sive field of sunflowers. *Sunflower field, that's what Matt mentioned earlier.* A queen-size bed stood against the far wall, to the right of the doorway. The dresser and desk had matching oak stain. The bed was made up with fluffy pillows and a quilt of a blue-and-yellow pattern. There was a plush yellow blanket at the foot of the bed, along with an oak hope chest loaded with more blankets, according to Leanne.

"Let me know if you need anything else. You can make yourself right at home here. Help yourself to anything in the kitchen."

Ashley stood awkwardly, then placed her bags down by the bed. "Thank you so much."

"Dinner will be at five tonight. Come down any time after you are settled in." Leanne smiled warmly.

"Thank you again." Ashley shut the door and looked around the room. She thought she should check on Sammy, but she was so tired. She looked at her bags and thought she should unpack too, but wasn't quite ready to go there yet. Sitting on the side of the bed, she ran her hands down the tops of her legs several times. *This is going to take some time getting used to,* she thought.

She lay back on the bed and closed her eyes, listening to the birds chirping, occasional voices off in the distance, car doors, and the sounds of the farm. Her mind swirled; her pulse beat fast as she shivered uncontrollably. Grabbing the blanket from the end of the bed, she wrapped herself in it and focused on calming breaths, repeating to herself that everything would be all right.

***

Ashley woke over five hours later to sounds of a delivery truck pulling up to the barn. It took her a moment to remember where she was. She sat up. The digital clock glowed. It was after 3:30 in the afternoon.

Sammy, she thought. She hoped he was doing okay. She hadn't heard barking, and nobody had awakened her, so he must be fine.

Sighing, she lay back down. She glanced at her bags in the corner. She had turned her cell phone off, not wanting to be tempted to check the messages or have any contact with her past life. *Stephen could somehow use my cell phone to track me.* She had to stop herself, avoid going down that path of paranoia, but deep down she knew Stephen was capable of anything.

She unpacked, putting a few of her clothes in one of the large dressers by the bed, but kept her other bag packed, just in case... She took out some clothes to wear and decided to shower before heading downstairs. Opening the door, she peeked out into the hallway, trying to remember where the bathroom was. She saw the open door past Leanne's room and quickly walked down the hall and into the bathroom, shutting and locking the door behind her.

She leaned against the door and sighed. "Get a grip."

The rustic country-style bathroom décor was simple. There were oak shelves loaded with thick white bath towels, wrought-iron rings, and simple decorative signs about hope and faith covering the walls. The shower was in an antique-looking tub that had been refinished.

Turning on the water and letting the steam fill the room, she stepped in. The shower felt wonderful, like a long-awaited respite. She let the hot water wash over her, thanking God she'd made it this far. This time was essential for her to gain back her strength and confidence and sort out where she would go from there.

Feeling refreshed, she made her way downstairs after dressing in clean clothes. She stood awkwardly at the kitchen entrance at first; then she saw Sammy eating out of the bowl they had set up for him.

"Hey, Sam." She went over and knelt to pet him.

"Hi, Ashley. Did you have a good rest?" Leanne smiled warmly.

"Oh yes, I can't believe how long I slept. The bed is so comfortable." She looked around the kitchen at what Leanne was prepping for dinner. "Can I help with anything?"

"Glad you asked. Can you chop vegetables for the salad?" She gestured to the assortment of colorful vegetables lined up on the counter next to the chopping board.

Ashley set to work and liked the distraction. She found Leanne easy to talk to. Or not talk to—it was a comfortable silence as they worked to prepare the dinner. Ashley was famished and could hardly wait to eat.

Matthew entered the kitchen with Jake, Cody, and Jess as it was getting close to dinnertime. Leanne had made a dinner of pulled pork, homemade rolls, potato salad, and pineapple-mango salad. The flavors were so heavenly. Ashley realized she hadn't eaten a real meal since escaping Stephen. She sat quietly and listened to all of them talking, joining in occasionally, but happy to take it all in. At the end of the meal, Ashley helped Leanne clean up.

"I'm going to head up unless you need me to do anything."

Leanne saw she was fading fast. "You go get some rest, Ashley. Tomorrow will be an early morning."

***

When Ashley finally sat down on the bed that evening, she felt relief wash over her. She brought the extra dog bed they had given her for Sammy upstairs for him to sleep. He circled a few times then settled in and fell asleep before she even had her pajamas on.

Her fears weren't taking center stage in her mind as they had earlier. She felt a brief hint of the freedom she so craved. She pulled back the quilt and crawled under the covers, closing her eyes and not moving until the early morning light shone through the curtains.

CHAPTER 10

Ashley woke up to the roosters crowing. She ate a quick breakfast and set to work for the day, navigating between helping Leanne inside the house and working with Jess in the barn. Jess showed her how to collect eggs from the chickens. Ashley was happy to keep busy, relishing the distraction from her dire situation. She had one break for lunch and worked late into the afternoon.

After her long, hot shower, Ashley joined everyone in the kitchen. Leanne had prepared a feast of roasted chickens, cheesy potato casserole, a garden salad, and more homemade rolls. This was a much heavier fare than Ashley was used to eating, but she was famished and loaded her plate.

"Ashley where are you from?" Jess passed to Ashley the basket with the freshly baked rolls.

She envisioned eating the entire basket of rolls loaded with butter, but she controlled herself, reaching for only one. Matt and the others were easy to talk to. She had rehearsed her story, hoping to avoid the many details about the darkness she'd escaped and her unknown future.

"Outside of Baltimore." She sliced the roll in half.

"Did you go to school down that way?" Jess inquired.

Her hands shook as she spread a generous amount of butter on the roll. *Would it be rude if I took a bite before answering?* she thought; then she wouldn't be able to answer the question.

"I went to school for art and graphic design in Baltimore. I'm hoping to find a job in the New York or Boston area. The advertising market is much better up there."

A new job and a new life, she thought. Regular adventures for a twenty-six-year-old, not someone on the run.

"That market has to be competitive," Matt interjected.

Jess continued, "Do you have any family or friends up there, or are you going on your own?"

Ashley swallowed hard, finding it more difficult to answer questions about herself than she'd thought it would be. "Uh, yeah, I have a friend from school that moved up there, so at least I have someone to show me around." She laughed nervously.

"Where, New York or Boston?" Jess persisted.

Cody spoke up, "I have family outside of Boston in Norwood."

Ashley nodded to Cody, unsure of how to answer Jess. *Should I say Boston? Or maybe lie further and say New York?* The fewer people who knew where she was going, the better.

"New Jersey. My friend lives in New Jersey. In Hoboken." She recalled the names of potential towns she'd researched before leaving Stephen. She prayed someone would change the subject.

"I worked and lived in New York City for ten years before moving back here." Matt scooped out another serving of the potatoes and then passed the bowl to Jess.

Ashley saw this as her chance to take attention off her. "Where did you work?"

Matt went on to talk about his and Anna's fast-paced life in New York before moving to the farm. That steered the conversation in an entirely new direction. She didn't know if Matt did that on purpose, but she was relieved. She didn't hear a word of what he said as she faded into the background. She didn't want to draw attention to herself and hoped no one would ask anything more about her future plans.

As soon as dinner was over, she explained she was tired from the day's work and went straight to her room, taking Sammy with her.

Exhausted from the physical labor of the day and the mental stress of weaving the lies for her life, she fell thankfully into bed.

***

The next morning, she woke up at seven o'clock, ate a quick breakfast, and was at work before eight o'clock. Since Jess had taught her the day before how to help with the chickens, that occupied most of Ashley's morning. Some of them were mean and gave Ashley a hard time when she entered the henhouse.

Eventually, Matt checked in on her.

"These chickens have some crazy personalities. Some are downright rude. It took me over a half hour to get past her," she exclaimed and pointed at the large, brassy-toned chicken that was pecking at the wooden trim of the barn.

Matt laughed and nodded his head as he leaned against the door of the coop. "Yeah, they can be strong-willed. Good thing you showed her who's boss."

She gave him a look and shook her head, picking up her backpack. "Yeah, I don't know about that." She tugged her bag over her shoulder. "I'm heading back to see what Jess has lined up for me now. Hope it's not herding the cows."

Matt laughed at her sarcasm. "I can give you a ride back and show you the rest of the farm if you'd like."

"Yeah, that's perfect."

They climbed into Matt's 1962 red Ford pickup truck and followed the dirt road from the henhouse, past an old horse barn, and ascended the hill toward the backside of the property. They passed old fields that had once been used to grow corn. There was a small barn on the right that Ashley hadn't noticed that morning.

"That's a cool barn. What's that used for?"

"Since we don't farm on this section as much, it's mostly used for storage." He slowed the truck as they neared the barn.

Ashley leaned forward in her seat. "What a shame. It has such a historical feel to it." Structurally, the barn looked sound. The outside was partially painted with a whitewash paint.

"My wife had visions for this end of the property. Her first project was to update and renovate this barn. She began the project before she got ill. Then…time got away from us. The final touches were never completed." Matt put the truck in Park, and they admired the serene setting in silence. The barn overlooked the rolling fields that were no longer used for crops.

"It's charming. Looks like a great place to have a party."

"You're observant. That was Anna's vision for the barn; it's a unique space." He was lost in thought.

"Oh." Ashley felt bad and hoped she hadn't brought up any sad memories. "I'm sorry."

Matt glanced at her, coming back to reality. "No, not at all. I love to come out here. It takes me back to a time when there was much joy, life, and excitement on this farm. I haven't been able to fulfill the rest of her dream. I…I'm not ready for that. But I do love to admire the work we started."

"Can we take a look inside?"

"Definitely." Matt led the way up the two steps to the small porch leading to the doors of the barn. He opened the large barn doors to a wide-open space.

The floors had been refinished with a dark-oak stain and were clean of the dirt and dust that Ashley had expected. There were two worn benches, wooden crates, and what appeared to be old window frames and wood panels stacked against the far wall. The barn had high, open ceilings that let in natural light from the original windows and dormers. Through the windows of the barn, there were views of the expansive fields. It seemed the walls only needed a fresh coat of paint.

Ashley imagined the finished project in her mind. "Wow, this would be a wonderful space. You should finish it." She scanned the ceiling and dormers that had been refinished and stained.

"I recently cleaned out the junk that had accumulated here and cleaned up the floors. There are so many other projects needing my attention, though." He shrugged and put his hands in his pockets. "Plus, I'm not quite ready to work on the rest of it."

Ashley understood how it would be hard for him to continue the work on this project. The painting and decorating with simple furnishings wouldn't cost much or take much time to complete, but she kept those thoughts to herself.

Matt turned to leave. "I have to get back to the house, so let's get you back to Jess."

Ashley had one last look around before she hurriedly followed him.

***

"I have an idea." She turned toward Matt as they were clearing the dishes from dinner that evening.

He studied her a moment, tilting his head slightly. "Yes, and this idea is…" He waited for her to continue.

"I could paint the barn for you," she blurted out. Ashley quickly explained before he had a chance to say no. "I need to help out here, and I'm obviously not good at dealing with the chickens or with the heavy lifting."

She tried to read his expression. He began shaking his head, and she knew this would take some convincing. "All it needs is some paint and a few decorations."

Matt hesitated. "I'll have to think about it." He carried the large platter into the kitchen.

Ashley followed with the empty salad bowl and utensils. "It wouldn't cost that much, either."

He smiled and placed the platter on the kitchen counter. "I'll think about it." He returned to the dining room.

Ashley understood. It would be a big step for him to move forward and trust her with the completion of the project that Anna began, so she didn't push it any further.

***

On day three, Ashley continued the simple routine of waking, eating, and going to work. The work wasn't easy, but it was therapeutic. She worked with Jacob and Cody, loading into the trailer hay to be delivered to a horse farm. She struggled to lift the small bales of hay as sweat dripped down her back, and the sun beat down on her. She stopped, removed the heavy work gloves to wipe the sweat from her forehead, and squinted while watching Matt's pickup truck drive toward her.

He parked the truck and approached her. "Hey, how's it going?"

Ashley huffed. "It's going." She drank from her water bottle and turned back to look at the piles of hay.

Matt followed her gaze. "So, you ready to take on a new project?"

She would be happy to give up this job for whatever project he had lined up for her. Even if it was fighting with the chickens again. "Sure, what do you need?"

Matt glanced around and then turned back to Ashley. "Well, I guess you need to tell me what supplies you'll need to paint the barn."

Ashley realized what he was hinting at. "Wait, you mean you're going to let me paint *the* barn?"

He laughed at her surprise. "Yes, I thought about it, and it seems like a good idea."

"Oh my gosh, that's terrific!" Ashley couldn't contain her excitement.

"I can drive you into town, or Jess can go with you to get what you need at the hardware store."

She wanted to hug him, but held back. This project was exactly what she needed. "Yes, I'll go; we can go now. I know exactly what I need."

He nodded and smirked. "Come on. I'll drive you to town." Matt turned back toward his truck as she grabbed her backpack and water bottle.

***

Ashley pulled on her baseball hat, tucking her hair inside. This was her first time out in public since she'd arrived at the farm. Suddenly, she felt a wave of panic run through her. *Maybe this is a bad idea,* she thought. *What if Stephen finds me somehow? What will I do?* That would put Matt in danger, too. All her actions from now on had the potential to hurt others, not only herself. *What if…?*

Stop, she told herself. This was the first step in living a new life. If she couldn't go to a hardware store for paint supplies, how was she supposed to move on and start the new life she craved? She had to take this one step at a time. *Baby steps.*

At the hardware store, Matt knew almost everyone he ran into. Ashley ducked down the paint aisle, searching for the right colors. She had the idea for an antique white, so she studied the assortment of white paint chips. Above all, she wanted to preserve the historic look of the barn, but she wanted to freshen it up with a whitewash. She remembered the old window panes and wooden boards that were stored in the barn. She could paint them and use them as accent pieces to hang on the walls.

Matt liked the vintage white and classic pewter colors she suggested and was impressed that the materials were not that expensive. He loaded everything into the truck, and they returned to the farm.

As they drove up the gravel driveway and the farm came into view, Ashley felt comforted. She breathed in deep and realized how tense she'd been while they were in town. She relaxed her shoulders and stretched her neck, happy to be back at her safe haven. This place gave her the peace and strength she needed to press on during this unsettled time of her life.

***

That evening, when she was in the quiet of her room with Sammy, she fixed her gaze on her backpack. Her sketchbook was in there. She hadn't touched it in the past six months. Drawing, sketching—they used to be her outlet, her way to relax. She hadn't had the motivation to start again...until now.

A vision of the completed barn was stuck in her mind. She knew she couldn't tackle all of the things she was imagining—the things that would make the barn a unique place to hold parties or even an annex to the main house—but she wanted to draw a picture.

She stood and retrieved her sketchbook and her pencils. Returning to the bed, she propped up several of the pillows and sat back against them. She stared at the sketchbook before opening it. *It has been so long,* she thought.

She opened the cover to a blank page and began to transfer her vision of a picturesque barn onto the page.

***

Ashley woke before seven o'clock. The bedroom light was still on, her book and pencils were scattered across the bed, and she had a pain in her neck from falling asleep sitting up. She dressed, ate, grabbed a coffee to go, and was ready for the day.

Jacob offered to drive Ashley to the barn on his way out to the horses. Matt had placed the paint, a small ladder, and other supplies in the barn the night before, so she was ready to get started.

She opened the barn doors and examined the space a little closer. She hadn't noticed there were a couple of lights hanging from the center beams. She located the wall light switch and turned it to the On position, pleasantly surprised that the lights worked. She envisioned chandeliers hanging from the beams.

Her first order of business was to clean up the walls and begin to paint. The wall areas she planned to paint were about eight feet high and had already been sanded and prepped by Matt prior to Anna getting sick. She only needed to wipe the walls down, prime, and paint. She lined up her supplies and started at the north-facing end of the barn.

As she worked, her mind wandered back to her life with Stephen. She always ended up asking herself the same question—*How did it get that bad?* She could recall moments when she should have left or should have done something, but most of the time she felt as if she were on one never-ending roller-coaster ride that she would never get off.

She poured paint into the tray and moved to a new section, priming, painting, and moving the tarp with her as she progressed. The therapeutic rhythm of painting and creating soothed her soul. She'd completed two of the end walls by early afternoon.

She heard a truck approach the barn and stood arching her back, realizing she needed a break for lunch. She stepped outside and saw Jess climb out of the pickup and walk over to the barn.

"Hey, wanted to see how you're doing up here. I knew you wouldn't want to walk all the way back for lunch." Jess came up the steps.

"Perfect timing. I'm starving." Ashley stepped back into the barn so that Jess could enter. "I got quite a bit done so far."

Jess peered through the door and entered. "This looks amazing. What a difference already."

Ashley grabbed her backpack. "I'm ready to take a break, though." She and Jess drove back to the main house for lunch.

Ashley didn't want to squander the afternoon. When she finished eating, she drove her car to the barn so she could get as much painting done as possible before dinner.

***

The next day, Ashley tackled the widest wall of the barn. She was nearly finished when Leanne brought lunch to her. Determined to complete this project by the end of the day, she hadn't taken breaks.

Ashley reflected on how calming it was to be able to have control over something in her life. Lately, so much had been spiraling out of control. She'd lived in organized chaos. To the outside world, her life looked perfect, but it was as if she were living in the eye of a tornado.

After she finished eating, she took one of the old benches outside and sanded it. She applied one coat of stain and left it to dry under the overhang.

She wondered what Matt would think of the barn when it was complete. He'd told her he didn't want to bother her while she worked, but he'd offered to help her if she needed it. She'd told him she would show him what she had finished by Friday.

***

By the end of the day Friday, she'd completed painting the walls, the trim, and staining the two benches and the old window frames.
Matt drove up to the barn midafternoon in his pickup truck and parked near the newly stained bench that was positioned facing the fields behind the barn. He smiled as he hopped out of the truck, walked up the steps, and knocked on the open barn door.

"Hello, are you ever coming out of there?" He peeked into the barn.

Lost in her world, Ashley jumped at the sound. "Oh my God. You scared me." She laughed, trying to calm her thudding heartbeat. She folded the tarp and placed it in the pile with the other supplies. "Perfect timing. I'm finished." She held her arms out and looked around.

"This looks amazing. What a transformation."

With his hands on his hips, he examined the walls which were painted an antique white, with one section a brushed grey. The remaining trim was the natural wood of the barn which altogether brought out the dark, exposed wooden beams above. The style was a mix of rustic and shabby chic.

"The colors are perfect."

"You like it?" She had been a little worried about what his reaction might be.

"Yes, I love it. It's changed the whole feel of the barn." He ran his hand through his hair as he walked the perimeter. "Thank you for this."

"It was my pleasure. Seriously, it was therapeutic for me." She showed him the old windows she had painted. "These could be hung on the walls as accent pieces."

"Those are perfect."

She picked up her backpack, and they walked outside as the sun cast shadows on all sides of the barn and through the windows.

"I love that you refinished this old bench. This, right here, will be the best view of the sunset." He motioned toward the bench that was perfectly situated for a view of the horizon.

Ashley sat, enjoying Matt's company and the satisfaction of completing this project.

***

Ashley and Matt drove back to the main house where things were quiet. The workers left early on Fridays, and the dogs were asleep on the porch until they heard Matt drive his truck toward the main barn.

Ashley hurried upstairs to shower before dinner. Afterwards, with a new yearning to create, she grabbed her sketchbook and pencils and took them downstairs. She settled into one of the large rocking chairs on the wraparound porch. The breeze was warm as it washed over her skin. The sun shone golden orange over the horizon, casting a glow over the fields surrounding the house.

The dogs were fed and were sacked out on the porch in their dog beds. Sammy even had his own bed on the porch, although he tended to extend a paw or his body across Tanner or Scout's beds, so he had contact with one of them.

Ashley smiled and tilted her head back to bask in the warm afternoon glow. If she could sketch this scene, she would name it *Freedom and Peace*—a drastic change from the life she'd escaped only one week ago.

Matt walked downstairs after taking his shower and strolled into the kitchen to check on dinner. "This smells delicious." He eyed the pots on the stove, hoping to sneak a taste, but Leanne shooed him away.

106

"Not till dinner." That was the same way she'd responded for years to his pleas for food before meals.

Matt glanced out to the back porch. Ashley was resting in one of the rockers. He paused before pushing through the door, hoping she wasn't asleep.

Ashley perked up at the sound of the door being opened.

"Hey. Mind if I join you guys?" Matt smiled and nodded toward her and the dogs.

"Sure, your house." She smirked and settled back in her rocker.

"I was going to have a glass of wine. Would you like some?" He put his hands on the top of the rocker next to Ashley.

"Yes, gosh, wine and this rocker—I may not ever get up."

"Be right back." Matt busied himself retrieving the glasses and a bottle of wine from the kitchen.

Ashley was enchanted by her surroundings, listening to the birds chirping and watching the sky turn shades of gold, orange, and pink. *This would be a beautiful place to live.* She contemplated staying another week, a month…and not having to worry about finding a new place to live.

She watched Sammy resting with the other dogs, and that warmed her heart. She knew if he could talk, he would say exactly what she was thinking—*Freedom and peace.*

Matt returned, bringing her back to reality. "Here you are. To a hard week's work."

She accepted the glass from him. "Cheers. I feel like I've worked harder this week than I have ever worked in my entire life."

"Yeah"—Matt grinned, that dimple showing—"this place will do that to you. I hope you're enjoying it here, despite the work."

She pondered her words before answering, turning the wineglass in her hands. "I like it here. The peace, the freedom"—she glanced at Matt—"and the work." The silence settled between them. "I'll be forever grateful to Faith. She saved my life by helping me." Ashley kept her gaze fixed on her hands. "I'm not sure how much she told you. She said she would keep most of the sordid details to herself." Ashley snickered, trying to sound casual, not sure how much she should confide in him.

He was quiet a moment longer. "I'm not sure of exactly what happened, but I'm thinking it was pretty bad since you had to leave rather quickly. I hope you feel safe here."

"Yes, I do. This is just what I needed." She turned to face him. Her hands began to shake, but she resolved to stay strong. "My boyfriend that I was living with became abusive. Things went bad. Faith gave me the courage to finally leave." Ashley stared across the wide-open field. "Now, I'm on the run." Her voice caught in her throat.

"I'm glad you found the strength to leave. You have a lot to offer the world. I would hate to see your spark diminished."

Ashley smiled, touched by his words. She saw him as a safe harbor, someone people relied on, someone willing to give anything to help others.

He continued, "I can help you with some things. I'm not sure what you have lined up after this, but you may have to change some things if you are trying to…not be found." Matt was careful with his words.

"Yeah, I was wondering about that. Like, what I would do about my ID and my cell phone…"

Matt nodded. "I can help you get a phone. And a new ID, for that matter."

She furrowed her brow and eyed him, confused.

He nodded and laughed. "I know people, and they owe me some favors."

"Okay, well, I'll take all the help I can get." Ashley exhaled loudly. The busyness of the past week had taken her mind off the daunting work that lay ahead in building her new life.

"All right. We'll figure it all out. But not tonight." He gestured to the beautiful sky and raised his glass to hers.

Ashley agreed. She couldn't get enough of this view of the sun glowing bright against the fluffy pink clouds. She considered her sketchbook on the side table. She had thought about showing Matt her design for the barn, but wasn't sure when to do it. That moment seemed as good a time as any, so she picked up her book.

"I want to show you something." She opened the book to the page with the barn sketch and paused. "I used to draw to relax; it was my outlet. I…haven't had time or wanted to draw for a long time, but I was inspired this week." She took a breath. "I drew a sketch of the barn." She observed Matt's expression. "The finished barn. Do you want to see it?"

"Yes, of course. When did you…?" He paused as she handed him her book. "Ashley, this is incredible." He looked at her and then regarded the drawing, smiling.

"I saw this in my mind the minute you opened those doors, and I stepped inside. I needed to put it on paper. The space has so many possibilities."

Matt couldn't believe the detail and the way the barn came to life on the page. The sliding barn doors on rustic wrought-iron tracks, as well as wrought-iron ring pulls for the décor, two chandeliers hanging from the center beam, and the refinished benches along the wall. There were wall sconces and string lights around the entryway. On the outside, she drew additional string lights along the overhang near the entrance and Adirondack chairs on either side of the door.

He smiled softly, the creases near his eyes showing. "This is amazing." He regarded the picture a moment longer. "It's so close to what we had envisioned." Slowly, he handed the book back to her.

Ashley tore the pages out of her book. "I want you to have these. Maybe, someday, you can complete your vision. When you're ready."

He nodded and held the pages in his hand. "Thank you. This means a lot. The fact that you finished painting the barn, it…it means a lot to me."

"It's the least I could do." She put her notebook to the side.

"You are incredibly talented. I hope you can find a job where you can use your creativity. It's a gift." Matt held the drawings, admiring them a moment longer before placing them under a coaster on the side table next to him.

"I hope so, too." Ashley drank her wine slowly, trying not to fall down the hole of wondering where she would work, live, be.

A cool breeze began to stir. Matt retrieved the drawings from under the coaster and stood, stretching his legs. "Are you hungry?"

"I'm starved." Ashley hadn't realized how hungry she was until he asked. "I can't wait to see what Leanne left for us."

"I'll get a fire started. And another glass of wine?" Matt held up the bottle.

"Yes. Sounds perfect." Matt carried the drawings and the bottle of wine into the house, while Ashley brought in the glasses and her book. She strolled into the kitchen and removed the covers from the platter of fried chicken and the bowl of quinoa salad. There was also corn bread, and brownies for dessert. "How much does Leanne think we can eat?" She eyed the expansive array of food.

Matt brought the dogs into the house, filled their bowls with water, then gathered kindling and wood for the fire. The two-sided hearth, one side facing the kitchen and the other facing the family room, soon spread warmth while they filled their plates and enjoyed the many flavors Leanne had melded together.

***

"I'm absolutely stuffed. She's an amazing cook." Ashley carried her dish to the sink.

"She is a godsend to this place. I don't know where I'd be without her." Matt wrapped and stored the extra food in the refrigerator. He noticed the fire had faded. "I'll put some more logs on the fire."

Ashley walked into the family room, admiring the oversized stone fireplace and the rustic but comfortable furniture. She sank into the comfortable chenille cushions of the L-shaped couch. "You've done an amazing job preserving the farm."

"I wouldn't have it any other way." He picked up a few logs from the rack next to the hearth.

Ashley, warmed by the wine and the fire, watched him as he tended to the fire, his strong back to her. She blushed, thinking about how attractive he was and how she wouldn't mind having his strong arms around her.

He sat down next to her and relaxed, leaning back against the cushions of the couch. "Thank you for an enjoyable night. I hope I didn't bore you too much."

"Not at all. Dinner, the view, the wine, the stories—this is just what I needed."

He turned toward her. "You can stay here as long as you like, you know."

Ashley was silent. How tempting it was to stay. *Running can wait,* she thought briefly. "I'll think about it."

They sat in silence. Ashley, mesmerized by the fire, felt something shift between them. All along, there had been a subtle spark, an underlying current that had now become apparent.

Matt placed his wineglass on the table and sat back against the couch. "I understand that you probably want to keep moving."

Ashley stared into the dancing flames. "This is the perfect place for me to be right now. I'm so grateful. You're right, though. I do feel like I have to keep moving." She glanced at Matt.

"Totally understandable." He shifted his gaze down toward his hands. "Too bad for me, though."

"Why is that?"

"You are a good worker—hard to come by these days."

"Thanks a lot!" She playfully swatted him on the shoulder.

"Seriously, I enjoy your company."

"Me, too. I enjoy yours." Ashley smiled, sinking back into the cushions. She wondered what it would be like to kiss him.

"Ashley, I…I want to kiss you, but… I-I'm sorry; is this too much?" He turned to face her.

She thought, *He must have read my mind.* She was good with this; it felt right. "No, it's okay. I'm okay."

Matt leaned over slowly and kissed her on the mouth.

Ashley savored every moment as her hands drifted up to his shoulders and pulled him closer. Their hands roaming, both searching, it felt good to be free and have no restraints.

Matt held Ashley's hand. "I've wanted to do that all week, but I didn't want to seem like a jerk. This isn't something I do often." He laughed, turning away. "Well, at all, since…well, since a while."

She smiled; her cheeks flushed a little. "Me, neither. I mean, I thought I wasn't ready, but this is different." She sighed as he held her gaze and leaned toward her to kiss her again. At the same moment, she moved closer to him, wanting more, not having felt this way about someone in an awfully long time.

Matt's strong hands roamed her body, making her feel so free and alive, and Ashley didn't want this feeling to end. He lowered her back against the cushions as the fire roared. Her hair fell against her shoulders; the glow of the fire on her skin reflected the heat she felt within. She pulled on his shirt, freeing it from his jeans, and began unbuttoning it, laughing at her fingers getting tripped up.

They removed each layer between them. Matt's hands on her back and the heat of her mouth on his combined to break down the walls they each had built in their separate worlds. They moved together as one until they used every bit of their energy.

Ultimately spent, Ashley remembered closing her eyes and the orange of the flames warming her face until she fell asleep.

***

The dim early morning light came in through the large bay window of the family room, and Ashley startled awake. For a moment, she forgot where she was, fearing this had all been some long dream and she was stuck in her old house, in that dark world with Stephen.

Finally understanding where she was and that she was safe, she took a calming breath and remembered the prior night. Matt lay next to her, the last of the small embers burning in the fireplace. She breathed in deep, pulling the heavy blanket against herself and realizing Matt must have brought this blanket in while she slept. She closed her eyes and drifted back to sleep.

***

Later that morning, bright sunlight warmed Ashley's face as she woke again, alone. Her clothes were folded and piled neatly next to where she lay. The French doors to the family room were shut, but she could hear the clanging of dishes and the sounds of cooking. Ashley brought her hands to her face, embarrassed that Leanne was there. Without Matt here, it was even more awkward not knowing what Leanne had seen and thought.

She pulled her clothes on under the covers and stood, placing the large blanket aside. Quietly, she opened the doors and crept down the hall. She ducked into the bathroom in the hallway and closed the door. She caught sight of her reflection and saw someone happy and relaxed. Gone were the black circles under her eyes, and her skin had a healthy glow. She smiled and thought to herself, *A hot night of sex does wonders.*

She needed to brush her teeth and hoped to make a quick run up to her room. Peeking out the door, she heard someone humming, but it wasn't Leanne. It was Matt. She walked toward the kitchen as he was preparing breakfast. There was no sign of anyone else.

"Good morning."

Matt turned toward her. "Good morning. Just in time." He continued working at the stove. "I hope you slept okay." He smirked.

"Like a rock." Ashley stood in the doorway, unsure of herself.

"Coffee?" He gestured toward the coffeepot and mugs.

Grateful for the distraction, she entered the kitchen. "I would love some, but, first, I need to brush my teeth."

"By all means."

"Be right back." She turned and dashed quickly up the stairs to freshen up, then returned to the kitchen where a mug of coffee waited for her.

"It smells amazing in here."

"I took the liberty of guessing what you wanted for breakfast."

She observed the pan of scrambled eggs, tray of bacon, large bowl of fruit, and platter of muffins, then looked at Matt. "You did all of this?"

"Well, I can't take all of the credit. Leanne prepped most of this, so it was pretty easy. She makes me look good." He shrugged.

"So, where is…?" Ashley peered around the kitchen.

"Leanne? She has the morning off. Which is probably a good thing, considering she would have gotten an eyeful this morning."

Ashley laughed, blushing.

Matt set his mug down next to hers on the counter. "Thank you for an amazing night."

She turned to face him. "Thank you. It *was* amazing." She hugged him, not knowing if that was appropriate, but feeling comfortable with him.

He wrapped his arms around her. It seemed they were both relieved to have broken the ice. Matt pulled out one of the chairs at the counter for her. "Bon appétit." He dished out the food, warmed their coffees, and then sat next to her.

"This is delicious." Ashley savored all the flavors. She hadn't eaten this well in months.

"I love to cook when I have the time. Leanne helps me along with that."

"What's the plan today—no workers?" Ashley noted the empty field where there was typically a lot of action.

"Nope. It's quiet here on Saturdays. I have to run errands, so you'll have the place to yourself."

"I can do some work here, so leave me a list." She finished her coffee. "First, I'll clean up the kitchen."

"I didn't make that much of a mess." He sat back and surveyed the room.

Ashley raised her brows at him. "Leanne would not be pleased."

114

Matt took another look at the mess of pans on the stove and the dishes in the sink and nodded. "This is true."

***

Ashley busied herself with cleaning the kitchen and the family room. She looked forward to having some quiet time. She needed to decide what her future would be.

CHAPTER 11

A shley exhaled loudly as she sat back in the booth at the roadside diner outside of Philadelphia. This task of trying to find a job was daunting. She'd been scanning websites and newspapers in search of jobs in advertising and marketing, but was open to working just about anywhere to get herself situated. She contacted a range of companies and considered positions from entry-level secretary at an investment firm to stock person at a distribution warehouse. She needed to establish an income as soon as possible.

Her thoughts drifted back to Matt and the farm.

***

Her last days there were carefree, and she was able to forget the darkness that pressed up behind her and the unknown world that lay before her. Leanne prepared a special send-off dinner for her on her last night. All the workers, her new friends, were there.

That night during dinner, Ashley felt as if she finally had a connection to something. *This could be a place I can come back to someday. Maybe, if things all go well,* she thought.

However, as her last night at the farm came to an end, and Ashley was alone in the quiet of her room, she knew she would never be able to return to the farm. She was on the run. She needed to put a lot more distance between her and Stephen. That old feeling came back in the pit in her stomach, the cold feeling in her hands, the uncontrollable shaking, and the fear that froze her, making it impossible to move.

She forced herself to stand on shaky legs and pack her bags as a distraction. She lined her bags up by the bedroom door, ready to go in the morning—or before, if the panic didn't subside and she decided to leave sooner. She could leave in the middle of the night without a trace; she'd done it before.

She decided she couldn't do that to Matt and Leanne; they had done so much for her. Ashley picked up the burner phone Matt set up for her. Her old phone had been cleaned and stripped, and the number cancelled—*no trace*. She placed the new phone, along with her new ID, on the side table and sat on the bed, exhausted.

She looked at Sammy, asleep in his bed. She'd thought about what to do with Sammy from the minute she arrived at the farm. In the back of her mind, she knew she wouldn't be able to take him with her to a city, not knowing where she would end up, if the apartment would allow dogs, and how many hours a day or night she would have to work to afford living in the city. That would be no life for him.

She and Matt decided Sammy's home would be at the farm. *Freedom and peace.* She wiped away the tears that were brimming. *Stamp it down; stay strong.* She needed to turn her mind and her emotions off and rest.

Tomorrow, there will be time to feel.

***

The next morning, as usual, the farm was busy. The pit in her stomach grew larger as her time there grew short. She could hardly eat the delicious breakfast—Leanne's fresh blueberry muffins and famous egg bake.

After breakfast, as Ashley packed her car and hugged Sammy fiercely, tears clouded her vision, and her stomach twisted into knots. Leaving Sammy would be the most challenging part of this entire new-life escapade.

He licked her face and hand, and then took off running with the other dogs, racing around the yard. She knew it was time.

Matt placed her bags in the trunk of her car, as she loaded up the back seat with packages of food and goodies that Leanne had packed for her. Before retreating inside, Leanne gave Ashley a tight hug good-bye, wiping away a stray tear. Matt stood aside, waiting for his turn.

When Ashley turned to face Matt, he smiled that warm, reassuring smile, reminding her once again of Faith. "Thank you…" She fought back the tears. There was nothing she could say to cover how grateful she was for all that he'd done for her.

"Don't forget us here…" His words couldn't convey how he felt, wanting her to stay, but knowing she had to leave. He pulled her close. "Please be safe. Send me a note at some point. Let me know you are okay."

Ashley closed her eyes, taking in the scent of him, the farm, and the safe feeling. "I will." She pulled away, keeping it together, and choked out a good-bye.

As she drove away, the tears came like a flood, guttural crying that was new to her. Her heart broke as she left Sammy and watched her chance at happiness fade from the rearview mirror.

***

She stared back out of the window of the diner, her past fading as a tear rolled down her cheek.

"Everything okay, miss?"

Ashley turned to the waitress and wiped away the tear.

"Can I get you anything else?" The waitress—an older woman, short, stocky build, with dark hair pulled up in a bun—stood patiently waiting for a reply.

"No, thank you. I'm okay." Ashley placed her hands on the table and gave a faint smile.

The waitress left the bill and walked away, looking relieved the customer hadn't confided in her.

Ashley looked down at the want ads on her tablet. She asked herself, *Why didn't I stay with Matt at the farm? Why did I shut them all out?* "I could have had a new life." Glancing around, hoping no one had heard her, she caught her reflection in the mirror behind the counter.

She would have to get used to this new woman who stared back at her. The dark hair caught her off guard whenever she glimpsed at herself. She decided the new hair color was one of her best decisions

118

so far. She'd bought the darkest hair color at the drugstore and colored her hair at a roadside gas station.

She laughed when she remembered draping one of her extra T-shirts over shoulders, dying her hair, and hiding in the stall for fifteen minutes to let the color set. Then, when the coast was clear, she rinsed her hair in one of the sinks in the back. A few women had come in, but hardly took notice. Maybe, they knew what it was like to want to hide, or they, too, were on the run… After squeezing as much water out of her hair as possible, Ashley slipped on her baseball hat, left the gas station, and let her hair air dry in the car.

Once she was settled in Boston, she would get a permanent color and clean up this half-assed attempt to change her identity. Gone was the shock of pale-blonde hair that drew so much attention. She hoped to blend in or fade to the back of the crowd.

When Ashley looked back at the job listings on her tablet, one practically jumped off the screen. The ad was for a graphic designer at an advertising agency located in the Back Bay of Boston. She swore she hadn't seen that ad before. She stared at the screen, deciding to call them from the car, then pulled her money out and paid the bill.

CHAPTER 12

A shley researched the towns within a twenty-mile radius around Boston, hoping to find an affordable apartment. Her criteria were to live in a well-populated area with access to the MBTA train system and within walking distance of stores and restaurants. On her drive to Boston down long stretches of highway, she called one of the real estate agents who was listed online next to two of the apartments in which she was interested.

The agent returned her call quickly. They planned to meet in Brighton at one thirty that afternoon.

The drive was lonely without Sammy. She cried a lot, feeling guilty, and the stress of the situation hit her harder the farther she drove away.

Freedom and peace, that is my hope for the future, she repeatedly prayed as she drove to her destination.

As she approached Boston on the Mass Pike, the landscape became more dense, larger office buildings and apartment complexes appearing. The busyness of the city was overwhelming, with one-way streets and speeding taxicabs cutting her off at every corner the deeper into the city she drove.

She found the apartment on Foster Street in Brighton, where the realtor had arranged to meet. To find a parking spot, she circled two times around a block filled with large brick apartment buildings and duplexes. Her stomach was in knots. She checked her rearview mirror, making sure no one was following her. *He's not here,* she told herself.

Climbing out of the car, she recognized the realtor immediately. Perfectly styled from head to toe, Caroline was waiting in front of the apartment building. Ashley approached and reached out her hand. "Hi. Caroline? I'm Ashley."

"Ashley. So nice to meet you. You found it okay?" She grinned and shook Ashley's hand.

"Yes, a little crazy driving, but glad to be here." Ashley crossed her arms.

"Well, let's find you a place to live." Caroline led the way into the first apartment on her list.

To Ashley's disappointment, the apartment was in a first-floor duplex, which brought on feelings of anxiety. In order to feel safe, she wanted to be higher up in a more populated building.

They looked at another space in the building across the street. The kitchen floor was dingy, the appliances were old, and the windows and doors were not secure. She was beginning to panic; her hands were cold and trembling. Maybe she was in over her head.

Caroline saw she was visibly shaken. "I have another one in mind that I think you will like."

They walked a block to Washington Street. The apartment was surrounded by apartment complexes, big and small, restaurants, and markets; Boston transit, which ran along the street, was a five-minute walk. The building and location met her criteria and would make it easy for Ashley to blend in or hide.

The small one-bedroom was located on the fourth floor of a walk-up building. The real estate agent informed her there wasn't an elevator, but laundry was in the building. Ashley nodded as she contemplated the looming four flights of winding, dark-wood stairs.

After trudging up the staircase, Caroline opened the door to a clean, sunny space recently updated with a fresh coat of paint in every room, newly installed wood-grain laminate floors, and a tiny, but efficient and clean, galley kitchen. The agent told her the rent included utilities and parking that was available in the front and the back of the building for the tenants only. The apartment was partially furnished with a sofa and chair, coffee table, and end table in the main living area. Caroline led her to the kitchen, which had a counter with two unfinished wooden stools. The cabinets were stocked with an assortment of simple dishware, pots, and pans.

Maybe someone left in a hurry. Ashley smiled to herself.

In the bedroom, there was a bed frame and dresser. She would need to purchase a mattress and extra bedding. Caroline talked about the benefits of living close to everything and how Ashley would rarely need her car.

"I'll take it. When can I move in?"

The realtor blinked, hesitating. "Oh, it's available as soon as we get your background check completed."

With shaking hands, Ashley pulled out the envelope of cash that she had brought in hopes of finding an apartment that day.

The realtor's eyes lit up. "Or we could arrange to have you in here as soon as you are ready."

Ashley smiled and thought to herself, *Money talks.*

While they sat at the counter to finalize and sign the lease, Ashley's mind drifted to her next mission, finding a job. Her hope was to hear back from the advertising agency she'd found while at the diner, the one that was looking for a graphic designer. Using her new name, phone number, and e-mail address, she'd e-mailed her resume; she was hoping they would respond soon.

While Caroline made a call to her office to find out information about a parking sticker, Ashley used her phone to check her e-mail. There were three new e-mails from three different companies, each responding to her inquiry about a position. She scanned the messages as her heart beat in her chest. One was from B&B Advertising. They were interested in meeting with her to discuss the position. She couldn't believe her luck.

As Caroline handed her a copy of the lease agreement and a key to her new apartment, she felt the tension release from her shoulders.

"Congratulations, Ashley, on your new home." Caroline beamed.

The smallest bit of hope filled Ashley; things were starting to fall into place.

***

Before going back down to her car to retrieve her few belongings, Ashley called the human resource director at B&B, hoping she wasn't too late in getting back to them. The director informed her they were still interested and wanted her to come into the office on Friday to meet with the staff.

She told them she was available and looked forward to meeting them. She ended the call while sitting on the floor.

Pulling her knees to her chest, Ashley looked around the quiet apartment and realized she was suddenly alone for the first time in her life.

CHAPTER 13

In her Brighton apartment, Ashley settled into a routine that was her new life as Ashley Banner—*New name, new place, and new life.*

She texted Matthew, letting him know she'd arrived and was safe. He texted pictures of Sammy, which induced another round of tears. Once again, she questioned her reasons for leaving the farm.

There were two small food markets located near her building, making it convenient to shop day-to-day. She learned the hard way that it was best to be efficient when shopping; whatever she bought, she had to carry up those four flights of stairs. *Forty-eight stairs.* She'd counted.

With Stephen, Ashley lived a life of forced order. To keep him calm, she made sure to keep everything in its proper place and to do what Stephen expected of her. His insistence on an appearance of order, combined with his manic episodes, led to what Ashley would characterize as a life of organized chaos. That was a pattern Ashley was determined to break in her new life.

So, the first week in her new place, she left things askew. One day the bed was unmade, or papers were left in a pile on the counter, or the day's clothes lay in a heap on the floor—because she could. There was no one to answer to. She made the rules now.

The day Ashley signed the lease, Caroline gave her the name of a secondhand furniture store located around the corner from her apartment. If Ashley mentioned Caroline's name, they would give her a 30 percent discount on her purchases.

The salesman loaded the foldaway twin mattress into the back of her car, along with two table lamps, a bedding-in-a-bag set, a set of new towels, and her new coffeemaker. After circling her building several times, hoping to snag a front parking spot, she realized she had to carry all these items up those dreaded stairs.

Her legs burned, and her back ached as she wiped the sweat off her forehead after lugging the last of the items into her apartment. She worked through the night, putting together her bed and decorating with what little she had, feeling a sense of accomplishment and satisfaction at starting this new chapter of her life.

The new bedside clock read 10:30 p.m. She knew it was time to get some sleep, but her nerves were fired up, and she flitted from one thing to the next, fussing with blankets on her bed and cleaning the bathroom for the second time.

Finally, she brushed her teeth, sat on her bed, and exhaled. The silence enveloped her; she jumped up to double-check that she'd locked the door and windows. She clutched her phone by her side and grabbed her pepper spray and a knife from the kitchen to keep by the bed. Leaving her light on, she sat up, huddled in her new bed and in her new place, alone.

No one else is here; no one knows I'm here. Sleep.

She lay down and pulled the covers up to her ears as she tried to stop trembling. She closed her eyes, praying to God that she would sleep and that Stephen would never find her here in her new space.

***

The interview was a success, and Ashley landed her new job. Her days consisted of waking early, eating a light breakfast, walking three blocks to the Washington Street T stop, and passing people while they were walking their dogs or during their daily commute to work on the bus or the train. She rode the Green Line B branch over a dozen stops to Copley Station in Back Bay, and walked two blocks toward her office building at B&B Advertising. Along the way, she stopped at Dunkin' Donuts and purchased a medium coffee, cream and one sugar.

When she sat at her desk, she busied herself with the work left in her in-box, typically finishing by lunchtime. Then, she'd ask her supervisor, Christina, if she had anything else for her to do. Her supervisor was usually surprised and commented on Ashley's speedy and accurate work.

At times during the day, her mind would wander to worrying about Stephen. She imagined his rage when he found she was gone, sure he would make looking for her his new obsession. Panic would set in— her hands would shake, her muscles tense, and her head throb. The impulse to run would begin to take over, and she would wish she could leave work. At those times, she would rush to the bathroom, soak a paper towel in cold water, place it on her neck, duck into one of the stalls, and tell herself, *No one can see me like this.*

These anxiety attacks were coming on more frequently and without warning. When they occurred, she closed her eyes, took controlled breaths, repeated her prayer to God that Stephen would never find her, and promised to live a life of doing good if God would answer that prayer. Then, she would steady herself, exit the stall, stand at the sink, lean toward the mirror, look herself in the eyes, and tell herself, *It is all going to be okay.*

One day, the uneasy feelings followed her during her commute home. She turned the corner, swearing Stephen was behind her. Her heart raced, and her palms became clammy as a silver pickup swerved around the corner, passing her, the tires skidding lightly on the pavement.

Ashley jumped then stopped in her tracks, watching as the truck with Massachusetts plates whizzed past. Her chest heaved; her shoulders tensed—*Not Virginia plates, it's not him.*

"Excuse me." A man brushed Ashley's arm while she was momentarily frozen in terror.

The jostling interrupted her panic attack and thrust her back into reality. "I'm sorry." She stumbled then turned around, switching directions. *I'm going crazy.* She needed to get a grip on her imagination and stop thinking that Stephen was around every corner.

She crossed Commonwealth Avenue at the crosswalk, blending in with a group of pedestrians. *A normal walk home on a normal day. No one is following me.*

Ashley kept her head down as she climbed aboard the Green Line and slunk into an empty seat. Her heartbeat slowed, and the adrenaline retreated while the train rattled along Commonwealth Avenue, the storefronts becoming a blur as it picked up speed.

Arriving at her stop, she glanced around the train and out the window, surveying faces before descending the steps onto the sidewalk with shaking legs. She kept a quick stride all the way to her building and then raced up the stairs to the safety of her apartment.

***

Ashley began to change her route home from work, boarding the train at a different location and then disembarking at her usual stop, but walking past the block where her apartment was located and continuing to the corner store, constantly looking over her shoulder. The feeling of someone watching, someone walking too close behind her—it was difficult to ignore. That foreboding was always with her, following her like a dark shadow.

CHAPTER 14

With deadlines, working late, takeout for lunch, overtime, and late-night dinners at her apartment, thoughts of Stephen faded to the back of Ashley's mind. But then, out of the blue, something would trigger her paranoia. It could be the way a man looked at her or a voice she heard on the crowded subway. Her hands would shake, and her stomach would clench with dread. She wondered what she would do if she turned around and Stephen was behind her.

Breathe. It's all going to be okay.

She wanted and needed to move forward, not backward. The distraction of work helped. She was overworked, but she didn't care.

The more work, the better.

With overtime and weekends, Ashley was making more money than she'd projected, which helped alleviate the stress of having to save every dollar. Her apartment was close to work, she had food and clothes on her back, and she didn't have to deal with anyone's bullshit.

This is perfect. Kind of.

Sometimes, she felt the weight of loneliness, the isolation of the safety net she'd created. During the day, she kept to herself—head down and work, work, work. At night, she was afraid. She would lock her doors after coming home from work, only to recheck them two more times throughout the evening. There were nights she hardly slept, jolting awake after vivid dreams and nightmares of running, of Stephen's hands encircling her neck, of not being able to breathe. She would wake in a cold sweat, sometimes remembering the awful nightmares. At other times, she couldn't remember the dreams, but she felt the lingering fear, the terror of something terrible looming or of someone chasing her.

She purchased an over-the-counter nighttime sleep aid to help her sleep through the night. She continued to leave a light on in her bedroom and to keep a knife, pepper spray, and her cell phone within reach on the bedside table.

She tried to look at the positive side. She was on her own and doing what she loved—creating for an advertising agency and learning from the designers and writers in the office. But she was alone. She figured this was the price she had to pay for running. Safety, no excitement, nothing to deter her from her routine—the new mundane life of all work and no play.

***

While eating lunch and flipping through the newspaper at her desk one afternoon, she found an ad for a women-only self-defense class. Women who wanted to "take charge" and "were against violence."

Well, shouldn't all people be against violence? she thought.

The workshop was being held at Boston Medical Center, through their well-being programs. She thought she could use some of that in her life. She tore out the ad and stuffed it into her workbag.

A week later, Ashley found herself at the door of Boston Medical Center, awkwardly waiting to join the self-defense class. The class was headed up by an instructor who was trained in martial arts; he specialized in self-defense techniques.

As she walked into the brightly lit room, Ashley thought, *What do I have to lose?*

In the group, there were a handful of women around her age and a few older women. The trainer, Brad, was probably in his late twenties and clean-cut; he was wearing a tight black Under Armour shirt and pressed khakis. With his bright-white smile and perfect hair, she thought he looked more like a model than an instructor. He introduced himself as an experienced self-defense trainer and gave the group a brief background of the clinics that he had led around the state. He then introduced his assistant trainer, Adam, another clean-cut, good-looking guy who didn't look a day over twenty-two.

The women were instructed to split into two groups on the large mats in the center of the room. The first drill was getting to know one other; each woman told the group why she was interested in learning self-defense. Brad called this an icebreaker.

Ashley wished she could be brutally honest—*Well, I'm hiding out from my fucking psycho ex-boyfriend that was a cop, who tried to kill me several times. I thought it might be helpful to know how to defend myself in case the situation presented itself again.* But she didn't dare.

Instead, she smiled, introduced herself as Ashley Banner, and said she was new to living in a big city and thought "one couldn't be too careful."

Using Adam as his victim, Brad began to show the group how to get out of dangerous situations. Then, he explained that they would use volunteers to show how easily one could be overcome by a stranger in a dark parking lot.

Ashley's hands were cold. She wished she could shrink into the background, but it was as if she had a sign on her that said, "Choose me, readymade victim."

Brad directed his award-winning smile right at her. "Ashley, is it? Would you mind being our first victim?"

That was supposed to be funny, right? Ashley thought.

Brad explained every move he was going to make; then he stood behind Ashley, hooking his arms lightly around hers.

Her heart raced and her hands began to tremble.

"Okay now, Ashley, are you ready to go?"

"Sure." Suddenly, she wasn't so sure. Adrenaline shot through her veins, sweat dotted her forehead, and her face began to flush. *Oh God, what am I going to do?* she thought as fear crept in to seize hold of her.

Brad talked the group through each move he made.

As he brought his arms around to lightly pin hers to her sides, Ashley's hands shook, and her heart thudded loudly. Ashley couldn't remember what came first. She snapped her arms up and back, breaking his hold on her.

"Hey, nice defensive move. You sure you haven't taken self-defense before?" He laughed lightly. "Okay, let's try another scenario. How to get away from an attacker that gets you in a rear choke hold. This is a vulnerable position to be in. We'll pair off and work on these movements together in a moment." He looked at her kindly. "Ashley, can I use you to demo this one, too?"

She swallowed hard. Not wanting to make a scene, she went along, determined to keep her cool. *He isn't here to hurt me; he is here to help,* she told herself.

As Brad moved to put his arm around her neck, Ashley's panic continued. He explained that she was to lift her arms overhead, slipping them under his, then snap them up and off her. She didn't hear a word of it as she saw his arm near her throat. She ducked down and reached her arms back, throwing his arm free of her neck. He didn't apply much resistance, making it easy for her to break free.

"Nice, job, Ashley." He turned to face the group. "Let's break this process down a bit."

Okay, this is not how an attacker plays, she thought. *The attacker would not give any leeway. His grip wouldn't loosen; if he wanted to hurt me, nothing would stop him. He would hold on to my throat like a vise. This is a joke!* Ashley's voice screamed in her head as her entire body shook.

"Find a partner, and we'll break the defense down piece by piece. Thank you, Ashley." Brad smiled at Ashley as if she were a five-year-old, putting his hand lightly on her shoulder.

The other women in the group were raring to go, wanting to get handled by Brad and Adam. Looking around, she saw they weren't serious; they only wanted the pretty boys to tell them how strong they were.

Ashley had had enough. She felt as if she had run a mile-long sprint; her heart was beating in her ears. *Coming here was a big mistake.* She realized she wasn't ready for something this intense and felt her panic attack raging on. As Brad moved on to his eager candidates, Ashley quietly grabbed her bag and snuck out the door.

***

Ashley wasn't able to fall asleep after the self-defense fiasco. She checked and triple-checked the locks on her apartment door and windows. Finally, after taking a long, hot bath—with a knife on the edge of the tub—and reading a trashy novel she found at the consignment shop, she felt relaxed enough to catch some well-deserved sleep.

***

It seemed the alarm went off early the next morning, and Ashley felt groggy at her desk most of the day. She was unable to concentrate and kept reliving the previous night.

"Hey, Ash, want to go out tonight? We are heading to Whiskey's for a few pops." Jim from sales was leaning on the wall of her cubicle, hoping she would join them that evening. She never said yes, but he thought he would give it another shot.

"Hey, Jim. I can't tonight. My niece is expecting me to pick her up at the airport and then give her a lift to my sister's house." *Nice, that rolled right off my tongue,* Ashley thought. She was getting good at making up stories of her life.

"Ah, too bad. We'd love to have ya come out. Next week, keep Friday open! No mattah what!"

"You got it, Jim." Ashley smiled, feeling a little bad for lying.

Jim was nice enough. He was a typical Boston guy—good-looking, Irish, and a strong Southie accent. Never pronounced an *r* in his life. "It's paht of the chahm!" he would always say. He sincerely wanted her to come to happy hour and unwind.

Why can't I? Everyone goes out for happy hour and a few pops on Friday at five o'clock in Boston.

She wasn't ready. That excuse was getting old, even to her—*Pretty lame*, she thought—but she was going to keep using it for a little longer.

***

The next day, Ashley met Lisa, one of the junior writers and photographers for the agency. She had been out of town when Ashley was hired. Lisa was to be Ashley's contact person on the new project she was assigned. Lisa was friendly, telling Ashley she could ask her questions anytime if she needed help.

Lisa invited Ashley to lunch the following week, but Ashley made an excuse that she needed to work through lunch. She tried her hardest to act cold and distant, but Lisa's personality slowly broke through her barrier. She had an addictive sense of humor, especially because most of the time she was making fun of herself. Lisa found herself in the most bizarre situations. As she would say, "shit" found her. While working together on the new ad layout, Lisa had Ashley laughing so hard it felt like a breakthrough. She hadn't laughed like that in months.

Lisa knew everything about what was going on in the office and in Boston; she was friends with everyone. She knew the city inside out. They went out to lunch once a week and grabbed coffee in the afternoons, which made the time during the week go fast and gave Ashley something to look forward to. In order to avoid suspicion, Ashley was good at keeping the deep questions at bay, while still giving Lisa some information about herself.

Finally, one Friday afternoon, Lisa strode over to her cubicle and slammed her workbag down on Ashley's desk. "That's it, girl; you're coming out for a drink tonight. I don't care if you promised your neighbor's grandmother that you would watch her cat for her, or whatever excuse you are going to drum up. Cancel your plans, and meet me by the elevator in ten minutes."

As Lisa turned on her heel and walked toward the elevators, Ashley didn't have time to protest or use one of her premade excuses. She thought, *Of course, Lisa caught on to me; she's no dummy.* Ashley shook her head and sighed. She logged out of her computer, grabbed her things, and headed for the elevator with a smile on her face.

CHAPTER 15

Lisa and Ashley sat at the crowded bar at Stephanie's on Newbury Street and ordered an assortment of small plates and two glasses of white wine.

"My husband owns a boxing gym in Back Bay. Well, I guess I own it, too." Lisa laughed then took a gulp of her wine.

Ashley's interest was piqued as she picked up a salted corn chip and dipped it in guacamole. "Seriously? Do you go all the time? Do you box?"

Again, Lisa laughed. "Yeah, I have been boxing for a few years. It's a good workout. I first took a self-defense class; that's where I met Vince. He was getting the program started. It was a great little class. Now, we have one of the best programs in Boston."

Ashley's memory of her self-defense-class experience still haunted her. She shuddered at the thought.

"You should come check it out. Meet some cool people." Lisa popped a piece of shrimp cocktail in her mouth.

"Yeah, I don't know…" Ashley was hesitant, the nervous feeling creeping in.

Lisa turned to her. "You need to branch out. This would be the perfect place! You said you were looking for a gym." She dipped a chip and crunched it loudly. Ashley was silent and looked at her hands as Lisa continued, softening her tone, "You wouldn't have to worry about anyone bothering you there. They're all cool people. I promise."

Ashley looked at her, surprised.

Lisa leaned her elbow on the bar. "Yeah, I listen, and I'm pretty good at figuring people out."

Ashley thought for a moment, turning her wineglass in a circle on the bar. "All right. Maybe I'll give it a try."

"Nice. You're going to love it." Lisa raised her glass and clinked it against Ashley's.

***

Lisa convinced her to meet at the boxing club in Back Bay that Saturday morning. Ashley had a knot in her stomach the entire car ride. She followed her GPS to the address of the Boxing and MMA Training Center on Commonwealth Avenue. She drove her car into the parking lot surrounding the large gunmetal-grey building that resembled a warehouse. Ashley circled the lot, looking for a vacant space among all the cars. When she finally found one and parked, the dread stayed in her gut, twisting and turning her insides and playing tug-of-war with her emotions.

Should I go in or should I leave? I can tell Lisa I'm sick. This is a bad idea. She took a deep breath. *Pull it together.*

Ashley stepped tentatively out of the car then retrieved her backpack from the back seat, pulling it onto her shoulder as she surveyed the massive building. Determined to follow through with this, she approached the double glass doors. A guy about one foot taller than she was, and probably a foot wider, pushed one of the doors open as he exited the gym.

"Excuse me. Here you go." He stood aside and extended his colorful, tattoo-covered arm to hold the door open for her.

She was momentarily stunned by the mere size of him; then she pulled herself together so she could speak. "Oh. Thank you."

"You're welcome." He nodded and smiled.

She walked through the door, and immediately her senses were flooded by the sights and sounds. Bright lights lit the entryway that led into the main gym. There was a front desk located on the left, where a young man sat at a computer and checked guests in. While men and women were coming and going, the steady beat of music reverberated, filling the space with instant energy.

Ashley stood off to the side, taking everything in, as she checked her phone. Lisa texted that she'd arrived and would meet her inside.

"Hey, girl." Lisa breezed in and walked over to Ashley, giving her a hug. "Sorry. Hope you weren't waiting long."

"Not at all. This place is unbelievable."

Ashley's gaze was drawn to the center of the gym while Lisa said hello to Jake, who was the guy working the desk. After a brief introduction to Jake, Ashley glanced around while Lisa finished her conversation with him.

There was a waiting area with benches. A refrigerator with water and sports drinks on the shelves was across from the main desk, along with cubbies for clients to store shoes and other belongings.

"This is it. Ready?" Lisa grinned and started walking to the exercise area of the gym.

"Sure." Ashley tentatively followed, amazed by this new world before her.

The walls of the main area were black with grey borders; framed posters of famous boxers hung on the wall. There were two full-size boxing rings set at the center of the massive space. In one of the rings, there were two men boxing, each with heavy gloves on. To the right of the rings was a line of heavy black boxing bags, where several people were practicing punching and kicking. On the opposite wall, there was a row of a dozen rowing machines and treadmills facing one of the rings. There were people running and rowing, boxing and working out. The energy of the room drew Ashley in.

"This place has grown so much since we started. We recently added this cardio area with the rowing machines. We have eight class instructors, six of them trainers. There is Trevor; everyone loves working with him." Lisa pointed to a guy who was talking with a group of males and females gathered on the matted floor; they were dressed in what looked, to Ashley, like karate uniforms. "That's a Jiu-Jitsu class, which is like grappling or wrestling."

As Ashley took in the constant buzz and flurry of activity, Lisa rattled off the names of other trainers who worked for them.

"Let's head upstairs to see Vince." Lisa led Ashley back to the front of the gym and up the stairs near the entrance. "Vince has his office up here with one of his managers, James. They oversee the fighters and the competition teams. There's a conference room up here, too. Debra runs the self-defense and fitness classes downstairs. We'll meet her later." Lisa led Ashley into Vince's spacious office.

"Hey, Lisa." Vince stood from his desk. He was over six feet tall and muscular; he had angular cheekbones and short dark hair with flecks of grey. His dark eyes were piercing. But despite his chiseled exterior, Vince was friendly and had a warm, welcoming smile that lit up his face as Lisa walked in.

"Vince, this is my friend from work, Ashley."

He approached Ashley and shook her hand. "Nice to meet you. You're new in town, right?" Smiling, he looked to Lisa and back at Ashley.

"Nice, Vince." Lisa smirked.

He winked. "I listen to my wife. She doesn't think so, but I pay attention."

"Yeah, yeah, sometimes. Yes, Ashley is the one I told you about. She's checking out the gym. We're going to get her started here." Lisa nudged her as Ashley gave her a look.

"Well, I'm checking it out. It's an amazing space." Ashley thought it would take a lot of confidence for her to join a place like this.

"Thank you. I'm sure Lisa told you how much it has grown since we started. Have you shown her all around?"

"Not everything, I thought you could give the official tour."

"Perfect. Let's go."

Vince walked them downstairs to the main training area and gave Ashley some insight about the trainers and classes they offered. They had traditional boxing, kickboxing (both American and Muay Thai), Krav Maga (a self-defense-style class), Brazilian Jiu-Jitsu, karate, and a list of others Ashley had never heard of. As she followed wide-eyed, Vince led the way past the boxing rings, pointing out the separate men's and women's locker rooms, both of which had showers and changing areas.

She was amazed at the athleticism of the boxers, the smoothness of their movements, their toughness, and their physiques. They walked beyond the rings toward an octagonal black-metal fight cage with grey-and-black padded flooring, where there were two guys grappling and another coaching.

"This is an MMA-style fight cage. Mixed martial arts combines kickboxing, boxing, and wrestling. We offer training programs for people interested in both fitness and competition. Some of our clients are more serious and want a career in fighting. We have every level here."

Ashley couldn't even believe that this world existed, much less that her friend owned a part of it.

There was a guy, with dark skin and short braids, jumping rope on the workout mat outside of the fight cage. He was light on his feet and made it look effortless, hopping from one foot to the other.

Vince led them around the perimeter where eight heavy black boxing bags were suspended from a metal beam that was secured to the wall. A trainer was working with a male client, demonstrating how to strike the large boxing bag. There were men punching and kicking the other bags.

One of them caught Ashley's attention with his loud strikes. Dressed in black boxing shorts, a grey T-shirt, and a grey-knit winter hat pulled down close to his ears, his moves were calculated and fluid, like those of a panther; he silently stalked his imaginary opponent and moved in, striking fast.

Intense. Extremely attractive, Ashley thought.

He was in his own world. His punches and kicks were sharp as they struck the bag, a loud echo reverberating with every controlled strike.

Lisa called out to him and waved, "Hey, James."

He nodded toward her and Vince.

"That's James; he's the head trainer for the fighters and the manager of the competition teams."

Ashley continued to watch as James worked the bag methodically.

Vince checked his phone then touched Lisa's arm. "Sorry, hon, I need to get back to my office for a meeting." He extended his hand to Ashley. "Nice meeting you, Ashley. I hope you try one of the classes sometime."

"Nice meeting you, too. I'm looking forward to it." She shook his hand.

Lisa turned to her. "See, I told you it's great! Come on. I'll show you the area downstairs." She waved for Ashley to follow.

Walking back toward the front of the gym, they passed the boxing rings where a young woman was sparring with a partner, both wearing protective gloves and shin guards. Their movements were quick and sharp. Ashley was in awe as each moved to counter the other's strike. A buzzer sounded, and the two paused their sparring session. The man in the ring noticed Lisa as she was passing by and waved.

"That's Justin. He teaches boxing and kickboxing. He was a competition fighter for us for a long time, and now he's a coach. Most of the trainers here have participated in competitions at one time or another."

The buzzer sounded again, and Ashley watched as Justin and his client started to spar again. They took turns throwing punches and kicks and defending against each other's strikes.

Lisa and Ashley returned to the area by the main entrance, where another staircase led downstairs to the lower level. It had another boxing ring, a group-fitness room, and a changing room with showers and lockers. Lisa told her they held self-defense classes and private lessons on that floor.

Ashley chuckled and described her bad experience with the self-defense class.

"Oh my God, that sounds terrible! You poor thing! The classes here are great. I'm not just saying that because we own the gym. There are different levels and instructors, depending on your comfort level. Our best one is Debra; she's in charge of the program. She's a hot ticket and doesn't take any shit."

They walked toward the group-fitness room and saw a few women talking. Lisa called out to Debra, "Hey, girl!"

Debra approached and gave Lisa a big hug; after which, Lisa introduced Ashley.

She thought, *Debra has a body to die for. Muscular and strong, yet she's super feminine. Her auburn hair and tanned skin enhance her bright-green eyes.*

"Nice to meet you. You here for a class, or you girls working upstairs today?" she said with an English accent.

"I'm showing Ashley around, and we'll probably get a workout in. I'm hoping she'll like it here and join." Lisa winked at Ashley.

"Well, class is over, so why don't you girls come in, and we can get a little workout in down here. Maybe throw some kicks on the pads?" Debra smiled, revealing a brilliant-white smile.

Lisa looked at Ashley and raised an eyebrow. "You in?"

Ashley thought, *How can I refuse?* "Sounds great!"

"Yeah, don't let the pretty exterior fool ya; she's a tough one." Lisa nodded toward Debra.

"All right, girls, let's warm up." Debra turned up the music and had them start moving with body-weight squats, push-ups, jumping jacks, and sit-ups.

Ashley hadn't run or worked out in months, and she felt the impact immediately.

Debra turned to Lisa. "Lisa, would you be a doll and grab some gloves for Ashley from behind the counter? I'll get the pads."

Ashley took this chance to take a drink from her water bottle and catch her breath.

Debra introduced Ashley to kicking and punching by demonstrating the strikes; Lisa held the pads. It was totally foreign to Ashley. At college, she had taken cardio classes, which included kickboxing, but that had involved nothing more than punching the air and feeling totally empowered.

Debra showed Ashley how to hold the pads, so Lisa could throw some punches. The pads were thick, rectangular black leather with

141

handles to slip your hands under and Velcro straps to make sure they fit properly.

Ashley held the pads awkwardly. Debra adjusted her arm position and instructed her to provide a little resistance when someone threw a punch at the pad. She demonstrated a high-five-type motion. Lisa threw left-right, jab-cross combinations. Once Ashley learned the rhythm of the strikes, hooks and uppercuts were added; they began to move around and add more speed to the strikes. After several rounds, her arms were like jelly, and her hands were shaking.

Next, Lisa took the pads, and Debra helped Ashley with her jab-cross combinations, showing her how to properly punch without hurting her wrists and how to move her hips to gain more power. Ashley started light with ten left jabs, then ten right crosses.

Debra demonstrated how to throw hooks and uppercuts and instructed her to try punching with a little more power. The first time she felt the crisp pop of her glove hitting the pad, she was hooked. Quickly, she fell into a rhythm with her punches. She and Lisa began to move around the matted floor while Debra set a timer for three 2-minute rounds. At the end of the final round, Ashley was dripping with sweat, out of breath, and elated beyond all expectation.

"What do you think, Ash?" Lisa threw her a towel.

"This is awesome! A lot different from cardio class." She wiped her forehead with the towel.

"Yeah, this is my favorite workout now. It's hard to go back once you start hitting things."

"I love it. I definitely want to come back." Ashley took a long drink out of her water bottle.

Debra came over and sat next to Ashley on the benches. "Well, that's wonderful! You did an amazing job. Nice, strong punches. We can work with you on technique. Would you be interested in coming to classes?"

Ashley put her towel around her neck to cool down. "I wouldn't even know where to start."

Debra explained the different classes she offered, as well as the boxing groups upstairs.

Ashley liked the idea of working with Debra separate from the big gym.

"Great, I have a list of times; you can come to whichever time works best for you. These are small classes, and sometimes it may be just the two of us. I think you'll learn quite quickly." Debra could see that Ashley was a little timid, but she also sensed a fire and an eagerness to learn. "I'm looking forward to working with you." Debra extended her hand, which Ashley shook.

"Thank you! I can't wait until next time." Ashley beamed.

"See, I knew you would love it." Lisa bumped Ashley with her hip as they walked out.

Ashley felt exhilarated and couldn't wait to do it again.

CHAPTER 16

Ashley cringed internally at the mere brush of the stranger's arm against her as she rode the train home from work. Using her peripheral vision, she could see that the guy next to her was preoccupied with his phone and paying no attention to her or anyone else. But, to her, any unsolicited touch was a threat, a trespass against her.

She gripped the pole tighter as the train descended underground, the darkly lit tunnel engulfing the train. She shifted left, brushing against another passenger. Glancing around, she saw a woman absorbed with her phone, oblivious to the world around her, while Ashley was hypersensitive and noticed any slight change in the atmosphere.

Letting out a shaky breath, she once again tried remembering the meditative breathing techniques she had begun practicing. *Inhale for six, hold for one, exhale for four...or is it inhale four, exhale six, hold one?* She realized she was holding her breath, while trying to figure it out, and exhaled audibly.

The train reemerged into the daylight aboveground, passing apartment buildings and restaurants. It slowed near its stops at Boston University stations, where the large brick academic buildings and dorms blended into the landscape of the city. Next stop, Griggs Street.

Three more until my stop.

As the automated announcement began, the train slowed and jerked to a stop, and the doors loudly retracted, opening to the street-level station. Awaiting passengers emerged from under the small overhang and moved toward the doors as passengers disembarked. Ashley moved nearer to the closed door behind her. She watched who was boarding the train.

The doors closed, and the train jolted forward. Ashley stared at the map of the Green Line route, which was located above the doors across from her, memorizing every name and counting them down until Washington Street.

Finally coming to her stop, Ashley clutched her bag, again scanning faces outside of the train, plotting her walk home, maneuvering away from oncoming crowds, and staying close to the inside of the sidewalk, close to the buildings, *just in case…*

As she closed the main door to her apartment building, comforted slightly by the fact that the security door was keeping the outside world at bay, her tension began to fade, exhaustion taking its place. She stood at the base of the staircase, surveying the trek ahead.

Four sets of stairs.

Sighing as she ascended, she couldn't wait to put on her comfy sweat pants and flop on the couch. Inserting the key to her apartment, listening again to the stillness of the hallway, she pushed through the door and turned on the kitchen light before closing the door behind her. She dropped her bag and keys on the entry table.

Double locks, triple-check the chain, turn on all lights, shut the curtains, check in every room and closet, shut the blinds… All is clear.

She washed her hands then ambled to her bedroom to rummage through her drawer for sweat pants. Finally, sitting on the couch in her apartment, safe and sound, she wrapped the blanket around her, was wide-eyed for about ten minutes, and then fell asleep with her pepper spray in hand.

***

Ashley decided she needed to make a change. She attended Debra's boxing class one time per week. Investing in a pair of twelve-ounce black-and-purple boxing gloves that Debra recommended, she packed her gear and took it to work with her. She rode the Green Line from Copley Square to the Kenmore Square stop and walked to the gym to meet Lisa after work on Wednesday nights.

First class on the pads, Debra taught her how to throw a rear kick to the body. "The power comes from your hip." Debra had Lisa hold the pads for her while she demonstrated the technique. She stepped out at an angle and powerfully kicked the pad with her right leg, landing it with a loud *smack*.

"That's how it's done. Your turn." She smiled and nodded to Ashley.

Ashley kicked the pads lightly at first, unsure of her footing. Then, once she had the technique, Lisa told her to hit with power. Ashley threw her rear kick, landing it perfectly with that satisfying *thud* of the pad. The addition of kicks brought the training to an entirely different level. Ashley knew she loved boxing, but she was now obsessed with kicking.

Soon, she added a second night of training with Lisa. The nights she worked out she felt amazing, but found it was difficult to wind down afterward because of the adrenaline rush. The positive side— she wasn't as freaked out on her train ride home anymore.

The nights became late, and she began to pay the price when she woke up early for work. The days would be long, and she would find herself losing energy in the afternoon, barely able to make it to the end of the workday. She decided to try an early morning class before she went to work.

Packing her gear the night before and setting her alarm an hour earlier sounded like a good idea. In the morning, however, when she hit the alarm button and saw 5:00 a.m. on the display, she regretted the decision as she dragged herself out of her nice, warm bed. Blindly, she dressed and drank coffee, hoping it would miraculously give her strength.

As she walked to the train in the dark, she thought, *This might not work so well.* The nervous feelings crept back in as she rode the train. Although the trains weren't as crowded as they were in the evening, to her surprise, there were a lot of people up and out at this hour.

When she arrived at the Kenmore Square stop, she was immediately alert on the two-block walk to the club; that feeling of being followed lingered. Once she entered the parking lot of the gym, she sped up her walk, hurrying to the door. When she opened the gym doors and saw the people working out, heard the beat of the music, and felt the energy of the club, she let out a sigh of relief.

Ashley began a steady routine. Three days a week she would attend class, shower, get dressed for work, and then ride the T to her office. On occasion, she would meet Lisa there at night or on the weekend and work out with her in the main gym, hitting pads or using the rowing machines, but she was most comfortable taking the classes. After three months of working together, she'd progressed quickly with powerful kicks, agility, and pad holding for others.

"You have a knack for this, girl. Have you thought about trying some of the kickboxing or boxing groups upstairs?" Debra asked as she stored away the kickbox pads after class.

Ashley was perfectly happy staying where she was—in her predictable, comfortable routine.

"No. I like working out here." She unfastened her gloves and stashed them in her duffel.

Debra pressed, "You could handle it."

Ashley smirked. "Well, we'll see."

"I'll take you up next week and introduce you to a few of the trainers. You would get a charge out of working with them." She sat next to Ashley on the bench.

Ashley busied herself with her wraps and gloves, avoiding eye contact.

"You would be safe there. They're not your stereotypical asshole-guy trainers."

Ashley looked at Debra. *She's probably figured out my story,* Ashley thought. She guessed she wasn't that hard to read, especially for someone who dealt with women's self-defense. Debra had been so welcoming and had taken her in without asking questions, knowing that Ashley needed this to feel strong again.

"I think you're ready to move to the next level. Step outside your comfort zone." Debra leaned over, making eye contact with Ashley. "I can tell it's difficult for you, but you're safe here."

Ashley felt as if she had been holding her breath for so long, and now she was finally able to release it. Debra was right; she had grown and learned a lot about herself in this short time.

"Thank you, Debra. For everything." She gestured to the gloves in her hands. "For this, for giving me confidence again." She felt a little choked up as she realized this was a big turning point for her.

Debra nodded in agreement. "You're definitely more confident. You have done awesome work here. Now, what do you say we clean up a bit and go grab a drink? I'm off for the night."

Ashley thought that was the best offer she'd had in a long time. "Sure. I'll see if Lisa is ready to head out." Packing up her things, she couldn't hide her grin. Her future was looking brighter every day.

CHAPTER 17

"James, I'm serious. This girl is good. She'd be great working in your area. She needs a little confidence." Debra stood before James at his desk, her arms crossed, and tried to achieve a serious tone in her British accent.

"All right, give her some confidence. Then, send her up." James sipped his coffee and continued working on the latest fight schedule that was spread across his desk.

Debra continued to stand there, determined.

He glanced up at her, eyebrows raised. "What?"

"I am serious, James. She can start with you now; she has done a lot of work with me. She's ready for something more… She's got something. Just do not stick her with that rookie asshole."

James sat back in his chair and smiled at Debra. She had the best way of telling it like it was, no bullshit. He knew what rookie asshole she was talking about, and he wouldn't stick anyone with that guy.

"No worries, Debra. I'll take care of it. Your little project will be fine." He smiled and took another sip of his coffee, knowing that would get her riled.

"James! She's not a project. What the heck is wrong with you?" She had her hands on her hips. "Put her with Trevor or with you."

"You have my word; I'll find a safe place for her." James held up his hands in surrender.

"Thank you, James." Debra smiled. She always got her way.

"You're welcome."

She handed him a piece of paper. "I'll tell you something; this girl has got a fire. You better keep an eye out for this one."

James loved her way with words. "Thanks for the heads-up." He smiled and took the paper from her.

"I'm just saying. You'll see; I'm always right. Off to teach now, ta-ta!!" Debra smiled that million-dollar smile and was off.

James shook his head, laughing, but then his thoughts drifted back to his previous realization about Debra—she told things as she saw them, and he trusted her judgment. She wouldn't be in his office, wasting his time, if she didn't feel passionate about this. Debra was usually spot-on, just as she was with her take on the rookie asshole, Josh.

James took the piece of paper Debra had given him with the name of the girl she was sending his way. "Ashley Banner" was written in pink in Debra's swirly cursive. "All right, Ashley, we'll see what you've got." He stuck the note on top of his pile for Trevor.

James didn't have room for any more clients, especially the ones who thought they wanted to be fighters, but were not willing to put in the hard work. He could teach them to fight if they were serious, but some of the women only wanted attention. It was tempting to work with some of those women and get involved with them, but James took his job seriously; he expected the same of his clients. If he became involved with them outside of the club, which had happened in the past, what was lost was respect for each other and for the sport. His remedy was to remove the temptation by working with only male clients and keeping his dating interests outside the club.

Except for Shawn...

***

After serving in the military for ten years, James wasn't sure how he was going to jump back into normal society. He began training in different martial arts, and that was how he met Vince. They shared a lot in common, trading histories of Vince's years in the Airborne Rangers and James's in the Army Special Forces.

Vince found that James's background made him a perfect match to run the self-defense program at his gym and recruited him. James created a program that included martial arts studies of Krav Maga, along with other self-defense programs. As time went on, the popularity of the program exploded, and James took on more of a managerial and coaching role.

James liked his alone time, hanging out at his apartment, either indulging his love of music and reading or going for a run. Better yet, he loved to leave the city to find hiking trails and get lost in the outdoors, away from the everyday stress. Friday and Saturday nights were spent either playing poker with the guys in his building or out at Boston's top clubs.

James was tight with a group of guys from the Boston Police Department that were a constant part of his weekend agenda. He befriended a few of the trainers from the gym, and they became part of this group. They frequented Whiskey Saigon, a trendy, upscale nightclub in Boston. It was a favorite spot for high-end spenders and affluent clientele on Saturday nights. Although similar to other big Boston clubs, Whiskey Saigon was definitely exclusive. There were VIP lists to get on, long lines to wait in if you were not on a list, and lots of beautiful women. Everyone was beautiful in this club; they dressed that way, too. No crappy clothes or ugly people to be seen. James wondered if people were allowed in based on their looks and their wardrobe.

His first time there, James had gotten the invite from a couple of the Boston PD Special Crimes Unit guys who were on the VIP list. Surely, the owners thought it was a good idea to have members of law enforcement as their top invitees. James had gone along and soon was a regular. It didn't hurt that he was the manager of one of the elite fight clubs in Boston.

James could be himself while he was with his friends. When he walked into the club, he was James. He was not the trainer or coach or adviser. It was nice to be able to breathe and let loose. There, he was the one getting special treatment. James and his buddies were the VIPs. They walked in without a wait or a question asked. They got whatever they wanted, whenever they wanted.

James took full advantage of the perks at the club—from the top-shelf booze, to the women, to the requests of special guests to have him at their table. He was well known in the boxing and fitness arena, and that was hot right then. Being seen with James, or known to be training at his club, was a huge plus. Some of the bouncers worked out at the boxing club or were on the fighting circuit themselves.

His cop friends introduced him to some FBI agents and members of the Secret Service. They hired James as their personal trainer. Deep down he was a humble individual with a true love for what he did for a living, but it was hard not to let this popularity go to his head.

Women made themselves readily available to him. In his nights of frequenting the club, he was rarely seen with the same girl twice. As time went on, he was exhausted trying to keep track of the different women.

The late nights, the different women—it never stopped, and it was draining. James began to limit his nights out to weekends only and was cautious about with whom he spent time. He formed a new friendship with Dean, a former Navy Seal, who gave James sound advice, telling him he should make it difficult for people to get close to him.

Stay exclusive, only spend time with people who would lift him up, not sap his energy. He always remembered those words and began to use that philosophy in both his professional and personal lives.

There was one remaining exception—Shawn. She was the one person who sucked the energy out of James—never giving, always taking. He needed to change that.

CHAPTER 18

Ashley stretched her legs out on the couch. She was looking forward to a relaxing Friday night. Her ringtone sounded. The caller ID was Debra; she reached for her phone.

"Hey, Ashley. I left word with our head trainer to get you started upstairs next week. He promised to put you with one of our top trainers, Trevor. Isn't that great?"

On the other end of the phone, Ashley bit her nail as Debra told her the news. "Yeah"—she hesitated—"that's great," she said flatly. She'd hoped Debra would set her up in a trial class, not make a full-blown commitment with a trainer.

"Oh, don't you get worried about all this. It'll be great. I can meet you there and take you up to introduce you. Okay, Ash?"

Ashley inhaled and leaned her head back on the couch. "Yes, yes. I'll see you there Monday. I'm excited…really."

"All right, see you then. Enjoy your weekend!"

"Thanks, Debra."

Ashley shook her head. *What did I get into?* She would keep busy for the rest of the weekend so that she wouldn't obsess over or back out of what was to come on Monday.

***

Sunday night, Ashley texted Debra to tell her she would be fine to meet Trevor on her own.

Ashley: *Time to get my big girl pants on. I can handle it.*

Debra: *Yes, you can, girlfriend. Come down afterwards. If I'm with clients, give a thumbs-up or -down, so I know how it went. I know it'll be a thumbs-up; you're going to love Trevor. He's a doll.*

***

Ashley's stomach was twisted in knots as she arrived at the gym early Monday morning. The floor was empty; hip-hop music beat through the open space. She made her way over to the benches, placed her gym bag down on the floor, and took a seat.

"Can I help you?"

Ashley turned, startled by the voice, and saw a guy standing behind the front desk. She hadn't heard him come in as she sat there. She stood and approached the desk, trying to stop her hands from clenching.

"Hi, yes, I have a meeting with Trevor. I'm Ashley Banner." Ashley thought he looked familiar, but couldn't remember which trainer he was.

He gave her a crooked smile. "Ashley, nice to meet you. I'm James Anson."

He shook her hand, surprised. Based on his conversation with Debra, she was not how he'd envisioned her. He also remembered her walking through the gym with Lisa and Vince a while back. He would never forget her face.

"Trevor will be here soon." James returned his attention to the computer at the front desk.

He is intense, Ashley thought. That jogged her memory; he was the guy she'd seen working the bags that first day when Lisa brought her to the gym. *Winter-hat guy.*

"Thanks." She returned to her seat on the bench, scooting her duffel bag aside, and sat on her hands to keep from fidgeting. "You're a trainer here, right?"

James was flipping through a file. He looked up hesitantly and smirked. "Ah, yes, I'm the head coach." He couldn't help but smile to himself.

154

"Hey, James, how's it going?" Trevor strode through the main doors and approached them.

"Hey, Trevor. Ashley's here to see you." James nodded toward Ashley.

She stood awkwardly and picked up her duffel bag, holding it close.

Trevor greeted her with a warm smile. "Ashley, I'm Trevor. So nice to meet you. I hope you weren't waiting long."

Trevor was tall and lean but muscular; he had dark hair, olive skin, and smiling dark eyes. She guessed he was a few years older than she was. All the girls downstairs talked about Trevor and how attractive he was. He was soft-spoken, but from what Ashley understood, he fought in competitions all around the country and had several trophies and medals to his name.

"Hi. Nice to meet you. I got here a few minutes ago." Ashley tentatively shook his hand with her cold hand, conscious of her every movement.

"James, hopefully you didn't scare her too much." Trevor walked behind the front desk and tucked his gym bag underneath.

She laughed nervously. *James.* She tried to remember what Lisa had told her about James, but she couldn't exactly.

James smiled, not looking up from his work on the computer.

Trevor opened a file drawer and looked through the pile; then he retrieved one of the folders. He leaned across James and took a pen out of the metal penholder. "James is our lead competition trainer. Keeps all of us instructors and fighters in line."

Oh yeah, that's what Lisa told me, she thought. She should have remembered that he oversaw the fighters and was Vince's right-hand man. Instead, she'd asked if he was a trainer. *Ugh.* Embarrassed, her cheeks pinkened.

James nodded to Trevor. "Have a great session." He grabbed his folder and jogged up the stairs to his office.

"All right then, Ashley, let's get started. Follow me."

As Ashley tried to keep up, Trevor led her past the boxing rings to a private training area with a set of benches against the wall. He sat and opened the folder, pen in hand.

"Debra tells me you've been taking her self-defense classes the past few months, and you're interested in boxing. Is this for fitness, or did you have other goals in mind?"

"Well, yes, I liked the self-defense class, but I'm looking to get more into kickboxing. Something a little more interactive and challenging." She felt her voice shake a little.

Trevor nodded. "Terrific. We offer a few different options along that line. There are small group classes for traditional boxing, kickboxing, both American and Muay Thai. There is Krav Maga, more on the self-defense side, and there's mixed martial arts that combines all the above with Jiu-Jitsu, which is a grappling-based martial art. All of these can be learned in a class setting or with one-on-one instruction."

"I think kickboxing. I liked punching and kicking the pads. Whatever program has that, I want in." Remembering the exhilaration of punching and kicking the pads in Debra's class motivated her to continue.

Trevor laughed, amused at her candidness. "All right. Muay Thai kickboxing or American kickboxing would be a good start. The difference is in the strikes. American kickboxing is limited to punches and kicks, traditionally above the waist, whereas Muay Thai allows many more striking options. Thai boxing is known as the Art of Eight Limbs because of its use of eight points of contact: punches, kicks, elbow and knee strikes."

Ashley thought boxing was boxing. She was fascinated that this style was considered an art form. "I'd like to try Muay Thai, but I'm kinda nervous about…getting hurt." She sat on her hands.

Trevor closed the file folder and placed it aside on the bench. "Do you have boxing gloves?"

Ashley nodded and reached for the gloves in her bag. "Yes, I used these with Debra." She held up the black-and-purple gloves, her new allies.

Trevor stood up and smiled. "Then, let's get to work."

Trevor's friendly manner helped calm Ashley's nerves. He had amazing attention to detail; he seemed to remember everything she'd mentioned about her limitations, and she was glad she was able to be candid about her fears of getting hurt. In the end, Trevor knew the right things to say to encourage and push her to go a little farther out of her comfort zone.

"We'll take it slow. One move at a time. Okay?"

She hesitated for only a moment. "Okay. I'm ready."

Trevor retrieved his kickboxing pads from under one of the boxing rings. The rectangular pads were thick crimson-red leather with black trim around the sides and sturdy black handles to slip his hands through. He showed her how Thai pads were curved to absorb the power of the kicks.

The first thing Trevor demonstrated was the correct fighter stance. The lead leg was the nondominant side, which for Ashley was her left. "The fighter stance in Muay Thai is different from traditional boxing. We stand with hips squared, not turned off to the side." He stood with his hips squared to her hips, not angled away.

"The other key is not to be flat-footed. One foot needs to be light, so you are ready to move to block kicks, throw kicks, or angle out to avoid getting hit." Trevor kept his front foot lightly tapping on the floor ready to lift and throw a strike or move out of the way of a punch.

"Next, gloves always have to be up to protect your face. It's a good habit to start early, even with pad work. Once you get to sparring, if you drop your hands, that provides an opening for your opponent. Keep hands up now; it becomes second nature." He kept his guard up and his hands loose, not pressed tightly against his face.

"Okay, ready to throw some punches? Let's see what you've got so far."

"Yes, ready." Shaking, Ashley slipped her hands into the gloves and secured the Velcro strap.

Trevor held the pads and signaled for Ashley to throw a jab or a cross, a hook or an uppercut. "Now, I'm going to show you how

Muay Thai strikes have a slightly different setup. The jab is the most important punch in your arsenal. It is the punch that will lead your combinations ninety-five percent of the time. You hit with your lead hand, and it's meant to throw your opponent off-balance and keep them at a distance, preventing them from returning strikes." He held his hands up by his face and slowly demonstrated the position of the punch. His eyes were intense, looking right through her.

"When you throw your jab, your shoulder, back, waist, hips, and foot have to move. Start with your jab tucked in close by your cheek, then project forward, not twisting the angle of the wrist until just before contact." In slow motion, he threw the jab and stopped a few inches from Ashley's nose.

She took a breath, staring at the end of his glove just inches from her face. She shook it off, determined not to panic.

They spent half of the session focusing on the correct positioning of her feet, hips, and shoulders in order to throw strikes with the most power. The punches and kicks were basically the same as what she had been practicing with Debra, but these upper-body moves required full-body movement and proper positioning. Trevor's motions were flawless and fluid; he made every punch or punch-kick combination look natural.

With the kicks, Trevor showed her that she needed to step out at an angle for her kick to be powerful and land precisely on its target. When Ashley attempted the movements, she felt awkward and not light on her feet. Trevor showed unbelievable patience in demonstrating and repositioning her. By the end of their session, she had become more comfortable with the patterns.

"Nice work!" He fist-bumped her gloved hand. "Congratulations, you have learned the first level of Thai boxing basics. What'd you think?"

Ashley removed her gloves, reached for her towel, and wiped the sweat from her face. "I can't believe how much I sweat. That was awesome."

Trevor smiled. "All right. Want to set up a time to meet again, or do you want to try a class?"

Ashley knew there was no way she was ready to jump in with a group of strangers punching and kicking her. "How much would it be to work with you one-on-one?" She was afraid she wouldn't be able to afford this customized training, but hoped she could continue with Debra's class and meet with Trevor every so often when she had the extra money.

"Typically, I charge eighty dollars per hour session when I'm training heavy for an upcoming fight. But my schedule is light right now, so I'm offering training for sixty for one hour and forty for thirty minutes."

Ashley knew it was worth the price to work with him one-on-one. She needed the direction, and she trusted him. "Okay. I can do that."

"Terrific. Do you have certain days or times that work for you?"

Ashley thought of her schedule and wanted to laugh about how empty her calendar was. She did absolutely nothing besides work, worry about Stephen finding her, and come here with Lisa.

"Early morning would be better, before work. Around six? I'm flexible, though."

Trevor led Ashley back to the front desk to retrieve his phone and check his calendar. "How about Wednesday mornings at six?" He looked up at Ashley.

She knew without looking that day worked, but wanted to look as if she had a life, so she rummaged through her duffel to retrieve her phone. "Yes, that works."

"Would you like to meet this Wednesday or wait until next week?"

"I can meet this week." She wanted to keep this feeling of empowerment going.

"Okay, Ashley. I'm putting you in for Wednesday at six in the morning. We can start with a thirty-minute session. I'll be honest; I'm going to put you through a tough workout, just as I do with the fighters. There'll be instructions, but we're going to work for those thirty minutes." He smiled, but she could tell he meant what he said.

"That sounds good to me." She entered the appointment in her calendar, thrilled to have something to look forward to.

"Great. I'll see you Wednesday, then." Trevor put his phone and her file behind the desk.

"Thank you so much." They shook hands; then she headed to the locker room, feeling the effects of the adrenaline rush from their workout.

Her arms shook with fatigue as she dried her hair after a shower. That amazing high and the grin on her face lasted the entire train ride to work; she never gave a thought to Stephen or the life she'd left behind.

***

The morning one hour sessions with Trevor were grueling. They met on the mats behind the boxing ring. He handed her a jump rope, and with a remote, he set the timer on the wall for three minutes. Her jumping was clunky, not smooth like the boxers she'd seen practicing. She had to restart constantly, losing her breath and pace quickly.

Next, he had her punch and kick pads with combinations he called out for three 2-minute rounds; then he slowed things down to teach her the techniques for the Muay Thai combinations. After that, he repeated the pad work with new combinations.

Part of her dreaded the intense work, the rounds of jump rope that she couldn't get the hang of, the ungodly number of push-ups that she could hardly perform, and the frustration of not knowing how to move her body in the new way. She wanted to be more in control.

The same things she dreaded also made her look forward to their sessions. The freedom of movement, the little victories she achieved when she would meet a goal—completing more than ten push-ups, mastering the jump rope a little. The powerful impact of her strikes against the pads was energizing, intoxicating even.

For hours after she left the gym, her spirit was lifted. Her mood brightened, adding peace to her days at work and calmness to her evenings at home. She finally felt she had a purpose.

***

Week number three, Trevor introduced new combinations that involved more complex punches and kicks. Trevor explained the switch kick was the kick thrown from the lead leg, the less dominant side. The concepts did not make any sense to her, but she followed his demonstrations and performed the movements as accurately as possible.

Over time, she learned hooks, uppercuts, leg kicks aiming for your opponent's legs, body kicks aiming for the rib cage, and head kicks, which needed no explanation. There were teeps or push kicks, a signature Muay Thai kick that resembled a pushing type of kick or foot jab; it was used for creating distance between opponents.

He taught her how to move at different angles as she threw and evaded punches. Footwork was a key element of the training. She learned to angle out in all different directions to avoid getting hit by an opponent. There was also bobbing, weaving, slipping, and parrying punches.

"To parry a punch means to deflect it away in another direction. It's more effective than blocking; you use your opponent's momentum against him. It's basically a way to quickly knock a punch off its path toward your face."

As she extended her arm in the jab, with his gloved hand, he would tap her glove to the side, away from his face. He also showed her ways to defend against kicks by using her leg when he threw a leg kick and using her arm tucked against her side to protect her ribs when he threw a body kick.

After eight weeks of training, Trevor introduced Ashley to sparring. "Sparring," he explained, "is supposed to be light in intensity, nothing over twenty-five or thirty percent impact or speed. It's supposed to be a teaching tool, learning moments, not a real fight. You'll need a mouth guard and shin guards. We sell them here if you'd like to purchase a set."

Ashley was dreading sparring. Putting herself in the position to get punched and kicked didn't seem appealing, but she knew it was part of the curriculum. So, she convinced herself to give it a shot.

She nervously nodded. "Okay, I'll buy a set." She swallowed hard, hoping she would not have a panic attack at the first point of contact.

Trevor retrieved from behind the front desk a black pair of fabric shin covers and a clear mouth guard. He handed them to Ashley.

She removed the plastic packaging from each with trembling hands and set them aside. She looked down at the foreign items and took a deep breath.

Trevor retrieved his gear from under the ring, pulling his shin guards on and tossing his blue boxing gloves into the ring. "We'll spar in the ring."

Trevor took out a mini stepladder to assist her in climbing into the ring, and she awkwardly stood staring at how to get under, over, or through the four blue-and-red ropes that encircled the blue, padded, square ring.

In contrast, with one swift movement, Trevor hopped up onto the ring, rolled effortlessly under the ropes, and jumped to his feet.

Ashley placed her gloves, shin covers, and mouth guard in the corner of the ring before attempting to climb into it. She thought, *There is no way I'm using a stepladder,* and hoisted herself up onto the platform of the ring as if she were pushing herself out of a pool. As she pulled her legs up awkwardly onto the platform, she was still contemplating how she would climb through the ropes as smoothly as possible, as if it were something she did every day. She prayed she wouldn't end up stuck in between the narrow ropes—or worse, fall flat on her face into the ring.

She carefully lifted the second rope down from the top and stuck her leg through, following with her body. *Step one,* she thought, *I'm in the ring.* Her nerves were stretched tight.

She sat in the corner on the canvas of the ring to slip her shin guards over her legs. The black, padded fabric encircled the lower leg like a sock, from below her knee to over the tops of her feet, and left her toes exposed. The padding was enough to soften the blow of a painful strike to the shin. She eyed the mouth guard again as she slipped a hand into one of her gloves. She could imagine how ridiculous she would look trying to place this guard into her mouth.

Everything she did here was awkward. Previously, Ashley had made sure that in her new life she was in control of all situations, of her body, and of her every move. Here, she was out of her comfort zone, yet Trevor did his best to make her feel at ease. He always asked if she was comfortable with what they were working on. At times, she would shut down and want to stop moving forward, but he kept things light-hearted and had her laughing at herself, relieving any frustration she might be feeling.

That day was no different. He actually made the entire concept of getting punched in the head and kicked all over seem normal. For the first round of their sparring practice, he instructed that she would alternate throwing punches and kicks at him, and he would defend only, not return with strikes.

"Remember, strikes are only twenty-five to thirty percent effort and speed." He smiled and pointed a gloved hand at her. "It'll be my turn to strike the next round, so be nice." Trevor smirked and put his mouth guard in, pressed the Start button on the timer, and secured his other hand in his glove.

She pushed the mouth guard in, slipped her other glove on, and nodded. They met in the middle of the ring and touched gloves. She started tentatively, her heart racing wildly, throwing light jabs at a slow pace. Trevor parried the punches by tapping her glove as it came toward his face. He began to move around the ring to encourage her to move with him. Her confidence increased, trying the jab-cross combinations, then hooks and uppercuts.

The next round, it was his turn to strike offensively against her. Each time he threw a punch, she would cringe, then realize it wasn't as bad as she thought. They took turns for two more rounds with the addition of kicks; then it was freestyle.

"Now, sparring. Anything goes, still at the twenty-five to thirty percent, but we can both throw strikes and both defend. Are we good?"

Panic set in as Ashley realized there was no control now. She thought of telling him she was all set and wanted to end the session, but then he flashed that reassuring smile before the bell rang. "Yeah, I'm good…I think." She nodded, not sure she could form words at that point.

"You'll be okay." Trevor adjusted his mouth guard and nodded, touching her glove, signaling to begin.

She struggled to remain calm, which hindered her performance. The more stressed she was, the more difficult it was to remember the combinations of strikes and, worse, how to defend against the incoming strikes.

There were teaching moments, many humbling moments, and a moment when she thought she'd landed a decent punch-kick combo.

"Try that move again." Trevor paused the timer.

She threw the combination—a high jab to the face and a low jab to the stomach.

"Now, try high jab, low cross."

She thought about it and then did as instructed.

"Again. Harder." He patted his stomach.

She landed the cross harder into the glove covering his stomach.

"Come on, harder. I can take it." Trevor grinned and placed his gloved hand over his stomach again.

She put the drive into her cross.

"Which one feels more powerful?" He looked at her intently.

There was no question in her mind. "The cross."

"Which one do you like better?" He leaned against the ropes.

She smiled. "The cross."

Trevor nodded. "That cross had way more force to push me back than that jab. Stay away from combinations that don't have purpose."

He tapped her glove, continuing the sparring session. Her heart raced as she dodged punches and angled out from his kicks. When he caught her leg kick, she froze then remembered how to free herself from his hold a moment too late as he swept her leg out from under her, catching her before she landed on her butt. He saw all things before she did them.

"Don't hesitate. Make your move; then know your next three moves. If you delay, your opponent will see the opening." He paused the timer, letting Ashley catch her breath.

They sparred for close to an hour. The last round, she barely had anything left. She couldn't defend against his strikes, and her reaction time slowed to a snail's pace; she wasn't able to catch her breath. When the final bell rang, she was relieved.

"Nice work." They touched gloves; then he removed his gloves and mouth guard.

"I'm so out of shape." She sat on the floor of the ring, chest heaving.

He crouched down next to her. "It's all right. We'll keep practicing. You've got it; you need to work on your cardio. The first thing to go when you're under stress like that is your breathing."

"Thank you for helping me. And not killing me." She chuckled in between breaths as Trevor offered his hand to help her back to standing. Ashley understood this would be a long road and wasn't sure if she would be able to master any of the moves, but she was ready to put in the work and give it her all.

Two things she did know for sure—she loved the adrenaline that ran through her veins and the feel of the impact when she nailed a kick. There was nothing better than that moment.

CHAPTER 19

What I want
Smooth and quick
Fast and sharp
Slow and precise
Heat my skin
Melt my heart
Weaken my knees
Don't ever stop.

Ashley added to her routine her own workouts in the evenings and on weekends, sometimes training with Trevor or meeting Lisa for sparring and pad work. As her strength and confidence increased, Ashley wanted more. She watched some of the other clients who had more training experience and the seasoned fighters, noticing how smooth their moves were and how comfortable they were sparring. Ashley felt clumsy on the mat and was still learning how to manage her space. These fighters were on a different level. The ring and the cage were their second homes. They moved swiftly and precisely, mastering layers of complex combinations and footwork.

That afternoon, after her session with Trevor and after getting her ass handed to her by Lisa while sparring, Ashley watched James sparring with his client in the ring. James broke down every move and made his client repeat each drill endlessly until it was perfect and smooth. Drill, repeat, drill, repeat. Again. Each move was precise and powerful, and he expected and produced perfection in his fighters.

At that moment, Ashley had an epiphany. She saw herself there. She saw herself fighting in that ring someday…working with him.

Ashley wanted to work with James because he was the best. He knew how far to push, even past the breaking point at times, then how to bring his clients back to where they needed to be.

She thought he would probably never consider her good enough to train on the competition teams, but she was willing to work for it.

***

"I'm interested in hearing about competition training and what it involves." Ashley was wrapping her wrists before her training session with Trevor.

He informed her of the different levels of teams, how many days per week the groups met, and how much extra time would be required on her part in order to commit to a team.

"They take their training seriously, and they expect the same commitment from all involved." He looked at her, his expression serious.

Ashley sat quietly a moment, taking in the information. Then, she looked at him with fire in her eyes and nodded. "I want to do it. I'll make the commitment."

He showed her the latest schedule for the competition-training group. Comparing it to her calendar, she saw there were times that Trevor could be her lead coach and others when James would be.

"I'll let James know you're interested. He has final approval on all fighters."

Ashley's hopes diminished. James was so serious, and she'd seen him shake his head sometimes when he was watching her sessions with Trevor.

"Don't worry. You have a good chance of getting in." He returned the schedule to the front desk.

"Yeah. Thanks. The waiting will kill me." She sighed.

"I'll talk to him. He doesn't mess around. You'll know by tomorrow."

***

That evening, Ashley constantly checked her phone as she waited to hear from Trevor. Her stomach twisted in knots.

Finally, late the next night, she received a text.

Trevor: *Hey, Ashley. I talked to James. He wants to see how you have progressed. He's joining our session tomorrow.*

Ashley had to reread the text a couple of times before it sank in.

"Holy crap."

***

Falling asleep that evening was impossible. She was a nervous wreck. She needed to block out the fact that James would be shadowing her session so that she could fall asleep and stay asleep through the night. She began writing in her journal to help take her mind off it. Drawing had taken a back seat to work and her new workout schedule. Writing in her journal had taken its place.

She would journal feelings of elation after her kickboxing sessions and feelings of depression on days she didn't work out or when memories of her past resurfaced. Writing freed her from stress and obsessive thoughts; she could clear her mind and set new intentions for the day ahead. As she wrote, she would get lost in her words, turning simple thoughts into poetry.

She drifted off to sleep with dreams of clouds and the pink glow of the sky from the farm.

***

She startled awake to the alarm; her notebook was by her side in bed. She dressed quickly, choked down a protein shake, and arrived at the gym early.

After completing a warm-up on the treadmill, she met Trevor in the ring. Her nerves were strung tight, causing her movements to be choppy. She tried to loosen up and establish a rhythm before James stepped into the ring.

"Come on, Ash; don't worry. Do what we've been doing. You've got this." Trevor moved her around the ring with light pad work, looking more for accuracy than power.

Ashley nodded, determined to stay focused and not let the runaway train of her thoughts and emotions get the best of her. *Not today.*

James jogged down the steps from his office and approached the boxing ring.

"Hey, James." Trevor nodded from the ring. He turned back to Ashley and continued with their warm-up pace, moving around the ring, increasing intensity and speed for a two-minute round.

She kept her eyes on Trevor, convincing herself not to stumble. *Don't think; go; you've got this.*

As the buzzer rang, James effortlessly lifted himself into the ring, hopping to his feet. He nodded to Ashley, his expression all business. "I'm going to have you work on your footing a little differently. That's what's slowing you down."

Instinctively, as she wiped sweat from her forehead, Ashley looked down at her feet. She thought she'd been moving pretty fast.

"The less you have to move and readjust your foot position, the quicker you can move in and out of ranges of punches." He moved quickly in and out of punch range to demonstrate.

"Let's see your jab, and freeze at the end of it." He slipped on the mitts and held up his hands for a jab.

She froze the position as instructed, and he went to work adjusting her legs and moving her foot angles. It took constant repetition to master his small changes; however, she felt she'd made the connection he wanted her to make. She began to move more freely. He had her do this with all the basic strikes, then had her freestyle spar.

As the session came to an end, her worry came back. *I'm not good enough. He thought I was terrible.*

She loosened the Velcro from her gloves, removed her mouth guard, and carefully climbed out of the ring on wobbly legs. She busied herself with her gear, arranging the items in her bag while Trevor and James talked about the competition-training schedule and who was in the group. There was no mention of her being in or out.

She thought, *Do they know I'm still here?*

James jumped down from the ring and turned to Ashley. "You'll need to work on your cardio. The team competes at a maximum of five 5-minute rounds. You won't make it past round two if you're completely gassed." He stood facing her with his stony expression.

Ashley nodded, feeling this was the cut. *Better luck next time.*

"The group meets on Saturdays. Nice work." He turned to Trevor. "See ya later, man."

"Thanks, James. See ya." Trevor hopped down to the floor from the ring.

James turned and was off.

"Nice work, kid. You made it." Trevor fist-bumped Ashley as she stood shocked, looking after James as he strode away.

"Oh my God. I made the team," she breathed, half asking if this was for real.

"Now, the work begins." Trevor smirked and nodded.

She was speechless, elated beyond belief, and truly scared. She thought, *This is what I wanted, right?*

CHAPTER 20

That evening after a long, hot shower, Ashley sat in her favorite chair, with a glass of white wine, her journal, and the gas fireplace lit. She wrote up a list of reasons why she should work with James as her coach. The list, of course, was never intended to be seen by Trevor or James, or anyone else, for that matter. However, it made Ashley feel proactive.

1) *Although a new student, I have the advantage of taking the self-defense course offered by this gym.*
2) *I blew through the workouts Trevor gave me, and now I'm on the competition team.*
3) *I can throw powerful kicks to the body, and I have a mean right cross.*
4) *I lived with a psychotic, abusive man, escaped from him, and am still in hiding; my adrenaline is through the roof, and my reflexes are on hyperalert—great for fighting!*
5) *I want to work with the best coach.*

Okay, number five is lame, she thought, but it was true. James was the best, and there was something about him. *Something about the way he works with me,* she thought. She couldn't tell if he thought she had no hope of becoming a fighter or if he thought she could make it.

He'd homed in on her weakness after the first few minutes. He had a deep connection to movement and how to improve it. The small tweaks in her positions gave her more power, more range of motion, and more energy to keep pushing through her sparring sessions. *Imagine how much further he could take me?* she thought.

She wrote more in her journal then sighed as she put it aside. A plan was starting to fall into place in her head, but she needed to make sure that her timing was right and that she got his attention one of these days.

***

Sometimes, I push through each session, feeling like I am on top of the world...but then, most times, not so much, especially when I fail. Next time, I will push harder. Next time, he will see. I can do this. I can be better than the rest. Next time, he will notice me...and, next time, he will not forget who I am.

***

James had been paying attention to Ashley as she progressed in her training with Trevor. When Debra pushed for her to start upstairs in the fight programs, James had thought this would be just another girl who thought she wanted to fight, who would give up once she got hit.

Now that he'd seen her in action, he had to admit he was intrigued. He'd watched her work with Trevor; her moves were raw, choppy, but something he could improve.

It wasn't long until word spread among the trainers that she'd joined the competition team. Often, James seemed to be drawn back to watching her as she progressed in the ring with Trevor and worked with Lisa. She was focused. He tended to watch the fighters' sparring matches on the monitors upstairs, realizing it could be a distraction if he stood by the ring.

The times he would walk through the gym or be talking to Trevor while she was in a sparring group, she would attempt over-the-top moves far above what she should be doing at her level. There was a discipline that needed to be followed to progress. Fighters needed to learn the art of fighting, along with aggressive combat tactics, offensive and defensive moves, and endurance; those were all important aspects of the sport. But Ashley rarely worked on any defense; she was always ready to take on the role of aggressor, especially when she thought anyone, particularly James, was watching.

At times, she would stumble through basic fight patterns. Then, other days, she showed glimmers of perfection: a round kick perfectly

172

placed at her opponent's head, powerful hooks, uppercuts, and complex combinations.

As James watched her in the ring, he knew he could make her better, make her moves sharper. He made them all better, but they needed to want it. Then, the grueling work would begin: the many hours of training, of being frustrated, and of falling and failing.

Finally, there was that moment when they became fighters. That one glowing instant they'd bask in their achievements, whether it was finally nailing a hook, landing a perfect kick, acing a sparring match, or winning a competition. They never forgot that spark, and they were never the same. They were willing to take the risks, the falls, and the failings to experience that one instant of perfection all over again.

Others believed they could get there without the work; they failed miserably and quit. James didn't think she would quit. There was a fire in her that couldn't be taught. He thought something was holding her back, but he knew how to get people past their obstacles and overcome their fears.

James began to plan his mornings so he could bump into Ashley. His thoughts and activities of the day circled back to her. *Great, I have become a stalker,* he thought. It started out innocently, not planned. He would run into her as she came flying in late for her session with Trevor. He'd be working with a client, and she would be nearby, wrapping her wrists and cursing that she could never get those flipping things right.

Then, he began to consciously make a point to be around when she was done sparring with Trevor or talking with Lisa. Watching her work with the competition team, he thought she had the potential to move up through the levels. He noticed her use of the techniques he'd taught her; her rhythm was better. Careful thought went into her moves now; he could tell she was replaying his instructions in her mind as she repeated the drills.

Putting it plainly, he realized he was attracted to her and knew he should probably walk away, but he didn't want to. Sometimes, he wondered if she thought about him. He caught Ashley watching him a couple of times while he trained other clients; then she would smile and look away. Other times, he could feel her eyes on him. He didn't mind; she wasn't creepy, psycho staring. She was only silently watching, but he wondered, *What does she see?* An overbearing perfectionist? A guy she would never think twice about? *Maybe this is crazy.* For some reason, she made him smile.

James shook his head. *What's wrong with me?* He probably had concocted this whole scenario in his head, imagining all the women were always looking at him. But, then, he justified his actions by telling himself he was only studying her to observe if she was ready to move up in the competition teams. *That's what I do; I study fighters.*

Except, she *was* different. One minute, he thought he had her figured out; then the next, she surprised him. Watching her in the ring, sometimes he saw someone who was focused, an athlete, strong and sure. Then, at times, he sensed weakness, someone who wanted to hide, not someone who wanted to fight; she was clumsy, too. She confused him.

The rarest was when she was calm and talking to him. She was warm; there was a feeling, an aura coming off her that surrounded him and pulled him in. That's what kept him hanging on.

All of it kept his interest. She was beautiful and strong, and he was drawn to her like a magnet, not able to pull away. That's what freaked him out the most.

Time to focus and get back to work, he told himself as he sat in the conference room, planning out the upcoming fights. Several of his fighters were slated to participate in high-level kickboxing and MMA fights over the next few months. The schedules were laid out in front of him, ready for him to juggle times and fighters, but his concentration was waning. The monitors for the rings were hanging above the conference table, and he couldn't help but glance up at ring number one, at Ashley doing her thing.

***

As Ashley worked with Lisa in the training group, she overheard James speaking in Spanish to one of his clients. The sound of the words rolling so naturally off his tongue melted her. *Beautiful*—that word came to mind often when she was thinking of him. Visually, internally—*beautiful*. He was intimidating, but he was also attractive, and when he smiled, she felt herself melt.

James stood close to her to help with the drill she and Lisa were working on, and she inhaled his scent, her senses on high alert. Inhaling the clean scent of soap, but mixed with his natural aroma—*beautiful*. He was standing in front of her; she wanted to reach out her hand and touch him—*sensory overload*.

She heard his words and knew she was supposed to be following directions at that moment, yet she stood there, frozen, until she snapped back to reality.

"Got it, Ashley?" He was turning to assist another client but hesitated. "Ashley?"

"Yes, got it." Ashley raised her glove and smiled, looking at James as if saying, "Yeah, of course!"

Luckily, he walked away and didn't make her repeat what he'd instructed.

"Hey, Earth to Ashley." Laughing, Lisa took a jab at her to snap her back. "Seriously, Ash."

"What? I was waiting for him to finish. Let's go." She slapped her gloved hands together.

"Do you even know what you are supposed to do?" Lisa shook her head and secured her own gloves.

"Um," Ashley peered around Lisa and then at the two guys sparring behind her. "Kicks and... No clue."

Lisa shook her head. "You, my friend, are hopeless."

CHAPTER 21

The challenge, the wonder, the question.
Never an answer.
Drawing in and getting stronger.

Ready to run, ready to soar.
Needing the heat, wanting it more.

Your invisible web draws me in.
Then, it is too late.
You have me trapped, ensnared.

But would I flee
If you set me free?

Ashley was willing herself not to think of James. She was reading too much into this, so she kept herself distracted. That worked...for a while.

With projects to finish, deadlines to meet, she would do well at work. Then, as she left work, she would swear that she saw James walking in the crowd as she headed to the train station, but, alas, it wasn't him. Her mind played tricks sometimes...

Trying to take her mind off James was difficult. Trying to convince herself she wasn't attracted to him was nearly impossible. Distractions—James occupying her thoughts—tugged her attention from work.

How ridiculous is this? she thought. Was her perception of reality that warped? Could she be that far from reality? *I can stop thinking about him anytime*—Ashley thought these words then repeated them like a mantra, *I am done thinking about James. I am done thinking about James.*

She inhaled deeply as she walked into the gym, determined to get her training in without distractions. *I am done thinking about him. I am done thinking about him.*

As she rounded the corner, James was working with his evening training group. She repeated her mantra stronger this time, *Stop thinking about him. I am done thinking about him.*

She exhaled loudly as she put her duffel on the benches and made a scene of gathering her fight gear. She glanced up, and he smiled and waved, looking genuinely happy.

Her stomach went into a cycle of tumbles, and her heart skipped a beat at the mere sight of him and his sideways smile. She smiled like a lovestruck teenager and waved back to him. *Pathetic,* she thought. *So much for the mantra.*

Sighing loudly again, she admitted to herself that she was a terrible liar.

CHAPTER 22

Trying hard to stay afloat,
Keep my head above the water.

Emotions pour out with every move.
Every punch and every kick,
Knocking the bag harder each time
Brings a little more satisfaction.

Blood pumping, lost in the rhythm.
Nothing can touch me when I am in the zone.

James saw Ashley as she walked into the gym, still dressed for work, her dark hair flowing down past her shoulders, and he watched her body move—

Thoughts of Shawn's upcoming competitions shook him back to reality. Shawn was unbeatable in the ring, and he needed to keep her head right. When he began training Shawn for the fight circuit two years ago, they started seeing each other outside of training as well and agreed to a no-strings-attached relationship.

The no strings attached only went so far with Shawn; she'd quickly become extremely demanding of him, wanting his full attention both in the ring as her trainer and outside of the gym. When she called late at night, her expectation was for James to drop whatever plans he had and meet her as soon as possible. As time went on, Shawn had become increasingly unhappy that James refused to be at her beck and call.

The urgency and secrecy were fun in the beginning of their relationship; James would be the first to admit that. At first, he thought they could build a solid relationship, but as Shawn's ego grew, her attitude became more difficult. She didn't lift James up or offer any emotional support, but she expected him to always be there for her and to give her everything. Over time, he began to distance himself, enjoying being on his own and away from her negativity.

***

James's watch read 5:20 p.m. He jogged down the stairs from his office and saw Shawn warming up on the heavy bags. She liked his style of intense training, so he worked with her individually as competitions approached. At one time, James thought she would be the perfect match for him, but she wasn't everything he wanted.

He leaned against the ring, and his gaze drifted to Ashley working the heavy bag down the row from Shawn. He couldn't shake it. *There is something about her…*

Ashley turned and glanced up at him. *Damn, those eyes,* he thought. They had a hold on him that he couldn't break. *Maybe I want what I cannot have,* he thought.

He gave her a thumbs-up, and she waved back. He thought he must be going crazy. *She would never think twice about a guy like me.*

"Hey, James," Shawn said, practically purring his name, as she approached.

"You ready to get to work?" He nodded up toward the ring.

"Always." Shawn gathered her things then hopped up into the ring as James followed, determined to keep it all business.

***

Having finished her training, Ashley was ready to cool down. Looking down the row of heavy bags, she saw Shawn working out. Shawn had a reputation around the gym, and not all good. Shawn was compact in stature, all muscle and no body fat; she had dark hair cut short in a pixie cut, close to the head with a little punk look to it. She couldn't have been more than five feet two inches, but she packed a mean punch and delivered killer kicks. She whipped guys' asses. *That's one tough bitch,* Ashley thought.

She saw James leaning against the ring, looking amazing in his formfitting shirt and black fighter shorts. He gave her a thumbs-up as she finished her work on the bags. Waving to James, she walked to the mats to cool down and stretch.

She knew she could never equal Shawn's level of fighting, but she envied her working with James. At that moment, she saw them talking together in the ring. There were so many rumors going around about the two of them—they were sleeping together, but they weren't a thing; they were a thing, but didn't want anyone to know. Ashley didn't want to look desperate, staring at their every move, so she finished her stretching and headed downstairs to the lockers, grateful to change out of her sweaty clothes and head for home.

***

"You're coming with me to the competition next weekend, right?" Shawn carried on a full conversation during her pad work with James.

"Yeah, of course, I wouldn't miss it." James didn't miss a beat, returning her strike with a countermove.

"I mean, you are staying with me, right." She glared at him. That was not a question, but a definitive statement.

He wasn't planning on staying with her, but he would be there as her fight coach. "Of course, I'll be there." He held the pads, bracing against the power of her kicks.

After several rounds of intense pad work, he called a break. James saw Ashley walking up the stairs from the lockers, and he turned to Shawn. "Grab some water, I'll be right back."

Before Shawn could protest, James hopped down from the ring to catch up with Ashley. "Hey, how's the fight going?"

Ashley was taken by surprise, and her face lit up at seeing him. "Hey, pretty good. I'm working on it." She playfully held up a fist and smiled from ear to ear.

How could she be this nice and happy? James thought as he listened to her talk about what she was working on and some of the obstacles she was running into. It was such a refreshing conversation, unlike what he usually encountered—someone always complaining about something. He leaned against the counter, listening to her, becoming relaxed around her, and getting lost in her eyes... He wanted to spend more time with her.

"Maybe you can jump in a sparring match with my group sometime." He looked at her intently.

Ashley's jaw fell open. "Seriously?" She couldn't tell if he was pulling her leg or truly serious. "Not sure I'm ready for that yet." She looked at him quizzically.

"Yeah, you are. Let me know; you can hop in tomorrow or another day if it works for you." He pushed off the counter.

She was caught off guard.

"Let me know," James repeated as he looked back to the ring where Shawn was pacing. "See you around." He turned and was gone as quickly as he'd appeared, jogging back to the ring where Shawn was now glaring in Ashley's direction.

Ashley turned to leave, shocked by the fact that he'd asked her to join his sparring group. Her stomach felt as if she were on a roller coaster. She needed to jump on this since she had a feeling he wouldn't offer it twice.

That night, Ashley's sleep was fitful. Her goal was to wake up early and drive to the gym to get in front of James before his busy day took over...and before she lost her nerve.

***

Ashley knocked on James's open office door. "Hi, can I come in?" She had to force herself to speak.

James looked up from his laptop, surprised she was there so early. "Good morning. Yes, have a seat." James waved her in, putting his work aside. "What's up?" He folded his arms on top of the desk.

Determined, she placed her duffel on the floor in front of his desk. "I would like to join your sparring group."

He leaned back in his chair and smiled. "Well, you're mighty eager to get started today."

For a moment, Ashley second-guessed herself. Scratching at her hand nervously, she thought, *Maybe this is a bad idea; maybe he doesn't think I can hang; maybe...* She shrugged off the self-doubt and stood firm. "I want to join your sparring group, like you mentioned. Would you have time to work with me before?"

James was impressed by her boldness. He couldn't hide his smile. "Yes, I have some time this morning if you want to work together."

Ashley took a deep breath; this was her chance. "Yes, sign me up."

James closed his folders and stood. "All right, let's do this."

***

In her corner of the ring, Ashley's heart beat like a bass drum against her chest as she waited while James set the timer and put on his gloves and shin guards. *This is crazy,* she thought. She readjusted her shin guards then concentrated on exhaling slowly to calm her frayed nerves.

"Let's start with light sparring rounds using hands only. I'll go first round, then your turn. I'll throw hand strikes; you can block and counter my strikes, but no kicks. Make sense?" He held his mouth guard, ready to pop it in, but waiting for her response.

"Yes. Got it." Ashley's voice cracked as she pushed her mouth guard in place, getting it caught on her lip; she then secured her gloves and nodded.

They moved about the ring. James kept his strikes light, but moved quickly.

She watched him carefully, looking for patterns, but her timing was off, and she got hit several times. *Get your head right,* she told herself.

She homed in and responded to each of his strikes. The buzzer sounded after two minutes; then they began again with Ashley as the striker. James kept his eyes on her, intent on every move she made. She began to find a rhythm and combinations that distracted him.

The next round was leg strikes and blocks only. Controlling the urge to use her punches was challenging. Kicks were her strength;

she confidently threw leg kicks, body kicks, teeps, and knees to the stomach. When it was his turn to use kicks, she had to be alert and fast to block his strikes.

Each consecutive round, James added another layer, increasing the complexity and the intensity of the sparring. Ashley needed to control her breathing because she was losing steam the more rounds they completed.

"Next, we'll spar for five 3-minute rounds, one-minute rest in between. We need to build stamina, and this is how." He jumped out of the ring and grabbed a belly pad from the rack.

She nodded and took a drink from her sports bottle, then shoved her mouth guard back in place.

"Make sure that when you are striking, you're breathing. Inhale then exhale as you strike. Faster strikes require quicker bouts of breathing." He demonstrated throwing his strike and exhaling audibly, forcing air out of his lungs.

She understood the concept and practiced a few strikes as he secured the belly pad around his waist. "I'll wear this so you can throw knee strikes without killing me." He smirked.

Ashley swallowed hard.

"All right. Let's go," James said as he pressed the timer.

They touched gloves. His movements were so quick Ashley was immediately forced out of her comfort zone. She had to utilize the entire ring in order to move out of the way of James's strikes. Punches whizzed by her head, nearly missing her face, forcing her to keep her block up and angle away or slip the punches. She found it difficult to land her punches as he moved quickly and snuck his punches in at different angles. He pushed her out of range, challenging her. Once, he waved her back in range, nodding when she connected with a jab-cross-kick combination. She understood she would have to work hard to earn this opportunity again.

James angled himself in the corner of the ring, encouraging her to practice at close range—quick jab, cross, knee, then knee repeaters. Her powerful punches and knees emphasized her breathing. Conscious of the sounds of his breathing and of how he felt as she pressed into him, Ashley found sparring with James both sensual and scary—raw pushing, hard breathing, heart racing, and sweat dripping.

To signal the end of the round, the bell on the timer rang.

"Nice!" James fist-bumped her glove.

Ashley was dazed, exhilarated, and exhausted. Even though she couldn't breathe, she wished for more. James was already climbing out of the ring, talking about how she was ready for the next level.

Ashley felt the slow satisfaction of finally getting what she wanted, while simultaneously struggling with her shaking limbs and burning legs. She then thought, not for the first time, *I should be careful what I wish for.*

CHAPTER 23

*I*t is a dance, unpredictable and raw, yet practiced and rehearsed. The hunter and the prey, luring in and pushing away, sensual and intimate. Their bodies touch; they move together, ebb and flow. Their hands leave their marks, legs finding their way around each other, sweat coming out of every pore. Yet their hands are protected, bodies are clothed; they are in separate worlds. Feeling vulnerable and exposed, pushing forward, and moving faster. The sounds of release echo from their lips as they thrust forward and endure the impact of force. Heat, power, strength, raw impact, capture and relinquish, corner and finish.

This was her new love—the love of Muay Thai kickboxing.

Still flying high days after her training session, Ashley couldn't remember a time she'd felt so alive. Thoughts of who she used to be, her timid self, and of past fears were fading, as memories tend to do. James was larger than life; he trained hard and expected all his fighters to fight harder. He was dark and serious, intimidating when she first met him, or so he seemed.

The next evening, she was revved with anticipation as she entered the gym to meet Lisa. She couldn't tell if it was because of the workout or because of James. Then, she heard his voice and knew.

He was running the advanced MMA fighter training in the cage. He coached from the side, his booming voice standing out above the noise of the gym.

Ashley's stomach flipped; her heart beat fast. It was James she wanted to see. She hesitated before walking through the gym to get to the lockers.

"Time!" The bell rang, and the guys exited the cage, fist-bumping each other. To put away some of the equipment, James crossed the floor and spotted Ashley. He called out to his guys, a little louder, hoping she would turn at the sound of his voice.

They caught each other in a glance. "Hey, Ashley." James smiled broadly.

"Hi, James." Ashley felt her cheeks heat up. Crossing to the stairwell, she felt eyes on her from the guys training in the ring and in the cage. Part of her hoped James was watching; the other part cringed, not knowing what he saw when he looked at her.

Lisa met her on the mat by the boxing ring on the lower level. "How's it going, girl?"

"It's going." Ashley tossed her duffel bag in the corner. They had the space to themselves, except for a few of the other members, some working on stretching and core workouts on the mat, two others practicing Jiu-Jitsu.

"Three 3-minute rounds on the timer. We'll alternate rounds. Kicks and punches. Ready?" Lisa set the timer and grabbed Thai pads.

"Ready." Ashley secured her gloves.

Lisa called out combinations, and Ashley fired them as fast and accurately as she could. If she didn't, Lisa made her repeat it until she perfected the move. Ashley continued punching and kicking until the timer buzzed; then they switched roles.

She moved Lisa around the floor, trying to increase her reaction speed. "Double kicks, four rapid punches, then double kicks on the other side. We're repeating this to the end."

"Got it." Lisa raised her gloves to her head.

Ashley kept the pace quick, and Lisa consistently nailed each kick. Next round completed, they took a minute water break.

"You are in for it, girl. Get ready," Lisa warned, waving the pads at her.

"All right, I'm ready." Ashley secured her gloves.

Lisa set the pace, moving quickly through combinations, first for power, then for speed. Ashley's kicks were solid. Lisa's kicks always landed perfectly, but Ashley's made the louder impact that turned heads. She felt eyes on her, but kept her focus on the pads. Jab, cross, hook, and kick pyramids, starting with one per side, then adding an additional kick each time. Each shot gave her more satisfaction.

The final buzzer sounded, and the session was done.

"Oh my God!" Ashley was out of breath as she flopped down onto the mat.

Lisa unstrapped her gloves, picked up both of their water bottles, and joined Ashley on the mat. "Nice work, lady." She held up her water bottle in a mock toast. "How's competition training?"

Ashley finished her water. "Good, I'm supposed to work with James's sparring group this weekend."

"Nice! Nervous?"

"Yes! Shoot, what if Shawn is there?" Ashley scrunched her nose.

Lisa pushed off to stand up. "Oh yeah, she'll be there. She has a bunch of fights lined up over the next couple months. Good luck with that."

"Great. I'll need all the luck I can get." Ashley dropped back onto the mat.

***

Saturday at competition training, James was short with Ashley in the ring. His constructive criticism turned into complaints about every move she made, and she felt the sting of his comments. *So it takes me a few times to get things.*

She could hear the tone of his voice change when he had to repeat the instructions for the third time. *Well, maybe it's the fourth.* She was left feeling like an annoyance or just any other client. *Get a grip,* she told herself. *That's what you are—a client, someone James coaches. No personal attachments.* She guessed it was easy for him to make that distinction, but for her it was personal.

Everything about this was personal for her, and James was getting her through it. She couldn't turn this on and off after her sixty minutes were up. The high usually stayed with her for the day and kept her going. Then, she would come down and need to be her own motivation until the next session.

It helped to be in the gym with all the fighters and trainers. Their energy and motivation pushed her to get better. Still, when she met with James, no matter how much she tried to convince herself to not take anything personally, she couldn't comply. He'd literally pull her in and immerse her in his intense world, even if only for an hour.

She was so attracted to his personality, to his aura. His eyes were deep and intense, his smile was rare, but it lit up his entire face when he shared it with her. His body, well, Ashley had to tell herself to stop staring at his chest, his muscular arms, and his back…his amazing legs, too…

Stop, she told herself.

It was hard to pull away so fast when their time together was over. It was even more difficult when she felt so…alone.

Ashley approached James. "What's up today?" She stood beside the desk, unwinding her wrist wraps.

"Nothing," he quipped and continued working on the computer without looking up.

"You seem off. Everything okay?" She stood uncomfortably.

"I'm fine." He shrugged, still not meeting her gaze.

"Huh." She frowned.

He stopped what he was working on and leaned on the counter, looking at her. "What is it with everyone around here? I have a lot of shit going on, okay?"

Her defenses went up, not liking his tone or how it made her feel. *Why should I care what is wrong with him? Maybe he is totally unstable. Best to turn and leave,* she thought. *Don't engage with him.*

But she couldn't help herself. "Good to know." She turned on her heel, left him there with his anger, and moved on to the treadmill. Her hands shook; she needed to brush off his negativity and move on.

Headphones on and tunes cranked, Ashley slipped into another world, forever chasing that high and running away from anything that reminded her of her past.

***

Covered in bruises—black, blue, and purple—Ashley covered up, hat pulled down tight, sunglasses on, long sleeves even though the humidity was high. She smiled, shaking her head. *How ironic…* Today, these bruises and black-and-blues gave her something to look forward to—a rush, a badge of honor. Unlike before.

Before, those bruises were a sign of weakness. Those were a source of pain and fear that ran deep. Now, these bruises were empowering, a sign of accomplishment. Her coworkers thought she was a little crazy, but she did not have to worry that they wouldn't believe her.

Ashley had Lisa, a witness and someone who'd paved the way for her. Showing up to work with bruised arms, and even a black eye once, Lisa never let anyone get away with judging her. They knew that under Lisa's lovely, always happy, glitter-loving, girly-girly exterior, she was badass and not to be messed with. So, no one batted an eye when, after her first competition-group training, Ashley showed up with black-and-blue marks peppering the insides of her arms from kicks to the pads and decorating her shins from kicking whatever was in front of her.

Today, Ashley covered the bruises because she was going to shop downtown and didn't want people handing her phone numbers for a hotline. Sparring with random strangers, learning to protect and unleash, not being frozen by fear—well, she was still working on that one—she felt strong inside when she remembered conquering those challenges.

There was improvement and growth that she never thought would come, but it was there. The change in her was painfully slow, but she'd made the turn. With so many on her side who wanted to help, Ashley was able to relearn that not everybody was the enemy, not everybody was out to get her or judge her.

Finally, she'd found something to be passionate about. She'd found her thing.

***

Strength and weakness. Going from feeling so strong, to struggling to keep up. Out of breath, off-balance, arms shaking, and legs like lead. I try and try, but fall further behind. Taking a deep breath, trying to gain control, and hoping to get it back.

***

Ashley's running routine helped her increase her endurance. Sparring, however, was a different story. That kicked her ass. She set a timer and decided to work the bag as if it were an opponent, ducking punches, slipping, and bobbing and weaving.

"Hey."

James's voice startled Ashley as she was hitting the heavy bags full force. "Hey," she answered shortly, not looking his way, and continued punching.

"I'm sorry about yesterday. For being such a jerk." He shuffled his feet and crossed his arms.

She paused and wiped the sweat off her face with her shirt. "Whatever." She shrugged, knowing he'd probably had a bad day and she'd probably overreacted, but she remained cool.

"No, Ashley, I had no right to take my bad day out on you. I'm sorry." He flashed the smile that made her legs weak. "Forgive me?" He grinned.

She was hesitant but smirked. *How can I stay mad when he looks at me like that?*

"Yeah." She smiled, relieved he was there because she was happy to see him, despite his being a jerk.

"Good. What are you working on?" He nodded to the bags, uncrossing his arms.

Exasperated, she looked at the bag. "I'm working on footwork. Or trying to. I'm struggling with that in the ring."

"Show me." James stepped back.

"Uh, okay." Ashley was self-conscious. She slowly started throwing combos, moving around the bag, bobbing, weaving, and slipping.

James watched intently as she moved.

She sidestepped the bag as it moved toward her after she threw combinations. Stopping, she held on to the bag to slow its swing. "Here, I'm good, but I'm not quick enough in the ring to get out of the way and plan the next five moves." Taking off her gloves, she grabbed her towel and water bottle, taking a long drink.

"You're definitely moving your feet more." He smiled, but she knew the "but" was coming.

"But…?"

"But the bag is predictable. It's not going to launch at you or duck to the side and throw a punch to your face or a kick to your head. You need to spar more."

She knew that was coming. "I hate sparring." She shrank down, rounding her shoulders.

"You need to do more sparring in order to get better at it." He smiled lightly, nodding.

"But I suck at sparring." She shook her head.

"Do it more, and you won't suck." He smiled.

"Argh. Will you help me get better?" She looked at James hopefully.

"Sure, but you have to do it my way." His smile faded, his face becoming serious.

She hesitated, knowing this would not be easy. "All right." She tried to sound lighthearted.

"You're going to have to work your ass off." He shrugged.

Ashley nodded, knowing that was the case.

"Probably harder than anyone else here." He put his hands on his hips.

"I get it. You're not going to scare me away." She smiled and threw a couple of jabs at the bag.

James thought about that and wanted to say, *Let's see what you'll be saying in a couple of weeks,* but he thought better of it.

"All right. Here's the deal. You need to train on the mats three days per week, pad work and sparring. One additional day needs to be dedicated to all sparring. I don't care with whom, spar. We'll work on it. The more you spar, the less scary it'll be. Include cross-training and conditioning another day. We can work together one or two times per week, sparring. You'll also get more sparring time with the competition-training team now."

Ashley knew it was a commitment, but that was a lot of time. She made a mental picture of her schedule and where she could drop in for more training. Maybe two or three early morning workouts, two evening sessions. She would dedicate Saturdays to competition training. She could run on any day off. She had a readymade trail outside her apartment, and it was heavily populated.

She nodded. "Yes, I can make this work. I want it to work."

James nodded. "All right. Sparring will be our priority."

***

"Again," James called flatly.

She stopped and stared at him.

"Come on. Your foot is facing out. Step across the body." Their session that afternoon was dedicated to sparring. He pointed to her feet, indicated where she should land.

She tried to duplicate his move.

"Across. Turn your hip." He turned her hip.

She tried again, this time moving in the direction he wanted, or so she thought.

"Again."

She stopped again this time, glaring at him.

He looked at her. "Try again."

Ashley was determined to get this, but he was driving her insane. "Can we do something else and come back to it?" she said through her mouth guard.

He shook his head.

"Ugh!" Ashley stomped and turned away, but he would not waver.

"One more time."

***

His eyes looked into my eyes. Did he know what I saw? I saw perfection, precision, and beauty, fast and sure, commanding attention. Never leave; do not break this tie. Keep me in your sight forever.

***

Ashley packed up her gear after an intense cardio workout and was ready to crash at home. As she came up the stairs, she heard the music blaring and a group of voices drifting from the ring. Usually, the gym was winding down at this time of night. She assumed this was a pre-fight-conditioning session since there were several fights coming up on the weekend.

Glad that's not me in there, Ashley thought as she glanced over and came up short.

It was James. He was positioned in the middle of the ring, ready to strike. Ashley couldn't take her eyes off him as intensity burned through his eyes, aimed at his opponent. He slowly calculated each move, positioning himself against the other fighter so he could pounce at any moment. His shirt was off, his muscles defined. By the looks of the sweat, the fight had been going on for a few rounds. A group of trainers and instructors were around the ring.

Ashley was mesmerized. His days of competing were long over, but he'd redirected his passion into training and teaching others how to master the art of fighting, making them great. Molding each one of his clients, showing them how to fight from their inner core, to embrace their transformation, and to dedicate themselves to perfection. As he was doing at this moment.

James threw a double jab, pushing his opponent back, then landed a cross and hard leg kick. He was playing with his competitor, drawing him in and then striking at the exact moment that would render his opponent helpless. His moves were precise.

Ash felt her face flush. She was embarrassed at her lack of fluidity when she was in the ring. *How can he work with us lowly, uncoordinated fighters and not be disgusted?* Why couldn't she learn to move the way he did? Or was it something that couldn't be taught?

James made his final move, holding his opponent's head in the clinch. He held on, not letting up, then thrust a knee to his ribs and swung him around, keeping his grip around his neck. Then, he swept his legs, bringing the opponent to the mat, as the final buzzer sounded.

All the trainers gave high fives and pats on the back, nodding their heads in acknowledgment of James's greatness. Not able to take her eyes from him, she wanted to sneak off before anyone caught sight of her. She felt as if she shouldn't be watching, even though all the trainers and other clients were there.

As she turned to go, James looked directly at her. It was as if he knew she was there the entire time. Her breath caught in her throat, and she froze as James smiled that crooked smile at her and winked.

Oh gosh. Her heart was beating out of her chest, and her legs were like lead. She smiled sheepishly, waved, then turned to go, but realized she'd forgotten her coat in the locker room.

How embarrassing. She slinked back down the stairs to the locker room to retrieve her coat and saw her makeup bag on the counter. *I would forget my head if it weren't attached.* She grabbed her things and ventured back up the stairs, head down, walking toward the doors.

James came bounding down from the ring with his hoodie on, half zipped, revealing his bare chest. He almost crashed right into Ashley as she was trying to sneak away. "Hey, Ash," he said breathlessly, making her stomach do a flip.

"Hey. That was awesome." She nodded toward the ring and pulled her bag up higher on her shoulder.

"Yeah, good to do that every so often. Work off my aggression." He smiled and winked, tilting his head sideways, sexy dimple showing.

Hmm, yes, Ashley thought to herself, her mind running away with her. She couldn't look directly at him because his bare chest was directly in front of her, and she wouldn't be able to form a sentence if she kept looking there.

"Well, I was heading home, and I heard the music… I thought it was…um…I thought it was some of the guys training for the competition, but obviously not." She laughed and then thought to herself, *Okay, you are a dork.* "I'm so beat; it has been a long day, so I'm heading home." *Oh God, I already said that,* she thought.

"Okay, yeah, you worked hard today, Ash."

James stood in front of the door. Ashley would have to squeeze by him to move through it. He kept his gaze on her with that side smirk, his hoodie unzipped…

What is he thinking? What if he asks me to get together? Her heart raced.

"Would I be able to get…" James spoke at the same time that Ashley gestured that she needed to get out the door.

"I should go…" Ashley held her bag tightly.

"Um, I want to get a water." He raised his eyebrows, innocently gesturing to the cooler behind her.

"Oh right." The refrigerator was right behind her. *He wants me to move so he can get a water.* "Oh! Yes, right. I'm sorry." She moved toward the right to get out of the way, and he moved in the same direction at the same time, her hands almost landing on his chest. Nervously laughing, she stepped aside holding up her hands.

He grabbed a water out of the refrigerator and drank it while standing in front of her, looking as sexy as ever. "Ah, perfect." He replaced the cap on the bottle.

She stood watching him, unable to move. *He takes the words right out of my head,* she thought.

"I'll see you tomorrow, then. Good night, Ashley." Those dark eyes of his were mesmerizing.

"Have a good night." She didn't know if she could perform the simple act of turning, opening the door, and walking…but she did, miraculously. As she walked through the door, she could feel his eyes on her.

Once outside, she could breathe again. *Wow, Ashley, nice job. He must think I'm a complete fool,* she thought.

Little did she know, James stood, leaning on the door, with his arm overhead, and watched her until she was out of sight, smiling at the thought that she had been watching him in the ring.

***

The next day, Ashley made her way back to the gym for competition-team training. On the docket were interval training and sparring. Half of the group completed interval training, which was comprised of battle ropes, box jumps, push-ups, and heavy-bag punching drills. The other half sparred in the ring—jab, kick, jab, cross, hook, body kick… repeat… Endless drills.

Ashley tried to mimic the moves she'd seen James using in his sparring session. She didn't feel as though the moves came naturally to her. She was used to her own routine and her own way of moving, yet something was missing.

"Come on, Ash; let's get a rhythm."

Trevor was working with the groups in the rings. James was running the rope drills and cardio intervals on the floor. That was next for Ashley. She hadn't seen him since last night and was trying hard not to keep gawking at him.

James watched Ashley as she worked in the ring. She was intense and focused on timing her combinations. He couldn't wait for her to get her confidence up and be comfortable competing in the ring. She would be unstoppable once he unleashed her on the circuit, if that's what she wanted.

His focus right then should have been on his group doing the cardio circuit he had set up, but he couldn't help checking out Ashley's body as she moved around the ring. He remembered feeling her eyes on him while he was in the ring; it felt amazing to know she was there. He was dialed into his fight, but the second it was over and he saw her, it was like a jolt of electricity when her eyes locked on to his. He guessed she wasn't expecting him to zero in on her because her eyes widened ever so slightly when they made the connection. She was caught watching him, like a deer in the headlights.

He still wondered what she saw. If he had a warning label on him, it would say, "Stay far away." She was flustered and guarded when he bumped into her afterward; it was frustrating not being able to read her.

Ashley bounded down from the ring to his station. "Hey, you ready for me?" Covered in sweat, now she was the one with the smirk.

"Always." James tossed the battle ropes toward her and set the timer. "Let's go, girl."

***

The problem was that she was trying to do too much in her sparring sessions. She would rack her brain for combinations. *Too many combinations.*

Words echoed in her head—*The best offense is a great defense.* She switched her frame of mind and concentrated on keeping her opponent at bay, moving out of the way, watching for patterns, throwing strikes to keep them back, and buying some time.

The new fighters gave away their moves early. They didn't have much control and hit full force. James's words played in her mind, *"Let them go, let them wear themselves out, save your energy, and strike when they are worn down."*

She kept her moves simple unless the opportunity presented itself to add a spinning elbow or a jump kick. She focused on jabs, crosses, hooks, teeps, and low and high kicks. She could do a lot of damage with the simple moves when she played it right.

***

The gloves are on, and I think I am ready, but I must wait. The teaching, the learning, the repetition of drills—wanting to unleash, but, still, I must wait. I want to go fast, but I need to go slow. Take each step and break it down. The need for control is more powerful than speed.

***

"Should I even be here?" She looked around the gym, feeling inadequate and suddenly small.

James was lacing up his gloves and looked at her sideways. "What?"

"I can't do this… I'm not ready." She stared ahead.

James stopped and looked at her, confused. "What are you talking about?"

Ashley shook her head and sighed. "I'm not that good. It's so frustrating, not knowing what is coming…being vulnerable. Look at my arms."

Seeing her black-and-blue and scratched-up arms, James had to admit they looked bad, as if she were a battered woman. "Ashley, we're all vulnerable in a fight. We can't predict the fight, the future; there isn't a script. Everyone starts somewhere." Nodding toward her arms, he added, "That's a blip on the radar. It won't last."

"I freeze when I spar." Ashley felt defeated.

"Come on; we can work on some drills, break them down. It's me you're working with." Flashing that smile at her, he nodded toward the ring.

This is difficult enough. Ashley felt so inadequate as a fighter, especially when compared to James's perfection, attention to detail, and the fact that he was so gorgeous.

He gave her some breathing techniques to help her be confident and ready, to prevent her from struggling for breath before she even started.

"Let's take it slow." Throwing punches in a slower motion and setting them up so she knew what was coming gave her the confidence to react and defend.

"Not so bad. Nice work." He fist-bumped her glove and jumped down from the ring. "You have the moves; now, you need a little more confidence. We'll get you there." He turned and walked off.

198

CHAPTER 24

The pain was radiating down her arm as she sat in the doctor's office two weeks after joining the competition team.

"Let's check your range of motion. How is this?" The doctor held Ashley's arm and gently tried to internally rotate her arm.

"Like you are ripping my arm off?!?" Ashley winced. "Yeah, that's not so good."

The doctor tested a few other ranges of motion. *Rip it off, for crying out loud,* she thought.

"It's most likely a strain of the rotator cuff, but it could be a tear. You'll need to get an MRI to confirm the extent of it."

Ashley didn't like the sound of that.

The doctor could tell she wasn't happy about the news. "Don't worry, it's probably small, and you'll need to rest and have some physical therapy for it."

That's not what Ashley wanted to hear. She couldn't afford to take time away from training.

As if he'd read her mind, the doctor said, "Take some time off from exercising. I'll give you a prescription for anti-inflammatory medicine to help reduce the swelling. Rest it and use ice, and you'll be feeling better in no time."

Yeah, no time. That isn't quick enough.

Lucky for Ashley, it was the weekend, and she was able to rest for a couple of days. She took an extra day to be sure and returned to the gym on Tuesday to meet with James. Dreading that conversation, Ashley arrived at the gym early to give her shoulder plenty of time to warm up and stretch before beginning her workout. The fear of tearing up the shoulder further was a major worry for her.

"Hey, killer, how's the fight?" Josh came bounding up the stairs toward Ashley. He was always friendly, smiling and saying hello. He was a little taller than Ashley and muscular, bulkier than most of the trainers and fighters. Josh leaned against the railing next to where Ashley was stretching. "What's up?" He nodded toward her arm.

"Obvious, huh? I messed up my shoulder. I checked in with an orthopedist, and it could be a tear."

Josh pushed himself off the wall and approached Ashley. "May I?" He gestured toward her shoulder.

Ashley eyed him suspiciously.

"I was a physical therapist for a few years, specializing in this type of rehab. That was before I got this gig." He was grinning from ear to ear, proud of having the experience.

Ashley thought she could probably trust him, and she needed all the advice she could get. "Sure."

Josh raised her arm gently, testing some ranges of motion,

Ashley felt no pain this time. "What is the best way I can avoid having surgery? That's the last thing I want; I need to train."

He put his hand on her shoulder and had her try different movements. He was knowledgeable and asked Ashley a lot of questions, reassuring her that she could train without destroying her shoulder. He talked about his past clients and some of the outrageous requests he would get from them. "I had a lady that came in for four months, and all she wanted was a massage. She never did any of the rehab work."

Ashley was relaxed and laughing, and for a moment, she forgot about her shoulder issue. As they were laughing about another massage story, James came down the stairs from his office and almost crashed right into them.

"Hey."

James looked from Ashley to Josh. Josh's hands were on her shoulder and arm. His anger flared up. He wanted to smack Josh's hand away from her; that guy was not one of his favorites. Moving around them, James walked toward the ring, barely acknowledging Ashley.

Josh showed Ashley a couple of stretches that he suggested would help.

Not long after he walked away, James came striding back toward Ashley. "Hey, Ashley. You are working with me today, right?"

Ashley dreaded telling him about her injury, so she was glad Josh was there as backup; he could tell James it wasn't as bad as the doctor said. "I need to talk to you about my shoulder. I met with an orthopedist. I might have a rotator-cuff tear. I'm supposed to take some time off."

James looked at Josh, then back at Ashley.

Ashley saw his look and hurriedly explained, "Josh was showing me some stretches that I can do to help." Ashley wasn't exactly sure why she felt the need to explain.

"Huh, okay, if that works for you." James's face was tense.

Ashley felt his anger. Was he angry at her about the injury? Maybe he didn't accept any weakness in his clients.

"Okay, then." James nodded, turned on his heel, and strode over to the mats where his clients were lined up and waiting for his arrival.

Ashley frowned, her stomach starting to twist in knots, and turned back toward Josh. "Thanks for the tips, Josh. I feel a little better already," she lied.

"Anytime, Ashley. Don't worry about James; he'll understand that you have to rest. Come see me anytime, killer." He winked and went off with his usual swagger.

Ashley huffed to herself. *Killer, I am not.*

Wanting to get the blood flowing, she made her way over to the treadmills. From there, Ashley watched James's group sparring and couldn't believe that she actually missed it. She popped her headphones in and cranked up the speed, trying not to worry about her shoulder...or James.

James left his group and marched toward Ashley. "Piece of advice? Don't take medical advice from that guy," he snapped at Ashley.

Surprised, Ashley fumbled and pulled her headphones off, slowing the treadmill. She hadn't heard him, but with the angry look on his face, she couldn't imagine that he'd said anything nice. "Excuse me?" She paused the treadmill and straddled the tread, facing him.

"Don't take any advice from Josh. Seriously, if you need help with that shoulder, stick with your doctor." He couldn't believe she would be gullible enough to listen to that jerk-off's advice. On top of it all, she'd blown him off when he tried to get her away from him.

Ashley was taken aback. *Is he for real?* "Um, I did go to the doctor, and I was trying to tell you about it... Josh was giving me some therapy stretches..." She pushed her headphones back in.

"He is twenty-three years old, for Christ's sake. How long could he have possibly been a PT? That guy doesn't give up..." James was shaking his head, looking over to the front desk where Josh was hanging out. "Don't do what he's telling you because if you get hurt, you'll be out of the game."

"I didn't think it was a big deal. He was trying to help. He started asking questions about how I was feeling, and next thing you know..." Ashley giggled nervously. She shouldn't have to explain herself, yet she was.

"Did he try giving you anything for it?" James pressed on angrily.

"What? No. Hey, he was offering to help. More than you are doing." Ashley was squeezing the rail of the treadmill, angry at James for coming at her so hard. Her jaw was clenched, her throat was dry, and old feelings surfaced, memories of fights and feeling at fault. She wanted to run away, yell at James for snapping at her, or kick him in his big-ass ego.

He saw she was getting heated. He took a breath. "Ash, I'm sorry. I got fired up."

She moved to resume her workout. *Too little, too late,* she thought.

"Tell me what happened with your shoulder?" He stood on the treadmill next to her and put his hands on the rail.

Taking a shaky breath, she relaxed her fists. He wasn't Stephen. She had no desire to fight about this. "Doc said I should rest and get some physical therapy." Forcing a smile, she shrugged. "Maybe it's a strain."

James had a hard time staying mad at her, especially when she flashed her smile at him. *I am such a hothead.* Josh was such a dirtbag, always trying to hit on the clients, and not one of James's favorite trainers. He wanted to get rid of him, but he was Vince's nephew. There was no shaking him.

"I'm serious, Ashley. If you want help on the shoulder, I'll give you one of our real physical therapists. Not Josh. Tell me what happened." James was surprised at himself for calming down so quickly. His typical manner would be to lecture and stew over this. But for some reason, she calmed him.

Ashley relented, taking her earphones out, relieved. She couldn't stand it if he was pissed at her. "I strained my shoulder, may have torn my rotator cuff. Doc said I need to lay off it awhile. This sucks." She threw her earphones into the compartment of the treadmill.

"I'm sorry, Ash. Don't worry; we'll figure it out. You're not out of the game." He softened his tone.

"Yeah, thanks." This couldn't derail her.

"Hang in there. I have to get back to the group. Can we still meet and talk more about it later?" James touched her arm.

"Yeah. See you later." She wasn't so sure about him anymore.

He nodded and jogged back to his group. James thought, *Talk to any other trainer in this place, not freaking Josh.* Josh's behavior had been so erratic lately that James suspected he was using steroids; James had even heard a rumor that Josh was dealing. James was angry, beyond all reason, when he saw Josh hanging around Ashley. He wanted to yell at Ash for taking advice from him.

"Come on, guys. Let's go!" James had his fight group start the session with cardio intervals of squats, jumping jacks, push-ups, and crunches.

Ashley watched as she walked on the treadmill, wishing she could be in the group. *This treadmill shit isn't cutting it.* She ran one mile, then decided to head over and check out the sparring. As she watched them, she thought, *This is ironic. I would give anything to spar right now.*

James saw her sitting on the benches, and his heart went out to her. He knew how bad it felt to be injured.

"All right, we're going to work on kick drills. Grab some Thai pads and a partner."

He called over to Ashley. "Hey, Ash. We're doing kicks. Want to jump in? I'll hold pads for you."

Hesitant, she wondered if she should walk away from this and from him.

James waved her over, giving her a smile.

Not everyone is like Stephen, she told herself. *Sometimes people probably get mad at things.* She was so grateful that James knew what she needed. "All right." Ashley grinned and hurried over to the mats.

There was a fire in her eyes that lit up her face. James realized that he would probably do just about anything to make her happy and to always have that smile be for him.

***

The MRI showed a small tear in the supraspinatus muscle of the rotator cuff. There was extreme inflammation, but all other tendons and ligaments were intact. Rest was a must, and the hope was that it would not tear further. Her doctor recommended physical therapy to regain range of motion and eventually strength. She could still train, but needed to avoid extreme shoulder motion for a couple of weeks while the inflammation went down.

She wasn't happy about it. The only good thing was she had a huge project deadline at work and would've had to cut back on her gym time, anyway.

James planned for her to focus on cardio, which meant mostly riding the bike to keep the shoulder stable. He put together a leg strengthening and core program for her as well. They would have her work with the physical therapist at the gym and get updates on when she could use full range of motion.

She iced, rested, and followed all the rules and instructions in hopes that she would recover faster. After the three-week mark, she was given clearance to add some resistance training and light pad work.

All went well, and by week six from her original diagnosis, she was back in full swing, except for extreme ranges of motion. She picked back up on her training schedule and continued with her rehab exercises.

Once she got clearance, James was back to riding her, just like old times. No more Mister Nice Guy, no more letting anything slide.

***

"What the hell are you working for? Get your head in the game!"

Ashley was about ready to snap. Exhausted, the group had been training for over an hour, the moves blending. *What the heck does he want from me?* She *was* working hard, and her head *was* in the game. *Well, until now.*

Ashley was easily distracted and frustrated during her sparring, and she wasn't sure what the problem was. Missing blocks when punches were aimed straight at her head, letting kicks slip by and feeling their sting, she just couldn't seem to get ahead of her opponents. Everyone else was able to respond to every punch thrown, their blocks up, their moves sharp. She couldn't afford to mess up, especially with competition training; she needed to get her shit together.

James was right; her head wasn't in it. Ashley hated when he was right. She had so much going through her head, but the main distraction was fear of Stephen. The thought that he was following her crept in again every time police cars passed her while she walked to her apartment or to the gym. She had received unknown calls from Virginia, spiking her paranoia about Stephen finding her. Constantly being on edge and worry at every turn were preventing her from sleeping well.

On top of that, the other distraction was Shawn. *Why did James have to bring Shawn into the sparring group today?* Ashley fell apart when she was around. She tried hard to have her best day when they were training together, but always failed.

Shawn was in an entirely different league. James knew that. It was part of the training to mix her in with different levels of competitors, but Ashley let Shawn get under her skin. When Ashley was upset, she couldn't concentrate.

James knew Ashley was struggling with her injured shoulder, but he didn't have patience. She was falling behind, but Ashley was determined to hang in there. *Toughen up.* As that thought crossed her mind, a pain shot down her arm as Shawn got a hook in on her shoulder.

"Get that block up, Banner. Come on!" James mimicked the block.

Ashley almost lost her mind. *Ignore him and keep moving.*

"Is that the first time anyone's thrown a hook at you? Get that block up!"

That comment pushed her over the edge. It wasn't her proudest moment, but she hauled off and landed an overhand hook, uppercut, and leg kick on Shawn. *Who needs this garbage?* She envisioned herself grabbing her gear, saying good-bye, and never coming back.

Shawn stared through Ashley as the final buzzer rang.

"Time! Nice job! Hey, Shawn, nice moves out there. You'll ace the competition this weekend." James was in Shawn's corner, stroking her ego.

Oh my God, I am going to puke, Ashley thought. She couldn't wait to get away from them and their ass-kissing. Shawn was so high on herself; she would never compliment anyone or, God forbid, give a fist bump.

"I'll be back tonight, James." Shawn unwrapped her wrists then dropped the wraps in her bag.

"Double sessions? Nice." James high-fived her.

As Ashley busied herself with removing her wraps and shin guards and stuffing everything in her duffel, Kendra, one of the other girls, came over to her with what Ashley would swear was a "I feel bad for you" look on her face.

"Nice job today." Kendra stood by Ashley and reached past her to pick up her own gym bag.

"Yeah, thanks." Ashley wiped the sweat from her face.

"Don't let him get to you. When Shawn's around, no one else can compare." Kendra shrugged and sat on the floor to remove her shin guards.

"Yeah, I get that." Ashley zipped her duffel then stood up to go. "Thanks."

Shawn is so darn perfect, she thought. *That body doesn't quit.* Ashley was sure James knew all about that. Too bad Shawn wouldn't go back to wherever the hell she came from so that Ashley didn't have to deal with her anymore.

She left with her focus on a hot shower and a cold glass of wine… and no psycho trainer.

***

James headed up to his office to wrap up some paperwork. He didn't feel bad for Ashley. She wouldn't learn if she couldn't get stronger in the ring. Being mentally strong was as important as the physical aspects.

"Little tough on her, don't you think?" Josh leaned on the door to James's office.

James wasn't in the mood for this rookie and his bullshit comments. "A little dose of reality. They all need it sometimes." He didn't make eye contact with Josh, hoping he would take the hint and leave. James stacked his papers and organized his desk, blatantly ignoring Josh.

"Ashley works her ass off; you should cut her some slack. Seriously, man." Josh pushed off the door.

"I know what I'm doing." *This guy better back the fuck off if he knows what is good for him.*

"You know, she's here more than a lot of the other chicks. Hell, she may be here more than some of the guys. She's dedicated." Josh looked out into the hallway.

This guy doesn't have a clue when to shut up. James was starting to lose patience.

"Or she's got some serious issues to work out. Ya know what I'm saying? She's fucking hot." Josh nodded and rubbed his palms together.

James pushed away from his desk. "What! You've got a thing for Little Miss Sunshine? I've noticed you smiling at her all the time, giving her advice. You think she's digging you, huh?"

For a second, James couldn't believe what was coming out of his own mouth. Why should he care? Of course, he agreed Ashley was hot. She was so much more than hot, though, and he didn't appreciate Josh talking about her that way.

"Hey, man, just saying. She's getting ripped and that ass…whoa." Josh smirked and shook his head again, looking out toward the gym.

He must want me to punch him in the face, James thought. *I should walk away, but…* James hopped up out of his seat and strode over to Josh. "You might want to stop talking now, Josh."

"What? You know she has a great ass! What are you scared of? Shawn will hear you talking about her and kick your ass?" Josh laughed, getting a total kick out of himself.

James moved in close to Josh's face and spoke calmly, "You better mind your fucking business, rookie. I'm seconds from knocking your ass out. Keep your comments inside your head from now on." He stared Josh down.

Josh held up his hands. "Take it easy, man. I'm effin' around with you."

James continued the standoff until Josh turned to leave. He didn't look nervous or as if he even cared. Maybe, being the boss's nephew, Josh thought he could do and say whatever he wanted. James didn't give a shit to whom he was related. It was pathetic how he was homing in on Ashley. He felt the need to protect Ashley from Josh, even though she could probably kick his ass.

Hell, someone should probably tell her to stay away from guys like me, too, James thought. After the way he'd treated her in the ring today, he wouldn't have to be concerned with her wanting to be near him. *Man, what the fuck is wrong with me? I'm the coach; she's the fighter.*

This whole thing wasn't sitting well with him as he paced the office. James was pissed at Josh and angry with himself. He didn't know why he was so consumed with Ashley. He was wound up and needed to blow off some steam.

He grabbed his sparring gear and headed out to the gym to find someone to punch.

***

"Stay away from Josh." James's eyes searched Ashley's. "He might be dealing."

"Are you serious?"

"I am serious."

"Can't you fire him?" Ashley shrugged.

"No one has proof. Vince doesn't want to face it. It's his sister's kid. He turns a bit of a blind eye when it comes to Josh."

"This is unbelievable."

"That is why I always wanted you to stay away from him. He is bad news. In more ways than that."

"Yeah, I got that feeling."

"I know you've got a good read on people. But I have to say it again. Watch yourself around him."

"Okay. Does Lisa know?"

James looked away. "Ah, I don't know. She usually doesn't miss a trick." He shook his head. "Again, people see what they want to see."

Ashley was shocked that Lisa would let it fly if she knew what Josh was doing. Then again, Ashley knew that families did weird things.

CHAPTER 25

Ashley woke up with a sense of dread; the pit in her stomach had returned, and she was reminded of the past she was trying to escape. The gnawing deep in her gut told her that something was about to go wrong. Begrudgingly, she rolled out of bed and pulled on her workout clothes as the scent of coffee drifted into her room, drawing her out to the kitchen.

Closing her eyes, she sipped the hot coffee, the caffeine filling her veins with enough energy to face the workout ahead of her. Fueled and ready, she drove to the gym, looking forward to the distraction of working out.

The group training was more of the same—conditioning for thirty minutes and kickboxing technique for thirty minutes. It was enough to get her heart level up into her max zone throughout the session. When it was over, leg muscles shaking, Ashley wobbled down the stairs to the locker rooms to shower.

Feeling refreshed and dressed in khakis, white button-down blouse, and black ballet flats, she pushed through the doors to the parking lot. The sun shining bright on her face lifted Ashley out of her early morning gloom.

Then, she saw it. Spray paint covered the windshield of her car. The words stung like a quick punch to the gut. A four-letter word beginning with a *C* was splattered across the window, and "slut" was sprayed across the hood of the car, screaming out at her. Frozen, her stomach dropped. *How did he do this? How is it possible? How did he find me? Or could this be someone spraying random graffiti? Why is no one else's car covered in these hateful words?*

Ashley felt light-headed, and her hands started to shake. *Too much of a coincidence.* She'd had an inkling that someone was following her and a sense of dread. Some might call it paranoia, but her intuition had been correct. Paralyzed with fear and unable to take another step, Ashley didn't know what to do. *Call the police? Tell James? Will I sound like a baby running to James first?*

People were starting to leave the gym and walk toward that part of the lot. Ashley lowered her head and walked toward the doors to the gym. Retrieving her cell phone out of her bag, she texted James.

Ashley: *Can you come out to the parking lot? I need help.*

She paused and hit Erase.

I can't hit the panic button and send this to him. Calling the police will cause a big scene, and then everybody will get involved. Maybe I should get in a cab and leave. Dump the car, get out of town, and run again. Keep running…

Determined not to cower or hide behind a text, she slunk into the gym to tell James face-to-face. *I'm not running.* Trust, that was a big order for her, but she had nothing to lose. If he said, "Hey, nice knowing you," then she'd know where she stood—alone, where she'd always been. But if there was a small chance this trust was two-sided, then he would have her back. Walking through the door, she hoped for the latter.

Ashley's heart hammered out of her chest as she climbed the stairs to James's office. *Turn and run; there's still time,* that nagging voice whispered to her, but she forged ahead.

Taking a deep breath, Ashley knocked on the open door and felt her voice catch in her throat. "James."

James was sitting in one of the chairs across from his desk. "Hey, Ash, come in. We're watching the video of Shane's fight."

Ashley hadn't noticed Shane sitting next to James. "Oh, I'm sorry. I…I'll come back." She tried to hide her trembling hands.

James saw she was visibly shaken. "No, come in. We're wrapping up."

Shane popped up from his seat. "Hey, Ashley." He gave Ashley a quick smile then picked up his gear. "James, I gotta go, anyway, man. I'll catch up with you later."

"Thanks, Shane. Nice work in the fight." James stood and fist-bumped Shane.

"Thanks, man." As he passed Ashley, Shane fist-bumped her. "Take care, Ashley."

She smiled weakly. "See ya, Shane." Ashley shut the door.

"What's going on? You don't look so good." James leaned back against his desk.

Ashley steadied herself. "Do you have cameras in the parking lot? The side lot, to be exact?"

"Um, yes. What's going on, Ash?" James crossed his arms.

"Someone vandalized my car." Ashley balled her hands into fists.

"What?" James was shocked.

"With some shitty words." Her voice caught as she trembled, fighting the tears and the urge to run.

James approached her and put his hand on her arm. "What? Here?"

Ashley nodded, unsure of her voice.

"You okay?" He held her arm and gestured to the chair.

She slumped in it, sighing. "You can't miss it, and I'm sure everyone is going to see it sooner or later." She hesitated. "It says 'slut' across the hood and...a fucked-up word across the windshield." Ashley looked away; her voice was cracking, and tears hovered.

"Show me." Shadows crossed his face. He had her lead the way downstairs and outside.

Silently, they approached the car. He glanced at her before opening the door. "Did you check if it was broken into?"

"No, I saw it and walked away." Ashley stood back, arms wrapped around her chest.

"Good thinking." James proceeded to check the doors, finding them locked and no shattered windows.

Ashley heard cars driving into the lot and chose to ignore them.

"Do you need anything out of the car?" He peered in the windows.

"No, I'm good."

"All right, let's go in and call the police. You should probably get this on record. We can check the video surveillance to see if there is anything on there." James softened. "It'll be okay, Ash." He led her toward the gym, steering as she was in shock.

James shut the door to his office and had her take a seat. "Probably some kids being stupid"—he snuck a glance at Ashley—"unless you can think of anyone that would do this?"

Ashley flinched, shaking her head.

Not very convincing, James thought, but he didn't push it. "Okay." James thought dragging the police into this might not be a good idea, seeing how shaken she was. "We could skip the cops. I can get that cleaned up for you and keep it on the down-low."

Her body trembled. "Yeah, that would be better."

"I'm on it. I can have Shane give me a hand. We'll pull it around back so it doesn't draw too much attention. You okay to stay here?"

"No, I can drive it around." She started to stand.

"No, Ash, I got this. You hang tight, all right?" James put his hand on her shoulder. "It'll be okay. I promise." He smiled reassuringly.

She handed him the keys. "Thank you."

James took the keys and jogged out the office and down the stairs.

Ashley released a sigh, not realizing she'd been holding her breath. Her hands were shaking uncontrollably; she needed to sit on them. *Deep breaths. Come on. You've got this.*

Ashley's mind wandered from one scenario to the next, each one worse than the next. *Was it Stephen? Someone random?* Of course, all thoughts pointed to one person, the only one who would do something like this, the only one who meant to hurt her.

A shiver coursed through her as her mind whirled. She needed to change her daily routine, stay with groups, maybe even see if she could crash with Lisa for a night or two. Paranoia filled her mind, leading her down the rabbit hole of doom and despair.

Controlling the flood of emotions, Ashley looked up to the ceiling. *Maybe it was just vandals being vandals.* She could only hope… and pray hard.

CHAPTER 26

"Hey, I heard it was the Shawn shitshow yesterday." Without missing a shot, Lisa carried on a full conversation while sparring.

Ashley loved that they got each other. They could spar and fight without overstepping boundaries and inflicting pain on one another. Unlike Lisa, however, Ashley had to fully concentrate while sparring, lest she get popped in the nose.

"Everyone is heading out tonight to check out a band at Whiskey Saigon." Lisa angled away from Ashley's kick.

"Yeah? You going?" Ashley turned and pressed on, trying to land a punch.

"Yeah, I'm going. Kendra and Debra are going. And you are, too." Lisa paused for effect. "James is going." She carefully watched for any change in Ashley's expression.

Ashley caught a hook to the side of her head. "Oof. Oh yeah? Maybe." She tried to sound casual. A night out was beyond overdue. In fact, she couldn't remember the last time she'd had a good night out...and James would be there.

"Come on, Granny. We won't keep you out too late...past your bedtime. You seriously need to get out." Lisa was insistent, and she was right, of course. "I'll even drive."

How could Ashley resist? "Okay, I'm in." She sidestepped Lisa's attempt at another hook.

"All right!" Lisa dropped her hands away from her guarded position.

Perfect timing, Ashley thought as she landed a nasty left hook.

***

A hot shower was heaven after any workout, but Ashley thought it was especially amazing that night. Lisa talking through the workout made time fly, but they hadn't even realized how many rounds they'd fought until Ashley's arms felt like lead. Lisa didn't cut anyone slack, even Ashley.

They tried not to let their competitive natures get in the way of their friendship. Ashley wouldn't let it. She needed Lisa. Lisa was the only person in her new life who truly knew her. Ashley felt she could confide in her about anything when she needed to. *Well, almost anything,* she thought.

She hadn't told Lisa about her past life and being in hiding, about her car being vandalized, or about her paranoia that her ex would show up any day now. Neither had Ashley admitted to Lisa that she had feelings for James.

Feelings? What the hell is wrong with me? Ashley thought. *This is ridiculous; there can't possibly be feelings.*

First off, she thought, *James would never even look at me that way. Second, that's the last thing I need right now.* No way should she get involved with anyone, especially someone like James. Besides, it would be totally unprofessional on his part. *Some lines shouldn't be crossed...or should they?* she thought.

Wait, what am I saying? She had to pull herself out of her imaginary world. *That can and will never happen.* She thought she might be going crazy. Lisa was right; she needed to get out more. Getting out of her own little world would be a good thing. She was ready.

Ashley couldn't shake the feeling of excitement, though, knowing that James would be there. "It's drinks and a night out with friends," Ashley said to her reflection in the mirror. *No big deal, right?* She inhaled deeply as she attempted to tame the butterflies in her stomach.

***

The bar was packed. The multilevel venue possessed every musical attraction, from DJs to live bands to a roof deck and everything in between. Everyone was meeting on the second floor to watch a band that Vince knew. The guitar player frequented the gym when he was in town and was friends with James, the trainers, and some members of the gym. They were supposed to be hot on the music scene, playing in many of the city's top bars.

Lisa and Ashley arrived a little late, per usual with Lisa. Music was playing and the crowd was pouring in as they made their way through the throngs of people. Hiding in the large group, Ashley felt safe with Lisa. *Imagine if Stephen showed up here?* Her eyes darted around the crowd. Her heartbeat sped up. *Stop.* She convinced herself to breathe and put those thoughts out of her head.

Ashley recognized a few faces from the gym and felt better. *Nothing will happen with everyone here.* Then, she immediately spotted James. He was talking with Vince and a few of the trainers gathered around the end of the bar. The group was so large they had cordoned off half the length of the bar to accommodate.

"There're James and Justin," Lisa yelled over the music.

At that moment, James looked up and met Ashley's gaze. Her stomach did a 360-degree flip. His gaze lingered a moment; then he turned back to the conversation he was involved in.

Okay, deep breath. Say hello…be cool!

Ashley bumped into Trevor and his girlfriend, whom he introduced as Julie. They exchanged small talk; then she continued through the crowd, following Lisa's lead.

***

James did a double take when Ashley walked in. She was as beautiful as ever, but tonight she glowed. He saw all the heads turn as she walked past, but she was oblivious to the fact that she was catching everyone's eye.

James kept it cool, though. He forced himself to refocus on what Justin was saying to him. He had no idea what that was.

217

"Excuse me, Justin. I'll be right back." He patted Justin's arm and approached Ashley and Lisa.

***

Ashley had to stop herself from staring at James as he approached. He looked gorgeous—his hair perfect, those intense dark eyes never breaking from hers, his fitted shirt showing off the shape of his shoulders and back, leaving just enough to the imagination…

Okay, enough! Ashley thought as she snapped out of her trance.

"Hey, pal. Look at you. You look terrific all cleaned up." James smiled that crooked grin.

"Hey, good to see you, too," Ashley managed to say. She pressed her ice-cold hands together.

"Can I get you a drink?" He motioned toward the bar.

"Sure, not like I am training or anything right now."

James gave her a sideways smile and asked Lisa for her order. After getting their drinks, James led them to a group of open seats at the bar.

Lisa was not long for sitting in one spot. She hopped up to speak with other friends.

James and Ashley talked for a while and, every so often, were interrupted by one of James's clients. Ashley noted he had quite the following. His people always wanted a piece of him. When they saw he wasn't moving from the spot near Ashley, they would wander off. She found him easy to talk to outside of the ring. He had her laughing with his stories about the people from the gym who made their way over to talk to him.

After they finished a couple of drinks, James nodded to the dance floor in front of the band. "Want to head over and check these guys out?"

"Yeah, they sound great!" Ashley followed him out to the main floor.

The band played original alternative-rock songs, as well as cover songs. They played good party music, and the crowd was on their feet, dancing. Lisa, Kendra, and their group of friends called to Ashley and James to join them up front by the band.

"Hey, girl! Glad you came out!!" Lisa wrapped her arm around Ashley and pulled her in to dance while the band played.

The band stopped for a break, and a DJ filled in with dance music, drawing almost everyone out to the dance floor. Lisa dragged James into the middle of the girls dancing. *And he can dance*, Ashley thought. She loved to dance, but wasn't quite ready to let loose with this group, so she stood off to the side, watching Lisa and her crew put on a show. James ate the attention up.

As the song ended and a new one started up, some of the group moved on to replenish cocktails. James strolled over to Ashley and motioned his head for her to dance.

"Come on, Ash; show me some of those moves out here."

Ashley was hesitant.

"Come on." He gave her a look that told her this was no big deal.

"Okay. Why not?" She felt as if he could talk her into doing anything.

The music pulsed through the club, drawing everyone back to the floor. The crowd was singing all the words to the song. Lisa sidled up to her with a replacement for her drink.

"Thanks, I think!" She was trying to space out her drinks, but had lost count after an endless number of rounds were bought. "It's so hot in here! I can't stop sweating!" Ashley pushed her sleeves up and fanned herself with her hand.

To be heard over the music, James leaned in closer to her. "Yeah, want to head back for a rest?"

Ashley nodded.

James took her arm gently, led the way to the bar, and ordered waters for them. Ashley needed a breather and wanted to pull herself together. The cocktails had kicked in, she was breathless, and her heart raced just being next to James. She wanted to regain control and make this business as usual, which it was…but she felt as if she was letting down her guard too much.

The next song came on, and James turned to Ashley. "Dance with me."

Smiling nervously, she chugged her water. "I need a little break."

James wasn't buying it. "Come on; let's have some fun." Standing close to her, he made it difficult for her to concentrate.

"I don't know, James. That'll give the gym people something to talk about." She nodded to the group at the bar.

James leaned on the bar, facing Ashley. She could see the rise and fall of his chest, and she could see the outline of his shoulders and his biceps through his shirt; the scent of his cologne was drawing her in. Pleading with those deep-brown eyes that pierced through her... *Oh, that smile...* James was crushing her resolve.

"Dance with me and pretend that world doesn't exist."

Her legs almost gave out from under her. *Did I hear him correctly? How can this be happening?* Looking into his eyes, that world did *not* exist. She only saw James.

Ashley conceded; he'd won this fight. "All right," she breathed.

James bit his lip and took hold of her hand. "All right, girl. Let's see what you've got."

As they walked through the crowd toward the dance floor, Ashley knew things would never be the same.

Everyone was jammed on the dance floor. James turned, facing Ashley, and moved in close, looking like a cat who had its prey right where he wanted it. She moved closer, and James locked eyes with her.

James didn't want to push it, but he tested the waters and moved even closer. When Ashley didn't pull away and smack him, he took a deep breath of relief. She flashed him a sexy grin, and immediately he was turned on. Right then, he lost all resolve of keeping this relationship strictly business.

Ashley was caught up in the moment and finally let loose. They both were working up a sweat as the songs blended. *I wish I could keep this night on replay.* They danced as if they couldn't get enough of each other, and Ashley didn't care who was watching.

***

James intruded on Ashley's thoughts throughout the day. Then, she would be distracted by something else and realize a little later that he hadn't dominated her thoughts for a while, which started the cycle of fantasizing about him all over again. She remembered his body...*especially his body*...when it was so close to her on that dance floor. And his smile...*oh yeah*...and his voice...*so deep and sexy.* And his eyes...*sparkled when he said, "Dance with me."*

He's a shameless flirt, she thought. *Am I reading too much into this?*

It was Ashley's day off, and she should be relaxing, but James consumed her thoughts. Maybe she should call Lisa to go shopping. Retail therapy could help, even though she didn't have the money. She picked up her phone and texted Lisa, and then put the phone aside as she cleaned the dishes that had accumulated in the kitchen sink.

She heard the phone buzz across the room. "That was quick." Ashley smirked as she crossed the room toward her phone. She could always count on Lisa. This would be what she needed to keep herself from obsessing over James.

She grabbed the phone and clicked on the text icon. Lisa couldn't pull off shopping today. Her grandmother was coming to town, and she had promised to take her out and spend the day with her.

Lisa: *I'm seriously hungover. This is going to be rough.*

Ashley laughed.

Ashley: *No problem. Enjoy your day despite the pounding headache! Drink lots of water. See you Monday.*

Lisa: *Yeah, definitely. Hey, how'd it go with James? Saw you guys hot and heavy on the dance floor.*

Ashley swallowed hard. There was no way she was getting into this over text.

Ashley: *LOL. We had fun. We'll talk Monday.*

Lisa: *Okeydokey. Looking forward to beating you;)* 🏃‍♀️🏃

Ashley laughed out loud. That comment made her want Monday to come even quicker.

Oh well, Ashley thought, *I'll still head out and do some shopping.*

As Ashley was heading for a nice long, hot shower to get ready for her day out, the phone buzzed again. Surely another wiseass comment from Lisa. She picked up the phone and tapped the text icon. Her stomach did a somersault.

James: *Hey, Ash. Great time last night! Have a great day off.*

Her cheeks heated up as she bit her lip. What the heck was she supposed to say back to that? "Hey, I cannot stop thinking about your sexy body next to mine and how hot you are?" *Hmm, not such a good idea.* She settled on something neutral.

Ashley: *Thank you. I had a great time! It was good to let loose a little.*

James: 😎

Well, there was no way she was going to get her mind off him now. Ashley knew she would need more than retail therapy. She decided to take a cold shower to cool herself down.

***

Fighting for it. Feeling the burn in my arms. Sweat pouring out of every pore. Not able to catch my breath. Heart beating out of my chest. Losing control. Stay focused on the goal. Needing control. Wanting the power. I cannot stop, and I will not stop until I get it. Loving the feeling. Wanting it more and more. Needing it. The fight.

***

She watches me intently. Every move I make, she takes it all in. I can feel her eyes, even after she has gone. All the others, they watch her; their eyes linger too long, but she does not see. She does not see them because she only has eyes for me.

James saw Ashley entering the gym as he jogged down the stairs from his office. He had to admit, he was looking forward to seeing her, and had been since Saturday night. He remembered how her body had moved close to him when they danced. He saw her let her guard down and was even more attracted to her.

Every guy in the place had their eyes on her as she danced and laughed...*but she was with me.* Well, she wasn't with him for any other reason than he was her coach, and everyone was out for a fun night. *That's what we had—fun. She didn't know anyone else besides Lisa, did she?* He didn't know much about her at all, except that she was distracting. He wasn't able to focus on much else.

Training was in full force at the gym; several fighters were gearing up for the weekend's big tournaments, and James felt the energy pulsating. As he scanned the training area, James saw Ashley scurry into the locker rooms, but he lost track of her after that.

Ashley wasn't avoiding James exactly; she was just prolonging bumping into him. She needed to get her head right before he came over and messed with it some more. Ashley popped her headphones on and went to work on the bags.

James took a quick lap around the floor and saw her at the bags. "Ash."

She didn't hear him since the music in her headphones was blaring.

James grabbed the bag midswing.

She jumped and pulled the headphones out of her ears. "Jeez, James! You scared me!" Her heart raced as she realized it was not Stephen finding her.

James had a devilish grin on his face. "Well, you looked like you were ready to take someone's head off."

She laughed and feigned throwing a jab at him, still calming her nerves.

"I would not want to be that bag." He let the bag steady, then let it go.

Awkward silence.

"How are you doing? Ready to train today?"

"Yes, great! I am ready. Lisa is supposed to be here today. Who else is in our group?" *I'm totally babbling,* she thought.

"Uh, yeah, I think Lisa will be here if she's not still hurting from the other night."

Well, there it is, she thought. *He brought up the other night.*

"So, you had a good time Saturday?" James smirked as he leaned against the wall.

Ashley threw light jabs at the bag. "Yeah, I had a great time." She truly did.

James smiled. "We'll have to do that again sometime."

Ashley panicked. She had to be blushing. "Yeah." *Pathetic.*

"Hey, I didn't want to bring it up last night, but is everything okay with the car?" James leaned in, speaking low.

He was concerned since they hadn't talked about it again after he and Shane cleaned the spray paint off. They scrolled through the security-camera footage for that day and saw people coming and going from the club after the time Ashley arrived. One person walked toward Ashley's car. He was tall, dressed in a dark, oversized hoodie, like many of the guys who came to the gym. The camera angle prevented a clear view of his face. The image of the man was blocked as a delivery truck parked in front of the camera. When the truck pulled away, the male figure had disappeared.

Ashley glanced at James and cleared her throat. "Yeah. Everything's okay." She swallowed hard, wanting desperately to change the subject.

"No one bothering you here or anything?" He watched her intently.

She shook her head. "Nope. It's all good."

He knew she was trying to avoid this discussion, but he couldn't let it go. "You're parking by the front door now, right? Cameras are right there."

"Yes, thank you. I feel safe here." She turned and smiled at him reassuringly.

"All right. Let me know if anything changes. Okay, Ash?"

"I will. Thanks for helping me out." She nodded and looked at her gloves. She should probably tell him about Stephen at some point.

James held on to the bag for her. "Take some powerful strikes." He demonstrated how he wanted her to take her time and go for power over speed.

Watching the shape of his strong arms as he demonstrated the moves was distracting. She worked as hard as she could, trying to emulate his every move, knowing she had a long way to go.

"Looking good. Let's get some pad work in." He turned and headed for the ring.

Ashley grabbed her gear, and as she was heading in his direction, she saw Shawn walking in. Her stomach turned.

Shawn walked up to James and punched him in the arm.

He turned, surprised to see her, and smiled. "Hey, kid, how's it going?"

Ashley's heart sank. She knew they had a "thing" going on, but she didn't want to see them together. It especially bothered her that he called her kid. *Well, he calls everyone kid*, she thought. It still bugged her to hear him use the same nickname for both her and Shawn. Everything about Shawn annoyed her.

Lisa entered the gym training area at that moment. She waved at Ashley, took one look at Shawn, and made a face as if she were gagging.

Ashley chuckled. Nodding toward the other side of the ring, Ashley met Lisa as she was pulling her gear out of her bag.

"What's up, Ash? Ugh, it's bad enough being here this early on a Monday, but now I have to see *her* mug?" Lisa pointed her chin toward Shawn and shook her head.

"I hope to God she isn't sparring with us today."

Ashley didn't want James to catch her watching him, but she couldn't help glancing over. She really wished she hadn't chosen that particular moment because Shawn was leaning into James and saying something that was indecipherable to Ashley, but Shawn's body language was loud and clear.

Ashley turned away. She would not get caught up in their drama. *Why should I even care?*

"Hey, dancing queen! You fighting today or what?" Lisa waved her glove around.

"Ha-ha, very funny. I'm ready." She threw Lisa a look and raised her glove.

Starting with a quick warm-up and a light sparring routine, they settled into a groove easily, able to read each other's moves. Knowing each other's weaknesses was one thing, but they were working to make each other stronger. Lisa was fiercely competitive and would never let anyone get a punch by her, but she would always offer encouragement or call out her opponent if they were distracted, just as Ashley was at that moment.

"What's going on, Ash?" Lisa circled around and tried to corner Ashley.

Knowing it was obvious, Ashley avoided the question and angled away from Lisa's trap. "I'm saving my best moves for later. I don't want to reveal all of my secrets too soon." She bobbed out of the way.

"You are so full of shit. Look at you. You cannot take your eyes off James."

"Bullshit! I cannot stop watching the two of them. They make me sick." Ashley threw a jab, an inside-leg kick, and moved around the ring.

Lisa stopped sparring. "Uh-huh, and you two dancing all night on Saturday has nothing to do with it, right?"

Ashley's mind drifted back to dancing with James. The way they moved together, the heavy beat of the music, and the rapid beat of her heart as his hand brushed hers. She smiled at the memory. There was something there…she couldn't be the only one who felt it.

"Uh, no, I… Don't be ridiculous." Ashley tried to cover her nervous laugh, but, apparently, it was obvious to Lisa. *Well, there it is,* she thought.

Lisa shook her head and laughed back at Ashley. "Woo-hoo, girl. You've got it bad! Worse than I thought!"

Ashley shushed her friend. She glanced over to James, who was now in the ring next to them. He was leaning against the ropes with his arms crossed; Shawn was nowhere to be seen. He was watching Ashley at that moment—quite intently, she noted. His eyes were alight with a fire, and he had that sideways smirk, which always sent Ashley's stomach into a tumble of butterflies. She felt her cheeks heat up, now self-conscious of every move.

She exhaled. *Oh yeah, I've got it bad.*

CHAPTER 27

"**A**shley, what do you say you come on over tonight? I'm having some people over from the gym, real casual. You up for it?" Holding his cell phone to his ear, James leaned against his kitchen counter.

When the call had come through, Ashley was curled up on her couch, sweat pants on, savoring her much-anticipated glass of Sauvignon Blanc. "Um, well, I was going to…" She glanced at her books and journal.

"Get your ass over here by eight, Ash." He laughed. "It'll be fun. Okay?" He pushed off the counter to answer the buzzer at the door.

Ashley sighed and resigned herself to giving up her couch for the night. "Yeah, I'll be there." Ending the call, she looked at the clock on the mantel. She had exactly one hour to get herself ready and over there by eight o'clock. She took a long sip of her wine and reflected for a moment. "I guess I better get my ass moving, then."

She hurriedly texted Lisa to make sure she was going.

Lisa: *Hey, girl! Yes, V and I are on our way. We'll meet you there. So excited you're coming!*

Lisa always made Ashley feel as if she were the only person Lisa hoped to see. She made everyone feel that way. Ashley was lucky to have her as a friend.

She bit the inside of her cheek. She had to make her way over to James's apartment alone. She sighed. "Get a grip."

With that, she hopped up and dashed down the hall to her room and started the race against the clock to put herself together, staring at the clothes in her closet and saying for the hundredth time in her life, "I have nothing to wear."

On the plus side, none of these people saw her in anything but workout clothes, so anything would look good. She decided on her Guess jeans with the frayed bottoms and a black, sleeveless cotton top that had a modest cut to it. Sexy, but casual.

She applied a little makeup, sticking with neutral tones, and a dark mascara. After being tied up in a ponytail all day, her hair needed some work. She fought with the straightener then decided to tie it back. Swallowing a last gulp of wine, she took one final glance in the mirror and was satisfied with her makeup and hair.

Ashley methodically went through her routine of checking rooms, lights, and locks on the windows and door, satisfying her compulsion to verify all was secure. She grabbed her cell phone and pepper spray, placed them in her small Coach handbag, which she'd splurged her first few paychecks on, and headed out the door.

Taking her time, she ventured down the old stairs, not trusting her shaky legs and the black wedge sandals. That's all she would need—to wipe out going down the stairs. James's apartment was about twenty minutes from hers. She called an Uber, making sure to check the license plate, car make, and driver before getting in the car.

She fidgeted with nervous energy. It would be a good idea to walk it off before she arrived at James's apartment. She asked the driver to drop her off two blocks before his place. The night was warm, but a light, cool breeze was blowing through the city. It felt heavenly against her skin. Toward her on the sidewalk, music and voices spilled out through the open-air bar fronts. The smells of the different restaurants' fare floated out as she passed—faint smoky barbecue, grilled steak, something sweet from the ice cream parlor on the corner... Ashley took it all in, inhaling deeply.

Summer nights in the city were filled with an energy and a feeling of connection. Everyone was elated and relaxed; conversations and laughs echoed from the restaurants. People slowed their pace as they walked through the city at night, no mad rush to get to work or make the last train.

Ashley felt a mix of nervous energy and excitement. Not knowing what the night held for her, she was trying to embrace the impulsive, unpredictable, and unplanned. She pushed aside the paranoid obsession of constantly looking over her shoulder. Ashley focused her thoughts solely on seeing James.

She wondered who would be at James's apartment—surely, some of the other trainers and clients. *What if they aren't? Then, what? What if Lisa is late?* Her stomach started to tumble. She hoped Shawn wouldn't be there, but she had to face the fact that was a possibility. *What will I do? Smile and wave.*

Deep breaths. No big deal, right? she told herself. *A casual night out with friends.*

Her hands shook as she rounded the corner of Beacon Street, realizing she'd reached her destination. She walked up the steps to the small entryway of the brownstone. The old character of the building showed the charm of this part of Back Bay. *Number seven.* She pressed the security buzzer, feeling excited, nerves building.

The speaker came to life with James's voice saying, "Come on up." There was a buzz, and the door clicked, signaling that it was unlocked.

After another deep breath, Ashley opened the door, entered the main lobby of the building, and was greeted by security at the front desk.

"Sign in here, please."

She signed the logbook, controlling the tremble in her hand, and then was directed to the elevator. The security guard told her James's apartment was located on the fourth floor. Her heart hammered in her chest, and her palms were sweaty as she waited for the elevator doors to open.

Cautiously entering the empty elevator, she pressed 4. *No panic attacks allowed on my night out,* she told herself.

As the elevator doors opened on the fourth floor, she heard muted sounds of laughter and followed the sounds down the hall to apartment number 7. The door was ajar, and the sounds of conversation mixed with music and the clinking of glasses and bottles drifted toward

230

her. She took another deep inhale and smiled as she reached out to knock on the door.

James appeared and opened the door wide. "Hey, Ashley, you made it. Right on time, too." He leaned against the doorframe and smiled, his dimple more pronounced than ever, and those intense dark eyes pushed her stomach into a cycle of somersaults.

"Yeah, I made it." *Duh,* she thought, convincing herself to speak like an intelligent human.

James was dressed in dark, faded jeans and a black, button-down shirt with black-leather shoes. He stepped aside and extended his hand to invite her in. "Come on in. I won't bite."

"What a great place." She took in all the details and charm.

The dark hardwood floor of the entry led down a long hall to a large, open living room and dining room with a minibar. There was a galley kitchen off to the side. The walls were exposed brick, and there were large windows that overlooked the other brownstones.

James shut the door and couldn't help but take in every inch of Ashley as she floated through his apartment.

Ashely felt self-conscious, so she tried to make light conversation as a distraction. "This area is a beautiful part of Boston. You must love being in the center of all the action."

"Yeah, I love it. There's always something to do, and it's peaceful up here…escaping the city. You found it okay?" He stood aside for her to enter the main living area.

"I took an Uber and walked part of the way. Such a nice night out." Ashley glanced around the spacious room that was lightly furnished with a navy-colored, oversized couch, love seat, and chair. There were about a dozen people there. Lisa and Vince, Kendra and Kali, who were both on the competition-training team, Shane, Trevor, Justin, a few other coaches, several clients whom she recognized, and to her relief, no Shawn.

Seeing Ashley, Lisa lit up, walked over, and gave her a big hug. "Hey, Ash. I'm so glad you're here."

Vince followed to greet Ashley. "Good to see you." He gestured to her empty hands. "You need a drink."

James was at the bar, already grabbing a glass. "Would you like red or white or something stronger?"

Ashley thought it would be wise to start with a red wine. That way, she could sip it and not chug it down, as she did the last time they were all together.

"Red would be wonderful." She turned to face James at the bar.

"I have the perfect red that will warm you up." He reached for an open bottle and poured a generous glass.

As if I need more heat, she thought.

Some other friends of James came and went throughout the evening. Ashley's nerves settled quickly; she had Lisa to rely on for introductions and as a safety net.

It was well after midnight when Ashley realized the time. She, Lisa, and Vince were the last ones there. Lisa was hinting about leaving shortly, so Ashley chimed in that she should be heading out soon as well.

"Another drink?" James was back with the bottle of red in his hand, ready to pour.

They all agreed on one more and settled down on the comfortable couches.

"Could you believe the story about Adam from Gold's? I mean, seriously, that guy…" Vince shook his head and set his glass on the end table.

Lisa was starting to fade and stifled a yawn. "Okay, big man, you need to get me home before I fall asleep."

Vince took his last sip of wine and put his arm around Lisa. "All right. James, thank you for hosting. This was a thoroughly enjoyable evening. Entertaining, to say the least."

They stood and James gave Vince a big backslap hug. "See you Monday. Thanks, man."

Lisa stifled another yawn and gave hugs good-bye. "See you Monday, girlfriend."

"Get some rest; you'll need it." Ashley hugged Lisa.

"Nice." She gave Ashley a squeeze.

Ashley reached for her handbag. "I can walk out with them and catch a cab."

"Hold on, Ash. It's late; I can walk you out. Not that you need someone to escort you. We could walk, get some air. What do ya say?"

He must have hypnotic powers, Ashley thought. She was useless to fight him, but thought it would be nice to have him walk her out this time of night. "Sure. Sounds good. Can I help you clean up first?" She began to busy herself by picking up empty glasses.

"You can put those on the counter. I'll straighten up after." He waved it off.

"I don't mind; you did all the work." She placed the glasses in the sink.

"Want a nightcap?" James placed empty beer bottles in the recycle bin next to the sink.

"Yeah, sure." She shrugged. *Why not?*

He fixed them both a martini. She listened to him tell stories of his family, all born and raised in South Boston. He had her laughing, near to tears, hearing about him and his brothers wreaking havoc in the neighborhood. Inevitably, he asked about her family.

The lies came out effortlessly, as she had practiced her story so many times—losing her parents at a young age, living with an aunt in Pennsylvania, having a sister she rarely spoke to—all easy, dead-end stories. No loose ends.

"I need to use your bathroom before we head out." Ashley was feeling the buzz from the cocktails, and she was settling into a blissful state of euphoria.

"Sure thing, first door on the left, down the hall."

She excused herself, and James tidied up the kitchen; then, he sat in the oversized chair and placed his drink on the side table. Laying his head back, he closed his eyes, the week catching up to him.

Ashley shut the bathroom door and steadied herself, placing her hands on the sink and looking in the mirror. *I am alone with James…in his apartment.* That was beyond comprehension. *Stay in control, girl. You do not need any complications.* She nodded to her reflection and freshened up.

She returned to see James lounging in his chair and thought, *Now is a perfect time to make my exit. Or escape.* "I should be going. You need to get some sleep." Her brain told her to move toward the door, but, instead, she stood frozen, watching James as he stood up and stretched.

"No, I'm okay." He walked over to Ashley. "I was resting my eyes." He smiled and nodded toward her cocktail sitting on the end table. "A few more minutes?"

Standing eye to eye, her legs wouldn't budge; she could feel the energy rolling off him. They stood looking at each other, neither trying to move away. Her heartbeat sped up, and she had visions of him kissing her. *Turn and leave,* she thought. Her conflicting thoughts raced as fast as her heart; she couldn't seem to complete one, let alone a full sentence, and she knew that wasn't caused by the alcohol.

James could feel her breath when she sighed, not able to tell if she was nervous or excited. His eyes settled on her lips, but he told himself he was her coach; moving this to the next level would change their working relationship. He had been wrestling with that. There was no way he wanted history to repeat itself with Ashley, but the scent of her citrus perfume drifted toward him, and he inhaled deeply.

"Ashley…"

"James…" She sighed.

The way she said his name had his senses reeling as he thought, *She should walk away from me…if she knew what was good for her…* He would only complicate things for her, but, then, he thought, *There is no way I can turn back now.*

At the same exact moment, both moved—James leaned in toward Ashley, and she moved in toward him. Their lips lightly brushed, sending a chill down her spine. He put his hand on her cheek, and the heat from him instantly warmed her.

Then, he pulled back slightly. "I'm sorry. Is this okay?" he whispered, half of him wishing she would want him to stop, and the other half wanting more.

"No, it's good." She could hardly breathe, much less make a sentence. Ashley put her hands on his arms, having wanted to do that from the first day she saw him. She slowly moved her hands up to his shoulders, feeling every muscle.

Her touch drove him crazy as he kissed her again. She let a sigh escape and seemed to hardly be able to catch her breath. He put his hands on her waist then slipped them around the small of her back. Nervous excitement, mixed with desire, made his hands tremble as he pulled her closer.

Fate had brought them together. This felt right to James. She fit him so perfectly; it was all messing with his self-control. As the curvy shape of her body pressed into him, his hands moved up her strong back. The need to feel every inch of her was taking over, but he didn't know how far this should go.

As if she'd read his thoughts, her hands were on his back, pulling him closer one second and then pushing him away the next. She stood back and looked in his eyes, trying to read the situation.

James smiled then trailed his lips down her neck, savoring the taste of her. Ashley breathed his name again as his hands roamed up the side of her body, pulling her back in.

A cell phone began to ring, pulling Ashley back to reality. She moved away and had to take a second to compose herself. "Is that your phone?" She looked toward his phone on the table, not believing that she could concentrate on anything other than his lips.

"Oh yeah." He laughed. "That can wait." James put his hand under her chin and turned her face back to his.

"Are you sure? It's kind of late. Don't you want to see who it is?" She peeked at the clock on the mantel behind him and couldn't believe it read 12:45 a.m. *Maybe I was saved by the bell,* she thought. The phone's ringing was enough to snap her out of this fantasyland and back to the reality in which she shouldn't be here, kissing him.

The ringing stopped momentarily, then started up again.

"Seriously?" James laughed and glanced over at his phone, then shook his head, and turned back to fix his eyes on Ashley.

"Someone really wants you."

He chuckled and raised his eyebrow at her. "Oh yeah?"

She stepped back, putting a little space between them. "No, I mean the call..." Ashley's face reddened. She laughed and turned sideways, glancing at the cell phone display before it stopped ringing.

She had watched his expression as he looked at the phone; he'd shown not even the faintest interest in the caller. The pit in Ashley's stomach grew when she saw exactly who was calling, the person she knew it would be, the reason she knew she should stop kissing him—Shawn. Who else would be calling him after midnight? And of course, other than to hook up, why else would she be calling at this time of night?

James inhaled deeply and tilted his head, looking into Ashley's eyes.

She averted her gaze before getting trapped by his hypnotic power.

"They'll leave a message if they want me. I'm sure it's not important." He moved closer. "Where were we?" He bit his lip.

Ashley's stomach clenched; she felt slightly dizzy. "I...I should be going home now. It's late..." She looked around to see where her bag was.

"Don't let that interrupt us, Ash. Please stay a little longer." His expression softened.

For one moment, she was tempted by his dreamy voice, but she knew better. *No way. I have to get the heck out of here,* she thought. *There is no need to get tangled up any further in this web with James and Shawn.* She pulled herself away.

"Ash?" Confused, James tried getting the mood back to earlier, but he could see she was distracted.

"No, I don't think this was such a good idea, after all." Ashley ran her hand through her hair, turning away, stamping down her attraction to him.

James stepped around her and looked skeptical. "What's going on? Are you okay?"

"Yeah, I'm totally okay." She wanted to tell him that she saw who called and that she knew exactly what was going on between him and

Shawn, but she didn't want to sound like a jealous girl. It was none of her business; it was time to make that exit.

"Come on, Ash. That was so… You had to have felt it, too…" His soft, dreamy voice was close to drawing her back in.

She turned quickly to face him and to put this to rest. "I know that was Shawn calling. I know the two of you are a…well, a thing." She wanted to blurt out, *I know you are sleeping with her.*

His expression changed to surprise. "Ash? That?" He gestured toward his phone. "It's no big deal. We are not together."

Ashley wanted to hear that they weren't together, but she didn't know if she could believe him. She was glad to hear it was nothing serious, but at the same time, she hated his casual attitude. James and Shawn were in a relationship and having sex. Everyone knew about it. Ashley hoped he would feel *something* about it, even though she wasn't sure what.

"Seriously, I have to go." Ashley grabbed her bag from the dining table and headed toward the hall to leave. Totally embarrassed, she tried to make light of it, but knew he thought she was being uptight. "This was a great night; thank you for having me." She continued down the hall.

He followed her. "Ashley, there's nothing going on with me and Shawn. I broke things off. This chance for us may not come up again."

Rigidly, she turned on her heel to face him. *Is he mocking me?* Anger bubbled up inside of her. She was angry with herself, with James, and with that bitch, Shawn, for interrupting them.

"Seriously, James?" Ashley snapped. "Is this my one and only chance to be with you? Get my chance now, and sleep with you, so I can be your favorite of the week?" She regretted it the minute the words came streaming out; she sounded like a crazy-ass bitch. *Oh no,* she thought, *I did not just say that.*

"That's not how it is, Ash." James shook his head and moved closer to her, trying to draw her back. "What I meant was you and I are never alone like this. Everyone is always around, watching. You said so at the bar. Where's all this coming from?" He held his hands out, smiling but totally confused by the direction of the conversation.

"I cannot believe I almost went through with this." Ashley shook her head. Backing up, she turned to go. "Good night, James. Thanks."

"Wait, Ash, don't end the night this way." He touched her arm lightly to stop her from leaving angry.

She turned on him, snapping her arm back from his reach.

"Whoa, I only want to talk, Ash." He held up his hands, backing off, knowing she was heated, and there was no way he would get through to her now.

"Listen, I'm not as casual about this as you are. We're looking for different things; that's all."

James was incredulous. "I enjoyed having you here, and I thought that you were enjoying it, too. We were messing around a little." James knew that was the wrong thing to say. *Why can't I say the right thing or, better yet, stop talking,* he thought. He saw disgust and hurt in her eyes, and he felt terrible. She was leaving. "Ash, I'm sorry. That came out totally wrong. Talk to me."

"I'll see you at the gym on Monday." She turned abruptly and walked out the door.

Son of a bitch. What the fuck was I thinking? I screwed that up after first screwing it up royally by leaving that phone out. Damn it, Shawn, James cursed. He and Ashley fit so perfectly together. His mind kept flashing to how she'd melted into him, to how he'd thought she wanted him as badly as he wanted her. *Now, I threw that chance out the goddamn window.* He cringed while he remembered saying that they were "never alone" together, that someone was "always around watching" at the gym. Now, after tonight, she would really make sure they were never alone.

He thought he was doing the right thing, ignoring Shawn, and it still blew up in his face. He'd been trying to break this off with Shawn for weeks, avoiding her outside of the gym, having no physical contact for the past month, but never finding the right time to actually tell her it was over. This whole thing was supposed to be no strings attached, but Shawn was taking and wanting more and more from him. *No strings and no commitment, my ass,* he thought. She loved the control.

James had liked spending time with Shawn in the beginning; it was exciting and a challenge. Then, her demands and late-night calls were over-the-top. She expected him to drop everything for her, even while he was at work—cancel plans, blow off clients, and take midnight calls, even when she knew he had other commitments. She was infuriated that he wouldn't see her earlier that evening, and he didn't want her at the get-together.

James wanted to spend time with Ashley. He didn't mind if there were strings with Ashley. He wanted those strings. He sighed. *That won't happen now.*

He couldn't get Ashley out of his head; being so wound up, he knew he would never sleep. He thought, *If this were the old days, I would call Shawn, after all.* Knowing she could take his mind off things, hooking up with Shawn used to be his fallback. But that wasn't what he wanted anymore.

James grabbed his phone and keys and headed for the door.

***

Why on earth did I let it go that far? Ashley berated herself. She knew better than to get involved with a guy like James. She hightailed it down the hall and into the elevator. There were so many reasons why it was a bad idea, not the least of which was the fact that James was her coach. This entire evening was against all of Ashley's rules.

Her heart was beating like crazy; she needed to calm down. Although she would have loved to erase the events of the evening from her mind, she couldn't help thinking of kissing James, his body close to hers, his hands on her…his wanting her, too. *This is insanity.* He didn't care about her, no more than he cared about the Shawn situation.

Nonetheless, she could not shake those images of James from her mind. Ashley made herself think of Shawn, and what Shawn and James would be doing if Ashley hadn't been there when she called. What they will probably be doing at some point again in the future.

That had to stay in the forefront of her mind, stopping all fantasies of James…and of his body against hers. *This isn't working so well.*

The cool air felt refreshing on her face as she pushed open the doors to the building and stepped into the night. Ashley wanted to walk to burn off some of her pent-up energy.

After walking a block from James's apartment, she felt eyes on her. She turned around, but no one was behind her. *Breathe.* Her palms were clammy; her heart began its erratic flutter. A man wearing a dark hoodie walked toward her. *The car. Stephen.*

The man glanced at Ashley as he walked past. He had a dark complexion and dark eyes.

She released her pent-up breath. *Not Stephen. God, what am I doing here?* She needed to get back to the safety of her apartment, fast. She was suddenly exhausted, her back aching.

She saw an empty cab parked across the street. It took everything out of her to walk over and give the driver her address. Ashley slid into the back of the cab and put her head back against the seat. She glanced out the window, making sure no one was following her.

Then, she glanced down the street toward James's apartment. She thought she must be crazy, half expecting him to come running after her like something out of a cheesy romance movie. *Those things don't happen.* She kept watching, even though she told herself she really wouldn't want him or any other guy to come running after her.

The cab began to pull away from the sidewalk as Ashley had the thought that James had probably ended up calling Shawn. *That is it,* she told herself, no more speculation or wondering. It would only infuriate her more if she kept wondering, *What if…?* She didn't have the energy left for that.

***

James held his cell and deleted Shawn's number from recent incoming calls. He pulled up Ashley's number and hesitated, thinking of her in his arms, of his mouth on hers, of her body and how it felt pressed against him, of his name when she whispered it… Those memories only made him want her more.

"Shit." He turned the screen off. No way she would take his call.

What am I doing?

He could have had Shawn there in minutes—no questions, no need to pretend, just sex. Then, she would have the control again. No, the games with Shawn needed to end, but he would deal with her another day.

I want Ash back.

***

Checking his watch, he saw it was after one in the morning. James took the elevator downstairs, stepped out of the building, and headed north. The late-night bar scene was going strong. It felt good to be out in the fresh night air, taking in the sights and sounds of the city. He sped up, hoping to catch Ashley.

James dismissed the thought of texting Ashley, figuring she'd ignore it. As that thought crossed his mind, he spotted her waving down a cab. She was walking at a fairly good clip, and he could tell she was pissed by her posture. James knew he had to fix things between them.

He jogged across the street to catch up with her. She slowed, suddenly looking wiped out as she approached the cab. James picked up the pace, and his heart quickened. *What the hell am I going to say?* he thought. *She'll think I am crazy.* Soon enough, he would know if she was going to tell him to go away or if she'd give him a second chance to explain or to apologize. Since she wore her emotions in her eyes, he would know the moment he looked at her.

As Ashley settled into the cab, James caught up to her and banged on the opposite window from where she was looking. "Ash, wait up."

She had a look of disbelief, followed by a shake of the head and a hint of a smile. She told the cabdriver to wait as she leaned across the seat and opened the door.

Good sign, James thought.

"What are you doing?" She looked up at James, not believing that he'd actually come after her.

"I couldn't let the night end like that. Want to walk with me?" He glanced at the confused cabdriver who was watching through his rear-view mirror. "Or can I hop in?"

"Um...oh right... Yeah, I guess we could walk." She turned to the driver. "Um, sorry, guess I don't need the ride right now." The cabdriver raised his hand and shrugged as she stuffed a five-dollar bill in the tip window.

All she wanted to do was to go back to her apartment, but she knew that things couldn't be left the way they were. She wouldn't have slept, and it would have been totally awkward come Monday at training. She had to clear the air with James.

Ashley tentatively climbed out of the cab and waited for James to circle back to the sidewalk. She knew James wasn't the type who did the chasing, so she was unprepared and didn't know how to react.

"Glad I caught up with you. You move fast." He shoved his hands in his pockets.

"Yeah." Ashley laughed nervously.

"Want to head up Newbury?" James nodded toward Newbury Street.

"Sure." Mimicking James's posture, Ashley put her hands in her pockets.

The noise and movement of the city were good distractions. After a couple of minutes of silence between them, James broke it, saying, "Listen, Ash, I'm sorry that things got messed up tonight. I didn't handle the situation as I should have."

"I didn't either. It's not my business what's going on in your life. I shouldn't have gotten involved." Ashley shook her head.

James stopped, turning to look at her. "No, I'm glad you were involved, that we were getting involved. That was the highlight of the night."

Ash tried not to get distracted.

"I ended up sounding like a complete ass. It's a little complicated with…Shawn." James didn't even want to say her name around Ashley, but he knew he had to explain the situation if Ashley was ever going to understand.

They resumed walking, and James let out a slow, long breath, tentative about how much information he should reveal to Ashley. He figured he would try for honesty. "I…we were involved for a while, no strings attached. The truth is…I've been distancing myself, personally, from her for a while. Things got complicated…"

"So much for no strings?" Ashley looked at James out of the corner of her eye.

"Yeah, that went out the window with Shawn a while ago. She likes to pull the strings and get what she wants, when she wants."

Ashley nodded, knowing exactly how Shawn worked. It was no secret she was vicious inside and outside of the ring, and she always got her way. However, she was not quite sure if she could believe everything that James was saying. Her guard was up, and she was determined to keep it there, despite his efforts to break her down with that sheepish grin.

"So, for her to call in the middle of us…well, you know…I didn't want to interrupt our time because of her." He inhaled deeply. "Ash, I wanted to spend more time with you, alone, without distractions." James looked sideways at Ashley to see her reaction.

Ashley's stomach flipped; a warm feeling spread through her chest. She had to concentrate hard on the words she was saying, "We both got caught up in the moment…don't you think?"

"I think it was more than that." His eyes lit up.

Ashley knew it was, but she stood her ground. "I can't have this get in the way… I want to work with you still…"

"Of course, Ash, that's not going to change. This shouldn't change anything; that's why I came to find you. Although, I probably looked a bit crazed…running across the street and ambushing your cab ride home." He shook his head and smiled that sideways smile.

Crazed was the last thing Ashley thought of when she saw James. She'd lived with fucking crazy. James wasn't that type of crazy. That dreamy sideways smile of his—now, *that* drove *her* crazy. Ashley didn't know what else to say.

James could tell he had gotten his point across, but didn't want to push any further. Ashley had built a little wall, and he understood. It would take time to chip away, but he was up for it.

"Let's get you a cab. Ya know, Monday's going to come up awful quick, and there's a lot of work to do."

Ashley was thankful for the out. They were her thoughts exactly.

The next cab that rounded the corner, James flagged it down. "All right, pal. We're good, right?" He looked at her nervously.

"Yes, we're good. Thank you for tonight. I had a great time."

"I did, too."

He wanted to be back in his apartment with her. Ashley envisioned the same, but neither made a move.

Ashley was tempted to say "screw this" and stay out for the night with James, but knew better.

"Get some sleep. See you Monday." James gave Ashley a hug and opened the door for her.

For the second time, she climbed into the cab to head home. But, this time, Ashley was in a much better place.

James tapped the glass and sent Ash off. He walked back to his apartment, but knew he would have a difficult time keeping Ashley out of his thoughts.

CHAPTER 28

"I kissed him." Ashley continued as if it were no big deal, "I kissed James."

Lisa stopped what she was doing. They were organizing folders for the upcoming meeting. It was quiet, so quiet you could hear a pin drop.

"Get the heck out." Lisa looked shocked as Ashley shrugged. "Oh my God. You kissed James."

Ashley smiled and continued stuffing the folders with copies of the agency's most recent magazine and marketing information.

"I knew it." Lisa nodded, taking a stack of folders and placing them in the box that was on the table.

Ashley burst out laughing.

"What?" Lisa put her hands on the table.

"You say that about everything." Ashley turned to retrieve more copies of the magazine.

"Well…" She held her hands up.

"Yeah, I know. You 'know things.'" Ashley waved her hands around.

"Exactly." It was quiet again. "Actually, I might not have known that. I thought you two had strong chemistry, but I didn't think you would act on it." Lisa continued loading the box. "You two are a perfect fit." She couldn't contain her excitement.

"We only kissed." Ashley wouldn't meet her gaze.

"There is more to it than that. This I know." Lisa picked up the box and handed it to Ashley.

***

James hoped Ashley still had that smile for him, the one that lit up her face. He sighed as he jogged down the stairs to meet her for training.

Thoughts of her had invaded his mind, every thought causing a major distraction over the weekend.

James cursed. *Fact of the matter is I fucked up, and my only chance of being with Ashley is in my fantasies.*

Walking in and seeing him there brought it all back; she felt a jolt of electricity shoot through her. She had been trying to keep thoughts of James at bay since Saturday, but it was challenging. The memory of kissing him… It was one kiss; it would not go any further. It was only one time—she had needed to kiss James once just to see what it was like. Ashley knew the temptation would be there to do more, but she had thought that maybe, just maybe, she would have enough self-control to keep from going any further than the one kiss. *When was self-control ever a thing? I am always all in. Nothing is ever halfway with me.*

"Hey, Ash." James's goal was to keep things light today.

Ashley was cautious, but tried the same game. "Hey, James. How's it going?"

"Great, you ready to spar with someone new today?" He had his hands on his hips.

That piqued her interest. She wondered with whom he was going to pair her. "Yes…I think."

"I thought we should put you in the ring and challenge you a bit. Let's see what you can do."

That was what Ashley had been wanting, but now she wasn't so sure about it. She adjusted the Velcro straps on her gloves.

"Can you handle it?" James smiled sideways at her, knowing that she was ready.

Her eyes flashed. "Yeah, I can handle it." Stifling her nerves, she played it cool, but was nervous about who would be her partner. "Who were you thinking?"

"Follow me." He turned on his heel and headed to the ring, smiling to himself.

Ashley took her gloves off, stuffed them in her duffel, and caught up. She didn't like surprises. As she approached the ring, she saw some of the trainers and other clients were hanging around, and Noelle, one of the girls who'd begun training around the same time Ashley started, was there, too.

He had matched her up with Noelle. Partly relieved that it wasn't one of the upper-level fighters or Shawn, for that matter, Ashley was still nervous because it was really happening. She pushed her gear into the ring and then climbed in.

"Hey." Noelle walked over to her with her mouth guard in hand.

"Hey." Ashley stood to face Noelle.

"Looks like we are working together today." Noelle popped her mouth guard in, fist-bumped Ashley, returned to her corner, and started loosening up her arms.

Ashley pulled on her shin guards, popped in her mouth guard, and secured her gloves.

"You ready for this?" James raised his eyebrow as he climbed into the ring.

"Hell, yeah," Ashley shot back.

James nodded, and a little smirk spread across his lips. "All right, get to your corner, young lady."

Ashley went to her corner. She glanced over at James and gave a nod.

"All right, we'll do three 3-minute rounds. Use what we've learned over our training time so far. Any questions?"

Each shook her head and waited for the bell.

When the bell rang, Noelle and Ashley met in the center of the ring, touched gloves, and nodded to each other. Ashley's heart raced; adrenaline shot into her veins. *Don't freeze; stay calm.* She took calming breaths and thought, *This is what I've been waiting for, right?*

Ashley was leery at first, but once they moved about the ring, she settled into a groove. Her shots were precise; she was dialed in. Everybody was watching, waiting. Some wanted her to win, but some expected her to fail—she would not let that happen. *Stay focused, and do not let them intimidate or distract.*

Jab, cross, and kick to the body—Ashley hoped it would leave a mark. She ducked the hook Noelle aimed for her left temple. Ashley kept her left side angled away from any blows Noelle could sneak in. She did not want to risk getting injured in this match. She kept moving. Noelle was getting frustrated at not being able to land a clean shot. Ashley kept her hands moving as a distraction; then, she slipped to the side and snuck in an uppercut.

Moving around the ring, Ashley lured Noelle into the spot where she wanted her. Double jab, cross, and a leg kick. As she moved away, Ashley threw a switch kick to the body then swept her legs. That was it. Noelle stumbled and fell to the mat.

The bell rang to signal the end of the third round.

Ashley looked up at James.

He slowly nodded as a small smile spread across his face. He knew he had a winner.

***

Constantly, James worked with Ashley on the form and precision of every move. He made her repeat and repeat and repeat moves, again and again, until she thought she would scream. She could throw a punch and kick, but needed to work on timing and accuracy. She was tough, but needed better defensive tactics. Then, there was her intestinal fortitude—the ability to fight through pain and obstacles—which many fighters couldn't do. You couldn't teach that.

Shawn had it. She was like stone. Nothing or no one could break her. Ashley, on the other hand, had the toughness, the fight in her, but she was breakable. There was something vulnerable about her. She needed the discipline and would probably hate him as they went further on this journey, but he could produce results. He could make a fighter great, could push one to the next level.

Dreading what he had to do to her, but knowing it was inevitable, James knew he was going to have to draw up a plan to break Ashley.

***

Ashley was pumped up after her fight, feeling higher than she'd ever felt. The minute she threw that last kick, she knew it was done. She watched Noelle fold over; the shock of the blow knocked Noelle off-balance and off her game. Ashley knew what that was like—being stunned and frozen—and that's when you knew it was over; there was nothing more you could do to recover.

When Ashley looked at James, she was nervous about what his reaction would be. He was a tough critic. But when she locked eyes with him, she saw the satisfaction and that slow, sly grin.

That was a great moment, a turning point. She felt strong, confident, and free of her past, of the chains that had kept her down. Ashley thought she could take on anyone, any challenge; she was ready for whatever came her way.

***

James was always intense and focused. At this particular moment, he was focused on the heavy bag. Knit hat pulled tight over his ears, gloves on, he was stalking around the bag with his unique intense look. Dialed in on his training, he threw some kicks and punches. The echo of the impact reverberated throughout the gym. It had such a different sound than when others hit the bag.

James looked up and caught Ashley's eye as she dropped her duffel. His gaze stopped her in her tracks. *Apparently, he isn't as dialed in on that bag as he lets on,* she thought. She saw the slight nod and small lift in the corner of his mouth. Ashley's heart sped up. Putting her bag away and getting her gear out occupied her for a couple of minutes. It was enough time to strategically plan where she was going to train. She did not want this to be awkward, although it would be until they broke the ice.

Standing up, Ashley glanced at the heavy bags, and James was gone. Her heart sank. Guess he did not want to stick around to see her. Ashley shook her head then popped her headphones on. She turned quickly toward the treadmills, and at the same time, James came around the corner. They collided.

"Whoa, hey, someone is eager to get going." James leaned back, tilting his head to check Ashley's expression.

Taken by surprise, Ashley pulled her headphones off. "Oh my God. What are you doing?" She laughed nervously, but was relieved to see him. Still wearing the knit hat and a little flushed from working out, he looked amazing to her. "Nice hat. You look badass out there." She nodded back toward the bags.

"Yeah, you know me"—he smiled sheepishly, his dimple showing—"that's the look I was going for. Where are you off to? You working out?"

"Yeah. Want to join me?" Ashley smiled, hoping he would. The gym was quiet, only one other person in their area and a few hitting the bags.

James looked around. "Yeah, let me put my gear away." He turned and was off again. He was always keeping her guessing.

When he came back, still wearing the hat, Ashley noted he had a wry smile on his face. "You ready to work me out?"

Ashley thought, *I could have a field day with that question.* "Yes, let's go."

CHAPTER 29

Fast punches, crouched low,
In tight, and pushed away.
Stand tall and gain control,
Then back in low, and punching fast.
Drills repeated, sweat pouring out of every pore,
Lungs burning, yearning for more.
When you think you cannot punch or kick any harder,
The bell rings…rest.

"Ash, there's a smoker in March. I think you should do it." James crouched next to her as she stretched her legs.

Ashley had settled into pigeon pose after an hour of kicking drills. She was in her happy space, smiling to herself. Then, his voice snapped her out of her Zen-like state. She felt herself tense and slowly lifted herself out of the pose before answering him. "Excuse me?"

"A smoker. It's an unsanctioned fight at a gym north of Boston. It's a great way to get you ready for the real thing." He was silent a moment. "It's the next step, Ash." He rocked on his heels, waiting for her response.

Ashley sat up and nodded. "A smoker, huh?" Biting her lip as she folded forward, stretching her hamstrings, she said, "Gosh, the real thing. Well, kind of."

"Yeah, it is. You go into it like it is. We would train for it like a fight."

Ashley knew this was the next step; that was the goal of the competition-training team—to get on the list for a smoker. She'd thought she had more time. Ashley sat up and looked at James. "Yeah, you're right. I need to get out there." She exhaled a shaky breath.

"That's my girl. Smokers are three 2- or 3-minute rounds. It's quick and dirty." He wished he hadn't said that, but she needed to know this wasn't a sparring match at the gym. This was the real thing, and it could get ugly.

"All right. Do we know who I'd be fighting against?" She pulled her knees into her chest.

"Um, no. We'll wait and see who they can get as an opponent. We'll do our research, make sure it's legit." He pushed up to stand. "Why don't we get some sparring in?"

"So, when will I know who I'm paired with?" Ashley stood slowly.

"Soon. Come on." He turned to go.

She eyed him suspiciously. *What isn't he telling me?* "James?"

He turned to face her. "What's up?"

"When will we know?" She shrugged.

"Sometimes, with these smokers, you don't know until we're closer to the date. Smokers are unsanctioned by the state, so not as organized."

She placed her hands on her hips.

He knew she wasn't going to stop asking him for details. "It could even be the day of."

"Seriously?" Her eyes widened.

"Yeah, it's fine. We'll know sooner. We'll be fine."

She rolled her eyes.

"Do you trust me? I've done a ton of these. You'll be fine. We'll get you ready for whatever they've got. All right?" He smiled confidently.

She nodded and smiled, excited and terrified, all at the same time. She picked up her gear and followed James to the ring while the visions of a smoker danced in her mind. *I've got a fight.*

***

The day of the smoker competition arrived, and Ashley was a wreck. James couldn't get her to focus or to calm down.

"James, I think I'm going to throw up." She bent over, hands on her thighs.

James pointed to the door. "Seriously? Then go into the bathroom!"

"I'm such a mess. I'm having a panic attack." She stood and took a big inhale and exhale.

"Ash, it's okay. Nerves. Let's focus." He motioned for her to come back toward him.

She wasn't having it—pacing, mumbling, and freaking out. Being closed in this room was like a steel cage for her.

"What if I fall walking out? Trip or something? Oh my God, I will look like a fool." She placed her hand on her forehead. "Wait, are my shorts right? They feel funny." She moved around, twisting to see if the shorts were too tight.

James stared, speechless, not knowing what to do with her. She was teetering on the edge; she could lose it at any moment.

"Ugh, my hair, too. I need to redo this." She ripped the ponytail holder out of her hair; the braid came loose.

"No, Ash. Don't take it all apart." *She's gone,* James thought.

Ashley readjusted her ponytail braid at least three more times.

James couldn't watch this anymore. "Come on, Ash; cut it out."

"I can't sit here. It's making me crazy." She paced the room like a cat.

"Well, then, let's get out of this room and get you moving." He grabbed her gloves and opened the door to the hallway, leading her to a back area away from the crowd. "Let's move. Come on." He jogged in place, nodding to her.

She copied everything he did. Boxer shuffle, light jabs, shoulder swings, hip openers, and breathing exercises.

James looked at his watch. It was time. "Let's go, kid."

Ashley shut it all down to focus.

They walked out to the darkened room in the gym north of Boston. In the center of the space, there was a cage; fixtures in the ceiling spotlighted the fighting arena.

Ashley's hands shook as James helped wrap her wrists; her breath was stuttering. He talked; she didn't hear him. All she could concentrate on was the fight going on in the cage. A guy swept his opponent, dropping him to the mat. She let a groan escape and turned away, fidgeting.

"Hey, look at me." He held her wrists lightly. "You've got this. Just like in the ring with me."

She nodded, believing him. He knew best; she wouldn't be here if he didn't have confidence in her.

"Remember, there aren't any points or winners; you go in and do what you do best. Throw those punches, land those kicks, and move out of the way. That's all."

That's all, she thought.

The bell rang and the two fighters in the cage fist-bumped and congratulated each other, looking worn out, as if they'd been through a war.

A guy came in and wiped the mat; the refs called in the next fighters.

Ashley was up. She strapped on her new black-and-gold gloves and entered the cage. The timer rang, and the battle began. Ashley didn't waste time dancing around the mat, trying to figure out the other fighter. James told her to go straight in with the goal of ending the fight before it started, and that's what she was going to do.

She moved straight in and threw a jab, a leg kick, and then angled away. Each time her opponent came at her with a jab-cross-hook combo—*What was her name again?*—Ashley threw two quick jabs and a leg kick and moved out of range. Third time, her opponent was ready, and Ashley threw a fast hook and body kick, pushing her opponent back. She moved in fast with a quick jab-cross, throwing her opponent off with the quick response.

Don't hesitate; keep pushing her back—James's voice in her head.

The first round ended.

James talked in her ear. "Get in; get out. Keep up the pace; keep her guessing; make her work."

Ashley nodded, fueled and ready.

Round two. *Janice. That's her name.* Ashley heard Janice's coach calling her name. Janice came in with her block up. Ashley used her leg-kick fake then switched to a front teep kick, pushing Janice back, then landed her cross. Janice guarded up, giving Ashley an opening for body hooks and a body kick. She moved away, avoiding Janice's strikes.

When she turned back to face Janice, she saw a face in the crowd that grabbed her attention. *Stephen.* She looked again, and the faces blurred. His face was gone. *Was it him?* She glanced around like a trapped animal.

Janice threw a jab that caught Ashley on the cheek. Stunned, she covered up and angled away, trying to sneak a peek toward the crowd. She backed up, scanning around the ring. She caught a glimpse of the face she thought was Stephen; it wasn't. She exhaled loudly and dialed back into the fight, shaken but able to focus.

Janice had fast hands, but Ashley was ready, countering with kicks, distracting her with an inside-leg kick and redirecting, then landing a hard cross-hook combo, ending the round.

Janice retreated, visibly shaken.

Ashley glanced behind her as she sat in her corner.

James stood in front of her. "What the heck happened out there? You could have gotten knocked out."

She turned back to face him and nodded. "I don't know. Light-headed, I guess."

"Stay focused." His brow furrowed as he handed her a bottle of electrolyte drink. "Here, drink."

Ashley grabbed the bottle and drank, glancing through the faces in the crowd. She was trying to convince herself it was only her imagination and to tell herself that Stephen was not in the audience.

"All right. Get back out there, and keep in control." James nodded and patted her on the shoulder.

Ashley hopped up.

He pushed her mouth guard in. "You've got this."

Final round. Ashley had control. Janice evaded punches and blocked kicks, but didn't counter with powerful strikes, obviously conserving energy. Ashley felt gassed and was experiencing a huge adrenaline dump. She needed to pace herself until the end. Hopefully, she would land a few decent combinations and not get tossed to the floor.

Things heated up during the last thirty seconds. James and their crew from the gym were cheering Ashley on from her corner. The crowd and Janice's coaches were calling for Janice to finish off Ashley. Wanting to throw a switch kick to end the round, Ashley powered up. She took a hook off the side of her head, stepped back, gained control, and feigned a punch, leading into her switch kick, which landed across Janice's side as she attempted a block. Ashley quickly retreated, avoiding Janice's last strikes as the final timer buzzed.

Ashley sat beside James and shook as adrenaline surged through her system.

"Ready to go out and celebrate?" He leaned into her side, smiling after high-fiving the other fighters from their gym and calling it a successful smoker tournament.

She needed food and her bed. She had nothing left; her body trembled with exhaustion. "I think I need to go home."

***

With the goal of increasing her endurance, quickness, and agility, James worked with Ashley on sparring. He had her run ladder drills, shuffle in and out, and practice her fast feet. She ran drills across the empty mat, did cone drills, and shuffled side to side. He needed her to be able to distract her opponent with constant movement, so she could get in with her punches and kicks.

The intensity of their sessions increased. He put the pressure on, moving in wider circles around the floor of the gym, drawing her in, and pushing her back with his strikes.

After a particularly grueling session, Ashley sat down on the mat, breathless and flushed, drinking her water.

James didn't take his gear off.

She continued to sip her water, avoiding his gaze.

"Ash, ready? We have one more set." He fastened his gloves and stood over her.

She pushed her hands off the mat and stood, nodding. "Yeah, ready." She bit down on her mouth guard.

"All right." He nodded and touched her gloves, starting the dance once again.

***

The smoker was in Rhode Island this time. Ashley sat in the back of James's car with Jamal, another fighter who was set to fight. James and Trevor sat in front. Ashley blocked out the conversation. She popped her earbuds in, getting her mind right. This time she would control the way the fight went. Her confidence was up; she was stronger and had a strategy.

The two-hour car ride passed in a blur. She looked out the window at the nondescript brick building that housed the gym where the smoker was being held. Keeping her earbuds in, she grabbed her gear and slung the strap of the duffel over her shoulder, following James, Trevor, and Jamal into the gym. They found a spot to settle into and began their prefight ritual. Ashley lined her wraps and her gloves on top of her bag. She sipped her water and stretched.

Jamal put on headphones, pulled his hoodie over his head, and then shadowboxed around the floor. James moved about, speaking with managers of other clubs, shaking hands with almost everyone who walked past him. Everyone wanted a moment to talk to him, see what his thoughts were on one fighter or another. He was well respected, and in turn, she could see that he treated everyone he met with respect.

Ashley turned the tunes up and began wrapping her wrists. Her time was coming. She was ready for this and finally felt confident. She was nervous, but she knew she had an arsenal of combinations that she could pull from to win this fight. She stood, shook out her shoulders, and added a little boxer shuffle and air jump rope to her prefight routine.

James was animated while speaking with a man. She saw his posture change—his arms crossed, his back became rigid, and his eyes alighted with fire.

She continued to move around, closing her eyes, breathing deep, and feeling the adrenaline fueling her drive. James's hand touched

Ashley's shoulder, forcing her out of the zone. She pulled an earbud out and raised her eyebrows. "What—"

"We're out. Fight's off." James pulled her aside.

"What? What are you talking about?" Now, he had her attention; she pulled the other earbud out of her ear.

"We are not fighting. Let's go." He nodded toward her bag, walking her backwards.

"James, what the hell?"

"It's not the right match. You're not fighting." His eyes were black, and he stood back, putting his hands on his hips. "Get your gear."

He glanced back at the ring, where the crowd increased their cheers for the fight that was happening. Jamal was listed to go on after three more fights, then Ashley after him.

Ashley stood looking at her wrapped hands and her gloves in disbelief; then, she looked up at James as fire burned through her. "No. I'm fighting."

"No, Ashley, you're not." He smirked, but there was a darkness that colored his expression.

"Bullshit." She grabbed her gloves and forged ahead, intending to rush to the ring, but was met with the wall of James blocking her. "Let me go. I'm fighting."

"Ash, stop." He was surprised by her attempt to get by him. He stood firm, but felt the force as she pushed against him. He braced against her.

"I can do this." Seething, she looked past him, not seeing him.

"No way. Not tonight." He stood firm and pressed on her body, but was unable to budge her.

"What, you think I can't do this? You don't think I can fight?" Her breath was ragged, and she was seeing red, pushing against his hold. She felt the heat of his body against hers.

"Do you think I invested all of my time with you to pull you out of a fight?" He looked at her intently, firmly holding his arm out to block her.

She tried to budge him, to no avail. Energy rolled off him; she felt the weight of his strength and tried not to waver. "Let me fight." Her voice broke, her resistance against him waning. She pushed against him with less force.

"Ashley." His face softened. "What is this?" He searched her eyes, seeing a desperation in them.

"I need this," she breathed and pressed her gloves into his chest.

"Ash." He placed his hands on her arms. "I've invested a lot in you. I'm not going to throw it all away on this." He nodded his head back toward the ring. "They paired you with a fighter that has at least eight fights that we know of under her belt. She is seasoned, and she fights dirty. This is the risk with smokers. They lied to us, saying she just came off the couch. I'm not having you get your jaw broken or your shoulder torn up for this shit. You're better than that." He lifted Ashley's chin to force her to look at him.

Ashley stared at him, her shoulders dropping, her resolve fading.

James breathed softly and smiled. "I'm protecting my investment."

Ashley's breath caught in her throat, and she bit her lip.

"We're getting you in the ring to fight, just not tonight." James wanted to hug her, to pull her close. Her determination moved him; he felt for her, but he knew this was all wrong.

She leaned against him then pushed away suddenly, stepping back from him. She tossed her gloves back onto her bag and placed her hands on her hips, sniffling loudly, biting back the tears and anger.

"Holy shit, James." Trevor rushed toward James with Justin.

James turned to face them. "Hey." He turned back toward Ashley.

"This is such bullshit." Trevor moved next to Ashley. "Ash, you okay?"

"Yeah, great." She shrugged and swiped her hands over her hair.

"No, Ash, there is no way you want to mess with that bitch. She is a psycho," Justin chimed in, bouncing from foot to foot. "I've seen her fight." He huffed, shaking his head.

Trevor nodded. "They totally lied about her experience. James was right to cut this."

Ashley tried to keep it together. It was beginning to sink in that this could have ended badly for her, but it was hard to separate that from the rush she'd felt about finally getting a chance in the ring.

"That is one crazy chick. She's still looking to fight someone, even a guy," Justin blurted out and laughed.

"Dude, seriously? Shut it." James threw up his hand, glaring at Justin, then turned back toward Ashley as she turned her back to him. James gave Justin a look.

"Sorry, man. Ash, don't worry about it."

James held up his hand to Justin. Then, he had an idea. "Hey, Ash. Get your gear."

Ashley frowned, turning to face him. "What about Jamal?"

"He's fine. Come on." James moved to his duffel bag and pulled out his shin guards, mitts, and belly pad.

Ashley stood frozen, watching him.

"Put on your gloves. Let's fight."

Ashley shook her head and grimaced.

"I'm serious." James pulled on his shin guards and stood, picking up his other gear. "Guys, come on." He nodded, leading them down the hall toward an area at the back of the gym.

Ashley watched as they all followed James. She huffed and grabbed her gloves, stalking after them.

James dropped the mitts and strapped the belly pad around his waist. Then, he scooped up the mitts, slipping his hands inside. "Trev, you got a timer?"

"Yeah." Trevor pulled his phone out of his back pocket.

"Set it. Three 3-minute rounds." He kept his eyes on Ashley while he spoke.

She stalked around, brow furrowed, then held his gaze.

"We'll treat this like a fight. I'll be padded up, but I can throw strikes with the mitts and kicks, too. You ready?" He nodded to the gloves in her hand.

Ashley pulled her mouthguard out of her shorts' inside pocket and secured it in her mouth. She undid the Velcro of her gloves and slipped in her hands, all the while keeping her eyes locked on James. He wanted to give her this little fight. She'd fight him, all right. *No holds barred.*

"Okay." James met her in the center of the floor and touched his mitt to her glove. "Ready?"

She nodded, holding her glove up, keeping her stony exterior.

"Right." He glanced at Trevor.

"Timer on." Trevor pressed Start and placed his phone against the wall, displaying the time.

Ashley kept her guard up, moving around the floor. James threw a jab, moving toward her, pushing her back. He moved side to side, eluding her attempts to make contact. His constant jabs distracted her and, at the same time, angered her. She launched forward with her one-two combo. Ashley tuned out that James was her opponent and went into her fight zone. She hit with full force then threw an inside-leg kick, angling away from him.

James backed up, making her chase him. She knew he was trying to wear her down. She stood firm and stalked around him, luring him back in. James threw a jab, then a double jab, and angled away, again, and again. She followed him, determined to make contact, and finally landed her jab-cross and a fast, hard kick to the body.

He wants me to fight him? He's got it.

The pace increased, and they soon fell into their groove. She anticipated some of the combos; he pushed and pulled, moving her into the dance, challenging her, pushing her harder, and taking the hard hits, knowing she was pissed at him and may never talk to him again after they got back to Boston. But at least he could give her this. The release.

She slammed him hard with her right cross. He covered up, but felt the impact against the side of his head. She nailed him with stinging leg kicks, wearing him down. He was impressed with her movement, her confidence. Her anger fueled her. That was something they needed to use in the future.

"Time!" Trevor yelled after the first round.

Ashley pushed back from James and turned to the wall.

Justin had run back to the setup area and grabbed waters. He handed one to Ashley. "Nice work, Ash." He fist-bumped her then tossed a water to James.

Ashley gulped the water, not realizing how much pent-up energy she had. She realized she needed to conserve energy to make it through two more rounds.

Trevor counted down until the timer started for round two.

James and Ashley touched gloves and began. James moved quicker, trying to break her down. He adjusted the belly pad as a reminder for her to throw teeps, knees. He wanted her to treat this as a real fight.

Ashley saw the signal and planned her attack. Jab-cross-front teep, pushing him back, then moving in with a cross-hook-cross. He closed the gap, throwing fast combos, distracting her with one hand, then kicking her leg, then back to hands. She moved out of range, then used the same technique, feigning a punch, then landing a kick. She pushed him toward the wall, threw a jab-cross, then moved in with double knees to the belly.

"Nice, Ashley. You've got this," Trevor called out.

"Come on, Ash. Keep that guard up," Justin yelled as James slipped in a hook-uppercut.

Ashley pushed herself to the end of the round, grateful for the break when it came.

Round three, Trevor called them to the center. Then, everything moved at lightning speed. James moved away, spinning out of her range, making her dizzy as she tried to follow his pace. Ashley angled away from him, keeping herself off the wall. She landed a head kick, then spun into a backfist. James caught her fist and pushed off, coming at her with a leg kick, hoping to sweep her. She caught her balance and moved away from him. She stalked around him, catching her breath, her movements slowing.

He threw punches that she defended and countered with her fast kicks, pushing him back. Her lungs burned as the bell rang for the third and final round.

"Nice fight, kid." James fist-bumped her.

CHAPTER 30

Back at the gym on Monday, Ashley felt distraught after missing the nonexistent fight. Then, she saw James and Shawn together, which only made her day worse. It was the first time she'd seen Shawn since the whole apartment fiasco. Ashley thought, *If it was such a fiasco, why do I keep thinking about his kiss?* She wished that damn phone had not rung. Shawn ruined that moment.

For one second, she thought, *What if…?* Then, she shook her head. It would never work between them. She should be glad Shawn's call came in. Especially now that she saw them together again.

Her heart felt heavy for no reason. Maybe because she was living such an isolated life, hiding behind the lie, trying to keep her life a secret from those around her. It was exhausting at times, and today she felt the weight of it. Ashley would not let herself go back to being depressed. *No way,* she thought.

The gym was what kept her going. Fighting, sparring, and kick-boxing—they made her feel free of the burden she carried. It was an escape, but she also felt that when she was training, she was truly herself. No one judged her or knew anything about her. At least, she thought no one did.

She couldn't shake the heavy feeling that had settled on her and was weighing her down. She watched others as they walked through their days, seemingly without a care. The black cloud of doom always followed her, threatening to unleash an uncontrollable storm.

***

She tried to forget me…but I knew she never would. I could tell by the look in her eyes when she saw me today. It was the first time she's looked at me like that since the kiss. That kiss started something, but it was left unfinished.

James approached Ashley and nodded as she worked the heavy bag.

She nodded back and kept moving around the bag, throwing strikes.

He crossed his arms and tilted his head, watching her. "Would you let me kiss you already?"

Ashley inhaled sharply. Her senses were overwhelmed by his being so close to her. "James! Shush," she hissed, her voice low. Ashley looked around then returned her focus to the bag, firing off rounds of punches.

"You know you've been thinking about it all day. Admit it."

She glanced at him, his laughing eyes teasing her and his crooked smile sending butterflies fluttering through her insides. "You are incredible. You know that?" Ashley continued to hit the bag hard.

"*It* was incredible. That's why you are thinking about it." James held the heavy bag steady for her, pushing his body into it.

"Humph." She landed a hard hook into the bag.

He infuriated her. She thought she had been playing it cool, but, truth be told, that kiss was all she thought about. She couldn't look at him longer than a moment before her mind would wander…her eyes would go straight to his delicious lips, and then she would think about that amazing kiss. No way she was letting on that he was right.

"Keep dreaming, James. It's not going to happen." She stopped what she was doing and bore her eyes into his to let him know she was dead serious.

Smirking and shaking his head, his irresistible dimples showed. "Okay, Ash, maybe not yet. But it will. And you'll be thinking about it until then."

James's singsong voice rattled her as he playfully flashed a grin and let go of the bag. He tapped her glove then sauntered off, leaving her there at a loss for words and unable to catch her breath.

CHAPTER 31

Feelings so strong
So intense
Blinding, burning,
Twisting, turning,
Draining me of energy

Needing to stay strong
Keep fighting
Intensity builds once again
Climbing

The higher the risk
The longer the fall
Hold on tight

Once more
So intense
Blinding, burning
Twisting, turning
Give me the courage before I fall.

"**W**hat are you thinking, Ash?" Lisa's voice made Ashley jump. "What? What do you mean?" Ashley was standing by the lockers, slipping into her fight shorts, and hadn't noticed Lisa walk in. Ashley looked at her, surprised by the sudden inquisition. She knew what Lisa wanted to know, but wanted to avoid that topic.

"Only wondering"—she paused for effect—"what you are thinking about James." Lisa kept her eyes on Ashley, searching for any change in her expression.

"Oh. Well, I...I like him..." Ashley rummaged through her duffel bag, hoping that was enough of an answer, but knew it wasn't.

Lisa continued, "I've never seen him like this before. I mean, he keeps to himself mostly, and I don't know the first thing about what he's thinking, but...I've never seen him this...this happy."

Ashley swallowed nervously. "I don't know what I'm thinking. Things are great, but...I'm...we are taking it slow."

"He would never hurt you, Ash..." Lisa wasn't going to let it go.

Ashley looked at her intently. "I know that. I'm taking this slow." She wasn't giving up any more information. She honestly didn't have any to give; she herself was still trying to figure it out.

"Okay." Lisa dropped her bag and chuckled. "Don't go and mess this up by hurting him. We all like him like this."

Ashley opened her mouth to say something, then shut it. There was nothing to say.

***

Ashley was feeling the effects of extreme fatigue. Her workouts began to suffer. In competition training, she fell behind, her cardio failing.

Her sparring partner swept her legs out from under her for the third time that day. Ashley wanted to cry, drop everything, and run out of there, never to return. She pictured leaving her gloves, shin guards, and wraps in a pile, slinking out, and not looking back. Mic drop.

She could do it now, and she wouldn't miss one thing about this place. Her anger and frustration boiled to the surface. Taking a deep breath, she felt herself shaking from the anger. *Breathe. Calm down.* Taking a few more deep breaths, Ashley closed her eyes. As her heart rate came down and she felt the stress roll off her, she thought, *Don't do anything rash.*

Ashley realized, if she left, she would realize in a moment of calm that she wanted to come back. There was so much that she looked forward to at the gym, so much that would be hard to replace. But this, this crap she was dealing with, she wasn't sure it was worth it.

266

"Ash, can I talk to you?" James's voice cut through her deep thoughts and drew her back to reality.

She looked at him, not saying a word.

"Can you take a walk with me?" He started walking, nodding toward his office.

"Yeah, sure." She left her things in a pile by the ring and followed James to his office. Glancing at the exit, she thought about her earlier vision of walking out and not looking back, but continued following James in silence.

He placed his phone on his desk and walked over to close the door. "How are things going?"

Nice open-ended question, she thought. Pausing, not quite sure how to answer, Ashley took a seat and sighed, shaking her head. "How's it going? You want to know?" Ashley wouldn't let her voice crack.

James pulled out a chair and sat across from her. "Yeah, Ash, I want to know. What is going on with you?"

Ashley laughed cynically. "Why is it that it's always something going on with me? Maybe everyone else is the problem?" She bit her lip. She knew it sounded as if she was the one who had the problem.

"Ash, that's not—"

She cut him off, "Let me guess. Do you want to know if it is 'that time of the month,' too?" She couldn't stop the words from spilling out.

"Ashley, I'm trying to have a serious conversation with you!"

"And I'm seriously trying to avoid it!" Ashley stood, ready to walk out.

James's eyes went directly to her hands, which were balled into fists. "I noticed." James lowered his voice. "Can you stop a second?"

She consciously tried to relax her icy hands. "Okay. What?"

"Maybe you need a break?"

Ashley knew he was pushing for that. She bit the inside of her cheek. "I'm good. I'm taking tomorrow off. I'll get some rest."

"Come on, Ash. You've been pushing too hard. You need to pace yourself, not just take one day off."

Shaking her head, she laughed. "Right. Stop pushing and then fall behind? The whole point is to get better, stronger, right?"

Using his words against him, he felt the sting in her tone. "Yeah, not like this. You cannot keep up this pace. No one can, Ash."

She sat back down, sinking into the chair, knowing he was right, but she would never admit she had pushed things too far. "I thought I knew what I wanted…actually, change that. At first, I had no idea what I wanted when I started here. I was clueless." She laughed a little, remembering exactly how clueless and withdrawn she was when she first stepped foot into the gym. "But everything seemed to come together for me here. I found an outlet, something to work for, a goal…and you helped me get there. But now, I…I don't know…I…" She wasn't sure of what to say as she shook her head, blinking away the tears that were threatening to come to the surface.

James remained silent. He'd seen his clients go through a range of emotions during their training, everything from elation to depression, anger, and quitting when they were overwhelmed. He knew the signs of overtraining, and they were apparent now in Ashley.

"I noticed your training has increased. You've been putting a lot more hours in here, right?"

She preoccupied herself with a pen that was on his table, pushing it around. "Yeah, I've been coming here a lot…mornings and most nights…uh, I guess weekends, too. Trying to fit it all in."

He knew how much she had been coming here. He'd looked up her check-ins. She was at the gym a lot and was now showing signs of overtraining. He carefully approached the subject, "For this week, you could try coming in once a day. Try not to overtax your body before your first match."

Ashley nodded, still fascinated with the pen.

James figured he was not getting through yet. "How's your eating been?"

She glanced at him, knowing he wouldn't like the real answer, so she lied, "It's been fairly good. I probably need to tweak a few things, but, overall, it's fine."

James knew she was lying. He could guess her sleep, too, was less than enough for the work she was putting in. "Well, let's get you down to one light workout a day, maybe take Saturday and Sunday off, then Tuesday and Thursday off next week. Refuel, rest your muscles, and see how you feel." He could see it coming; she wouldn't like this plan at all.

She stood up and crossed her arms. "I'm fine, James. Only tired today, that's all."

He nodded, knowing he had to say something. "Ash, you need to watch it, or you are going to crash and burn, and your competing will suffer. There will be a longer recovery from that if you don't step back a little. Trust me."

She shuffled around, getting increasingly uncomfortable with the conversation. *What am I if I'm not working out?* Pushing herself made her feel alive, lifted her so high she didn't want to come down.

Except, maybe not so much lately. Her energy wasn't there. She had been crashing hard at work, and random aches and pains were popping up, limiting her range of motion. She wasn't sleeping well; she'd started getting headaches. All of those things were making her bitchy and depressed, which made her want to work out harder, but she couldn't... *Maybe I could use an even longer break, take it down a notch.*

"Take the weekend off. Next week, we can start back, make a plan so you can keep your energy up."

Ashley nodded, reluctantly accepting what felt like a prison sentence. "Yes, sir."

James was skeptical.

She smiled and held up her hand. "Okay. I'll lay low. Honest."

"All right. Have a good weekend." He put his hands on his desk and called after her, "And rest!"

CHAPTER 32

Ashley left the gym and called Lisa on her drive home.

Lisa answered, "Hey, what's up?"

"Nothing, heading home from the gym, to rest apparently." Ashley couldn't mask the sarcasm in her voice.

"Everything all right?"

"Yes, fine. I'm beat up this week." It was great to hear Lisa's voice.

"Want to come over tonight? Vince and I are having some apps and drinks. Come by!"

Ash had visions of lying on her couch, her usual Friday-night routine. This sounded like a good diversion. *I need to relax, right?* This could be just what the trainer ordered. "Okay, I haven't showered, but I have all of my stuff…"

"Come straight here, and you can use my shower." Lisa's excitement made Ashley smile.

"All right. Thank you."

"Can't wait!"

Ash made a quick pit stop for some wine and other provisions, and then she set out on her mission to relax, avoiding thoughts of the gym, training, and James.

***

The night sky was turning shades of violet and cobalt. Ashley was beyond relaxed at Lisa's house; the fire, the wine, and the aura of the night—it was all perfect. She felt herself melting more into the sofa by the minute as Lisa told her about her day.

The doorbell rang, and Vince yelled from the kitchen, "Got it!"

Lisa was telling one of her stories—how she would always be in the right place at the wrong time—and Ashley was wiping tears from laughing so hard. She and Lisa heard voices as Vince walked into the family room.

"Hey, look who is here."

Ashley looked to the entryway and could not believe whom she saw walking in—James.

Lisa hopped up to greet him with a hug. "Oh my God, look what the cat dragged in! What's up, James?"

Ashley had to take a moment to process that James was, in fact, there. She stood slowly, gathering herself so as not to look like a fool from all the wine she'd already consumed. "James."

"Ashley. Hey." He approached her and greeted her with a hug.

"I'm getting started on my relaxing." Ashley held up her glass of wine.

"Yes, I see. Nice job." There was an awkward silence; then, James continued, "I had no idea you were here." Clearing his throat, he looked at Vince.

"What? I told you Lisa was having a friend over…" Vince held his hands up.

"Yeah, grab me a drink." James turned to Ashley and shrugged.

Ashley wasn't disappointed that James was there. She felt warmth spread throughout her chest as he sat next to her on the sofa.

As the night went on, more stories were told. With each one, the space between Ashley and James shrank. Her arm brushed his; his leg was next to hers. Slowly, they inched closer.

It was late, and Ashley was fighting to stay awake. *No way am I breaking up this party*, she thought. Soon, James, Vince, and Lisa began rehashing old stories, and Ashley started to drift off.

"James, no way did it go down that way, no way!" Lisa stood up to grab more wine and nodded toward Ashley. She had wedged herself against James, her head on his shoulder. "Guess you got her to relax. I should get her up to bed."

"No, don't wake her," he whispered. "I can sit with her until she wakes up." James looked at Ashley, inhaling the scent of her perfume. He never would have guessed she was here tonight when Vince called him. Now, she was this close to him, and there was no way he was moving from his position.

***

Ashley moved and felt her neck cramp. She sighed and repositioned herself, eyes still closed. She moved her hand, felt something—someone's arm—and snapped open her eyes, surprised to see James.

"Hey, sleepyhead." He made eye contact with her.

Ashley moved her hand across her chin. *Oh my God, what if I drooled on him?* "Hey." She looked around as she sat up and put some space between them.

"Good dreams?" James smiled, looking at her sideways.

"Oh gosh, I was out. I'm so sorry." She motioned to his shoulder.

"Don't be. I was pretty comfortable myself." He had a smug look on his face.

She thought, *What if I talked in my sleep?* "Where's Lisa?" Ashley looked around.

"She and Vince went upstairs." James looked sheepishly down at his beer. "I told her not to wake you."

"Thanks, I guess I needed that." She laughed, running her hand through her hair. She looked at James. "I'm staying over here tonight, so…"

He stood quickly. "Yeah, I should go, let you rest."

Ashley followed, nervously clasping her hands together. "Thanks for letting me crash on you." She laughed.

"Anytime." James walked to the kitchen and disposed of his empty beer bottle in the recycle bin.

"Are you working tomorrow?" Ashley followed behind, rubbing her eyes.

"Yeah, it's a light day." James leaned against the counter.

Ashley yawned, leaning against the doorframe.

"You better get to bed, kiddo."

She nodded. "Yeah"—stifling a yawn—"good seeing you."

"You, too, Ash." James hesitated…then opened the door and left.

Through the window, Ashley watched him leave, wondering why she was left wanting something more.

CHAPTER 33

Heat rising, working against the force of it.
Heat flowing, pushing in and out of my core.
Twisting, turning, falling, rising.
Heat, close enough to burn, but so far out of reach.
Mesmerized by it, yet scared of all that exists there.
Coming close, drawing in, I won't get burned.
Pushed away, blinded by the intense fire.
Drawn back again for more.

"Is it safe?"

"It's safe, Ash." James held on to her arm. "Don't look down. Hold on to me."

Ashley gripped James's arm as if her life depended on it. "I can't do this. It's too…" She thought for a moment. She could insert so many descriptions there: scary, high, dangerous, fast…terrifying! She did not have to say anything else.

James smiled at her and whispered in her ear, "But that is the fun of it, Ash." His words sent a chill through her.

Her heart rate began to soar to an unspeakable speed as she stepped onto the edge of the wooden platform. Zip-lining at a course located in Berlin, Massachusetts, with James, Lisa, and Vince—Ashley thought, *How did I let James talk me into this?*

He circled his arm around her waist, and she felt her body trembling. Partly from the fear of heights. Partly, she was fairly sure, from having James so near her.

"We're up next." He moved her forward then turned her toward him. In one quick move, he snapped the harness around her waist then his. Nodding to the technician to whisk them through, James held on to Ashley and smiled that killer smile. "Keep your eyes on me. Trust me."

Ashley locked her eyes with his and thought, *Yes, I can do that. I could do that all day long.* For one moment, all her fear subsided, and she thought of kissing James. His arms were around her, pulling her near. *That's what he wants, to be near me—*

The floor was swept out from under her feet, and she was flying, soaring through the air. Squeezing her eyes shut and hugging James even tighter, Ashley couldn't catch her breath.

James's voice broke through her fear, "Ashley, breathe! Open your eyes; it's not so bad. I've got you."

Trying so hard to slow her breathing down, Ashley feared she would puke or die of heart failure if she opened her eyes. She began to squint and grabbed on to James's arm harder than before. "Oh my God, James! I am going to kill you!"

When she looked at him, he was smiling. They weren't going as fast as she had first thought. They were on a beginner track, which still was quite harrowing; however, she could sense that they weren't as high as she thought, either. Even so, she didn't dare look down.

"Keep your eyes on me. You okay?" He was hopeful that she might possibly end up enjoying it.

"Yeah." Ashley ventured to look at the trees and the skyline past James. Beautiful shades of green covered the mountain. Flowering trees outlined the horizon and contrasted with the deep blue of the sky. It was breathtaking—if she could find her breath to begin with. Inhaling slowly, she told herself, *Nothing will go wrong.* She wanted to enjoy this moment with James and not let it slip away from her.

"Check this out." James pointed to a flock of white birds that were taking flight up through the trees.

They neared the end of the trail, and Ashley once again felt her stomach flip as she clenched her hands on the harness and on to James. Landing seemed as bad as the takeoff. At the last moment, she closed her eyes and prayed for a safe landing. They coasted into the landing track with James holding on to her for added support.

"We made it, Ash! You did it!"

Keeping ahold of James's arm, Ashley didn't trust her wobbly legs as the technician unhooked the harness. She watched the others come in for their landings. "I can't believe it. I am still shaking!" Ashley felt exhilarated, energized, and exhausted, all at once.

***

Watching her struggle with the fear she battled inside herself was baffling to James. On the one hand, she was so brazen and strong. Then, when it came to real-life situations, she fell apart. *Well, this might not be considered a real-life situation; it's zip-lining. Lots of adrenaline and risk, I suppose.* James needed to lighten the mood, or she would dig her stubborn heels in and refuse to go.

James placed his hands on her waist to calm her and, selfishly, just to put his hands on her waist. He thought, *I can't lie; she feels good next to me.* Although, she was trembling. James told her to hold on to him, to look at him, and to forget about the major drop-off below her feet, even though he knew, in about sixty seconds, her stomach would feel as if it were in her throat. *Trust me…*

Then, when her eyes locked on his, he nearly forgot where they were. James thought he couldn't describe those eyes adequately, or the way they made him feel. *It sounds crazy, but they look like she doesn't have eyes for anyone else, that all she sees is me, like she wants me to be closer to her… to kiss her. Totally ridiculous. She can't need me as bad as she makes it seem. We tried, and things got messy.*

Maybe this is a second chance. Her eyes on mine, we move forward slowly. Teetering on the edge, holding on tight. We'll take this leap, and see what happens next.

CHAPTER 34

*T*heir bodies worked in unison as she threw punches, and he took the hits. Navigating his way around the floor, he drew her in, harnessing her power. Promising to make her great.

***

The uneasy feeling comes on fast, without warning and for no apparent reason. But there is a reason. A big one. It hovers below the surface, threatening to flood over and pull me under. It takes over, making me question everything…but there is no answer. No life preserver thrown my way. I'm left wanting, waiting for someone to answer my silent cries for help, wanting someone to see…but also wanting to drown in the deep, dark sea.

***

Why is it so hard to keep the dark thoughts away? Nightmares disrupt my sleep; flashbacks of abuse haunt my mind. This is not the time for it to come out; that would ruin everything. Everything I worked so hard to avoid, everything I planned. I cannot have this take over now… Push it down; push it away.

***

Punches flying.
Heat rising.
Anger and rage boiling up inside,
Bubbling under the surface of her skin.

This was her release. She needed this, craved it. Her emotions were overwhelming, threatening to drown her. Every ounce of anger, hate, and rage came out of her as she unleashed on the pads.

James, being the recipient of this rage, didn't realize how close to the edge Ashley was teetering.

Ashley kept her workouts light for a few weeks, but the hope of an upcoming fight pushed her to train harder.

James felt her force, but saw a lack of technique. He stopped Ashley and looked back at her stance. "Can you stand like a fighter? Come on."

She complied, but nothing was good enough today.

"Move back."

"Move over."

"Again."

This had to be the hundredth time today she did this drill. *Why can't I get it right? Mental block,* she told herself.

"Again. Stop at the end." As her target, he held his glove up by his face.

Ashley threw her cross, and he held her glove.

"Look where you're standing. Your feet are way off, your cross not centered. This will throw your entire sequencing off. You'll get hit or swept like this." To illustrate, in one swift move, he swept her legs out from under her, catching her before she fell to the mat.

She bit down hard on her mouth guard as she pulled herself back to standing and pushed him away. She had no patience for his constructive criticism. She was easily frustrated, which, in turn, made her mess up more. Her depressed mood and anxiety attacks of late had taken their toll on her mental function. It was all she could do to try and stay in the moment.

"Again." James pushed her back with his gloves. "Jab, cross, slip, cross."

Her shoulders burned. *This is the last time,* she thought. *I'm out of here if he tells me to do it again.*

"A little better. Again."

That is it! she thought. "This is the last time I'm doing this. If it's not right, I'm outa here." Seething, she clenched her jaw. She threw her cross, and it landed square on the mitt with a loud echo, inches from his jaw.

"Nice shot. Guess you're staying." With his smartass smirk, James picked up his cell phone.

Ashley started taking off her gloves, hoping for a break.

Without turning, he commanded, "Keep your gear on. Speed rounds are next. Then, we'll spar."

Ashley drank her water, shaking her head. *No point questioning him because, once he makes the decision, that's what we are doing.* Strapping the gloves back on and trying to stay focused, she nodded.

Timer on, punches flying, kicks next, and no break.

"Faster shots, come on, Ashley." James wouldn't let up.

The timer beeped.

"Burpees, let's go. Twenty." James stood looking at her. "Come on."

Ashley grunted. She wanted to haul off and punch him; she probably would if she had the strength. Her lungs were burning. She wouldn't give him the satisfaction of beating her down. Sweat dripped off her face; she could barely catch her breath as the timer buzzed.

"Time. Grab some water; then, come on back."

Ashley didn't hear him. Her ears were ringing. Hopping down carefully from the ring, she walked it off, breathing heavily. She wasn't sure she could keep water down at this point. Her emotions were raging, her stomach churning.

Things were already bad. She'd thought this session would help squash those feelings, but everything was worse. Not knowing how much more she could take, she took her time walking around and taming her breathing. *Come on, Ash; get through this,* she repeated to herself.

"Come on, time to spar." His voice, usually music to her ears, was like nails on a chalkboard.

As she climbed back into the ring, Ashley had to blink to keep her focus. She kept repeating her mantra, *Get through this...*

"Ready."

James nodded, started the timer, and popped his gloves on. He threw fast combinations, testing her defenses. This was her first area to weaken when she was tired.

Each blow sent her back even further into herself. Trying to keep him at bay, she threw sloppy combinations and forgot to cover up to defend, which made him throw harder and more frequent shots at her.

Finally, Ashley had had enough of it and let loose. She went at him with unbridled force, pissed at herself, at her past, at him. Blind with rage, her punches flew, and he countered every single one, frustrating her even more. He caught her foot and lifted her leg out from under her, sending her crashing down on the ring floor.

Tears started to fill her eyes and threatened to spill over. *No, don't do this now,* she thought, fighting back the tears and biting down on her mouth guard as hard as she could as she stood back up. Her rear kick didn't land right; her power had dwindled. Ashley caught a leg kick wrong on her upper shin, sending a splitting pain straight into her knee, sparking the anger that had been brewing into a full-on assault.

She moved in toward James's face and hauled off as many jab-cross combinations as she could as he covered up. Then, her tears spilled over.

"Ashley, hey, that's it. Whoa." James backed up and kept his guard up.

Ashley tore her gloves off and threw them down hastily, wiping at her tears as she spit out her mouth guard. "I am done!" She turned away, not wanting James to see any more of this than he already had.

James removed his gloves and mouth guard. "Hold up. Ashley! Talk to me," he called, shocked at her tears.

She stood staring off, sweat pouring off her. "No, I'm done… I have to go," she choked out as she climbed out of the ring. She could hear James calling after her, but she walked straight to the locker room.

James had expected a breakdown with this intense training, but not like this. He tapped the timer to turn it off. The gym wasn't crowded, but a few of the members were there cross-training or working with trainers. He gave Ashley a few minutes to cool off, figuring she'd return when she was ready.

When she didn't return, James was worried. He leaned over the ring and called out to Kali, one of Ashley's friends, as she passed by. "Hey, Ashley is in there; can you make sure she's okay?" He nodded toward the locker rooms.

Kali had seen the latter part of their session and thought James had pushed Ashley too hard. She shook her head at him and walked into the locker room.

James tossed his head back, not believing this was happening.

Kali returned after several minutes, stood with her hands on her hips, and looked at James. "Ya know, she's not doing so hot, so leave her alone." She turned and walked back into the locker room.

"Yeah, thanks." James tossed his gloves aside and hopped over the ropes. He walked into the lady's locker room, calling out to the other women in there. "Excuse me…sorry…I need to get in here."

There was a woman in the locker room, removing her things from a locker.

"You might want to go upstairs and change." James smiled at her. "Sorry."

Grabbing her stuff, she walked out, totally confused.

Kali walked back around the corner and stared at James.

James held his hands up. "I'm here to talk to Ash."

"Haven't you done enough?" Kali shook her head.

"Do you mind?" He crossed his arms and leaned against the lockers.

Kali shrugged and walked past James, then turned toward him. "I'm staying outside this door. Don't push her anymore." She eyed him, then left the locker room.

James put his hand to his forehead. "Dear God, is everyone losing it today?"

He heard the shower running and called out, around the corner from the stalls, careful to make sure any stragglers knew he was in there, "Hello, it's James here, checking on a few things. Anyone else in here?"

No answer, so he rounded the corner. "Ashley, it's me. I came in to see if you're okay," he called then retreated to sit on a bench.

***

Ashley let the hot water stream over her, calming her tremors. She breathed in the steam, trying to steady herself. *What happened out there?* she asked herself. She'd been so good at holding it all together. She leaned into the shower, soaking in the warmth, escaping reality. Then, she heard a man's voice, snapping her out of her tranquil moment.

"What the hell?" She peeked out of the shower door and saw James, looking sheepish, sitting on the locker bench.

"Ash, you okay?"

"Oh, dear Lord." She shut the shower door. *Why can't he leave me alone?* Tears welled up in her eyes again; she couldn't stop them, no matter what she tried telling herself.

James called out to her. "I'm going to hang here…till you're done. No rush, no one else is here. Kali's waiting outside in case I freak out on you or something." He spoke loud enough for Kali to hear.

Shaking her head, Ashley leaned under the water stream once again, knowing she couldn't hide in there forever, although she would have liked to. She also knew James wouldn't leave until he talked to her. Reluctantly, she shut off the water, grabbed her towel, gathered her things, and steadied herself before facing him.

Slowly, she opened the shower door. James looked up from his seat, worry creasing his face. He noticed she looked drained and so small, her big fighting presence a memory.

She tugged the towel tighter around herself and took her shower bag off the hook. "I'm going to get dressed." She pointed to one of the dressing rooms.

James looked at her with brows furrowed.

"Don't worry. I won't hurt myself with my hairbrush or anything."

He nodded, smiling a little. "Okay, I'll be here. No one else will come in."

Ashley sighed and closed the door to the changing room. Taking her time, she dried off, pulled on her underwear and bra, jeans, and a T-shirt, calming herself before facing James. She walked over to the lockers and retrieved her gym bag, trying to keep it together.

James broke the silence. "Ash, what's going on?"

So much is going on. Where to begin? she thought. Her back facing him, she shook her head and let out a shaky breath. Her legs suddenly felt unsteady; she held on to the locker, closing her eyes, and then turned to sit. She faced James, eyes red and swollen.

Kali knocked and called in, "Everything okay in there?"

Ashley walked over to the door and smiled faintly. "Yes, Kali, thank you. I had a tough morning. It's okay with James here." She nodded back to where James was sitting.

Kali gave him a look then glanced back to Ashley. "Okay. I'm here if you need me." She touched Ashley's arm and left.

James shook his head, trying to stifle a laugh. He knew Kali was the biggest gossip there. She wanted to know what was going on.

Ashley locked the door and hesitated. She inhaled a shaky breath and returned to sit across from James. "I don't even know where to begin."

He clasped his hands and leaned forward. "It's all right, Ash. You've been training hard. This happens."

Ash turned her head aside, not able to control the tears. They flooded down her cheeks. This wasn't how she wanted him to see her. He saw her as strong, a fighter; he knew nothing of her emotional weakness.

Crouching down in front of her, James took her hand. "You can tell me anything. Or nothing. Or yell at me, or tell me you hate me, or ignore me. I'm here for you, in every way."

Incredulous, she looked at him, and at that moment, she knew she had to tell him…everything. She had to release this unrelenting nightmare that was destroying the walls she'd so carefully built. There was nothing left to hide behind anymore.

"My life is so fucked up. I can't do this anymore." Her anxiety spiked at the mere thought of speaking about her past.

James was worried. "It's all right. Breathe, Ash." He held her hand.

She looked away, determined to draw strength from God only knows where and face this head on. She steadied herself and looked at James, ready to confess her hidden past. "I've been running for so long." She looked down at his hands holding hers. "I ran away from a life that was something I couldn't bear to be stuck in. Then, I ended up living in another nightmare."

James rubbed his hand over his jaw, listening quietly, waiting.

"Before I moved here, I was in a terrible relationship with a man named"—she swallowed hard, barely able to get his name out—"Stephen. Things spiraled out of control. He was violent. I had nowhere to go, so I ran. I ran away to start a new life." She looked at James. "My life here."

Ashley steadied herself, knowing she had been living a lie, telling the lie so many times that it almost seemed real. Yet it wasn't.

"No one knows where I am. I changed my name. Only my last name. I changed my life story. Basically, I'm living a lie." She looked at James and could see the confusion and hurt in his eyes. "I didn't lie to you about everything, but a lot about my past wasn't true. Like where I was from, my family, my friends…" *What friends?* she thought.

At that, the tears started again, and her hands trembled. She put her head back against the locker. "James, I'm so sorry. I thought I could push all this bullshit behind me. But it reared its ugly head. There's so much." Full-on sobbing at this point, Ashley wanted this over.

James was silent but attentive.

"I was careful to leave no traces; nobody knew where I was going." *Except Faith,* she thought. She smiled at the memory of Faith and all that she did for her.

James broke the silence. "Has anything happened that's making you worried now?"

Ashley thought of the paranoia. "I'm always worried. I always look over my shoulder. Hiding, living the lie. If he ever finds me"—Ashley shuddered at the thought and looked at James, her voice barely a whisper—"he'll kill me."

James clenched his jaw. He would never let that happen! Stunned by her admission, he knew he would do whatever it took to make sure she was safe from this guy. Then, he had a realization. "The car...?"

She nodded. "Yes, I thought that was him. There have been other things, but I don't know...maybe I'm paranoid."

"I'll make sure to keep you safe, Ash." James's eyes bored into hers.

She smiled faintly. "I know. I know you would." She swallowed hard. "But that's not all of it. I'm dealing with so much... Before I met Stephen, I already had a mess of a life. My family, I..." She broke down.

James sat next to her, putting his arm around her. "I'm so sorry, Ash."

She hadn't realized how much she was holding in...until now. "James, I have to tell you everything. I have been living this big fucking lie, and I can't do it anymore."

"All right"—James steadied himself—"you can tell me anything. I'm your friend above all else."

Ashley inhaled deeply, determined to get her story all out.

"My father was abusive. He drank. He yelled at my mom and us. My parents would fight or not talk; the tension in the house was high. Then, he would be home for a while and try to make it up to everyone. He"—she inhaled deeply to keep her voice from cracking—"sexually abused me when I was young."

James was taken aback by her confession. Saddened deeply, he took her hand. With his voice barely a whisper, he said, "I'm sorry."

Ashley flinched initially at his touch, but then continued in a daze, "My mother acted like nothing happened, so either she didn't pay attention to what he did or she didn't care. I never said anything. Then, I went into a deep depression. I had anxiety attacks, but I didn't know what was going on or why. I found a therapist, and she helped me through all that mess. I confronted my family, but no one took ownership.

"It took a few years, but I recovered from that and was getting back on my feet when I met Stephen in college. Things were going well... until they went terribly wrong. He was crazy. He *is* crazy. I can't believe I ended up in that situation. He turned on me, and I stayed. It was almost too late...but I finally left."

She paused, looking at his hand on hers. "I was doing so well here, finding this place, you... You have helped me so much. But I knew something was going to give." She swallowed hard. "It has been eight months since I ran. I came down off the adrenaline from it, and it hit me all at once."

James looked into Ashley's eyes and saw a darkness, a sadness.

"I was numb for so long. But here"—she looked around and gestured toward the gym—"here, I'm alive. You brought me back to life."

James pushed Ashley's wet hair out of her eyes. His voice was soft. "You kept yourself alive, Ashley. You're so strong." He looked at her with eyes so deep, and he began to tear up. "We'll get you through this. It's going to be all right, Ash." With his other hand, he touched her arm. "I'm sorry for what you went through. I'm here, whatever you need from me."

She wanted to believe him; she needed to believe him. He motioned toward her, and she embraced him tightly. She held on to him and his strength; it was the only thing keeping her from drowning in the sea of black.

***

James met Ashley outside of the locker room after she finished drying her hair and gathering her things. He was leaning against the wall with his bag, ready to leave. "Hey, want me to follow you home? I want to make sure you're okay."

Ashley had wanted to ask James to follow her home, but felt funny about it. She was glad that he'd asked. "Yeah, okay. If it's not too much trouble." She pulled her bag onto her shoulder and wrapped her coat tighter around herself.

"Definitely. We can order some food if you want."

She nodded, feeling the weight of the day settling on her. "That would be great."

They left the gym. He drove behind her all the way to her apartment, not letting her car out of his sight.

***

"Will you stay with me?" She hugged the fluffy pink blanket close around herself, doe eyes wide, fighting the exhaustion.

James had finished eating the takeout he ordered, grinders and soup, but Ashley had barely picked at hers. It broke his heart right down the middle to see her like this. Even though unsure of what he should do or say, James knew there was no way he would leave her alone in that condition.

"Sure, I'll stay." He brushed a stray hair away from her wide eyes. "I can crash on the couch."

"Okay, there's a blanket in the hall closet."

Ashley's heart began beating out of control, panic setting in. *Should he stay in the room, just in case I have a panic attack during the night or a nightmare?* she thought. *I can't even hold my shit together.*

James saw she was shaking and how fragile she was. "On second thought, I'll stay in here with you, and we can talk until you fall asleep. Okay?" He smiled, reassuring her that everything would be all right.

She nodded, barely able to keep her eyes open. "Thank you." Ashley grabbed her lavender essential oils from the bedside table and inhaled the scent deeply, hoping a small wave of calm would settle over her. Trembling and feeling cold, she pulled the blankets tighter around herself.

"I'll get you another blanket. In the hall?" He gestured out toward the hallway.

Ashley nodded.

James grabbed another heavy, fluffy blanket from the hall closet, probably the one she had meant for him to use on the couch. Even after placing it on top of her, she didn't settle down much. James didn't want to violate any boundaries, but he knew that body heat would be the best thing to warm her up.

"Can I try to help you calm down? Can I sit here?" He motioned toward the bed.

At that point, Ashley would try almost anything to calm her nerves. "Okay." She scooted over to make room.

"All right, I'm going to put my hands over the blankets. I'm not trying to do anything weird."

She nodded, trusting him, and lay down on her side. His strong hand pushed downward, adding pressure from her shoulder, down her arm, toward her legs, and then starting over again. It took a couple of times before Ashley began to relax. Her trembling stopped; her breath deepened and slowed. The warmth of his hands had a hypnotizing effect on her. The rhythmic motion calmed her, and soon she felt she could fall asleep.

"This all right, Ash?"

"Yeah, thank you," she said, her voice a whisper. She couldn't keep her eyes open. She fell deep asleep, dreaming of colors, light, and floating in a cloud of warmth...finally feeling safe.

***

James could tell the moment she fell asleep. There was a different kind of quiet and calmness that settled over her. Easing up on the pressure, James continued the steady movement to be sure she didn't startle awake.

After a short while, he stopped and pressed the blanket down around her. Deciding to camp out on the chair next to her bed, he grabbed his bag from the hall so he could do some work. He'd fallen behind on planning the schedule for the upcoming fights. He pulled out his tablet to go over his spreadsheets and get organized.

This is a perfect quiet time, no distractions.

He watched Ashley; she was still and breathing steadily. He hoped she could stay that way through the night and get caught up on her sleep.

Work, he commanded himself; he needed to concentrate on work.

After some time of organizing the spreadsheets and forms for the upcoming competitions, the names and dates started to blur as his eyes grew heavier. Placing his hand next to Ashley, he closed his eyes, his memory drifting back to that one kiss they'd shared.

***

"James."

Her voice snapped him out of a deep sleep. "Ashley, you okay?" James jumped out of the chair.

She was sitting up in bed, looking around and a little confused.

"Ash…?"

Seeming to snap out of a dream, she looked at James. "I'm sorry. I was dreaming. I was trying to find you… I'm sorry I woke you."

"It's okay. I'm here. My heart is beating out of my chest, though." James smiled and sat back down in the chair. He brushed his hand over his hair. "Do you want some water or anything?"

She smiled sheepishly. "Water would be great."

James stood and stretched, hands on his lower back.

Ashley stole a glance at his exposed torso as his shirt crept up, away from the waistline of his jeans. She quickly turned away before he saw her.

He headed to the kitchen and filled two glasses of water. Returning to the bedroom, James handed Ashley a glass. "Cheers," he said, raising his glass before he took a sip.

"Thank you."

James nodded. "No problem…"

Ashley looked down at her glass. "No…thank you for staying with me. I…I'm glad you are here."

James moved to sit next to her on the bed. "Anytime, pal. It's going to be okay. Try to get some sleep."

As James was brushing her hair back again from her eyes, Ashley leaned into his hand, loving the warmth, the safety she found with him. "Yeah, I'm wiped out." Her eyes burned with fatigue.

"Come on, back into your cocoon," James ordered. He made light of it, but, the moment she'd pressed into his hand, he wanted to kiss her again. *Jeez, James, nice…with all the hell she's been through…* He shook it off and tucked her under her covers.

She murmured something about blankets for him and then was fast asleep.

James stayed seated on the bed, propped against the headboard, finding comfort in being next to her and feeling her warmth; finally, he gave in to sleep.

***

His strong hands moved over her, pulling her curvy hips closer. He couldn't get enough of her. Her warm mouth was on his; she moved to whisper his name in his ear, her warm breath sending a shock wave through him. His hands were on her body, roaming and needing more.

Ashley was smiling and teasing him with those round red lips, drawing him in with those deep-green eyes. Nothing could stop them. Moving, pressing, and pulling…wanting this, wanting her more than anything—

Bzzz…

"James, James…" her low voice called his name, her soft hands on him—

Bzzz…

A slight hum in his head was getting louder and pulling his attention away, but he wouldn't let it—

Bzzz…

It wouldn't go away; it was still there and getting louder.

"James…"

She was all he'd ever wanted…her body and his together. He reached to touch her face as she leaned down to kiss him, her mouth on his, pressing in—

Bzzz…

That humming noise again! He pulled her closer and tried to ignore the sound that kept getting louder—

Bzzz...

***

James startled awake to hear his cell phone vibrating on the side table next to him.

"Son of a—"

He reached for the phone and silenced it. Losing that glorious dream filled him with frustration. He leaned his head back on the headboard. "Damn it." He looked at his phone and saw it was Vince who'd called.

James placed the phone on the side table and sighed, glancing at Ashley as she moved in her sleep, murmuring his name. He smiled and placed his hand on top of her blanket, willing himself not to go any further.

"Ashley, you make me crazy, even in my dreams," he whispered and closed his eyes, still seeing the vivid images of them together in that dream.

CHAPTER 35

Several weeks went by, and James made sure to keep Ashley's workouts light. Slowly, they resumed their training routine. Regularly, he checked in with Ashley to make sure she was okay. When they worked, he was all business. They hadn't talked much outside of their sessions; James had a full schedule training fighters.

Ashley realized she was wasting brain space on James as she sat at home, wondering what he was doing. Was he thinking about her? *Apparently not.* Was he working? Was he out? Was he with Shawn? He'd said he was "done with that," *but who knows?* He didn't owe her any explanations.

Needing a distraction, Ashley turned on the TV, hoping to find a movie to watch, but that didn't help keep her mind off James. She picked up her journal to write or draw—anything as a distraction.

After a few minutes, Ashley realized nothing was going to take her mind off James. She needed to figure this whole thing out and soon. This tug-of-war and flip-flop of emotional turmoil over wanting/not wanting James, facing reality/running away was eating at Ashley. How could she tell James that, yes, she wanted to be with him, after she so adamantly made it clear that there was no possible future for them? And that was after they hooked up in his apartment and things went bad...then good...then bad again.

This is ridiculous! See, this is a sign that things won't work between us.

Worst case scenario, she tells him how she feels, and he says, "Sorry, I'm not feeling it." That would be embarrassing, but she could get over herself and maybe get back to concentrating on fighting.

But that wouldn't be the worst case. Even worse would be if he thought she was a freak and decided he didn't want to train her anymore. That would be devastating.

Maybe I shouldn't say anything and just see what happens. No, that's what I've been doing.

Ashley tossed her journal aside. Tomorrow would be the day. Fate would be her ally…or her enemy.

***

"James, I have to tell you something…"

James threw her a sideways look and, raising that eyebrow, responded, "Okay, I'm intrigued. Go on…"

Damn. Ashley took a deep breath. *Here goes nothing…or everything,* she thought.

"I…I can't stop thinking about you." James squinted and shook his head, but she couldn't get sidetracked. "Ever since that night at your place, I've thought about you…about us. I know I said this could never work between us. This is probably the worst timing, but I needed to tell you…I think of you…of us…all of the time."

He looked at her intently, on his face a mix of shock and something Ashley couldn't read. James drew his hand over his forehead.

Oh gosh, this isn't good, she thought, her stomach twisting in knots.

He turned and strode toward the stairs, apparently heading to his office.

Ashley froze, then quickly followed James. *What is he going to do? Is he going to tell me this is over? Is he done with me?* He would probably palm her off on some other trainer. Or worse! *What if he kicks me out of the gym?* She would die. She would grovel, do anything to stop him from kicking her out.

She called to him to stop, but James was strides ahead of her.

He strode into his office and turned to face her.

"James, what are you thinking? I…" She held her hands out in front of her.

"Shut the door." His jaw was set tight.

Biting the inside of her mouth, Ashley entered his office and shut the door, cringing inside.

"What's going on with you? You're here every day, training like a maniac...you're all into me one second, then push me away, and now this? Do you even know what you were saying down there?"

"No, I...I don't know...I mean, yes, I know what I was saying, and no, I don't know what's going on with me. This sounds crazy..."

"So, why say things if you don't mean them, Ashley?" He crossed his arms.

"What? I don't know. Wait, I meant I know what I was saying downstairs... Oh my gosh," Ashley fumbled, trying to save herself and failing miserably.

"Ashley, either you mean it or you don't." He shook his head again.

She didn't like the look of disappointment on his face. She took another deep breath. James was right. She was talking like a fool. She sank down into a squat against the wall behind her, knotting her hands. She needed to tell James how she felt, once and for all.

"I meant what I said, James"—her voice cracked—"I think of you constantly, probably more than I should. That's probably weird, but I know what I feel...and I need to know"—Ashley looked up from her hands—"I need to know what you're thinking." She shook her head. "I know I must sound crazy. I get it if you are done with me." She braced herself for the worst.

He walked toward her.

Here it comes, she thought.

"I can't believe you said that." His voice was low and hoarse.

She couldn't tell if he looked angry or confused.

Standing over Ashley, James reached his hand out to her.

Swallowing hard, she took his hand, not trusting her shaky legs as she stood. Closing her eyes, she couldn't bear what was coming.

James placed his hands on the wall on either side of her. "Ashley. I don't know what to do with you. You make me crazy."

Ashley opened her eyes, determined to stay strong. "I wasn't going to say anything; then, I knew I'd regret it. I don't want to waste time anymore."

James's gaze softened.

As Ashley looked into his eyes, she felt as though she could get swallowed up inside them. Neither wanted to say anything that would break this feeling.

Without any warning, James touched her lips with his so gently she had to catch her breath. Not having known how he was going to react to her and then having him kiss her sent her emotions swirling. Her breathing increased; her heart beat as loud as a drum.

The kiss. It was everything she'd dreamt it could be.

He touched her cheek. "Ashley," he breathed, kissing her with more force this time.

Ashley's mind raced as quickly as her heart. Kissing him back, her hands drifted toward his chest. Starting at his shoulders, she slowly let them trail down his arms.

His breath quickened. He put his hand to her chest, feeling her heartbeat, moving to kiss her again, deeper, longer than before.

She could feel every emotion at war inside of her. Each emotion pulling her in a different direction. This was more than she could take, but everything she wanted. As James kissed Ashley, his hands tangled in her hair. A sudden moment of clarity hit her—*This is not a war at all. This moment...this is paradise.* Ashley pulled James in toward her, craving him against her.

James leaned into her, pushing her back against the wall. Raw instinct kicked in, and they moved together. James's hands roamed to Ashley's waist, the heat of his hands warming her skin. James looked in Ashley's eyes, searching. Her eyes revealed everything as she pulled him closer. He pulled her into a hug, holding her tight. "You are beautiful, Ashley."

Ashley wrapped her arms around his waist, inhaling his scent as euphoria set in. They heard voices in the hall and pulled away from each other. She had to steady herself.

"I'm sure you have to go back to work." She knew he had more clients.

James ran a hand over his hair and glanced at the time. "Ah, yeah, I do have a client in a few, but he can wait." He smirked that wonderful smile and leaned his forehead against hers, holding her hand. "I'm so glad you changed your mind about me."

Ashley smiled and shook her head a little. "I've always felt this way about you. I…I didn't know if I was ready."

James held her hands to his chest. "I'm glad you are ready now." Then, he kissed her hand. "Can I see you tomorrow?"

"Yes. Definitely."

James drew her into his arms. "I don't want you to go. You won't regret this tomorrow, will you?" He leaned back, looking in her eyes.

"No chance." She kissed him then turned for the door.

"Let me grab my gear, and I'll be right behind you."

As James gathered his gear, Ashley carefully walked, as if on a cloud and using her shaky legs, down the stairs to the locker room, smiling to herself the entire time. When she returned, James was standing at the front desk. As he caught her eye, he stopped what he was doing, his face reflecting how Ashley felt.

Ash broke the spell, looking down, embarrassed, biting her lip.

Right at that moment, Trevor came through the doors. "Hey, how's it going?"

"Great, just leaving." Ashley pulled her duffel over her shoulder and fidgeted, turning toward the door.

James walked to the doors as she was exiting. "Hey, I'll call you later. I'm heading out of town tomorrow for competitions in New Jersey."

"Sounds good."

He nudged her side; his eyes were smiling.

She blushed under his stare. "Bye, James." She walked to her car, unable to hold back her smile.

James watched her till she drove away, his hand pressed against the glass.

***

Ashley's phone buzzed at ten o'clock that evening.

James: *Good night. Sorry, I've been nonstop with work. I can't stop thinking of today.*

She felt her cheeks heat up as she smirked.

Ashley: *Me, too.*

Ashley smiled as her phone buzzed again.

James: *I'll text while I'm away. Wish I could see you before I leave.*

Ashley: *Me, too.*

James: *Night and sweet dreams.*😄

Ashley: *Good night. Good luck on the trip.*😄

Ashley held the phone to her chest and smiled, closing her eyes, replaying each moment of how their bodies had moved together. *Oh yeah, I'll have sweet dreams, James.*

CHAPTER 36

That morning, she was easily distracted by the buzz of the gym. She turned away from the sparring group briefly and saw James was there in the center of the commotion. After returning from the competition over the weekend, everyone wanted to know how the fights went.

The timer rang loudly, bringing Ashley back to her training.

"Want your water? Earth to Ashley." Lisa waved her water bottle in front of Ashley.

"Wait…oh yeah, sure." Ashley watched as James spoke enthusiastically to the other coaches. She grabbed her towel and water, trying not to stare.

James flashed a smile at her and a brief wave.

"We still going or what?" Lisa held up the pads.

"Yeah, we're going."

Ashley grabbed the pads, and Lisa reset the timer for three minutes. Ashley flashed the pads for punches, always following the combination with a signal for a kick, testing Lisa's reaction time at how quickly she could position herself to throw powerful kicks. She moved around the floor, changing angles and combinations until the timer sounded.

"Nice work." Ashley high-fived Lisa as they walked toward the benches.

James continued to hold court as other fighters came over to hear the updates on the competition.

Ashley hung back, waiting for him to break free, then ducked into the locker room to change. When she returned, James was still there.

He nodded to Ashley as she approached. "Hey." He smiled and feigned a punch toward her, ducking to the side.

"Hey, welcome back." She held up her hands and feigned a punch back, then gave him a hug. "How was the trip? We missed you here."

"Good. Great. Our fighters were amazing. I'm ready to be back, though. How's your training? You look good." He nodded out toward the floor. He had been watching her as he gave the guys the update. He'd missed her while he was away.

"Hey, James. Man, welcome back." Justin walked in and slapped James on the back.

"Good to be back, man."

"Fights were awesome. I saw footage of that amateur grappling match. What the hell?"

"Yeah, that was something—"

Justin cut him off. "The video was unbelievable; that guy couldn't have won…"

James nudged Ashley's side as Justin continued about the fight. James stood so close to her she could feel the heat radiating off him. After what seemed like forever, Justin finished.

"Hey, Ash, can you swing by my office? I want to go over our training this week."

Ashley was caught off guard. "Sure. Now?"

"Yeah, come on up."

She followed him up the stairs in silence, noticing every move his body made.

James put his duffel bag next to his desk. "Shut the door."

"What is it?" She was worried by his serious tone.

He turned to face her, and his eyes were dark as he flashed that sexy sideways smile. "This. I can't be in the same room as you without kissing you." Immediately, his arms were on either side of her as she stood against the door.

"Oh really?" She smiled, teasing him.

"Yeah. I've been wanting to kiss you all day."

She laughed. Her heart beat so loudly he had to hear it. His hands were warm on her skin. His mouth was on hers. She was breathless as she came up for air. Ashley locked the door and turned back to him. "No interruptions."

"That's exactly what I had in mind." He put his hands around her waist, smiling that wicked grin of his.

She put her hands on his chest. "When I am around you, I feel so much."

"Is that a good thing?" James leaned back, looking confused.

"I feel the intensity of you, which is absolutely amazing." Ashley smiled and touched his arm. "Sometimes, it's overwhelming. I can only concentrate on those feelings, and that's it. Nothing else can get through."

"I'm flattered that I occupy your thoughts so much." James used his seductive voice and pulled her close to him.

"James!" She feigned pushing him away, then settled against him.

"I like feeling you next to me." He moved her hair away from her neck so he could kiss her there. "It's hard for me to be away from you."

"Yeah, me, too." Ashley was blown away by how intensely she reacted to his touch. She couldn't get enough of it. Her mind and heart raced. "You know what you do to me, right?"

He looked in her eyes, curious. "No, what?"

She moved her hands to his waist and under his shirt. "Let me try to show you."

His breath caught as her hands touched his skin. Her kisses became deeper as her hands roamed and pressed against his flesh. She backed him up to his chair and straddled his lap. He was lost, heat rising, desire burning, barriers breaking away; he experienced the thrill, the peak, and the stillness.

***

The next day was a grueling double session of strength training and kickbox class. *Sometimes the best part of the day is when it's over,* Ashley thought. Just crashing on the couch sounded so appealing.

James came bounding down the stairs and headed toward the training area. "Hey, Ashley. Got a minute?"

She couldn't exactly say no, but thought about it. "Yeah. What's up?" She placed her wraps aside.

"Come with me." Full of energy, he turned and bound back up the stairs, two at a time.

You have got to be kidding me, she thought. "Can't we talk here?"

"Come up!"

Figures. I want to crawl home and get into bed. She sighed. Even taking the stairs at a slow pace, Ashley's legs were wobbly.

James, already in his office, peeked back out the door. "Ash? Oh, come on." He waved her on excitedly.

"This better be good," she mumbled under her breath.

He stood at his round table with papers and files askew. "What would you say if I told you I can get you an amateur match next month?" His eyes were electric, energy rolling off him.

"What?" She was looking at the paper in his hand.

"Next month in Rhode Island. It's not a huge venue, but it's something. It's perfect, actually."

Ashley couldn't believe what she was hearing. She looked from the paper in his hand to him. She stood stunned.

"This is going to be great. There are two main cards, and you'll be up fourth." James was pumped. "We have a lot of work to do, so get home and rest up. Tomorrow, we start right in." He practically shooed her out the door.

"This is crazy. I can't believe it." She was dazed.

"There are four others representing from our gym. This is big. Congratulations."

"Thanks, James."

"You got it, pal. See you bright and early tomorrow." He placed the paper on his desk and walked her to the door.

Ashley turned to go, shocked and scared to death. She was trembling, her hands shaking like a leaf. She'd gone from flat-out nothing left in the tank, to full of adrenaline and energized. She felt a little nauseous and light-headed, and her heart was hammering inside her chest.

Despite all of that, she beamed; she couldn't contain her smile all the way out to her car.

***

This meeting was going longer than Ashley hoped, but the only saving grace was that James was there. Ashley could not concentrate, her leg bouncing nervously as she tried to focus on anything other than James's lips. They sure grabbed her attention. Oh yes, and when he moved any part of his body, it was a huge distraction, one she could not avoid…one she did not want to avoid. Those lips, so smooth and full, inviting…

At one point in the meeting, she had the feeling he knew what each move he made was doing to her. The sexy smirk, flashing his eyes at her, raising his eyebrow…*Ugh*. She felt her cheeks start to flush. *Oh no, not now*, she thought.

Luckily, James said something witty that caused laughter among the others. Not having any idea what he'd said, because of the sexy-smirk distraction, Ashley just laughed along, trying to blend in.

She pictured herself biting that lower lip before kissing him… *If he could read minds, I would be in trouble*, she thought.

"Ashley, you good with all of this?"

She did not have any idea what he was talking about. What she knew was they were planning the fight schedule for the competition, but her input? *No idea*. Ashley had two fights coming up back-to-back. They needed a break in between each for her to recover. The time span could not be too long or too short. The placement of each competitor was crucial to their success.

"Uh, Ash? We good?"

Everyone turned to look at Ashley, awaiting her simple yes.

"Yes, those times will work. If you think there is enough of a break, then I'll be okay."

James nodded and smiled, which made it all okay to Ashley. He knew her strengths and her weaknesses.

James knew she could do this. He knew Ashley's confidence level could either make or break her. He needed her to own it. Her wry smile reassured him that she was in a good place, but it also had him wondering what was going on in that pretty little head of hers.

CHAPTER 37

Heat pulling, pushing, twisting, turning
Spiraling away
The force is so strong
Make it last forever.

Ashley finished her training for the day. She hadn't seen James, so she decided to check in his office. She hated to disturb him and felt everyone was watching as she ascended the stairs to his office. She knocked lightly on the door.

James was on a call and smiled, waving her in. "Sounds good, man. We'll get him on the schedule. Talk to you soon." James ended the call and stood from his chair.

"Ash, thank God you're still here. I've been stuck in here all day." He came around the desk.

"I wondered where you were. Thought I'd check on you before I left." So glad to see him, she smiled as he approached her. His hands found her waist, pulling her against him, not able to resist being this close to her. She could feel the heat of his chest pressing into her, the warmth of his hands on her skin.

"How was your day?" He brushed the hair away from her neck and kissed her sensitive skin.

"James, there are people still here." She looked toward the door.

"I know. They won't come in." He continued kissing her.

"You don't know that." Her hands trailed down his arms, which encircled her waist. Her strength was waning. "I need to go home so I can get to bed."

"I would love to join you." His dark eyes were dancing.

She smirked and raised an eyebrow.

He pressed his mouth to hers. "Please."

"Maybe."

James pulled back smiling. "Maybe? Seriously?"

"Yeah, I may need a little more convincing, though." She placed her hands on his chest.

"Okay. I can do that." James kissed her a little bit deeper this time, pulled her toward him, and lifted her up.

Ashley held on to his shoulders.

Slowly he lowered her down, his lips never leaving hers.

Breathless, Ashley was overwhelmed once again by him and his hold on her.

"Need more convincing?"

"No. That was good." Dazed, her legs feeling weak, she held on to his shoulders.

"So, can I come home with you?" His dimples emerged with that devilish grin.

"Most definitely," she breathed.

He took her hand in his and smiled.

***

On the way to her apartment, Ashley stopped to pick up chicken, vegetables, and pasta for a pasta primavera with grilled chicken on the side.

James insisted on cooking for her.

"I'm going to shower before we eat. Is that all right?" She nodded toward the stove as James sautéed the chicken and vegetables. "Need any help out here?"

"No, I'm all set here. You need help in there?" James smirked and nodded toward her room.

Ashley's face reddened. "Um...no...I'm all set." Smiling, she turned and quickly walked into her room.

She shut the door to her bathroom and leaned against it, imagining him giving her a hand in the shower. Then, she pictured him standing outside her door. If she opened it, and he was there, she would pull him into the shower with her.

Steadying herself, she opened the door a crack. *No one there.* Laughing out loud, she shut the door again and turned on the shower.

***

James heard the door shut and shook his head, smiling, imagining her in the shower. He would have loved to have joined her. He glanced at her room, wondering what she was up to, as he heard the door open, her laugh, and then the door shut again.

His phone beeped and vibrated as texts were streaming through. Checking the phone to make sure nothing urgent was happening, he silenced the ringer. *My night off,* he thought.

He returned to prepping dinner. Chicken was simmering, he sauteed vegetables, and Ashley had the wine chilled in the refrigerator. As he was pouring a couple of glasses of wine, Ashley emerged from her room, refreshed.

She wore blue jeans and a slim-cut sage-colored T-shirt and looked amazing to him. He wanted to scoop her up, go straight to her bed, and forget all about the dinner.

***

She inhaled the scent of his skin, a mix of cologne, soap, and him—sexy, deep, and sensual. Deeper, she breathed him in, not wanting to waste a single breath.

He was lying still, feeling like her prey, not sure of what her next move was, but listening to her breathing. His hand was lightly on her back as he felt the deep rise and slow fall of her breath. Her mouth trailed across his chest, her hair cascading around him. Hands roamed; a sigh escaped.

Every move, each touch sent a trail of electricity through James, yet he stayed still.

Then, Ashley locked eyes with him, and a slow smile spread across her face. She took his hands in hers and stretched them up over his head.

He was exposed and vulnerable—two things James was not accustomed to feeling. He usually made others feel that way. *This is totally different*, he thought, *and amazing*. He watched how she looked him over then released one of her hands so she could touch him.

Her hand slowly pressed down his arm, but then Ashley stopped for a moment. "You have the best arms." She leaned over and put her mouth on his bicep, kissing around his arm.

James breathed deeply. "Ashley…"

"Mmm?" She teased and kissed him until he thought he would explode.

"You're driving me crazy…" he breathed as she trailed her mouth down his arm then locked eyes with him once again.

"That's the point." She smiled.

***

"Don't forget me while I'm away." James smiled, looking down at Ashley in his arms.

She looked up to him, mesmerized by his eyes. "That could never happen." She leaned in and kissed his inviting lips. "I'll miss you."

"Me, too. I'll call you when I get in. It might be hard for me to call after that. I have to be there for the guys, but I'll try." He absently traced his fingers along her back.

"I get it; don't feel like you have to. You'll be busy."

He kissed her again then held her close, breathing in her scent. "I'm going to miss this." He lifted her up with an exhalation and spun her around.

Ashley laughed and squealed with delight. The feeling was euphoric. She didn't want to break free of him, or of the spell he had cast on her. She held on to him tighter as he brought her back down to him.

"When I come back, we'll have a weekend together. I promise." His eyes held hers steadily, until she had to look away, blushing. He kissed her cheek, sighing.

She knew it was time. James had to drive to meet the guys, and they would all drive together to New York for the fight. "Good luck."

He held her at arm's length, keeping a connection with her hand as he pulled his duffel onto his shoulder.

"Bye, Ashley." Lingering a moment longer, embracing her hand, then he was off.

***

Ashley couldn't concentrate on anything other than the flash of memories from that morning—the flood of sunlight streaming into her room...the white sheets...his lean, muscular body next to hers...his bright smile...the heat of his skin... those smiling eyes teasing her...

She could feel those wonderfully inviting lips on her neck, his warm breath on her as he laughed when she asked if they were ever getting out of bed. She could still feel the heat of his palm from where it had rested on her waist.

He said he didn't want to leave. She absolutely didn't want him to leave.

***

"I don't think we're leaving this bed today." He smiled and kissed her throat, sending a magnificent sensation down to her core.

"I'm definitely not leaving," she breathed.

As he touched her face, he looked at her as if there were only her in his world. "Wild horses couldn't drag me away from you."

James kissed her so beautifully Ashley could only lie there motionless, his power over her making her dizzy.

Smiling, his hand trailed down her side. "Nothing could entice me to leave you." Then, James lay back, hands propped behind his head, gazing at the ceiling. "Except...maybe coffee."

"What?" Ashley snapped out of her dreamlike state and rolled over to look at him.

"Yeah, coffee." He nodded, looking at her sideways. "Wanna get me some?"

"James!" Ashley swatted at him.

"What? I like my coffee." He laughed, blocking her punch, then took hold of her wrists and rolled on top of her. He looked down under the sheets at her body and smirked his adorable smile. "Like I said, absolutely nothing could drag me out of your bed. Besides, I don't need any caffeine right now."

She knew exactly what he meant.

***

Ashley smiled at the memory. She had to complete her markup of the marketing piece today in order to meet the Monday deadline. Distractions weren't helping.

Her phone vibrated as she settled into her seat. Hopeful it was James, Ashley picked up her cell with butterflies in her stomach. As she unlocked the screen, she had a moment of doubt. Biting her lip, she checked her messages.

James: *I never should have left your bed today.*

Her stomach flipped.

Ashley: *Big mistake. I'm still in it.*

Ashley chuckled, knowing James would answer immediately.

Bzzz…

James: *What?? You're killing me.*

Ashley: *No, I'm working, but having a difficult time concentrating.*

Her memories filled with thoughts of the morning.

James: *Same here. Can't wait to get back.*

Ashley: *Me, too.*

James: *I'll see you on Monday.*

Ashley: *Of course. For my Monday torture.*

James: *You won't be disappointed.*😎

It would truly be torture being next to him, but not able to touch him. As that thought crossed her mind, her phone buzzed again.

James: *It'll be torture for me not to touch you. Sweet dreams.*

She sighed. *This is too good to be true.*

Ashley: *Same here.*😄

Her dreams would be the sweetest as she replayed each moment of the previous night. If she could ever fall asleep, that is.

CHAPTER 38

The night of the competition seemed so far away, an elusive goal that was talked about, hyped, and announced every day for weeks. Then, it was here, and the hours were humming by in a blur. Ashley couldn't get a handle on the day. She would focus on completing one task, time would fly by, and then she was behind schedule.

Her phone was buzzing constantly—coaches, friends from the gym, James—all wanting to know how she was doing and to wish her luck.

I need more than luck, she thought.

Her stomach was tied in knots. She needed to fuel up, but lacked an appetite. Panic set in when she thought of the fight or looked at the clock.

The group was meeting at the gym at one o'clock. They planned to stop at a restaurant and drive to the fight venue together. She'd underestimated how difficult the waiting would be.

Once she was with the group, everyone's energy picked her up, but when they arrived at the arena, it was difficult to relax. There was so much time to sit and ruminate. Learning from experience, she had to get ahead of the possibility of runaway emotions taking over.

Music, meditation apps, her heavy hoodie sweat shirt, water, and her fruit ropes. Chomping on a few of those calmed her nerves. She sighed heavily as she paced the dressing area. While she was waiting, she had to choose slower songs to calm her racy nerves. Right before it was time to walk out, she would crank up the heavy metal.

James was nearby, keeping calm and keeping everyone organized and focused. She didn't know how he carried that off.

"You set, Ash?" James brushed her shoulder, checking in on her mood.

Pulling the headphones off, she breathed easier seeing him. "I think so. It's the waiting game now." She fidgeted.

"Yeah, let's get you moving around. Come on." James waved her on.

She followed him to an open section away from the others. He worked with her to loosen her up, making her move around and get her mind right.

The announcements came on, and Ashley froze, not believing the time had come.

"Let's go; they're almost ready to begin."

They walked to the front of the venue to see the first fight. Fighters were lined up, waiting for their turns. James talked with the other fighters from the gym as Ashley stood by, her excitement and nerves rising by the minute.

The announcers called in the first pair of fighters, and the music began. She and James stood outside the curtain that was blocking off the main event from the waiting area.

Not long after the fight began, Ashley had to walk away. She couldn't watch as her anxiety increased. She ducked back to the area behind the curtain and grabbed a water bottle off the table set up for the competitors.

James noticed she'd left and followed. He quietly came up beside her. "Ash, you okay?"

She turned her head sideways to glance at him. "Yeah"—she sighed—"I can't believe it's time. Jittery, that's all." She sipped her water.

"You'll do great, kid. Remember what we've been working on. Keep it simple."

"Right, simple. Got it." She gulped her water.

"You're up in two fights. Want to get some air?"

"Yeah, you sure? Can you leave the guys?" She nodded toward the curtain.

"They're fine. Come on." He tilted his head in the opposite direction from the ring.

Ashley followed James toward a back entrance so that they could step outside for a while. The security guard stood by the door, nodding, and let them by.

The cool air felt like a cold splash of water against her skin; she breathed it in, already feeling better. She started moving around, bouncing, doing a little boxer's shuffle, and throwing light jabs. While James talked with the guard on duty, Ashley escaped to her world, blocking out the distractions, tuning out the voice in her head that said, *You can't do this.*

After several minutes, she heard the distant cheers from inside the arena and felt a surge of adrenaline. *This is it.*

James turned to Ashley. "Ready to head in?"

She nodded. "Yeah. I am ready."

***

Walking down the hall toward the arena, the sounds became louder. Her senses were on high alert. She heard everything—the crowd yelling, the sounds of the fighters hitting the mat, the ref banging on the mat, and the bell ending a round. The spectators started moving around during the brief intermission before the next round started.

Kendra was slated to go on next. Ashley to follow. Ashley told Kendra she would be there for her, watching her match.

Behind the curtain, Ashley heard the buzz of the competitors and coaches, ones that were lining up and ones that were done for the night—winners and losers, emotions ranging from elite happiness to extreme lows, anxiety and nervousness to pumped energy. It was easy to get sucked into everyone's drama, but Ashley tried to stay in her own bubble.

James led the way, keeping her close and shielding her from the crowds. They stood by the side of the arena, close to the waiting area, so they could watch the fight up close and not be stuck out in the stands.

The music started. The energy of the audience increased. The seats were filled.

"Go get 'em, Kendra," James called out to Kendra as she walked past.

Ashley cheered her on as Kendra climbed into the ring. "You've got this, Kendra!"

She gave Ashley a thumbs-up and a big smile. Kendra stood before the ref for the prefight check then entered the ring.

Once the bell sounded to start the round, Ashley felt her adrenaline surging. She needed to step away again. She'd watch the video footage of Kendra later. Ashley returned to the waiting area and stepped into the bathroom one more time before she was up.

To stay on schedule, James retrieved her gear from the back room. When Ashley returned, he had her wraps lined up and her water bottle out. "Sit, I'll do your wraps." He shook out the first wrap.

Ashley smiled. James knew she struggled with the wraps when she was nervous.

He swiftly wrapped her wrists perfectly. Unlike when she did it, James's were never too tight or too loose.

"Thank you." She stared at her hands.

"You're welcome." He held her wrapped hands a moment longer. "I got your gloves."

She drank some water then took her mouth guard out of its case.

"Let's do this." He gave her a high five, and they walked out to the holding area.

***

Ashley paced while James looked through the curtain. It seemed as though Kendra would take the win. James turned to Ashley as she sidled up to him to get a better look.

"You've got this, Ash. Keep your head in the fight. Make sure to breathe." He smiled, and she nodded as her gaze lingered on his lips.

At that moment, the bell rang, and the final round was over. The judges took a moment to review and ruled that Kendra had the win. The ref raised her arm; the crowd cheered. She held her hands up and looked to Ashley, elated.

Ashley waved back, excited for her friend. Kendra worked hard and deserved this win more than anyone.

Ashley's nerves were frayed. She was excited but a wreck; she hoped she could pull this off without panicking and forgetting combinations.

James was talking to her, helping to keep her mind from wandering to a bad place. "All right, Ashley, are you ready?"

She was distracted by the crowd, Kendra, and all the celebrating.

He turned to her and put his hands on her shoulders. "Look at me; stay focused. Okay?" He bent closer to her and smiled.

"Yeah, I'm ready to go." She nodded, trying to convince herself.

Her walk-in song played as they stood behind the curtain, waiting for the cue. She shook her arms out, staying loose and breathing.

The guy at the curtain nodded to them, signaling their entry.

***

Elated. That was how Ashley felt. She was getting the chance to fight her first real fight. Then, a pit settled in her stomach. *Now, I'm scared to death.*

She could get her ass kicked and get seriously hurt. A black eye, a bloody nose, or worse—broken ribs. *I must be crazy.*

Still, the thrill of the fight outweighed her fear. Adrenaline coursed through her veins. *Am I ready? Or has this all been smoke and mirrors?* she contemplated, as she looked around the arena.

Suddenly, silence and calm enveloped her; then a sudden surge filled her. She heard a voice in her head telling her, *You are ready.*

***

James and Ashley walked out together, the music blaring and a small spotlight following their path. Adrenaline shot through her veins. She stopped in front of the ref.

He patted her down, checked her gloves, her ears, and her mouth. Then, he nodded to James that she was good to go.

James popped her mouth guard in for her. He hadn't been this close to her lips in a while.

Ashley laughed a little as her lip got stuck on the guard.

Clearing his throat, James adjusted it to fit, his eyes lingering on her mouth. "All set?" He was all business now.

"Thanks." *No time to dwell on wanting to kiss him...not when there is a psycho chick ready to kick my ass,* Ashley thought.

Ashley climbed into the ring and started her warm-up, loosening up her shoulders and hips. Shadowboxing, moving around the ring, staying loose, and keeping it light. Her opponent, Sam, did the same. Ashley could barely look at her.

The referee directed them to their corners.

In her corner, James held her shoulders, talking in her ear, giving her his strength, his voice, his words, pulling her into focus, into the moment. She was ready, no matter the outcome.

The ref signaled them to the center of the ring, the bell rang, and they touched gloves.

***

She planned out every scenario and counter for any possible attack. She would show Sam that she could fight. She might get pummeled in the process, but she would do this. The key was in her killer hooks and kicks and watching for patterns. Sam always threw the same combo, starting low with a rear hook-jab, then moving in high to an overhead hook.

Ashley laughed once she noticed the frequency of it. It was not even that good a combo, except for the fact that it had caught her off guard. So, she supposed it must have been a fairly good move, after all. But she knew that overhead hook, which always surprised her, came after the low hook-jab to the belly. Every damn time. She thought, *Time to get out of the way and throw a body kick or a body hook. Or a low cross, high hook.*

She felt the moves as she pictured how this fight would go. Sam was theatrical with spinning kicks and punches. Ashley knew those took a lot of energy, and if she could avoid contact and prolong the fight, she could wear her down. Her own side kick to the belly could do damage if Sam didn't catch her kick. Sam loved to catch kicks.

She imagined the combination playing out, imagined the push and the force behind each move. Her moves needed to be sharp, she needed to be three steps ahead, and she needed to get out of Sam's way. Then, she had to kick fast, kick hard, and kick through her.

***

The back of her opponent's glove landed with a thud against Ashley's nose. Her adrenaline moved her forward until her cheek and nose started throbbing.

Am I bleeding? Ashley touched her nose and checked her glove. Nothing there, but the feeling of her nose filling up was unmistakable.

Her opponent moved in. Ashley knew it was a matter of time. She sniffled, moved around, and checked her glove again. This time, there was a bright-red splotch on the gold band of her glove. *Blood.*

Sam saw the blood, nodding toward Ashley. "Hey, you're bleeding."

No shit, Ashley thought.

James saw the amount of blood and yelled to the ref for a time-out. The ref called it since the blood flow was heavy and spattering around the mat.

Ashley sat on a stool in her corner, feeling queasy. James stood by her side as the physician made his way up into the ring. He applied light pressure to Ashley's nose with an ice pack and a towel, having to change the towel because the blood flow was so heavy.

James held her shoulder. "You hanging in there, kid?"

"Yeah." But she wasn't. She knew she should have gotten out of the way quicker, kept her guard up. She swallowed and tasted the tinny taste of blood. "Yuck." She grabbed the towel and spit out a clump of blood, feeling light-headed.

"Here, Ash, rinse out." James held the water bottle and a bucket for her to spit into.

Glamorous, she thought. She watched the cleanup crew mopping up the blood from the floor of the ring. *My blood.*

James could see he was losing her, and he stood in front of her, blocking the view. "All right. Look at me."

The doctor continued holding the ice pack lightly against her nose, and James held an ice pack against the back of her neck. He needed to redirect her focus to the fight.

"You have to keep those kicks going; she gets distracted by them. She's all about punches, so guard up and kick. Got it?"

Ashley nodded, feeling herself regain confidence. The bleeding stopped, and the throbbing was gone.

"Nose is good. Feeling all right to continue?" The physician was concerned and wanted to make sure she was strong enough to fight.

"Yeah, I'm okay." She inhaled deeply and nodded.

The doctor made his way out of the ring as quickly as he'd appeared.

James rubbed her back with the ice pack. "Get back out there, and remember—kick."

Ashley stood up, ready to go in strong as the bell rang.

Taking the punches and the kicks, she felt nothing; she was numb. Jab, cross, backfist, kick. Averting punches and defending kicks, Ashley struggled to conserve her energy. Jabs coming in faster, hooks off the side of her head—she fought them off sloppily. She threw jabs, front kicks, and leg kicks, keeping her opponent at bay for the time being.

After throwing a body kick, her kick was caught, and Ashley froze. *How many times did we do this in sparring?* She felt herself falter, and then she was down. Hurriedly, she popped back up and went into her fighting stance.

The bell rang and the second round was over.

Ashley went to James for her water and pep talks. He instructed her to concentrate and not get distracted. She was feeling overwhelmed and trying to rein in her emotions by focusing on her breathing.

The bell rang, and Sam came at her hard.

Ashley tried to stick with defensive moves, watching and trying to predict Sam's next attacks. Then, she homed in and started kicking. Ashley's punches were not solid, but her kicks were fast and hard. She was able to hold Sam back with teeps, front kicks, and double body kicks. Punches flew and a jab slipped through Ashley's guard, catching her off the nose again.

Ashley had to get her bearings, but her opponent didn't let up. Ashley angled out of the way, gaining a moment to come up with a plan. Sam caught her kick, and this time she was ready, punching her way out. Her leg was thrown, spinning her back to her opponent. She used it to set up a spinning backhand, landing across Sam's cheek, pushing her back. Sam came back fast with punches as Ashley returned with a body kick. Sam caught her leg and swept her other leg out from under her, dropping her to the mat.

The bell rang, signaling the end of the third round. The fight was over.

The ref came to the center and had both girls stand with him as the judges made their decision. It wasn't a knockout, so the winner would be decided based on points. Ashley knew she didn't win. There were so many times Sam outshone her in technique.

The judge gave the signal, and the ref raised Sam's arm for the win.

Ashley nodded and hugged Sam. "Nice work."

"Good work out there." Sam grabbed Ashley's gloved hand.

Sam's coaches ran in and pulled her aside, high-fiving as she received her medal.

Ashley grimaced.

"Ash, it's all right. Come on." James pulled her away from the crowd.

Lisa was there in a heartbeat. "Hey, you looked good out there. That girl was tough to beat." Lisa hugged her friend. "Seriously, nice work. Don't be down on yourself."

"Yeah, thanks." *Easier said than done.*

James moved them along to the back room, knowing Ashley wouldn't want to see too many people.

Lisa stayed with them for a while before meeting up with Vince. "We are heading out. You coming?" Lisa held her hand.

"I don't know. I'm wiped." Ashley shook her head.

Lisa knew she was hurting, and going out was what she needed. "James, work on her. Okay?" Lisa gave James a hug.

"Thanks, Lisa. See you later." James turned back to Ashley. "Ash, look at me." He placed his hands on her shoulders. "You were solid out there. This was a huge step. Don't let the points get to you."

"Yeah, but I still lost." She wanted to scream and cry, all at the same time.

"Okay, yes, you didn't beat her. But you put on a show. You kept up, hit for hit, lasted the full three rounds, and landed more kicks than she landed. It was impressive."

Ashley had to laugh. She didn't think she could have looked impressive out there, but she appreciated his sentiments.

"You know I wouldn't bullshit you. I was impressed, Ashley." His voice and his expression softened. "Be proud." He put his hand on her shoulder. Having his reassurances and his words now meant as much as a win.

"Thanks, James." She fought to hold back her tears, but they poured down her cheeks.

James pulled her into a hug, squeezing her tight. "It's all right, Ash."

CHAPTER 39

Dreamy violet sky
Smoldering dark eyes
Burning red heat
Hands pulsating against my skin
Cool breath on my lips
Soft smile brightening my days
Blinding star-filled nights

A shley bounded up the stairs to the "beach cottage." *This is much larger than a cottage,* she thought. James's client had told him he was free to stay at the cottage while the client was out of state at his other home for a couple of months.

She knocked on the door, even though James had told her to come right in when she arrived. She cautiously pushed open the large mahogany door and called out to him, "Hello?" She walked lightly through the entryway, glancing around. Soft music drifted down the hall. "James?" She walked toward the front sitting area.

The late afternoon sun was shining through the windows, giving the room a warm glow. The room was furnished with rich-cream furniture surrounded by pale-yellow walls with white trim and wainscoting. Large, white built-in cabinets flanked the oversized stone fireplace. She stopped to look at pictures on the shelves.

"Hello, Ashley." James had entered the room without her hearing him.

She jumped slightly. "James."

He walked over and gave her a hug. "I'm so glad you're here."

Ashley felt perfect in his arms. "Me, too. This house is amazing." She looked around the decadent room.

"It's quite a home. I'll show you around. Would you like some wine first? I have a delicious red that's perfect for you." He raised his eyebrow, putting her under his spell with his beautiful, crooked grin.

"Hmmm, yes. Sounds perfect."

James lightly brushed his lips over hers.

She felt her legs go weak.

"Shall we?" He motioned toward the kitchen. He poured the wine as she took in the details of the kitchen. Pretty maple-wood cabinets and flooring. State-of-the-art appliances and beautiful granite counters. James followed her gaze. "Some cottage, huh?"

"Um, yeah, that's what I was thinking."

He handed Ashley her glass. "Cheers." They clinked glasses.

The wine filled Ashley with a warm feeling.

"This is my client's third residence." He led her toward the living room and stood aside so she could enter.

Not believing her eyes, Ashley took it all in. The room was beautifully decorated in grey and white tones, maple-wood floors, a mahogany bar, and a wall of windows overlooking the view of the ocean and rock ledge. The room was adorned with dozens of lit candles.

"Oh my gosh." She caught her breath and looked at James; the glow of the candles reflected in his eyes.

"I thought you'd like this room." He kissed her, smiling. "You like?"

She was convinced that her legs were going to give out on her once and for all, so she held on to his arm. "Yes, this is incredible. Where did you get all of the candles?" Looking around, she saw there were even more than she first realized.

Sheepishly, James looked around. "I went to a bedding store downtown, and I think I bought them out." He laughed nervously. "I wanted this to be…memorable…for you and me. I bought a few other things for us while I was there. Some blankets for the beach, and I saw these candles and…" He brushed a stray strand of hair away from her eyes.

She could see him scanning her face, searching her eyes. "Thank you, I love it."

His eyes softened, and he kissed her again. He led her over to a table set with small plates—a display of olives, meats, cheeses, and crusty bread. "Let's eat." He pulled a chair out for Ashley. They enjoyed their wine and the view of the setting sun over the shore of Marblehead.

The house was situated on two acres of lush green lawn that spread from the front of the house to the back, where a landscape of rocks cascaded from the backyard down to the ocean. The windows on the rear side of the house overlooked the rock wall, where waves crashed during high tide. There was a sandy trail that led to a small beach. Houses lined the shore around the bend of rocks, ever increasing in elevation. The beach side of this house was private and led to more residences with private beach access.

"If this was my house, I would never leave this view." Ashley took in the view, and James nodded in agreement. "How often does your client stay here?"

"Not as much as he would like. He has an interesting job that takes him out of the country frequently."

Curious, Ashley asked, "What does he do for a living?"

"No one knows what his actual job is." James chuckled, knowing that his client had a supersensitive position in the CIA, but not many others were privy to that information. James kept his clients' secrets to himself. That was one of the reasons they chose to train with him.

When they were finished with the food and wine, Ashley helped James take the dishes into the kitchen.

"Leave them here." James took the dishes from Ash.

"Let me clean up since you did all of this work."

He took her hand. "Let's leave them. Besides, we should not leave all of those candles unattended."

Ashley giggled and followed him into the living room. The sun had started its descent behind the fluffy pink clouds, and the room was lit by the glow of the candles. James took Ashley's glass and set it with his own on the coffee table. He drew her toward him and kissed her long and deep.

Ashley pulled his body closer to hers. Her legs were fine now. She felt a surge of energy and heat as his hands moved down her back. She kissed him a little harder and put her hands lower on his hips. He leaned back and looked at her, bringing his hands to her shoulders, lowering the straps of her dress. He kissed her along her shoulder and up toward her neck.

Ashley's breath caught in her throat, and she let out a small sigh.

"Is this all right?" James's voice was so low she could feel the heat from his breath on her.

She could hardly form words. "Yes."

He slowly lowered her dress. Ashley started to remove her shoes, but he stopped her. "Keep those on." He smirked and helped her step out of her dress.

She felt self-conscious, standing in the middle of the room with only her bra, underwear, and high heels on while he was fully dressed. *Not for long,* she thought.

James touched her and looked at her as if she were a work of art. "You are so beautiful." He took away any feeling she had of being self-conscious.

He kissed her shoulder, her chest, and down toward her belly. His hands followed his kisses and felt amazing over her whole body. He stood back up and led her to an oversized chair. The chair, Ashley noticed earlier, was a lounge, but with a circular shape at the head, enough for two to sit comfortably. Or roomy enough for something other than sitting.

Ashley started to unbutton James's shirt. Her hands were shaky, and she hoped she could get all the buttons undone.

He began taking his shirt off, and she stopped him. "No, let me."

He watched her intently, his breath quickening as she touched his chest. He let out a sigh. Slowly, she slid his shirt off him, always keeping her hands on him. She undid his belt and pants, hands shaking. She was so nervous and excited she could not contain it anymore.

He kicked his shoes off, and she slid his pants down as he stepped out of them. She slid back into the chair as James climbed in toward her. His movements were so sexy and animallike as he crawled on top of her. He stopped and slid her shoes off, slowly pausing to kiss her calf, her knee, then her thigh…he looked up at her with that eyebrow raised and his crooked smile.

Ashley's heart beat out of her chest. He continued his slow ascent, stopping along the way to touch or kiss random parts of her. By the time he was face-to-face with her, she was shivering.

Looking amused, James leaned on his elbow. "Are you cold?" He smirked, enjoying this. He leaned over to get a blanket. "Our beach blankets." He grabbed them off the couch and was back in an instant. He lifted Ashley's body with one arm and laid one of the blankets under her. Then, he covered her with the other.

Ashley grabbed on to James, pulling him down on top of her. "I'm not cold." She needed to feel his body heat against her.

He could see the fire in her eyes and feel the heat of her skin against his. She brought his head down close to her so she could whisper in his ear, "I want you so much." Her hands roaming all over his body.

"Ashley, you have me." He looked into her eyes and outlined her jaw with his fingers. Kissing her mouth, he took in her taste, her smell, and the feel of her hands on his back. Her body.

The heat between them was making him crazy. He wanted to take his time with her, but she was pressing into him, breathing his name, and wrapping her legs around his hips. With each breath, he was losing more of the control that he was trying so desperately to keep.

In those moments that he was able to look at her face and see the light in her eyes, she reflected the way he felt inside. Two becoming one, ebbing and flowing. Crashing and then calm. Energy spent, bodies entangled and encircled by peace.

James lowered himself, his head resting next to hers. Their sweat-covered bodies molded together as one. Her lips brushed his cheek as she held his head in her hands. The candles gave off an auburn glow in the dark of night that reflected off their bodies.

James started to move, but Ashley held him in place, not wanting to break this moment.

"Am I squishing you?" James whispered hoarsely.

"Not at all." She smiled and closed her eyes. "You feel...perfect."

He kissed her ear then her neck, sending a shiver and a wave of warmth through her core.

"This is perfect," James repeated back to her and held her so close, not wanting to ever let go.

They drifted in and out of sleep as they lay on the chair.

"Want to head upstairs? I can get you a shower started." He traced her jaw, followed by a kiss.

"I would love a shower...if you join me." She smiled, leaning into him.

He smiled. "Let's go."

James wrapped one of the blankets around Ashley, then slipped on his boxers. Their clothes were in a heap, so James scooped them up. They giggled as he led her into the hall and up the stairs. Ashley felt as if she were a teenager sneaking through the house with her boyfriend.

He flicked on the lights to reveal a beautiful guest suite with an oversized king bed loaded with pillows and comfortable-looking blankets. A bathroom, with a Jacuzzi tub and a walk-in glass shower, was situated off the far end of the room. There was a picture window above the tub, overlooking the ocean.

James placed their clothes on top of the bed, then started the shower. While the shower was warming up, James lit a couple of candles in the bedroom and bathroom. "Why don't you get started, and I'll be right in." The three dozen candles burning in the main room had him nervous. He wanted to run down, blow them out, and return for the shower.

"Okay." Ashley dropped the blanket and made her way past James and into the shower.

He stood there with his mouth open, speechless.

"Don't be too long, or I may finish before you come back."

He was about to jump in with her and be damned if the whole house burned down…but he had to blow those candles out. His nerves would not allow him to enjoy this moment if he left them burning.

"I'll be right back!" he called into the room. James turned to go downstairs, but stopped and returned quickly to the bathroom, opening the shower door. "Do not go anywhere," he warned with his most serious look.

Ashley laughed and thought, *There is no way in hell I will leave this shower before he comes back.*

James hurried as fast as he could, thinking he'd broken a record for extinguishing all those candles in under a minute. He hopped over furniture and used his fingers, anything to speed the process and get to that shower. *Motivation,* he thought.

Once he was positive all possible fire hazards were taken care of, he raced back up the stairs, taking two at a time. His boxers were off in mere seconds, and he was opening the door to the shower. He was out of breath from racing around like a lunatic, but seeing her made his heart race even faster.

"What did I miss?"

Ashley made room for him under the double showerheads. He moved his hands over Ashley's slick body, lathering up the soap on her skin. When James concentrated on slowly stroking up and around her chest, Ashley moaned slightly, tilting her head back. He put his arm around her hips, pulling her closer, then gently moved his hand up to her throat, carefully massaging the soap into her neck and shoulders. Then, he moved those amazing hands back down to her chest and back, around her hips and down her front.

"My turn." She took the soap from him and began to lather his chest, his arms, and his beautifully sculpted back.

They rinsed off and held on to each other, not wanting this moment to end. Ashley rested her head on his shoulder and closed her eyes. Lifting her chin so delicately, he kissed her beautiful lips.

"Ready to get out?"

"Yes, for sure."

He turned off the water and retrieved two thick sage-colored towels from the linen closet. Wrapping Ashley in her towel, he kissed her again.

She grabbed another towel and wrapped her hair up. After drying off and walking into the bedroom, she noticed more candles were lit. "When did you light these?" She towel-dried her hair as James turned down the bed.

He smiled. "While you were in the shower. Almost broke my leg blowing out the ones downstairs."

She laughed, returning to the bathroom and using the hair dryer that was set out on the counter. She went back into the bedroom as James dropped his towel and pulled on his boxers. He stood there with his perfectly sculpted back and butt to her, and she admired the beautiful view. He was so comfortable with his physique.

He turned, caught her watching, and was immediately flattered. "Is it warm enough in here?"

She nodded, still admiring James.

"Yes," Ashley lied as she looked to the bed and felt herself shiver, but she knew the shivering was nerves and excitement at the thought of being here with him.

"You're a terrible liar." James winked and clicked on a heated blanket covering the bed.

The bed was the largest she had ever seen, with a luxurious comforter and lush blankets. She couldn't wait to sink into that bed with James next to her. She rummaged through her duffel to find her sexy sleep T-shirt and undies. She slipped them on then returned their towels to the bathroom.

James waited for her to return and turned off the lights once she was in bed. He climbed in and snuggled up to her. He leaned up on his elbow, brushing aside her damp strands of hair. "Better?"

"Yes." She snuggled against him.

This was not so scary anymore. This was pure and true. She felt a beginning without an end, a trail that led to endless possibilities. She felt deep, red-hot passion, and a cool-blue calm from him. There was no black or hate, no control or jealousy, only a golden light and a bright glow of warmth.

Surrounded by James's love and protected wholly by him, she finally felt at ease. And that night, she slept peacefully.

***

Ashley awoke to warm sunlight coming through the plantation blinds. She felt herself smile before she even opened her eyes. *Who wakes up smiling,* she thought? *Me!* She was reminded of the beautiful, hot, steamy night she'd shared with James. Her smile grew as she stretched toward his side of the bed.

Blinking her eyes a few times to wake up, she saw that James was not there. Lying in what felt like a cloud, Ashley stretched out and brought her hand to her body, trailing the path that James had covered with his hands, from her lips down to her throat, remembering how he carefully stopped at her throat and let the heat of his hand heal her, reminding her that the past was behind her. She breathed in his scent and longed for him to be next to her at that moment.

Slowly, she rose from the bed. After using the bathroom and brushing her teeth, she opened the plantation blinds in the bedroom to let in the light and take in the view of the ocean. To her surprise, James was below, standing on the beach and taking in the same view as she was. He stood, beautifully, in his jeans and white T-shirt, bare feet in the sand, holding his cup of coffee. Ashley touched the glass as if she could touch him. She felt a connection to him from deep within her.

Then, her heart began to race. *What am I doing?* she thought. She should grab her clothes and run. *This can't be real; it is all too perfect; something is going to go wrong.* Last night, the candles, the shower—all of it. *Is he feeling the same way I am? Was he smiling, as I was, when he first woke? Did he have that deep warmth inside of him as he thought of me? Or did he want to turn and run, or jump in the deep blue sea and swim far, far away from me?*

As if he could feel her watching him, James slowly turned and looked up at Ashley with her hand on the glass, watching him. Her fear was pushed aside the minute their eyes connected. That smile, those warm eyes squinting to see her—they answered all her questions and squashed any doubts she had.

He nodded to her and waved for her to come down. Ashley nodded back and held up a finger, mouthing, "One minute." She rummaged through her bag and pulled on a bra, T-shirt, and jeans. Her hair was a hot mess as she combed her fingers through it and made her way down to see James.

The smell of coffee greeted her in the kitchen. A cup was placed out for her, as was cream and sugar. Quickly, she fixed herself a cup and walked out to meet James on the beach. She followed the sandy walk to where he stood, looking picture-perfect, his profile outlined by the golden morning sun. Her heart raced, in a good way, as she approached.

He turned to see her and stood still, watching her come toward him. That look, he realized, was for him, and he caught his breath for the hundredth time that weekend. *How is it that she is here with me?* he thought, and silently prayed that he would not fuck this up.

"Good morning, gorgeous." He leaned toward her and kissed her.

Ashley melted into him and put her arm around his back, careful not to spill her coffee on him. "Good morning." Ashley kissed him back and let her free hand slide across his back.

"You should wear your hair like this more often." James stood back with that smirk and tilted his head. "On second thought, no, you shouldn't."

Ashley was totally confused. "Um. Okay…"

"No, don't get me wrong. You look amazing, sexy…uh…and yeah…that's why you shouldn't wear it like that anywhere else…unless you're with me." He laughed.

She felt amazing and sexy when she was with James, so she wasn't entirely positive that it was the hairstyle making her look that way. "You make me feel amazing."

She looked up and saw her reflection in James's eyes. His eyes were crystal clear and perfect. She could stare at them all day. At that moment, Ashley felt that he could read her thoughts. She blushed and looked away.

"Last night was incredible. Did you sleep okay?" He brought his lips to her cheek.

"Yes, like a rock." She hugged him closer.

"I hope you'll spend the day with me. We can do whatever you like. We can take out the boat for the day, grab a bite to eat… Your wish is my command."

"Sounds like a perfect day, then!" She stepped back from him, nodding.

"All right. Shall we?" James raised that persuasive eyebrow, and they walked toward the house. They sat in two white-wood Adirondack chairs on the dark-stained, wraparound deck that overlooked the rocky shore and had a view of the bright-blue sky.

James was smiling, looking deep in thought, staring at his coffee. "Ashley…I mean it when I say last night was amazing. Uh"—he looked down, and she noticed a hint of blush in his cheeks—"I keep replaying it in my mind and…"

Ashley knew what he was going to say. She reached for his hand. "Me, too. I wish we could do it all again." Now, it was Ashley's cheeks that heated up.

James leaned over to kiss her. "Ashley," he breathed.

It sent chills up her spine. She moved closer to him. James had his hands in her hair, and she climbed out of her seat. She stood over him, kissing him as his hands moved up and down her legs.

James stood and, with a sexy smile, nodded toward the house.

She laughed, took him by the hand, and started walking backwards toward the door.

With a devilish grin, James teased, making it look as if he were chasing her down. She shrieked and laughed and ran into the house as James playfully chased her up the stairs. She stopped abruptly at the bedroom door, turning toward him, her heart racing. He stopped short and was breathing heavily.

Turning his sexy gaze on, he tilted his head and moved toward her slowly. She felt as if she were his prey as he taunted her, lured her. She went willingly into his arms, letting her hands roam as he kissed her deeply, letting out a small groan as she grabbed on to his hips.

She moved him back toward the bed, which was all in a heap from their fun last night. Now, it was her turn for control. She pushed him back onto the bed, and he willingly submitted.

She took her time coming closer and then crawled on top of him. Ashley kissed his stomach and worked her way up to his chest, his neck, then his jaw and his lips, so full and ready for her. James put his hands on her, wanting to pull her even closer than she already was. Ashley needed to feel the heat of his body against hers.

James took full pleasure in having Ashley assume control and do whatever she wanted to him. Their bodies moved together and began to perfectly meld into one, while their coffee was long forgotten on the small end table between the Adirondack chairs.

***

The sun warmed her skin as she sat in the stands. Hearing children and families enjoying the day at the baseball fields pulled at Ashley's heart. For a split second she felt a sense of loss, or maybe it was longing. Longing for the life that could have been. She thought she was headed there so long ago, but how wrong she was.

She didn't long for her past life; she longed for the stability of a life in the country, with kids and baseball fields. The smell of fresh-cut grass and the taste of home. That's the feeling she had deep down. That feeling was here; that feeling was with James.

Her heart skipped a beat. For a moment, she felt the need to run away creep in again. *It's too soon. This is too perfect.* James looked up at her from the field. She saw his slow smirk light up his face. Sunglasses shielded his eyes, but she felt the heat from them and knew the sparkle that was there for her. Warmth spread through her again, and her heart began to race in that good way. She realized she wanted to run toward him, not away from him.

Family meant a lot to James, especially his nephews. When he asked if it was all right if they stopped by the athletic field where the boys were playing, she didn't have the heart to say no. He himself looked like a little boy when he saw them. His eyes lit up, and his excitement showed through, as much as theirs showed for him. They loved him like a father. Ever since his brother-in-law passed away, James had made a point to be present for them as much as possible. They had an unconditional love for their uncle and liked when he invited them to the gym. Ashley cherished seeing how he was with the boys. It brought out such an unguarded side of him that not many saw.

James tossed the ball with the older nephew before his game, laughing and giving him tips on how to field the ball. When it was time for him to join the team, James gave him a hug and pulled on the brim of his cap. His nephew jumped up and gave a big hug back, then ran off to his teammates. James stood watching for a moment then headed back up to Ashley.

"Sorry to leave you up here."

"No problem. They are cuties, and obviously they love having you here."

"We won't stay long. I appreciate you coming out here with me." James took hold of her hand.

Ashley felt the warmth of his touch and melted toward him. "I don't mind. I wouldn't want to be anywhere else." She meant that with all her heart.

They sat for a couple of innings and then walked down around the fields to check out his other nephew's game that was ending.

James leaned against the fence. "What would you like to do today?" James placed his hand around her back.

Ashley's mind wandered back to that morning in bed and wished to head back that way soon.

As if reading her mind, James leaned close and spoke low in her ear, "I would like to get you back to the house soon."

Delicious chills ran up her spine. "I would like that." She stepped back. "Well, we should enjoy this beautiful day for a little bit longer. Do you want to stop for a bite to eat, then head back to the house?"

"Yes, ma'am." He kissed her nose and held her hand as they walked to the car.

CHAPTER 40

Monday morning came quickly. The gym was busy; the regulars were all back to their training schedules after the weekend. Most of the fighters trained outside of the gym on the weekends. Spending so many hours there during the week could get monotonous, so the coaches encouraged most of their clients to try other forms of training a couple of days per week and to take one day off.

Some of the fighters took a midweek break. Ashley typically took Saturday as her day off or her light workout day, sometimes only walking. By Friday night, her body usually couldn't take any more.

She needed to train hard this week. Competitions were coming up, and she wanted to get in on as many as James thought she could handle. *James.* The thought of him made her insides feel twisted, in a good way. Nothing like the knots she used to get from Stephen…

She checked in at the desk, trying not to be obvious by glancing upstairs toward James's office. At that exact moment, he walked out of his office and looked right at her. That slow smile crossed his lips, and he nodded for her to come up.

In her mind, she raced up the stairs, crossed the floor, and looked straight into his eyes. Then, as she walked in his office, she kicked the door shut behind her, dropped her bag, pushed him up against the wall, and…

In reality, she clumsily walked toward the stairs, adjusting her hair, fidgeting with her duffel bag, and clearing her throat.

James watched her with his hands in his pockets. "Hey, pal. How's it going?" He gestured for her to come into his office.

Ashley entered the dimly lit office, holding her bag on her shoulder. *Talk, yes, talking would be a good thing right now,* she thought. "Great." She nervously laughed, trying to sound as if she had it all together.

"This is going to be tougher than I thought." James looked down toward the floor.

She was hoping this wasn't *the* talk. She imagined him saying, *Well, now that we are at my work, we can't let anyone know...*

"Yes, um, don't worry. I won't say anything to anyone..."

James's brow furrowed. "Ash, that's not what I meant. I would tell everyone here if you'd let me. What I meant was it's difficult seeing you here and not remembering...this weekend." He looked at her with a soft smile.

"Oh!" Ashley's face reddened.

"We have a lot of work to do to get you ready for competition. I don't want to be a distraction."

Yeah, too late for that, Ashley thought.

"You know I still have to be a hard-ass." He looked down to the floor for a moment, then returned his gaze to Ashley with a concerned expression. "You probably won't like me too much."

Ashley knew this was the risk of them being together. She'd need some thick skin because James was tough, but she knew he'd be especially hard on her. "I'm sure I'll hate you some days. And you won't be happy with me. I get that it's gonna get ugly. We knew what we were getting into." She swallowed hard. "Right?" She felt desperate for a second, wondering if he would turn her over to another trainer.

James moved closer to her, his eyes drawing her in deeper.

Stay focused, she told herself. "We'll make this work. We have to," she said and shifted her position, holding her bag tighter.

He stared at her a moment longer; then he leaned toward her.

Ashley froze, not knowing what he was going to do here in his office, where anyone could walk in.

James looked in her eyes and whispered, "Of course, we'll make this work." He lightly touched her arm. "Now, get your ass out on the floor. It's the beginning of hell week, my dear."

***

Hell was an understatement. Ashley's arms would surely fall off with all the push-ups, battle ropes, and sandbag drags James inflicted on her. *This apparently is arms day. No chance of lifting my arms to shampoo my hair later.* The drills didn't end. Interval after interval of punches, uppercuts, speed bags, and body-weight exercises. Then, an unending number of crunches and ab work. She thought she was going to die by the end of the workout, and that sounded appealing.

***

Ashley slowly walked downstairs to the showers. The rest of her group stuck around to tell each other how strong they were and how they would kick ass at the next fight. *Don't these people have jobs?* She couldn't wait to shower and get the heck out of there. She'd love to shower and go home to bed, except she had to go to work.

As she was heading out, James was still out on the floor, working with one of his guys, preparing him for an upcoming match. Ashley hoped to sneak out without a pep talk.

"Hey, Ashley, nice work out there. Don't go lifting anything too heavy today!" James called out to her as she passed.

He's an ass, she thought. "Yeah, have a good one, too," she called back.

James laughed.

Ouch, she thought. Carrying her duffel was even a chore.

CHAPTER 41

*I*ntensity builds the closer we get. In low, guard is up, fists are flying, and kicks are strong. No break, hard to breathe, move away, duck, and counter. Sweat pours out; adrenaline spikes. Move in close; do not stop until the bell rings.

Hell week was not something that Ashley ever wanted to experience again. She was beyond tired, severely exhausted.

James had started this new regimen, and it sucked. Waking up and seeing 5:00 a.m. on the clock, she wanted to pull the covers over her head. She was in the gym by six o'clock for warm-ups, stretching, and cardio, then to the ring for sparring.

James added in a weight-training regimen for her to follow one to two days that week. Ashley's body was totally spent by the end of each day, muscles screaming and craving rest. The best part on those days was sinking into a warm bath at night. That almost made it all worth it. *Almost.*

James also lost his sense of humor during hell week. Not that he had much of one to begin with at work, but now he was all business. Some days, he manhandled Ashley in the ring, making her repeat drill after drill, moving her into the exact stance, time after time, until she couldn't take it anymore.

He needed her ready for anything. This was a big competition, and Sam would be ready for her this time. She needed to be strong and focused. She thought she could win; she *needed* to win this fight.

***

"Ashley is going to ace this competition, James. You know that, right?" Lisa stood in the doorway to James's office.

Without looking up from his work, James answered, "She's working hard; she will be ready."

"Working hard? Are you kidding me? She is beyond that. She is freaking ready! You're riding that girl too hard. You're going to break her, James."

He put his pen down and sat back in his seat, crossing his arms and giving Lisa "the look." He thought, *Now she is going to tell me how to train my fighter?*

As if she read James's thoughts, Lisa looked at him sheepishly. "I know. I'm not telling you how to train your client. But she is fucking ready. I'm just saying…" With that, she turned and left. Lisa knew when she had pushed James to the edge, and then she knew when to leave him alone.

He was aware Ashley was ready. He couldn't let Ashley know that, though. She would lose her edge, that small amount of doubt that kept you wanting more. So, it continued for the week.

Ashley showed up at the gym in the morning. James worked her down to the bone during group training, as well as when they were one-on-one; she didn't know which one was worse. James homed in on Ashley and called her out, even if she was merely thinking of dogging it. *Damn him.* She couldn't get away with anything, even when she wasn't really trying to get away with anything.

He was right about one thing—she didn't like him much this week.

She was sapped of energy. Every day was eat, train, work, and sleep. After training, she hit the showers then headed to work, eating her premade and proportioned meals throughout the day. Aside from her one deadline that week, she luckily had a light schedule. She dragged herself home after work and up those bloody stairs to her apartment. Dinner was a necessity, but she was so dog-tired some nights she didn't even enjoy it.

James checked in with encouraging words via text. He knew not to push it, and he needed her to be headstrong.

James: *Only 2 more days in hell week. Stay strong, pal.*

James: *How's the shoulder? Nice job today.*

Then…

James: *I miss last weekend.*

Ashley missed it, too.

She also couldn't wait to crawl into bed. Then came heavenly sleep. Ashley slept like the dead. Thank God for that because that alarm came up fast, and then she went at it again.

Ashley craved the rest and recovery that she would get in a couple of days. Maybe she would see James, but not at the gym.

James: *Good night. Sweet dreams. J.*

Ashley was already there.

***

Finally, Friday rolled around. This was the last intense workout Ashley would have to endure of the four-week cycle. Today was a group day with high-intensity intervals for cardio. Next week was recovery week—lighter workouts with a concentration on sparring and fighting technique more than strengthening.

James waited outside of the locker room for Ash. Now that this intense week was done, he hoped to see her over the weekend. He was on edge, not knowing how she would feel about that. Everything that week had been intense. Day and night, he had had clients whom he was prepping for competition. He was getting burned-out and truly looking forward to a break…with Ashley…away from this place, he hoped.

She came out of the locker room, freshly showered and looking as if she was ready for a break as well. She was surprised to see James waiting by the door. "Hi, James."

"Hey, great work out there. How are you feeling?"

"I'm glad it's over; let's put it that way!"

"Yeah, I can't wait for this week to be done. I have a few more sessions today and one tonight."

There was an awkward silence.

"Well, I have to check in at work, but I'm off early this afternoon. I'm looking forward to a warm bath and bed."

James had the most delicious vision. He went for his most seductive smile. "That sounds inviting. Do you have any time to spend with me this weekend?"

Ashley was so beat and, a moment ago, couldn't envision anything but pj's and her comforter. However, the thought of seeing James outside of the gym was appealing. "Yes. What are you up to tomorrow?"

He wished to see her tonight and into tomorrow, but he could wait. "I'm yours for the day. Want me to pick you up? We can get out of the city. Or we can walk up by the Charles. Anything you wish."

Ashley felt her cheeks flush as she looked down to the floor. "Come over tomorrow. We can make a plan once you get there." She could not contain her smile.

"All right! Great, wherever you want to go."

He didn't get it. Her plan wasn't to go much farther than her bedroom...or the couch...or... She raised an eyebrow and gave her most devilish grin.

"What?" He was irresistible when he was clueless.

"Well, we don't have to go anywhere..." Ashley bit her lip and let that statement hang in the air for a bit.

"Oh! Yeah, oh... Definitely! Now, I'm not going to be able to think of anything else." James did his best seductive stare into her eyes, which was his usual gorgeous look.

Composing herself, she wondered if she had the same effect on him as he did on her? She leaned in and whispered, "Good, that was the point." *Touché.*

Now, he looked as if he had to catch his breath. That answered her question.

***

Ashley wandered through her day in a haze. She was walking, crossing busy intersections, riding the T, but not seeing anything.

She dragged through her workday, hoping she didn't make any careless errors, but knowing she probably had. Editing would be all over her on Monday. As 4:00 p.m. showed on her computer display, her body started to seize up, and her muscles were starting to realize the brutality of the work they'd endured that week. She needed to get up and walk before she couldn't.

Time to call it a day; her bath and bed were calling.

CHAPTER 42

"*Y*ou are a fool. You have no place here.*"
Sam's words echoed in Ashley's head as the ache seeped into her side. She felt the implosion of pain as her opponent's fist struck her lower ribs. The sound of the blow to her already weak ribs and the splitting of her skin sent waves of piercing pain throughout her body.

What a fool she was to take on this rematch. Take on any fight, for that matter. Sam had been busy, training hard and working her way up through the fight circuit.

Who am I kidding? Do I have a place here? Ashley was driven and had learned to love sparring, but real-world ass kicking? Could she handle this? Was she a fool?

Pain. She had lived with pain for so long now; that part was easy. It was the mental torture and head games that she agonized over. Through her blurry vision and haze, she felt someone take her aside, to her corner.

James. He was talking to her, trying to calm her, trying to help ease the pain of the blow.

Other hands on me now. Cool ice packs on her head and the doctor's hands checking the injury, Ashley flinched from the acute onset of pain that felt like a knife in her side, forcing her to come back to reality. The flood of feeling, noise, and light flew at her at full speed. She remembered the buildup before the match, the adrenaline rush, and the mental game of staying headstrong. Then, she received the blow to her body—and to her ego—and was pulled out of the fight. *What does this mean?*

"You are a fool," echoed in her head. *"You have no place here."* Sam had said that as Ashley entered the ring.

No way.

As the medic wrapped her injured ribs, Ashley thought of why she'd started this in the first place. There were too many reasons to count. The only thing holding her back was her vulnerability and getting hurt. *That's life, right?*

At least, in the ring, she could make her own destiny. Fool or no fool, she felt empowered there, even when she lost. There was always a next time to try for the win. Always getting better, climbing to the top—slowly, but making her way there.

James came around to face her. He had his concerned look on—arms crossed, chin resting in his hand, serious eyebrows.

Ashley smiled at him and then winced quickly at the ache in her side. "I'm okay," she said to James, but also to herself.

James shook his head slightly, keeping his gaze intent on Ashley's expression to see if she was lying or telling the truth.

The ref came over to him. "What's the call, boss?"

James looked at him then back to Ashley. He squatted down to her eye level. "Ash, you have to be honest; only you know how you feel. You up for this?"

Ashley breathed in slowly and carefully. The pain was starting to dull as the doctor eyed her nervously. Wrapped and padded under her sports bra, she felt she could protect her side and still pull off some powerful moves with her crosses, kicks, and knees. The challenge would be to protect the weak side. There was that vulnerability again. She was exposed, no doubt about it, but she must draw the attention away from her soft spot.

"I can do this. I have to," she breathed.

James didn't like the odds, but, God knows, she'd surprised him before when she was backed into a corner. "You have to keep that elbow in the entire time. You have to stay protected, but not look restricted." James had his arm tucked in by his left side, fist guarding his face, but it looked natural, not an obviously guarded stance.

Ashley knew her opponent could ruin her if she left her side exposed. She felt confident she could pull this off using her dominant right side to kick, while keeping her left side away from Sam.

It was as if James could read her mind. "You need to get that head kick in right away. Sam will be on your weak spot as soon as that bell rings."

Ashley's heart was racing. She nodded. *Protect and unleash.* That rear kick of hers was deadly.

James thought about it. "Get those leg kicks in, too. Wear her down."

She nodded and breathed out a long, slow breath. "I'll only have one shot." Searching James's eyes, needing his reassurance, she held her breath again.

"Good"—he smiled slowly—"one shot is all you need."

***

The bell rang as each of them came out of their corners with their own idea of how this would go down. Each hoping to be the victor. James watched as Ashley came out loose, looking ready to fight, but not drawing obvious attention to the pain. Hands up, she led with a right cross and began to keep that left elbow in tight.

James's stomach was in a knot. He wished he had a headset to talk Ash through this. Shaking his head, he knew, if that were possible, she would rip it off her head in a second. She was going to do her own thing here. He prayed it would work.

***

Adrenaline pumped through Ashley's veins as she circled around the ring. Keeping things loose, she kept her elbow in and tried to distract Sam with her cross, her front leg bouncing, she was ready to launch a front teep. She landed a cross to Sam's head then quickly ducked as a fierce jab-cross came at her.

Ashley backed up, gauging how much time she had before landing her finisher. Sam kept jabbing, knocking Ashley back, watching her pull that left arm in close to her ribs. Ashley knew her jabs were out. Sam was now homing in on her exposed ribs, trying to land a hook or a kick to that weak spot.

The minute Ashley moved that arm away, Sam came at her with a rear kick to the body, searing her side. Ashley crouched low as Sam moved in and threw a close hook. She felt the impact of the blow against the side of her head, near her ear; then it skimmed across her cheek toward her nose. Ashley was shocked by the intensity, but fired back punches quickly. *Cross, hook, cross.* They were in close proximity, all punches.

As she glanced up from her guarded stance, she saw the next blow coming and was ready this time. Leaning into the punch, she used it to gain momentum and fire back that cross-hook combination. Then, she pulled Sam into the clinch and landed knees to the stomach before pushing her off, leaving Sam temporarily stunned.

Ashley was on borrowed time; she knew this needed to end quickly. It would have to come as a surprise. She had been predictable, safe, throwing crosses, push kicks, and hooks.

Give her the most unpredictable. Countering each strike Sam made, Ashley moved in. Duck, low kick, switch kick. She saw her advantage. Sam wouldn't expect a swing kick to the head.

Side throbbing, heart pulsing in her head, Ashley took quick gasps for breath; she needed control. Sam came at Ashley with a jab and started to turn for a nasty liver hook. Her hook started too far back, and Ashley quickly pivoted and released her swing kick to the head.

"Kick as if you are kicking through your opponent," James's words echoed in her mind. *"Take that spin all the way through."*

Ashley moved through the kick at a fast pace. *There's no time left to think; just do it.* Her body shifted back as she spun and whipped her rear leg around to land squarely on Sam's head. The force of the blow spun Ashley around and set her up for a perfectly placed spinning backfist to the head as Sam fell forward. Ashley let that backfist fly and felt the pain ripping at her side. The kick took Sam out, and the fist sealed her fate. Sam dropped to the mat and was down.

The ref rushed over to make the call.

Is she getting up or is this the end? Ashley held her side and knew she was out at this point, no matter Sam's outcome.

Pain seared through Ashley's rib cage as she heard shouts from the ref and the crowd. James burst through the ropes to meet her; then the ref grabbed her right arm and raised it high, announcing Ashley the winner.

"You did it, kid." James stood by her side.

"Holy shit," Ashley muttered and turned to him.

He gave her a hug, putting his hand on the back of her head, avoiding her bad side. "Nice fucking job, kid." Stepping back, he took one look and knew her side was bad. "Let's get you looked at; come on."

Ashley turned back to look at Sam struggling to sit up. Her coach and her squad were all around, carefully helping her to stand. Ashley moved toward her, extending a hand. "Nice job."

Sam grimaced, nodded, and turned away.

Ashley turned back toward James. "Who's the fool now?"

***

James sat with Ashley while the doctor checked her ribs. "They're not all broken, but there are most likely small fractures along the lower ribs. You did suffer deep trauma to the area."

"Yeah, no shit," Ashley mouthed to James.

He chuckled. Not able to sit still due to the adrenaline and excitement of the win, he was out of his seat and pacing. James replayed the fight in his head—what worked and what didn't. That amazing kick to the head. *Ashley dropped Samantha like a bad habit.* As always, she'd surprised him.

"So, what's the treatment?" Ashley already knew the answer.

"Plenty of rest, lay off sparring for at least eight weeks, realistically sixteen weeks."

That's not what she wanted to hear.

"You'll heal quickly, Ash." James put his hand on her shoulder and forced her to focus on him. "Hey, it'll be okay. We're on a break now, anyways."

As the doctor was cleaning up his gear, he cleared his throat. "Yes, but the important thing is to rest, Ashley. Allow enough time, or you'll be out longer than sixteen weeks." He looked pointedly at James.

"Yeah, sure, Doc. Whatever you say. Rest, it is." He gave one of his most convincing smiles and put his arm around the doctor's shoulders to usher him out. "Thanks again for your help. See you next time."

"Thank you," Ashley chimed in.

The doctor turned back and waved to Ashley. "Take it easy."

James closed the door and returned to Ashley. "You okay?"

She adjusted the ice pack that was strapped around her side and attempted to hop off the table. "Yeah, a little tender, but the meds are kicking in." A jolt shot through her side.

James was at her side. "Take it easy, Ash. No rush to get outa here."

Nodding her head, she sat down on a nearby chair.

Once Ashley was settled, James couldn't contain himself any longer. "Awesome work out there! Holy shit, Ash, you dropped Sam with that kick; the backfist was a bonus!"

"Yeah, it felt pretty awesome, except for the stabbing pain in my side." Ashley had been pumped for a win, and it felt great to have earned James's confidence in her.

The door opened and in came the other coaches. "Okay to come in?" Without waiting, they poured in.

"Nice work, ass kicker!" Trevor gave her a hug, careful of her bandaged side.

"We weren't sure after we saw that blow to your ribs. Are they broken?" Justin gave her a high five.

The questions and the congratulations continued. They replayed Samantha's hook to the ribs and then Ashley's devastating kick to Sam's head, giving Ashley a good laugh and a distraction from the pain.

James knew she had the fight in her, she had the focus (sometimes), she had the skill (when she could focus), and, now, she'd proved that she could put it all together. He needed her to work on the technical side, but the drive, the hunger, and the focus under pressure were not easy to teach; that was something deep inside. She had it, and James needed her to harness it.

Then, he couldn't wait for her to unleash it.

***

Ashley saw an orthopedic surgeon recommended by Vince. The X-rays confirmed what the event doctor already diagnosed. Physical therapy was in her future.

Three days postfight, Ashley sat home, nursing her wound and bored out of her mind. *Thank God for texting.* She had friends from work and from the gym checking in on her with texts, scheduling times to stop by, or seeing if she needed anything. To keep moving, she'd been going for short walks with whoever stopped by. James checked in daily. He wanted her to stay mentally strong.

One day, he dropped by to visit and brought coffee. "How about I stay with you for the weekend? Make sure you are not overdoing it or anything… I have some time off. I promise to give you my undivided attention."

Ashley was speechless as James kicked the idea around with her, literally shuffling his feet and looking at her sheepishly. *An uninterrupted weekend with James?* She thought, *That would be amazing, even if I am laid up.* "Um, yeah, I'd like that," she managed to say. "You sure you want to spend your entire weekend off here, taking care of me?"

"Yes, I can't think of anything else I would rather do." James's confident way was back, and he leaned over to kiss her fully on the lips. "I'll make sure you stay in bed for the entire weekend." He smiled and kissed her again.

With her good arm, Ashley pulled him down next to her on the sofa. "That sounds perfect."

***

His hand trailed down to her waist and then settled on her hip. "Ashley…" Not waiting for an answer, James kissed her mouth fully on the lips. Breaking the kiss, he kept his face close to hers. "Fess up. Where's my phone?"

Ashley tried not to laugh. "What? What are you talking about?"

James propped himself up and held her hands over her head, laughing. "You're a terrible liar, by the way. I know you hid it. Tell me where." His eyes trailed down her body. "Tell me, or I'll torture you."

"James, I put it aside for a little while. Come on; you're supposed to be here taking care of me. Remember? I am injured." She inclined her head toward her ribs, reminding James of his promise to give her his "undivided attention" for the weekend. She wanted it to last a little longer.

"Okay, your injury didn't slow you down too much last night." James held both her hands with one of his and brought his other hand down to her waist again, this time to inflict torture by tickling her good side.

She laughed uncontrollably then winced, feigning pain in her side. "My ribs, come on! We have to be careful." She laughed.

James kept it up.

Twisting away from his torture, Ashley rolled onto her side. "Shit." Certain angles sent searing pain shooting through her side, and they still caught her off guard.

James sat back, putting his hand lightly on her back. "Ash, I'm sorry!"

"I'm okay." She downplayed it, but James could tell that one was real.

"You okay? Lay on your back." Looking worried, James turned her gently to her back and laid his hand over the bandage. He leaned over and kissed her cheek. "I'm so sorry."

Ashley played it off. "It's not your fault. I turned wrong...and I hid your phone." She glanced at him and sighed. "I loved having you here with me this weekend. I...I don't want you to leave." She looked away, embarrassed by her confession.

James lay down on his side next to her, smiled, and spoke softly, "I'm not going anywhere." With those deep, dark eyes, he told her more than any words could say. Then, he leaned over and kissed her, making her forget about any pain she had felt moments before.

***

Three weeks postinjury, her phone rang. Checking the ID, Ashley saw it was James.

"Hey." She smiled, glad to hear from him.

"How are ya? Hanging in there?"

She could tell he was in his car. "I am bored out of my mind!" She leaned back, sinking into the couch.

"Can you be ready in about twenty minutes? I'm coming to pick you up. Oh, and wear workout clothes."

She sat up. "What? You know I'm not supposed to get back to training for a couple weeks, according to Doc."

He sighed impatiently. "I know all about that. Can you be ready?"

Ashley decided she would go along and see what he had planned. "Sure. I'll meet you down front."

***

Ashley already had on stretch pants and a fight T-shirt; she liked getting dressed in her workout stuff even though she wasn't going to the gym. It made her feel as if she was heading in the right direction. She grabbed her sneakers, phone, and keys, and headed downstairs to meet James.

As she went down the stairs, she realized it felt great to be out on her own, and her heart started to race. She saw James's car circling around the corner and ran out to meet him.

James pulled up and leaned across the seat toward the window. "Hey, want a ride?"

"You know, I would probably hop in the car with anyone at this point." Getting in, she was still careful to nurse her side.

James leaned toward Ashley and kissed her. "Feeling better today?"

She thought, *Now, I am.* "It's all good. Keeping things stable, *like the doc said*." She put emphasis on that last part, not knowing what James had concocted for the day.

"Yeah, yeah." He pulled the car away from the curb.

"Where are we headed?" Ashley turned to face him.

Smiling, he looked sideways at her. "To the gym, of course. No worries, we won't focus on the upper body. It's leg day."

"Leg day?"

James nodded. "Leg day. Trust me."

Ashley sat back in her seat.

***

As James drove into the gym lot, Ashley's heart sped up—that old, familiar feeling she always had before entering this place. She remembered the adrenaline surges and her energy level going through the roof. She couldn't wait to get in there and see her friends and all of the trainers. And get to work.

Then, she remembered she was injured. She didn't want to go in and face everyone if she couldn't do anything.

James parked and looked like a kid, all excited. "Ready?"

She wasn't as raring to go as James thought she would be. "What?" He looked confused.

"I don't want to go in there like this, James. It looks like I am desperate. Well, I am."

Raising an eyebrow, James looked at her pointedly. "Come on, Ash. We're going to work. I'm not parading you through the gym. Let's go." He hopped out of the car and was at her door in seconds.

She waved him off. "I'm not crippled. I can get out of the car."

James smiled and grabbed his bag out of the back.

Here goes, she thought as she took a deep breath.

Walking in the gym, she felt a sense of both relief and belonging. Trainers came over and asked how she was holding up; they wanted to know how long it would be before she could get back in the ring. They commented on her knockout. Having been missed in the gym made her feel better.

"Can we get some work done now?" James was leaning against the front desk, putting on his best "you are wasting my time" look.

"All right, I am ready." Ashley grinned.

***

James had her warm up with light walking on the treadmill. Then, he took her back to the weight area. "Doc said to rest, especially around the ribs, which pretty much cuts out all upper-body work besides your physical therapy. However, he said nothing about resting your legs." James loaded the plates onto the leg press.

"Are you joking?"

He stood aside, shaking his head. "No joke. Get on."

Ashley lowered into the leg press, positioning her feet on the plate and holding on to the handles.

"We're starting light. Push from your legs; try not to grip tight on the handles. All legs, girl."

"Light, huh?" She shook her head. Nervous about overdoing it, Ashley started slowly. As promised, it wasn't too much. She completed one set and was smiling.

"All right. Ready for another set?"

Ashley started more confidently. As she neared the end of the set, James leaned on the bar holding the plates, adding more resistance. "You're so mean."

"No rest, kid. I need you to stay strong." James needed that mental toughness, and this was the way to do it. Having her see that the injury didn't beat her was his number one goal right then. He didn't care how many reps or sets she completed; he needed her to know she could do it.

***

Two months later, it was the first time she had been in the ring since the injury. *The* injury—it was as if it weren't hers. It was something that had intruded on her life. *The uninvited guest.* Nonetheless, it occupied the same space, even though she was determined not to own it. The phantom pain still lingered; the fear of reinjury was fresh.

The ring stood before her, large and enticing. She wanted to be back, but hesitated. Ashley didn't know what it was going to feel like, but she was scared it would be too painful, or that she would feel as if she were starting all over again.

Taking a deep breath, she hopped up into the ring and rolled under the ropes, as always, then hopped up onto her feet. Gloves on, mouth guard in, she was ready.

Her partner climbed in and was prepared to spar in the blink of an eye. *Of course, he was. He doesn't know what I've been through.* He hadn't seen her pain or felt even an ounce of that pain in his short career here. *He will if he keeps up with this,* she thought. *We all face it at one point or another.*

The sparring came easy. It felt great to move, even if it was awkward and a little slow. Combinations flowed smoothly; she was back in her groove. Punches, hooks, kicks, and blocks. Each strike building upon the other, power increasing with each combo. She was in her zone and in the ring, where it all came together.

CHAPTER 43

"I can't do this!" The anger was boiling up to the surface. She was losing control and needed to get out of there.

The past three months, she'd jumped back into training headfirst. Now, there was too much pressure to train, to get strong enough to compete in the next fight in three months, to work, and to be in this relationship with James. She felt old feelings closing in on her.

Ashley grabbed her things and started to leave James's apartment.

"Ash, Ash, wait." He grabbed her arm. "Please."

She turned, eyes piercing through him and rage boiling over. "Don't," she hissed.

James released her arm, putting his hands up. "I'm sorry."

"No! No, you do not get to do this!" She seethed, shaking her head.

"Ash, come on," he pleaded, looking exasperated.

"Don't give me that look. I want out." Immediately, she wished she hadn't said that.

James looked at her, stricken. "You want out? What does that even mean?"

"I mean... I don't know. I...I need some space," Ashley stammered, looking around nervously. She wanted to run away and put space between them. She could come back and start this over another time. *A redo.* She needed time. "Everything is overwhelming right now." Her mouth was dry as she swallowed hard.

James stood before her, looking perfect in his grey, worn jeans and soft sweater. Looking at him this way, part of her wanted to run to him, hug him, and never let go. But that scared her to death. *I have no control over my feelings.* That was her life now—out-of-control emotions both in and out of the ring.

"Why are you running away?" He crossed his arms.

She stood awkwardly, turning away from him. Staying was more than she could deal with, and she didn't know why.

"Ash…I…I wish I could change things. But I can't…and I can't stop you from leaving." He turned away.

She hated doing this to him. *Doing exactly what Lisa said not to do.*

"James, I'm sorry."

He leaned back against the counter, arms still crossed, not making eye contact.

Her anger was dissipating; she didn't want to fight. Pulling her bag up on her shoulder, she turned to go. Pausing, she placed her hand on the door. "Don't give up on me, please. I need time…"

James kept his gaze down.

"Bye," she said softly, turning the knob and then walking out the door. The sound of the door closing echoed through the deafening silence.

***

The phone buzzed. Notifications came in from texts and social media apps. She decided to take a break from all that. She needed to disconnect and disassociate herself.

She deleted the apps and turned the notifications off on her phone to eliminate the temptation. *I'm not answering texts this weekend.* She knew no one would be texting except Lisa, and she knew Lisa would have a few choice words for her. *There will be enough time to face Lisa's harassment at the gym.*

Ashley couldn't settle down; her book was not holding her attention, and she'd cleaned her apartment already. Eyeing her sneakers sitting by the door, she contemplated going for a run but knew that would be pushing it. She was supposed to be keeping her workouts light.

The sun was out; there was nothing stopping her from going for a walk by the Charles River. *That's what I need. Fresh air, blue skies, and a little sun on my face.* She grabbed her book to ensure that she would not turn this into a workout. *Go for a walk and maybe sit on a bench and read.* The day was looking up. Going out of her comfort zone, she left her phone behind and headed off, not caring who was trying to reach her.

***

After resigning herself to the fact that she was "taking a break" from the gym, her training, and people, Ashley settled into a routine, relishing this rest period. The day was set before her. She had work, but she also had freedom.

No prepacking two bags for the day, or making sure she had her workout gear and work clothes ready. She picked out one outfit to wear for the day. Unlike her usual two- or three-times-a-day change, depending on her training. *Put it out of your mind,* she told herself. *Embrace the freedom. No ties, no pressure to perform, to keep up, or to worry about not being good enough.*

She thought about her day. She could take a full lunch break; she didn't have to eat at her desk because of a rigid workout schedule. Her thoughts drifted to the gym. *Pay it no mind.* She planned to sit in the sun for her lunch hour that day. Maybe even buy lunch, not even take her prepped meals.

Ashley smiled, looking at her reflection before she left for work. She felt lighter. Grabbing her things, she prayed that this feeling would last.

CHAPTER 44

Holding on
Don't let go

I need to fly, to soar above the clouds
I need it a little more but
Not able to keep up
Or maintain the height
But trying each day
Through every fight

Keep me close
Forever near
Keep me strong
Help me lose my fear.

"I think about you all the time." James looked at her, hopeful, as he paused the twisting of his coffee mug on the table. He was there at her request.

Ashley had had time to cool down. After a few days, she reached out to James to apologize, feeling terrible for blowing up at him. She'd asked him to meet for coffee after work.

"Do you think of me, Ash? At all?" James shrugged then averted his eyes, looking out the window as he thought better of having asked. "Wait, don't answer that."

She didn't break eye contact with him. "All the time."

He turned to face her and leaned across the table. "Damn it. Then, why does it have to be this way, Ashley? If you do think of me, why are you fighting this?" His dark eyes held hers.

She thought he could see all her feelings welling up in her eyes. It was her turn to look away. "I don't know," she said, her voice so small that it cracked. Tears threatened to spill over; she willed them back. "There's so much, I..." That was all she could say.

James moved closer to her, wanting to take her hand. "I don't mean to pressure you."

Ashley stared out the window at the cars driving by, absently twirling a strand of hair. She broke the silence between them. "Sometimes, memories are the worst form of torture."

James waited for her to continue, but she continued to stare at whatever was outside the window.

"But the good memories...don't they win out over the bad?" He leaned his arms on the table.

"Sometimes, the good memories are harder to face than the bad ones." Her voice was gruff, her tone bitter.

The silence built once again between them. There was no way he could comprehend what she'd been through. He'd tried everything to make it right, make life perfect, but there was no way to turn off her memories. Reaching out, he took hold of her hand.

In the time they'd been together, her startle reflex had almost disappeared. No one else might have detected it, but James still saw the flicker in her eye, felt the slight twitch in her hand. Then, there was recognition, a warmth and a comfort in knowing he was there for her through all of her idiosyncrasies.

"Well, I'm betting I can give you some memories that'll win out over all the rest." Raising her cold hand to his lips, he paused then kissed it.

"I'm willing to see if you can do that," she whispered as he melted her icy heart, making her want those beautiful memories.

James tilted his head toward the door. "Then, let's get out of here."

Ashley nodded, glad to leave. He kept his hand on her arm, then across the small of her back, warming her skin and calming her frayed nerves as they walked to the parking lot. He opened the car door for her.

As she settled into the seat, she watched him walk over to the driver's side. She studied the angles of his face and the way his body moved; he was so sure of himself. *Is it possible he could be the one for me?* That seemed too good to be true.

As he slid in the driver's side, he caught her looking at him with a small smile on her face. "What?" He paused, looking around.

"I was looking. Making a memory." She nodded.

"Oh, well...can I add to that memory?" He leaned his arm on the steering wheel.

"Of course," she breathed.

He leaned over the seat toward her, drawing her in, gently touching her face, and then kissing her, melting her again and breaking down another layer of that wall. She felt hypnotized by his touch. *His lips are so soft,* she thought. *Memory, commit this moment to memory. This is one I need to recall.*

His warm lips on hers—she wanted that feeling forever. Those strong hands, so gentle when he touched her—she never wanted him to let go. Eyes drawing her in so deep—her heart skipped a beat as she committed those deep, beautiful eyes of his to memory.

"You okay?"

His voice drew her back to the moment. "Yes. Perfect." Breathlessly, she held his hands close. "I don't want this to end."

"It doesn't have to, Ash." He kissed her again. "Can I take you home with me?" He smiled slyly at her.

"Yes." Ashley had to remind herself to breathe.

He started the car and drove off, not able to stay under the speed limit.

CHAPTER 45

James: *Can I see you tonight?*

Ashley: *It's midnight…um…*

James: *I know. I need to see you.*

Ashley: *What's going on?*

She was squinting, trying to text. The letters all jumbled together.

James: *I'm out. Can I come over?*

Seriously, it's midnight, and I'm in bed, she thought. Then, wondering what was going on, her heart began to race.

Ashley: *Sure. Are you okay?*

James: *Be there soon.*

Throwing back the covers, she huffed out of bed and threw on some joggers and a hoodie. She tried to tame her wild hair, then threw it up in a bun. She shivered as she crossed the room and entered the dark living room. The temperature had dropped, and the night air had a chill. Grabbing a blanket, she wrapped herself up and sat down on the oversized couch.

There was a soft knock on the door, and Ashley jumped up to get it. Quietly unlocking the latch and turning the knob, she peeked out to see James standing there, hands in pockets. He looked worn down, and he had a few drinks in him.

"James"—she pulled the blanket tighter around herself—"what's going on?"

"Ash, can I come in?" He was swaying a bit. The look on his face worried her. She felt a small sense of dread starting to creep in. She stepped aside and let him enter.

"What happened?" She turned to look at him; he had his head down.

His voice cracking, he said, "It's Vince…he was shot." It had hit him hard; speaking of it made it more real.

"Oh my God! No!" Ashley tried to steady herself. "What? When?"

James lost his footing a bit, and Ashley reached out for him. "Come sit." Holding his arm, she walked him over to the sofa.

He steadied himself on her and was starting to break down. He needed to keep it together. "Ash, I didn't know where else to go… He's in the hospital and…I had to get out of there. Someone drove by the bar when we were leaving… I-I stopped to say hi to someone… I should have been with him. He left ahead, and I heard it…" He put his head in his hands.

Ashley put her arms around him. "I'm so sorry."

"Fuck. I don't know what happened or why, or if this was something random."

"Oh my God, Lisa." The thought was like a punch in the gut.

"She's at the hospital with her sister. Justin and Trevor were with us; they stayed… I couldn't. I needed air, and I kept going. I texted Lisa; she said she'll call. She's a wreck."

"Do you want me to go back with you?" Ashley kept her hand on his back as he trembled.

"Yeah." He was in shock.

"You'll want to be there when there's news. You have to be there."

"Yeah." Brushing his hand back over his hair, he seemed to snap out of it. "I have to go back."

"Let me change. I'm going with you." Ashley stood to go in her room.

James caught her hand. "Thank you, Ash, I couldn't sit there. I needed to see you."

"It'll be okay. I'll be right back."

In a blur, she threw on clothes and grabbed a baseball hat, her heart racing. *What is Lisa going through? Was this random?* Nothing was random to Ashley. *What if it was Stephen? What if that was meant for James? What will happen if Vince dies? Pray, pray that Vince will pull through.*

Eyes welling up, she threw on a pair of sneakers and headed out to the living room.

James was pacing. He stopped, searching her eyes for hope, for assurance that this was going to be all right.

She gave a nod and grabbed a jacket. "Ready?"

"Yeah." Crossing the room, they headed out. "I called an Uber; they should be here any minute." James's voice was hoarse.

An Uber drove up to the sidewalk as they walked out of the apartment. Ashley clutched James's hand as they rode in silence, lost in thoughts of Vince and Lisa. The warmth of Ashley's hand permeated through James's ice-cold skin as he tried so hard to keep his frayed nerves from coming apart.

Dread seized Ashley's insides as they entered the emergency area. This time of night was chaotic; there were lots of car-accident victims, late-night illnesses, and gunshot victims. Her mind whirled; her eyes darted around.

"We are here for Vince." James placed his hands against the check-in counter.

The attendant handed James and Ashley visitor stickers and allowed them through the security doors.

Ashley felt as if her legs weighed a hundred pounds each; she was dazed by the noise and commotion.

Lisa was sitting in a chair by the doors to the operating room. "Ashley." Lisa stood unsteadily.

Ashley hurriedly approached her and caught her in a hug. "I'm so sorry, Lisa." She continued to hug her friend fiercely, trying to will this nightmare away.

"Thanks for coming." Lisa held her at arm's length.

"Of course. You should sit." Ashley lowered onto the bench with Lisa and sat, silently watching the nurses and doctors as they walked past.

"He's in surgery. We're waiting to hear…" Lisa's voice trailed off.

Lisa's sister came over and sat with Lisa, so to let them have time together, Ashley went back over to where James was standing with Trevor. They sat and waited for what seemed an eternity.

She caught a glimpse of Lisa talking with a doctor who'd come through the doors from surgery. Then, everything slowed down.

Lisa grabbed the doctor's arm, covering her mouth, doubling over as if in severe pain. Someone grabbed on to Lisa to catch her, and Ashley realized it was James; he had vanished from her side so quickly. Trevor was also there, helping Lisa. James stood to face the doctor and looked confused, refusing to believe what was happening.

As if waking to a splash of cold water in her face, Ashley snapped back to reality, and the world seemed to speed back up. She raced over to Lisa.

"Ashley," Lisa barely choked her name out. She held on to Ashley's arms for support, tears streaming down her face. "Vince, my Vince. He's gone. He can't be gone!"

No! Ashley's mind screamed. *Why is this happening?* She hugged her friend tight, tears running down her face. Darkness and dread filled her. Still holding Lisa tight, she looked up at James. His face was ashen as he stood against the wall.

Trevor hugged him.

Ash reached out her hand and touched his shoulder. "James," she said, her voice barely a whisper.

James closed his eyes, blocking out the images, not able to face this new reality.

***

"It's not going to be okay!" James slammed his beer bottle into the wall of his kitchen.

Ashley cringed and noticed he'd barely missed the clock on the wall. The time read four in the morning. They had stayed at the hospital with Lisa until there was nothing left to do; then, they returned to James's apartment because Lisa's sister was planning to stay with her.

364

Ashley drew a sharp intake of air. She knew he wouldn't project his anger at her, but she had never seen him like this. "Please, James. Don't shut me out." Ashley felt desperate. The feeling of being separated from him was making her anxious. He was everything to her now. Seeing him in this much pain hurt her. She needed to be there for him, no matter what. "James…let me stay. You don't have to talk. We don't have to do anything. Let me be here with you."

James's back was to her, so his expression was hidden from Ashley. She wanted so desperately to approach him and put her arms around him, or put her hands on his shoulders, if only to show him she was there for him.

His hands were on the counter, and his head was down. He turned slightly to look at the broken bottle on the floor by the wall. Feeling the weight of what had happened was wearing him down. He didn't have any energy left to fight or to do anything at all.

Ashley saw the slump in his posture and knew he had nothing left. She walked over to him, took a deep breath, and moved to put her arms around him. She knew he would not lash out at her, but, still, she was leery.

The initial touch made him flinch slightly; then, he felt her warmth against him, and he relaxed into her.

Ashley hugged him close and put her cheek on his back.

"I'm so tired." His voice was hoarse, and she felt all of the energy go out of him as he put his hands over hers.

"Let's go." She took his hand and led him to his bedroom. She turned down the bed for him while he went into the bathroom.

When he came out, he looked as if he'd aged. He climbed into bed, and Ashley lay on the covers next to him, wrapping her arms around him from behind, his back to her front.

"I'm here for you. It is going to be okay."

He laid his hand on top of her hands on his chest.

Kissing his cheek, she realized his breath was slowing down, and he was falling asleep. Holding him close, she stayed the night, knowing tomorrow would be even harder for him to face.

***

James startled awake, covered in sweat, swearing he heard a gunshot. His first response was to feel around the bed for Ashley. He thought he'd dreamt that she stayed over. Then, he heard noise coming from the bathroom. Glancing at the clock, it was only 6:30 a.m. and still dark in the room. He rubbed his eyes, not wanting to remember yesterday, and not ready to face the day.

Relief washed over him as Ashley came back into the room. He could see the outline of her body covered by one of his T-shirts.

Climbing into bed, she realized he was awake. "Hey." She assumed her position of spooning him into a bear hug.

James rolled over to face her and put his arm around her. "Ashley, I am so sorry for—"

She silenced him before he could go any further. "It's okay. I'm here."

He was thankful she knew what he needed. He held her close and didn't let go as they both drifted back to sleep.

***

The next two days passed in a blur of trying to support Lisa and James. Ashley notified the people at her job that she needed time off for the wake and funeral. She planned to take a couple of extra days to be there for James.

The day of Vince's wake had come. *How the hell am I going to get through this?* James thought as he looked in the mirror. What he saw in the reflection surprised him. There were dark circles under his eyes, and he looked as if he'd aged ten years this weekend alone.

Then, he saw Ashley's reflection as she entered the bathroom, wearing his gym T-shirt and carrying a mug of coffee. He felt his face soften, and he smiled a little. *That's how I'll get through this,* James thought.

"Morning." Her voice was soft, but James could tell she was nervous about how he would handle this morning.

Turning toward him, she set the mug on the counter and stood before him. Then, she leaned into him, hooking her arms around his waist. At the same moment, James moved toward her for a hug.

Ashley breathed James in as she held him close, feeling as if he would disappear if she let him go. Leaning back, she touched his face. "I'm glad you slept." *I love you* were the words that she wanted to say, but held back because she didn't know if this was the right time to drop that on him. *Would it be too heavy, too deep?*

She didn't want him to feel he had to say it back. She didn't need to hear him say it, but she wanted him to remember that there was a life for him here, a reason not go into the darkness that kept pulling him in. She wanted him to hear the words, feel them wash over him, and find a reason to get through this. Hope for a future where light and happiness were possible again—two things that he'd lacked since Vince was shot. Darkness and despair were pulling him under. She wouldn't let him drown.

He sighed. "Thank you for being here." He held her close, brushing his hand over her hair.

"I love you, James." She heard the words come breathlessly out of her.

He held on to her tightly as a tear rolled down his cheek.

***

"Are you all right?" She placed her hand on his shoulder as he stared absently out the window of Vince and Lisa's sitting room.

"Yeah, I'm fine." He looked at her briefly.

"You sure? We can go anytime."

"I'm fine." His voice was clipped.

She knew he was on overload. They had been to the funeral service and the burial, and now had to face the gathering at Lisa's house afterward. She kissed his cheek and held his hand, leading him into the living room.

She knew the feeling of being overwhelmed; she knew it well. Guiding him off-center of the crowd, she tried to divert attention away from him. They would all want to talk to him. Everybody wanted to share condolences, sympathies, and well-wishes, which led to stories, rehashing, and asking, "How's Lisa doing?" and "What happened?" Even asking, "Will you take over the gym?"

James had to deal with these questions at some point, but not now. Small doses he could handle.

Ashley was the buffer keeping them moving. *Nothing to see here...*but it was unavoidable.

The first surge came on slowly, then built like a tidal wave and slammed him full force into the spotlight. She held his hand, intervening with a thank-you, a handshake, or a hug, which she could then use to steer them off toward another area.

James was trying hard to keep it together for everyone else.

Almost two hours flew by in a blur of faces. "We can leave anytime. Give me the sign."

This time, he nodded, looking exhausted. "Maybe in a few."

Her heart went out to him. Although he hadn't left her side much of the day, between them, she felt a wide chasm that was growing deeper by the hour. The past few days had taken their toll on everyone, but she'd seen a drastic change in James. She'd tried to hold him up and keep him treading water, but it was becoming more difficult.

He needed to be alone. He saw faces, heard their voices, but he was having difficulty staying glued together. Time was up for him. Ashley was trying hard, but he didn't even have the patience for her anymore. Craving solitude, he ducked down the hallway when Ashley was occupied by other friends. He opened the slider doors off the small office that faced the yard on the side of the house and stepped outside. He stood against the wall and breathed in the fresh air, feeling as if it were a lifeline.

People were walking to their cars on the street; some were smoking on the front lawn, taking a break from the stifling air and crowd. He thought, *I could leave, go for a walk, and come back, or maybe keep walking.* He knew Ashley would send out the troops for him, but he could envision himself leaving for good.

James leaned his head back against the wall. As he closed his eyes, he heard a car nearing the sidewalk, then an engine idling. Turning toward the direction of the car, he saw it was his car, and Ashley was in the driver's seat. She motioned for him to get in.

James smiled faintly, relieved he had a reason to leave. He pushed off the wall, kept his head down, and walked to the car. He opened the door, sliding in without a word, numb.

Ashley put the car in Drive and took off in silence. James couldn't shake the feeling that he could have walked off without feeling a thing.

***

Without a word, they moved about his apartment. Ashley busied herself cleaning the kitchen, sensing James wanted his space. She didn't want to leave him alone yet.

James came out of the bedroom with his shirt partially unbuttoned and his belt, socks, and shoes off. He looked fragile, broken.

She broke the silence. "Why don't you head in to bed? I can sleep on the couch if you want to be alone."

James had had that exact thought…until he heard her voice. Then, he looked at her and saw the love in her eyes, the concern on her face. Deep down he needed her to stay; he couldn't face this alone. That's what bothered him—his weakness.

When he didn't answer, Ashley turned away from his eyes. "I could go if you want…"

"No, Ash. Stay. I-I'm just…I'm tired."

She took his hand and led him into the bedroom, drew the sheets back, and fluffed the pillows as he stood frozen, in a daze. He seemed to forget what he should be doing. She sat him down. Swiftly, she finished unbuttoning his dress shirt, helping to remove it. For a moment, she thought of all the times she'd taken his clothes off, but this was different. She wanted him to rest.

He swung his legs up, and she helped remove his pants. He could already feel his eyelids getting heavy as she pulled the covers over him then turned to switch the light off. Hands light as a feather brushed over his forehead and hair; her lips soft as a whisper touched his cheek. He saw her silhouette, felt heavy, and then didn't think again until the next day.

***

Ashley slept on the couch, not wanting to disturb his sleep. She needed to be up early in the morning to get in touch with the office. She had to check in on the deadlines for her big project. She set up the coffee, as well as her alarm, to go off early.

Turns out, she didn't need it. Like clockwork, she awoke at 6:30 a.m.

James slept the deepest sleep he ever remembered. The last hour he had fits of dreams. They ranged from fast-moving, vivid colors to soft whispers of light and sound. He felt Ashley's hands on him, warm and inviting; then, they turned into steel blades pressing toward his chest. He woke with a start and realized he was in his quiet apartment, in his bed alone.

Light streamed in through the shades, and the scent of coffee drifted into the bedroom. There were faint sounds coming from the kitchen as he rolled over to see the time was 9:00 a.m. He never slept this late. Feeling as if a Mack truck hit him, he could barely sit up without feeling the pounding in his head. Slowly and steadily, he walked to the bathroom, then to the kitchen where Ashley stood.

"Morning." She smiled and poured him a large mug of coffee. Sensing the wall he was building, she waited for him to make a move. Last thing she wanted to do was smother him. It took everything out of her not to run over and hug him tight and never let go. Instead, she poured cream in his coffee, stirred in a little sugar, and busied herself with fixing her own mug.

370

James approached and took his coffee, touching her arm. "Thank you." His voice was gruff with sleep and stress from the preceding day.

"Sure. You sleep okay?" She sipped her coffee.

"Yes, like the dead." He looked off and grimaced. He saw the blankets folded neatly on the couch where Ashley had slept. "You sleep okay?" He placed his mug down and turned to Ashley.

"Yeah, not so bad." Looking up at him, she smiled.

He put his arms around her, kissing the top of her head. "Thanks for everything. For yesterday…"

"Of course. No need to thank me." She squeezed him harder, knowing she had to leave at some point and go back to work. She also knew that James had to get back to his work, restart his life.

James pulled away, as if he was preparing for the separation.

"I have to leave in a bit for work, but I can come by later if you want me to, or if you need anything…"

"Yeah, I know. I have to go to the gym. There's so much…" His voice trailed off. "I'll let you know how it's going. It will probably be a long day."

"Sure, let me know. I'll get my things." Ashley took her coffee and her bag to the bathroom to change.

When she came back to the living room, James was staring out the window, lost in thought. Walls were going up around him; she sensed it.

Putting on a bright face, she went toward him. "All right, I'm off. Call me."

He turned to her, hesitating a tad longer than usual before putting on his mask. "I will." He hugged her close.

That urgency was beating in her chest—the sense that this was the last time she would see him. *But that's ridiculous,* she told herself. *Give him space; it will be fine.* Ashley brought her hand up to touch his face and kiss his cheek. "I love you."

Again, he hesitated a moment then answered, "I love you. See you later."

With that, she picked up her bag and left. Closing the door, Ashley felt a sense of unease settle deep in her gut.

***

"Nice work, you guys! Let's get this cleaned up!" Justin clapped once and marched off.

My muscles are screaming, and he wants us to keep moving? Ashley thought as she peeled her gloves and shin guards off.

Two weeks after Vince died, she was back into her routine at the gym. One and a half hours of pad work, intense sparring, and sweat-inducing muscle burners. There were hand mitts, Thai pads, and jump ropes strewn across the floor.

"Now, you guys. We have a class coming in ten minutes. Get moving." Justin didn't take any crap, and he wasn't the one to put everything away.

Ashley wrapped her towel around her shoulders and set about collecting the jump ropes. They had brought out some extra equipment from upstairs, so she and Kendra set about returning all of it to its rightful place.

"I got the Tombstone pads. You got the ropes, Ash?" Kendra called as she piled the pads up in a stack. Kendra laughed, knowing the trek up the stairs would be painful.

"Yeah, right behind you." Ashley draped the jump ropes around her neck, grabbed a set of Thai pads, then made her way upstairs. Adjusting the pads while turning the corner, she almost ran into James as he darted out of his office.

"Hey, whoa…sorry!" She fumbled with the pads.

"Hey." James stood with his jacket on, a duffel bag in one hand, and a large overnight bag in the other.

Ashley eyed the bag. It was his travel bag. "You're leaving…" It came out more of a statement than a question.

"Yeah, I'm heading out tonight." He stood stiffly.

"Oh. I thought you were leaving tomorrow. I thought I would see you before."

"No, tonight's better. I want to get there, get settled."

Ashley awkwardly shifted, the pads slipping, the ropes around her shoulders sticking to her shirt, and cold sweat running down her back.

"Oh"—she hesitated—"were you going to say good-bye?" Her hands began to shake.

"Uh, yeah, I was going to call you. I'm running behind." He looked at his watch as Kendra came breezing by.

"Hey, guys." Kendra looked from one to the other and saw the tension between them, then kept moving.

"Hey, Kendra." James didn't look at Kendra and wouldn't meet Ashley's eyes. "Well, I gotta head out. Shane is waiting."

"Oh yeah, sure. Okay then." Ashley stood awkwardly, wanting to drop the pads and hug him, keep him from leaving.

"Bye, Ash." He kissed her cheek hastily, turned, and was gone.

"Bye." Ashley stood still, holding the equipment. The spot on her cheek burned with the abruptness of his touch. She continued to stand in the same spot, tears burning her eyes, unsure if she could move or even breathe, not even sure of what just happened.

***

Sadness settled in. Tears welled up, threatening to spill forth as my heart broke. Did he know how much it hurt to hear those words? Did he know how long I had been waiting for what I thought was our destiny? Then, to have it torn from my heart? The knife, the twist, the pain. The sadness. Worse than all of that was the empty hole that I was left with. The hole that stayed with me when he walked out and the silence that ensued after he shut the door to my heart.

CHAPTER 46

*D*id you ever have that feeling when you woke from a dream that it could have been true? It felt so real that you almost couldn't believe it was a dream? Everything so real you could feel it, taste it, and see it with such clarity. It was so utterly amazing and so much better than what was happening in your real life that you would do anything to return to it? Give up anything, even your own life, to feel that way for one more moment in time.

***

Ashley woke abruptly from a dream, taking a minute to get her bearings. The dream seemed so real; she still felt the same emotions, even the heat and the warmth, that she had experienced in the dream. Not wanting to face the day ahead, she longed to return to the dream—seeing flashes of their bodies together, feeling James next to her, even hearing his voice. It was too real.

And yet, not a possibility. He was still gone.

Ashley put the pillow over her head, willing herself to fall back asleep. Sleep, like so many things lately, eluded her.

"Damn it."

Tears stung her eyes. Biting the inside of her mouth, she willed the tears not to spill over. *Why is this happening?* Ashley thought she would be fine going forward…*without James—There, I finally said it. He has been gone for six days and nine hours, not that I'm counting or anything,* Ashley thought.

Although he'd texted a couple of times, checking in, Ashley had to come to terms with the fact that James was gone. He had bigger and better fighters to work with. She thought she was fine; she thought she could do this on her own, but everything was ramped up and more challenging.

The flowers James brought her had withered in their vase on the counter. James's sweat shirt was folded neatly on the dresser by her bed. Everything was frozen in time. *Waiting.*

Rolling onto her side and hugging the pillow close, Ashley felt a warm tear sliding down her cheek. She hadn't heard from James for days. He kept things inside and never let anyone too close. It shouldn't bother her; he had a lot on his plate at the moment. James was in charge of the entire gym now; he was dealing with the legal side of the business, not to mention the tragic loss of his friend.

Right now, I'm literally just a blip on his radar, she thought. *But, still, an important blip.*

The loneliness could not be put into words. It lived deep within her belly and drove all the way to her heart. Why couldn't she control this surge of sadness? She inhaled slowly, swearing she could smell his scent.

Silently, she said a prayer. Even if he didn't want them to be together now, she still needed him in her life. There was no way she could imagine him being gone from her life for good. She hated to admit that she relied on him for so much, but she needed him. Ashley was holding on to hope and faith for his return because that was all she had left.

She needed to get out of there. She knew working out would help. Besides, going to the gym would help her feel closer to James, even without him there... *Maybe I should go shopping or call someone and have some fun, instead. Maybe I need to take a step back. Maybe I need serious psychological help.*

She decided she needed the workout, needed to feel something. Anything.

***

I'm on my own now; I was made to find my own way. Who will guide me through the dark? How will I overcome all the obstacles I face? You are the only one who knows, the only one I trust. Now, you are gone...moving on to your destiny. Bigger and better things, I do not doubt. You are meant for greatness. I was blessed to have a glimmer of that golden light shine on me, if only for a moment. But it was enough. Enough to make me strong again, enough to teach me how to fight. Enough to give me new courage to move forward through the darkness, through the unknown, and into a new light.

***

Ashley fell behind in her training. There had been no time the past couple of weeks. When James left, she didn't feel like going back.

Her heart raced in anticipation of returning to the gym. *Things will get better.* She should use this time away from James to find what worked best for her. *Is fighting truly my passion?* Everything was about to become real, hard, and messy. *Either I run and hide, or I push myself and stick with it.* Did she have the courage to move out of the small comfort zone she and James had created? One that she had been happy to stay in…until change came and forced her out?

As she parked her car in the lot, Ashley thought, *Is this going back a good idea? Maybe I should go home and go for a run…*

This is ridiculous. Pull it together, and walk through the door. Palms sweaty, insides trembling, and legs a little wobbly, Ashley approached the front door. Deep breath. *Here it goes; walk through the door.*

As she opened the door and stepped in, Ashley was immediately drawn in by the sights and sounds of the gym. Her senses flooded with energy and light. She felt herself gain confidence and lose the self-doubt that had dominated her brain just moments before.

Ashley retrieved her gloves and wraps from her duffel bag. She expected to see Lisa waving to her from up in the ring, but Ashley's heart broke when she realized that wasn't going to happen. Trevor and Justin were working with fighters in the cage; the bags were being punched and kicked by all different levels of fighters and members of the gym.

Ashley breathed in deep. It was at that moment that she realized she was here to stay, no matter what.

***

Justin called to Ashley from the cage, "Hey, Ashley. We have competition training starting in a little bit. Want to join?"

What do I have to lose? "Sure. I'll be right there."

She pulled out her gear quickly and caught up with the group as they warmed up. The session was an endless amount of cardio, pad work, and sparring. A couple of times, she got winded and felt nauseous. After an hour, she wanted it over, and tears threatened to spill when Justin said they were doing another round of pad work and cardio intervals.

She told herself she would rest on the weekend. *Please get me through this without breaking down in front of everyone,* she thought. This was different. *So different without James.*

"Come on, Ashley; stay headstrong. Finish strong."

She put her head down and went to work. Jab-cross combos, push-ups, squat jumps, repeat, repeat, repeat. *Keep breathing, even though every muscle is searing; stay focused, even though I want to drop; maintain control, even though I want to scream and cry. Finish strong.*

"Time!" Justin hit the timer.

As Ashley struggled through her last push-up, her arms gave out. She was done physically, but still holding her emotions in check. *Get up, get your stuff, and go to your car. You can cry the whole ride home, just not here.* She stood up as Justin approached.

"Nice job." His jaw was set, and he was serious.

Ashley was able to choke out, "Thank you."

"You should get some rest. Take a break from here for a couple days. See you after the weekend." Justin nodded and walked off.

Ashley put the towel up to her head, wiping away more sweat than she thought was possible. Arms trembling, bruised, and banged up, Ashley was not sure she could gather her stuff and carry it to the car.

"Nice work, Ash." Eli nodded to Ashley as he collected the pads.

"Hey, Eli. Thanks for not killing me today." She stretched her trembling arms.

"Get some rest. See you next week."

In a haze, she walked to the cubbies, packed her bag, and dragged herself to her car. There were no tears the entire ride; she was numb.

Climbing the stairs to her apartment, that was when she wanted to cry. Counting them down, she knew exactly how many were left. *Get there; a shower and bed are waiting.*

After unlocking the door, she pushed through, dropped her bag on the floor, and shut the door, not even bothering to go through her triple-locking routine. Leaning against the door, she slid down to the floor and cried.

***

"It's God's sky." The colors painted across the sky changed with each passing moment. Ashley had taken dinner to Lisa's house. They were sitting on the deck with their dinner and glasses of wine. So much had happened since their first night out.

"You believe that?" Lisa turned to her friend.

"Yes." Ashley stared off, tracing the outline of the clouds. "I would not be alive if I did not believe that. God has gotten me through the darkest parts of my life."

"Wish I could say the same." Lisa looked to the sky as a tear rolled down her cheek.

Ashley grabbed her hand. "You can. Have faith that everything will get brighter."

Lisa looked off. "How can I do that after this?"

Ashley didn't have an answer. Why did bad things happen to good people? How can someone go on after the darkness? Ashley had been in a different darkness, but it was still dark. Ashley squeezed Lisa's hand. "There is still hope and a way back to brightness."

Lisa closed her eyes, not able to see it.

"I'm here for you, always." Ashley hugged Lisa, wanting to take away her heartache and pain.

"Thank you, Ash. For everything."

"Anything I can do for you, at any time, you just have to let me know." Ashley pulled back from Lisa, hands on her shoulders, looking at her pointedly. "Promise?"

"I promise." She pulled Ashley back into a hug and cried.

***

Feeling lost, but feeling strong.
Needing to stand on my own.
Relying too much on everybody else.
Strength.
It needs to come from me.
Step away.
Find your soul, your strength, your balance…
Everyone else will be there when you are ready.
Stand tall.
Don't go back to being weak…don't go back to falling behind.
Stay centered through it all.
Be your own warrior.

***

Intensity builds, drawing me in and lifting me up until I fall…flat on my back. Moving in sequence, trying to follow, trying to be good enough, strong enough, powerful enough. Time and time again, I fall short. Wanting more, needing more, craving more…it never seems to be enough.

***

"Will you listen to me? Hear me out on this, Ashley?" Justin's voice rose slightly, trying to get her attention.

Ashley was punching furiously at the heavy bag, taking out all her frustrations on it. Turning to face Justin, she felt her blood pressure rising. "What?" Her breaths were shallow, she was covered in sweat, and her patience was running thin.

Justin took a breath and steadied himself. He had to set her straight. "James will be back. I need you to hang in there. Be patient a little while longer."

Ashley shook her head and looked away. Removing her glove, she grabbed her towel from the floor and wrapped it around her neck. *How did this get so messed up?*

"This is not what I signed up for," she snapped bitterly. That could have been interpreted in so many ways. She'd signed up to work with James and to progress up to fighter status, not to work with the rookie trainers now leading her through basic training.

Also, this crazy relationship drama—she didn't want it or need it. Ashley turned away and covered her face with her towel, not wanting to show her emotions.

Justin continued, "He'll be back. Trust me. When he's back, you'll be ready, and you'll have the best training out there."

She knew it was true; that's what aggravated her. Ashley threw the towel down and returned to focus her anger on the bag, not Justin. She knew she had to wait it out. Leaving would be worse than staying. There was no other gym that could compare. Begrudgingly, Ashley knew she had to stay if she wanted to progress as a fighter.

"Ash, go through the training; fine-tune the basics. You'll get stronger, faster." Pausing, he chose his words carefully, "James will be back...for you, Ash. He will."

That hit Ashley hard. She came up short, not able to throw another kick. Desperately, she wanted to believe that he would be back for her. But that sense of dread, abandonment, insecurity—all those feelings resurfaced.

She didn't trust her voice not to crack. She nodded her head and turned, locking eyes with Justin. He knew James almost as well as Vince had known him. She had to trust Justin.

"I'll work with you, Ash, as much as I can. I'm strapped now with running the gym and training the fighters for the next competition, but I'll do what I can when our schedules match."

The fight was out of her now, and her shoulders slumped slightly. "Okay. I'll keep training...and waiting."

Relieved, Justin knew he'd made progress. "Stay strong, Ashley. We'll get through this." Justin smiled, reassuring her that all would be back to normal soon. He patted her shoulder and hurried off to his next appointment, leaving Ashley there with her heart in her throat.

"Stay strong, Ash." Those were James's words echoing in her head. Ashley knew she needed to work extra hard over the next two weeks… and until he came back. Shaking off that thought, Ashley checked her phone. Nothing. She grabbed her water bottle and sat on the mat, knowing what she had to do. *Keep it together and get stronger, faster, better.*

Looking around the gym, she began to map out her strategy. If she couldn't work with James or Justin, she would make her own training schedule, work every possible angle that she could. It was a bit over-whelming as she thought of the work she had to do. Strength, cardio, building stamina in the ring, perfecting combinations and defense strategies, training with Justin when he had time for her… So much to do. This would keep her busy…preoccupied.

To start, Ashley would focus on what was available to her right then. Working the bags would take the edge off, and she needed the conditioning. She took her last sip of water and grabbed her gloves.

As she returned to the bags, she passed the ring. Stopping in front of it, she felt a tug. Ashley touched the red canvas floor of the ring, pressed her hands into it, and wished she could go back in time and relive the moments with James. The ones she'd taken for granted. So many hours, so much sweat, and lots of tears.

Touching the black fabric around the ropes, she felt exhilaration run through her. She remembering how he maneuvered her around the ring and introduced her to this way of fighting. How he flashed the bright-red pads in front of her, testing her recall of offensive and defensive moves…so many combinations. How, when he backed her into a corner and she froze, he gave her subtle hints on how to take back control.

Ashley's heart raced as she pictured James leaning up against the ropes as he motioned to make her move and cued her to dominate with knee thrusts into his pads. She remembered how their bodies shook with each strike. James, literally, swept Ashley off her feet when he caught her kick midair and lifted her leg higher, demonstrating how quickly power can be taken away. Ashley stood breathlessly gripping the ropes while being assaulted by the flood of memories. But, most of all, she recalled James's eyes boring into hers as their close work became more intense and they communicated without a word.

Get it together, Ash. Taking a deep breath, she told herself she needed to focus and get to work—no more distractions.

Ashley slipped on her gloves, enjoying the sensation of sliding her hands into the soft leather. She felt loose, relaxed, and ready to work…while she patiently waited. Feeling the impact of her fists hitting the worn black-leather bag, the burning in her arms increased as she fired off round after round. The power of her kicks intensified after every blow. *Repeat, repeat, correct the tiniest flaw, repeat.* There was no room for error.

CHAPTER 47

Through the phone, Ashley felt James's coldness and the emptiness in his responses. She hated not seeing his face. "Is everything all right?" Ashley tapped her leg.

"Yeah, I'm good." His short answer told her to let it go, but she couldn't.

"Are you sure?" She held her breath.

"Things are good. Busy." James rubbed his forehead. He was not having this conversation now.

Ashley waited a moment, biting her nail. "But are you happy?"

"Yes, Ashley. I'm happy." Exasperated, James began to pace.

Ashley couldn't help herself. "You don't seem it. What's going on?" Her insecure side was screaming in her head, *Are you mad at me? Did I do something? What can I do?*

"It's nothing," he breathed.

Frustrated, Ashley was losing patience, but she knew that the more she pressed, the more James would shut down. "Okay. Well, let me know how the fights go." She heard muffled sounds on the other end.

"Hang on. Yeah, yeah, I'll be right out. Hey, Ash, I...I gotta go. The guys, they're ready, so..."

"Yeah...no, I get it. Good luck." Ashley pulled her knees to her chest.

"Love you. Bye."

"Love you, too." She hung up the phone and felt so far away from him. She knew he needed to be training, to be busy. But the emptiness in his voice filled her with a deep void that spread across her chest like an ink stain.

***

James: *Our schedule is behind. I probably won't be able to talk tonight.*

Ashley read the text later that evening, already anticipating that they wouldn't be talking. There was nothing to say.

Ashley: *Okay. Good luck. XO.*

James: *XO.*

Time went by without a call. She placed her phone on the coffee table and lay back on the couch with her book. Sinking into the cushions, she knew she'd fall asleep if she closed her eyes. *One moment to rest,* she thought, and Ashley felt herself drift to that place where you feel as if you were floating. Then, all became an endless sea of grey.

***

The phone's ringing jolted Ashley out of a deep sleep. Her heart hammered in her throat as she clamored to get to it and squinted at the caller ID with a sense of dread. *No one calls with good news at 2:00 a.m.*

It was James.

"Hello?" She did her best to sound as if she had been awake for hours.

"Ash. Hey. Sorry, were you asleep?" His voice was scratchy.

"Um, no, of course not. It's only two in the morning." She ran a hand through her hair.

"Oh yeah, right. God, I'm sorry. I didn't look at the time."

"James. Is everything all right?"

"Yes. I…I wanted to call. It has been so crazy. I…"

He can't give me the time of day during the day, but wants to talk now? She sighed, not wanting to fight, but she couldn't let this go. She sat up and rubbed her eyes. "So, now you want to talk?"

"Yeah, I—"

"You had no time for me the past few days when I wanted to talk. But you call at two in the morning, and I'm supposed to pop right up and start talking." She was heated, but trying to calm herself.

"Ash, I-I should have known this was a bad idea. I honestly forgot the time difference. The fights ended, and I finally got a minute." He sounded exasperated. Silence grew between them. "The guys won.

They did great. I wanted to tell you." He was trying to make light of the situation, trying to take her mind off how much of a dick he was.

"Oh, that's great. Awesome." Ashley pressed her hand to her forehead, trying to fight off the headache that was threatening behind her eyes.

"I miss you, Ash. I'm sorry for being such a dick. I'm sorry for leaving the way I did. I'm sorry."

Ashley closed her eyes. "James, I'm trying to give you space…"

"I know. I'm sorry."

Ashley leaned her head back on the couch, inhaling deeply.

"I'll be back next Monday. Final competitions are this weekend. I promise to make this right. I miss you, Ash."

"I miss you." She had so much to say, yet nothing could be communicated properly…now…at 2:15 a.m.

"I'll text you when we get settled tomorrow. If you want."

"Yes, of course."

"I love you, Ash." James held his breath. What if she didn't say it or if she didn't feel the same anymore? He couldn't blame her. He loved her, whether she said it or not, but he couldn't handle the rejection right now; he was teetering on the edge.

"I love you, James."

He closed his eyes and thanked God. "I promise to make this up to you, Ashley. It's been tough…after Vince…" His voice shook. *Damn it,* he thought. James didn't want to get into this over the phone. He owed her more than that. "Gosh, you should get back to sleep. I'll text at a decent time from now on."

"It's okay, James. Are you sure you're all right?"

"I'm okay. I'm trying to hang in there. It will be okay when I get back." He paused, wishing he were with her right then. "Sweet dreams, Ash."

"Night, James."

***

As she brought the towel away from her eyes, she saw James walk in from the parking lot. He'd come straight to the gym from the airport, she guessed. Her heart froze; so did she. She hadn't realized how long it had been since she had seen him. He looked a little worn, and his face was scruffy, as if he hadn't shaved in a while. Ashley stood still, but she was elated to see him.

James walked through the door, stopping to greet Justin and a handful of people; then, he looked in her direction. He gave a smile, nodded, and waved as Justin cornered him, talking to him as he approached the stairway. James shrugged at Ashley and waved for Justin to follow him up the stairs to his office.

What did I expect? James to come running over and pick me up off my feet? Does he even want to talk to me? Fight it back; stamp it down; do not cry. Ashley repeated this command numerous times as she collected her things. She wasn't going to wait around for him; she had to get home.

Walking across the gym and out through the front doors, Ashley crossed the parking lot to her car, obeying her own instructions until she started her car and drove away. Then, the tears came, hot and streaming down her face.

***

She pulled herself together before she made it to her apartment. As she climbed the stairs, her phone buzzed. James. She let it go to voice mail. Rounding the stairs to her apartment, the phone beeped, signaling a message. Ashley fumbled with the key, opened her double-bolt locks, then stumbled inside her apartment. Turning on lights and throwing her stuff in a pile, she pulled her phone out and checked the voice message.

"Hey, Ashley. It's me. I was looking for you at the gym, but I think I missed you. Uh, I mean that I did miss you. Sorry. Justin had my ear. Can we talk later? I'm sorry I didn't get to see you. Bye."

Ashley smiled at hearing his voice; she'd waited for so long to hear from James, and finally had, but she was drained. There was no way she could have this big conversation with him tonight, especially over the phone. She dropped the phone on the kitchen counter and busied herself with emptying her gym bag, throwing her workout clothes in the wash, and airing out her gloves and shin guards for the next day. She needed a shower, food, and bed.

After turning on the water, steam filled the bathroom. Feeling as though she could fall asleep while standing under the hot shower, Ashley scrubbed her skin and washed her hair, thinking of James's call. She would text him and tell him that she'd be at the gym tomorrow; they could meet then.

Grabbing her towel, she dried off, threw on sweats and a T-shirt, and towel-dried her hair. Walking back into the kitchen, she realized she hadn't eaten since that afternoon. There was a dish of quinoa and chicken from the night before. Sitting down at her counter, she inhaled her dinner.

After cleaning up, she stared at her phone, knowing she wouldn't sleep well if she didn't respond. She had no idea what to say and no energy to be creative. Finally, she decided to text.

Ashley: *Crashing hard from training. I'll be at the gym tomorrow. Can we talk then? Night.*

She powered off the phone and fell asleep the minute her head hit the pillow.

***

Memories. Flashes. Light. Heat. Sighing, feeling so much, but not able to bear it; then, it reverberates and shakes you to the core. Calm, quiet…peace. His hands in my hair then slowly roaming down the length of my spine. Arching toward him, needing him closer. My hands on his shoulders, down his back, bracing, holding on, pressing, almost as one, but not yet.

He moves me quickly, pulling me on top of him. I feel like I am floating. Heat building. His eyes intent on mine, boring through to my soul. Then, he touches my face, so gently, wanting more, guiding my mouth toward his.

The kiss. It has always stopped me in my tracks, freezing me and melting me at the same time. I melt into him as my world, our world freezes around us. His mouth is so warm, so soft, but intense. There is no stopping now. Hands roaming, pulling my hips onto him harder. Breathing accelerates. Our bodies flow together. In perfect sync, wanting more, pushing till we cannot bear to hold off anymore. Tremors shuddering to complete stillness. Pure bliss.

***

"Hey." James approached Ashley as she unwrapped her wrists.

"Hey." She continued unwrapping, playing it cool as her stomach swirled and tumbled.

"Do you have time to meet?" His voice is soft. James gestures to his office with a look of concern on his face.

On the one hand, she could say, *No, I've had a long day and am heading home.* She could just say no and walk away. Why offer him an explanation, when she hadn't been given one inkling of an excuse for his actions? Or she could be civil and go along, then say her piece.

Finally, she decided to go along and hear him out. "Yeah, sure." She turned to Lisa. "I'll catch up with you later."

Lisa had returned to the gym to assist in managing the finances. Ashley had convinced her to stay for a short workout.

Lisa nodded to Ashley and mouthed, "Call me."

Ash blushed, hoping James hadn't seen Lisa do that. She put her gear in her bag and hoisted it on her shoulder, following James upstairs.

James stood aside at his office door as Ashley walked in; then, he closed the door. He stole a glance at her. "Have a seat?" He gestured to the chairs.

Ashley remained standing, bag on her shoulder. "What's up, James?"

"Okay, we can stand." Sighing, he looked at her a moment. "Ashley, I want to work with you again if you'll...if you still want to."

Ashley slid the bag off her shoulder. "You're back for a while?"

"I had to work some things out...I..."

"What was there to work out? You left...left me." *There it is.*
Silence followed.

"I didn't feel like I could train you..." He held out his hands.

"You were fine to work with Jonathan. Oh, and Jamal."

"I know. It was bad…" He shook his head and shoved his hands in his pockets.

"Bad for you? Yeah, how do you think I felt?" *Oh well, so much for playing it cool.* Sighing, Ashley crossed her arms.

"Ash, I'm so sorry. I was not strong enough to stay, not strong enough to work with you, to be with you. I'm sorry."

That stopped Ashley's full-steam-ahead plan of telling him how wrong he had been.

"I couldn't have given you what you needed. I…was… Losing Vince, it wrecked me. It wouldn't have been fair to you." He ran a hand through his hair.

Ashley had taken his desertion as a selfish move to leave her behind.

"After the funeral, the loss…I wasn't in a good place. I panicked and did the only thing I knew would help me. That was to leave and to keep moving—"

"Without me." She couldn't stop herself.

"I know, without you, and I'm a jerk…without you." He looked at her as if reliving the feelings all over again. "It was without you so that I wouldn't hurt you. I wouldn't have been good for you mentally. My mind was not here. Being out on the road for the tournaments and fights, that was constant movement, constant change, no need to focus. Get everyone pumped and keep them on schedule. It was totally selfish. When I had downtime, I would think of you and how I left; it killed me. I figured you would bitch me out if I called, which I deserved, so I checked out. I'm sorry."

She knew Vince's loss was a lot for him to bear, but she hadn't realized he was running from the pain, not her. "James, I'm sorry that things were so bad. I tried to help."

James moved toward Ashley, taking her hand in his. "You did, Ashley. You helped me so much. God, you put up with my tantrums and my moods. I felt okay then; I did. But, getting back to work and trying to keep that same regimen going, I couldn't do it. I saw I was holding you back. You were too worried about me, and I was too worried that I was going to miss something in your training and that you would get hurt."

"I was so worried about you." Tears threatened at the corners of her eyes. "I thought you gave up on me. Or forgot about me."

James felt that like a knife to his heart. "Never. Never, Ash," he whispered and kissed her hand. "I'm an ass. I was too stupid and selfish to see straight. I'm so sorry." Ashley held his hands close as James pulled her to him. "I will never leave you again. I promise." James leaned back and looked in her eyes. "Never again."

Somehow, she believed him. *Trust.* This time she felt it.

"I'm here for you. Whatever you are going through." She hugged him fiercely, not wanting to let go.

"Whatever it takes, Ashley, I will do anything to make this up to you."

When Ashley pulled back from James, she thought, *This could be good. It's my turn to call the shots.* "I have conditions if we are going to work together again." She crossed her arms. "But that can wait until tomorrow." Her head ached from the stress, and her body hurt from overtraining that week. "But, now, I need to go home. I'm beat."

James understood. He could see it in her eyes; she needed to rest. Selfishly, he wanted to see her that night, but didn't want to push it. "Okay, Ash."

She wanted him with her, but she didn't want to appear desperate or too weak. Then, she thought, *Who cares? Haven't we wasted enough time?* "Would you want to come over if you don't get out too late tonight?" Ashley held her breath.

"Yes, I'm done in an hour. Would that be okay?" Now it was his turn to hold his breath.

"That would be perfect. I can go home and clean up."

"I will bring dinner. I can't wait, Ash." He hugged her close.

"Me, too. See you later." Ashley turned to leave and felt a huge weight was lifted off her.

She felt light on her feet as she walked out to the parking lot. As she climbed into her car, she noticed a beautiful orange glow to the sun, with rays of yellow, pink, and purple streaking the sky. *God's sky.*

It was a sign of hope and a promise that they'd be together for the long haul.

***

"I missed you so much. I missed this!"

Ashley was working with James in the ring the next day. She'd stuck to her word and given him her list of requests—things she wanted and now expected of him as her coach. He knew her goals and her desire for a big-name fight; she was training with him exclusively. If he was not available, then it would be Justin working with her. James had to make this happen. No ifs, ands, or buts.

It's like no time has passed. He's back; we're back in the ring.

She'd anticipated this moment for so long, but Ashley was too nervous to properly appreciate it. It was not how she'd imagined. She was anxious, unsure, and unsteady; she hadn't practiced beforehand, so she was shaky out of the gate and not very confident.

On the other hand, James was steady, strong, and sure of himself. His movements were smooth and precise; he exuded confidence. His voice was warm and reassuring; it calmed her nerves and squashed any self-doubts.

It's perfect.

Moving methodically around the ring, timing combinations, and testing the limits—this is what she'd missed. At first, they worked at a lighter pace, not landing any punches or kicks with full force; then, the intensity increased with each consecutive round.

Final round, they were sparring with even more speed and power. James caught her leg kick and tossed her. Ashley spun, knowing what he had planned; she avoided his incoming kick and surprised him with a side kick to the gut.

"Nice." But, then, he was ten steps ahead, as usual.

James grabbed Ashley in a clinch; she froze at the surprise of it. She always froze—trigger response. James lightly threw a knee up against her side, getting her to play along. Once she settled in and started breathing again, it was okay; she knew what to do. *Breathe, get to work.*

They worked back and forth, trading knee for knee, swimming in and out of the clinch, their bodies pressed together. *If I let my mind wander...but this is work.* They flowed together around the ring until the bell rang.

"You've been working hard since I've been gone." James bumped her glove. "Nice."

"Yeah, thanks. Well, there wasn't much else I could do." She paused. "I wanted to get stronger; I needed it."

James knew exactly what she meant. "You definitely got stronger." Taking off his gloves and putting them aside, he turned to Ashley, smiling. "Up for some heavy pad work? Finish with some kicks?" He knew, out of everything in this sport, Ashley loved kicking the most, and he loved holding pads for her.

"Sure, if I can still move."

He hopped out of the ring and retrieved his Thai pads, while Ashley took advantage of the time for a water break. Too soon, he was back and raring to go.

"Let's go." Moving across the floor of the ring wordlessly, he positioned the pads in ranges from low to high kicks, to switches, to crescents, and to body kicks. After three rounds, she was exhausted.

"You've got this; come on." He pushed her through one more round, knowing she had a rest day coming up.

She wanted him to work her, and she got what she requested. Ashley was so thankful for that annoying timer as it blared out, ending their session.

CHAPTER 48

The warmth in his eyes was back. His entire demeanor had changed. His aura pulled her into that calm circle of comfort. She liked it there. The sound of his voice, when he spoke her name and shared all that had happened during his day, was smooth and deep, a melody to her ears.

He would drift away at times; she could see the hurt in his eyes, but he would come back and give her hand a squeeze or hug her so hard she thought he was going to break her or break down. He did that a couple of times, and she held him through the tears, the sobs, and the "why did this have to happen to Vince."

Ashley told him she would always be there for him; he could scream at her about it, cry, or say nothing at all. Lord knows, James had been there for her more times than she could count. She wanted to be his rock, his shoulder to lean on. She couldn't bear him shutting her out.

James needed her. He could not bear the thought of losing Ashley, and he promised to never leave her again. He would try to be present and share what he could. Her hand in his was all he needed to know there was hope in this world for something beautiful to begin again.

Ashley's connection to James was more intense than before he left. Watching him across the gym, she could feel his emotions, his energy, and every nuance of each move. Occasionally, he caught her eye and raised his eyebrows suggestively. She smiled, blushed, and then looked away.

God, he can read my mind; he knows everything I think about him, she thought.

She tried to concentrate on the rowing machine, absorbing every movement and thinking about each stroke and push of her legs.

Breathing in and out, Ashley felt her heart race. She tried not to look back at James, but that didn't last long.

She watched his body move—his back so strong, his arms punching and blocking, and his sparring dance. Those arms that held her close, that held her down, that made her feel like the most amazing woman in the world. Hearing his voice in the gym put her at ease. It soothed her soul, but at the same time, it sent her insides swirling with excitement and desire. No matter where she was or what she was doing in the expansively large gym, whenever Ashley heard James's voice, she was distracted. Even if she couldn't see him, she wanted—no, she needed—to hear him.

Ashley tried to focus on her breathing. She could see James in her peripheral vision. Glancing to the side, she saw he was watching her with a smile she couldn't explain. He was at peace, happiness crinkling the corners of his eyes. That made her heart soar. A month ago, he'd come back to her from the darkness.

Ashley slowed her rowing after seeing that her heart rate was in the 95-percent maximum zone. She needed to be mindful of recovery for the next several days. The upside—she would have more energy and time to spend with James.

James jumped down from the ring and spoke with his client, looking ahead at the week's schedule. He wanted to make sure he kept some time open to see Ashley—if she wanted to see him, that is. He hoped so; he was still feeling a little insecure. He knew she cared about him. She loved him, but he didn't know why at times. He'd been such a jerk to her this past month; he couldn't see why she'd stuck around.

He watched her and thought she was the most beautiful woman he had ever seen. Her inside radiated outward and outshone any woman he'd ever encountered. No one could compare, and he didn't care to even try to find someone who could.

He only had space in his heart for Ashley. She was everything to him, and he vowed to prove that he could live up to what she deserved.

James had an amazing weekend planned for the two of them after her competition. He needed to run it by her and see when their schedules lined up to make it happen.

CHAPTER 49

The uneasy feelings flooded back at times. No matter how hard she tried, there was no way to build a dam to stop them. The bruises on her arms brought it all back. How could she feel so amazing and strong, and then revert to that insecure person she was so long ago?

This situation is totally different, though. This is my sport. I fight. That's what I do. The result of that is getting hurt. Bruises, black-and-blues, cuts, and bumps. Those come with the territory. Face it.

"Am I ready for this?" She stared at the tickets to the fight; her name was printed across the bottom. *Ashley Banner v. Shawn Doubak.* They were almost sold out. Just reading Shawn's name evoked an increase in the pace of her pulse and stomach churning.

"Yes."

James exuded the confidence Ashley lacked. He'd answered as if there was no question she would win. His confidence in her was what she needed. She was packing her gym bag nervously and fussing so that everything was perfect.

"Will you wait for me?" She looked up at him, hopeful.

"Of course. I'll be there, only a little later this time." He touched her shoulder.

This was harder than she'd imagined. James had always been there at the start of her fights; he was the voice of reason, her motivation. This time, Justin would be there with her; he was good, but still...not James.

***

She loved the intensity, the feeling of freedom after hitting the bag or the pads; even the sparring was liberating. But she hated that she was so fragile. *No one else has bruises like this. Why me?* she thought. Laughing to herself, she wondered when she had ever gotten an answer to that question? Over her lifetime, she'd learned to face it, deal with it, suffer through it, or grin and bear it.

This situation wouldn't be any different. Ashley was better and stronger, and she hoped that would ensure getting hurt less. *Stay strong,* she repeated in her head. Physically, she'd become stronger over the past year. But she knew she needed a different strength to beat Shawn in the ring. The strength that comes from within.

CHAPTER 50

This was the fight of her life. Ashley knew there was a lot at stake here; she needed to win, make her mark, or break a record—do something. Once and for all, she had to end this game between her and Shawn.

The anticipation was more than she could stand. Ashley's heart was beating out of her chest, and her palms were sweaty. She needed to get control of this situation.

Deep breathing, tune it out. The noise of the crowd and the music blaring—she needed to ignore it all and breathe. Her nerves were on high alert, her body on fire. The waiting would kill her; she could not stop moving and fidgeting. *Relax; be calm.* A part of her longed for this to be over. *This fight will be well worth all the nerve-shaking, tummy-twisting excitement. I will win…breathe in…this will be over soon…breathe out.*

Shawn was the toughest opponent she had ever faced. *The end of the fight—so far away. The fight—moments away.* Later, there would be time for peace, serenity, and rest. Until then, she had to be present in the moment. *Focus. Concentrate on being precise.*

"Five minutes." The voice blasted her back to reality.

"I'm ready." Ashley did not even recognize her own voice. She was ready.

The team came in to lead her out. Walking with them, she heard the buzz from the crowd; the faces and sounds blurred together. Ashley answered questions from Justin, but was hardly paying attention to the conversation.

"Make sure you listen to the officials."

"I will." She loosened her shoulders.

"Take advantage of the breaks when you can get them. Don't blow all of your energy early…"

"Uh-huh."

She tuned it all out; her vision tunneled with only one focus. *Keep your eye on the ring,* she told herself.

What if Stephen is here…?

No, stop!

Adrenaline shot through her veins; she could feel the rapid rise in her heart rate. With each step, she felt the excitement build.

With sudden clarity, Ashley knew she had this fight. Everything fell into place around her. She knew she had the upper hand. The feeling hit her like a bolt of lightning. She felt it, and she knew it deep in her core because she saw him—*James is here.*

***

James felt Ashley's energy, and he wasn't even in the same room with her. He was running late from his last competition and had told her he would meet her down by the ring. He would make it, not to worry. He could imagine how fired up she was. He had been around her enough prefight to know what she was going through—extreme inner turmoil, but appearance of calm to all who were around her. James was the only one she let in behind the mask. Calm versus panic, ready to unleash versus ready to go over the edge and snap.

He prayed she kept it together long enough to take Shawn out. He had confidence that she could win, but as she came into view, he thought she looked a little lost. The group was pressing in on her— telling her the rules, he assumed—but he could see she wasn't focusing on them.

"Come on; come on; you've got this, Ash," he whispered to himself. Suddenly, he saw a shift in her posture; it was as if she'd heard him. He saw the transformation instantaneously as she approached. The fire was in her eyes; she was focused.

Ashley locked eyes with him and held his gaze.

Damn, she is ready.

"You're here," she said in a voice that seemed strong, but Ashley had felt it almost crack.

"Of course, I'm here. What'd you think?" He shrugged, melting her with his smile.

Ashley knew he was going to be there, but when he texted that he was stuck in traffic from his last competition, she'd begun to panic a little. *Well, a lot.*

James placed his hand on her shoulder. "You've got this; remember that."

She nodded.

Ashley couldn't get distracted by him, by those eyes. She was thankful he was there. No matter how crazy he made her, no matter how much she couldn't stand him at times during training, he grounded her. His voice could bring her back from wherever she went when the panic set in.

James blocked off Justin and the others. "I've got this now. I'll take her from here."

Justin looked crushed. With James not around, he was all set to take the lead, but James had put an end to that. No one but James would be up in the ring with Ashley.

Justin stepped back. "You've got this, Ash. See you after."

"Thank you, Justin." She reached out and fist-bumped him.

James couldn't hold her hand all the way, although Ashley would have liked that right now. She chuckled at the thought. James would die if he knew that. She'd kill for a hug, for some reassurance that it was all going to be all right—a pat on the back, even. *God forbid.* Again, she had to chuckle.

"Glad you are finding this so amusing. Focus." James glared at her sideways. *What the heck is she thinking?* He was hoping this wasn't the start of one of her manic prefight moments.

James is right, Ashley thought. *We are past the time for warm and fuzzies.*

"I'm good; let's go."

They walked in silence. James led the way, keeping Ashley close. Always a hand guiding her, brushing her side, her arm, or her back.

It was as if he thought she would run away if he was not close, not touching her.

The music started. Her entry song.

Ashley was giddy inside for a second. *This isn't possible,* she thought. Then, the platform came into view. *This is it.*

Ashley released a long breath, which she felt she had been holding in for so long. This is where she and James wanted to be, what they both had worked so hard for.

The Ring.

***

Ashley's world slowed down. The guards patted her down, checked her gloves, and her mouth guard. James put the mouth guard in for her and strapped her gloves on tight. She then walked up to the ring and under those ropes, as she'd done so many times at the gym.

This is it.

The warm-up, the talk. Ashley prayed to God that she would be granted strength and that she would somehow be safe.

James was there now, in her ear, giving her reassurance. "Stay head-strong. You've got this. Control your breathing. You know what to do."

Today, those words meant so much. It was as if he were breathing strength into her, one word at a time. His energy radiated off him in waves and flowed into her. The heat of his body next to hers was pulling her to him.

Ashley remembered his instruction. *"Focus."*

James fed off Ashley's energy. She was quietly taking it all in, but he felt that she was jazzed and ready for the fight. His adrenaline was through the roof, and the energy from the crowd was giving him a rush. He could only imagine how she felt. James needed to get inside her head and keep her in the moment. This was not the time for Ashley's mind to start wandering to the dark places.

James knew what worked for her and what did not. He would not bring her down, only pump her up and keep her floating. Being so close to her was distracting; her breath and her scent were so intoxicating he had to be careful. *Focus, damn it.* He had to keep her close; standing next her, he felt as if they were magnets.

The bell rang, snapping him back to reality.

Once again, James looked into her eyes and saw the fire.

It's time.

Ashley locked on to Shawn when she entered the ring, her senses razor-sharp. Shawn looked ready and pissed. She always looked that way. Ashley could never tell if she had any other emotions. With wiry muscles and a lean body, Shawn was near perfect, except for that miserable look.

Shawn was intense; her stare seemed to pierce straight through Ashley. *Breathe.* Ashley nodded quickly at her then turned away. Shawn would never put aside her pride for good sportsmanship, and Ashley was prepared for that.

The ref called them in, and Ashley and Shawn were now face-to-face. All that James taught Ashley needed to be accessible and had to come together in some semblance. James had taught Shawn, too, but Ashley had a slight advantage. James had schooled Ashley on Shawn's weaknesses, which only he knew, having trained her for so long. There were not many, but Ashley only needed one.

Always the professional, James would never have revealed a client's secret, but Ashley was not just another client to James. In a fit of jealousy, Shawn had dropped James as her trainer and had left the gym to train elsewhere, shit-talking his gym and bad-mouthing him and all the trainers from his facility. Shawn had drawn that line in the sand. So, James felt no loyalty to her anymore. Now, he only had one thing on his mind. Winning.

Shawn did not waste time when the bell rang. She came at Ashley with a cross-hook combo. Ashley blocked her punches as if she knew what was coming. Feeling light on her feet, Ashley maneuvered around the ring and returned Shawn's punches with a jab-cross-hook to the body. She attempted a rear kick, but Shawn moved out of range.

The round flew by like that. Neither of them gained much of a lead over the other. Shawn took some cheap shots, but she was good at hiding them. She did it in such a way that no judge could detect her cheating, but Ashley certainly felt the results.

Obviously, Shawn had also done her homework. She was aware of Ashley's weaknesses and her strengths and seemed to know what Ashley was going to do before she did it. Shawn homed in on Ashley's injured shoulder as if she had X-ray vision and could see the injury. She knew how to inflict intense pain, and Ashley was trained to hide the pain she felt.

Shawn watched her like a hawk to detect any type of change in Ashley's face, her stance. Any small flinch would give her satisfaction, and she would hammer away at that body part. The plus side—Shawn was obsessed with reinjuring Ashley's shoulder. While Shawn was focusing on Ashley's shoulder, Ashley was taking advantage of the opportunity and getting in some body shots.

Shawn needed to be weakened. Ashley knew that Shawn had suffered from broken ribs a while back; they'd never quite healed right. If she kept landing those shots to Shawn's side, Ashley knew she could chip away at her slowly, subtly.

As the bell rang, Ashley thought, *Thank God this round is over.*

James had seen that Ashley was slowing down, so he got in right next to her, putting ice on her back and shoulder. "Ash, you are doing great, kid. Don't let her mess with your head. Got it? Protect that shoulder." James looked into her eyes and tried to will strength back into her.

Justin was over the ropes, icing her legs, telling her to stay focused.

James gave her the nasty green goo that she hated so much, but Ashley knew she needed to replenish her energy and fluids. So, she took it willingly, listening to his words and nodding her head. She knew what had to be done.

James massaged Biofreeze into Ashley's shoulder. Usually, he let the others deal with these details, but he needed to be in Ashley's ear, to touch her skin, and to keep her together. He wanted her to know he was behind her, no matter what happened.

James did not underestimate what Shawn was capable of; he knew what she was made of, and it was not pretty. If Ashley let her guard down or fell apart, Shawn could severely injure her. James would never let it get that far; he would pull Ashley out if her shoulder got much worse or if her energy was zapped. No way James would let Ashley know this; she would be pissed at him for doubting her in any way. Ashley wanted this win as much as he did.

Finally, regaining her energy, she spoke, "I'm good. I've got this."

Their eyes locked a moment, electricity flowing between them. James leaned close to her and whispered in her ear, "There is nothing that can stop you, Ashley."

It was exactly what she needed to hear. She was filled with confidence, and the fight was back in her.

A second later, the bell rang.

***

Shawn did not take her eyes off James and Ashley the entire break, watching and waiting to see if her shots were taking a toll. She watched as James talked to Ashley; she could imagine exactly what he was saying to her. Shawn had been on that end before.

Her jaw dropped when she saw James touching her, massaging her shoulder. The connection between them was visible. Suddenly, Shawn realized what was going on between them. She had been *there* before, too. *What a joke, he must be desperate*, she thought. Seeing James whisper in Ashley's ear, another possibility hit Shawn; James most likely told Ashley about her weak ribs.

Shawn's eyes reflected the rage that was boiling up inside of her, filling her with fire. The bell rang, and Shawn was ready to unleash her fury.

***

James crouched against the side of the ring. Shawn had come out full force and backed Ashley into a corner. She was relentless, positioning Ashley so she had nowhere else to go. *No, she can get herself out.* As that thought entered his mind, it was quickly erased when he saw the look of rage in Shawn's eyes as she hammered away at Ashley's shoulder and threw knees to her ribs. James felt helpless as he watched Ashley cornered.

Ashley cringed as a bolt of white-hot pain shot into her shoulder and radiated all the way down her arm again and again as those punches kept coming. *I have to stop this,* Ashley's mind screamed. In a split second, she looked up into Shawn's face and saw the hate, the rage seeping out of her.

Ashley moved her body to get out of the line of fire. Shawn kept pushing her toward the ropes and blocking her in. Ashley felt her heart race; panic was creeping in and taking over her breathing.

No, panic cannot take over now. This is it—do or die. Kick this psycho's ass or fail miserably. I am not going to lose.

In her head, Ashley heard James and all the encouragement he had given her. She remembered how hard she'd fought to overcome all the shit that had happened to her in her life. *No, this bitch is not going to take me down.*

James was close to calling the fight at any minute. This beating could not go on; he could not watch Shawn demolish Ashley like this. He wanted to jump in there and ring Shawn's neck. "Come on, Ash; come on!" James banged the side of the ring.

With Ashley still backed into a corner, Shawn pulled her into a clinch, holding her tight, throwing knees into her side. Ashley freed herself and spun away from the ropes, landing in the center of the ring.

Then, James saw it. There was a transformation in Ashley's expression—from fear and pain to something else. James saw her eyes and froze. Her voice echoed in his head, *"Bad things happen when I'm backed into a corner."* He remembered her saying it half in jest, but he knew it was the truth.

James's first thought was *Holy shit, she's going to kill Shawn.* He let out a nervous laugh. Not believing his eyes, James watched Ashley rise, take all that anger, pain, and struggle, and start to use it as fuel to take Shawn down.

Ashley landed a quick jab, high hook, and low hook, temporarily pushing Shawn away from her. Ashley dodged a cross and countered with another nasty body hook into Shawn's ribs, followed by a rear kick to the body, landing perfectly on Shawn's weak spot. Shawn was thrown off guard, and Ashley unleashed repeated kicks to her body, followed by hook after unmerciful hook into her weakened ribs.

Ashley came at her with such force that Shawn was thrown back into the ropes by her blows. Ashley saw red as she landed a double uppercut in Shawn's now-broken ribs.

Shawn grabbed her side as she dropped to her knees.

Ashley didn't even hear the bell ring.

James saw the intent in Ashley's eyes and thought, *She's not going to stop.* Ashley was heading straight for Shawn, ready to land a knee to the head. It would have been a perfect end to a fight if they were in a movie where the heroine finally killed the evil opponent, but this was no movie.

No way James was going to let Ashley throw away this win. He hopped the ropes and ran to Ashley as the bell was ringing. He stood in front of her and placed his hands firmly on her shoulders. "Ash, you won. It's over!" James could feel the force as Ashley tried to forge ahead toward Shawn. "It's done! Don't throw this all away."

Ashley shook as she stared at James blankly; momentarily, she was still in her other world. Then, all the tension left her face and her body. James caught her as she leaned into him, losing her balance.

Ashley grabbed hold of him in disbelief. "Oh my God, James." Her full weight was leaning on him. She couldn't hold herself up any longer.

He held her and smiled. "You did it, kid. We won."

CHAPTER 51

I *need to stop for the night. This driving through the boonies is making me crazy. Middle of fucking nowhere. I'm pulling off at the next exit, no matter what. Says there is food and lodging. I can only imagine what I'll get stuck with. If there's a bed and a beer close by, I'm good.*

Looks like my wish has been granted. Roadside motel and townee bar-and-grill next door. Not too crowded, but enough cars that you know both are good. This night is looking up.

Stephen checked into the Gas Lamp Inn and settled in a "deluxe room" that was on the far corner.

"Lots of privacy." The lady at the front desk chewed her gum and gave him a once-over.

She could be my mother, for Christ's sake, but I'll smile and give her a wink back. No need to start trouble here.

"How's the place next door?" Stephen nodded toward the bar.

"Food's always hot, and beer is cold. Gets a good crowd." She handed Stephen his key, and her hand stayed on it a few seconds too long. "Call if you need anything."

"Will do. Thanks a lot."

Grabbing his bag, he jumped back in his truck and pulled up to the room's private entrance. *Lucky number seven,* he thought. *Ridiculous, they all have their own entrance.* His unit was on the end; there was no one to bother him next door, and the unit upstairs was empty.

Stephen threw his bags into the room, cleaned up a little, and headed next door, hoping his good luck would continue.

***

Music was playing in the bar-and-grill when Stephen walked in and took a seat at the bar. The place was packed with what looked to be locals and maybe some out-of-towners from the motel. Based on the front-desk clerk's recommendation, Stephen asked the bartender for a tall, cold beer. Scanning the patrons, he noticed a couple of girls giving him the eye from the opposite end of the bar. He was sure he stood out here. A new face among the townees. One of the girls had blonde hair; she was the one he would set his sights on for the night.

This was the distraction he needed after all the stress he'd been under, the stress that Ashley had caused. Stephen felt his grip tighten on the beer. *No, I will not let that bitch ruin my night.* He glanced at the doe eyes down the bar. *Perfect.* It was a matter of time before she would be begging to go back to his motel room with him.

***

Stephen threw her down on the bed as she laughed. *This girl is so drunk.* Stephen had other ideas.

As he took his shirt off, she sat up smiling, liking what she saw. "You have an amazing body." Working her way across the bed, she started to take off her shirt.

Stephen climbed in bed on top of her, pushing her down. He held her hands down.

Her long, blonde hair spilled over her shoulders, like Ashley's. Her legs wrapped around him, like Ashley's.

Stephen bit down on her neck, pressing against her. "Ashley..." For a moment, he felt as if he were back in time, loving Ashley, holding Ashley close.

"What? My name isn't Ashley." She shoved him hard. "You're drunk! Or stupid!" She laughed and rolled over, pulling her shirt back over herself.

Stephen snapped back to reality, not realizing he'd said Ashley's name. Enraged, he grabbed her by the hair and shoved her back onto the bed. "Shut up, bitch. Use your mouth for something else." He pulled at his pants and got free of them while holding her down.

She was stunned by his behavior and thought it best not to fight him. She had been beat up by guys before; she'd learned it was better to go along and get things done without a fight. Then, she could leave and be free of this crazy guy.

She did her thing, which seemed to pacify him.

Then, as quickly as he'd grabbed her, Stephen pulled the girl off him and shoved her aside.

"Okay, baby?" She was trying to read him, hoping he would give her a little satisfaction in return.

"Yeah, great. Get your clothes on." He stood and walked to the bathroom to clean up, leaving the door ajar.

Dumbfounded and shaking, she grabbed her shirt and the blanket that was on top of the bed and covered herself. Being drunk was not helping her judgment. Maybe she could entice him to come back for a little more. She stood, wrapping the worn blanket around herself a little tighter, and walked toward the bathroom. "Come on back. I can do something else for you."

Enraged, Stephen had had enough. He bolted out of the bathroom, pushing the door open so violently that it hit her with enough force to throw her to the floor.

She let out a loud cry. "You stupid ass!"

This sent Stephen further into hysteria. He lunged at her, grabbed her by the throat, pushed her against the wall, and held her there. "Who is the stupid one now?" He seethed. "You came back to my hotel without knowing anything about who you were getting in bed with. Now that, my dear, was stupid." His hand tightened around her throat, and he raised his arm until the girl's feet were off the floor.

She struggled to catch her breath, clawing at his hands for relief.

"You stupid girl." With each word, he slammed her hard against the wall.

Her airway was cut off, and her limbs became weaker as she faded then blacked out completely.

His anger unabated, Stephen continued squeezing, harder and harder. As he loosened his grip, the girl slumped down the wall. Breathing hard, he completely let go, and she crumpled to the floor, the blanket falling away.

Stephen's hands shook violently. He tried to check for signs of life. "Get up." He shoved at her shoulder, but she further slumped into a heap. "Fucking great!" Stephen punched the floor as rage turned to panic. His eyes darted around as he came to the realization that he had killed her.

"Shit. I gotta get out of here." Stephen wrapped the girl in the blanket and stood staring down at her, weighing his options.

Should I leave everything as it is? Or wrap her up, hide her in the trunk, and dump her somewhere? Neither option ever worked out well for anyone, he thought.

He began to pace then set about the room, making sure the door was dead-bolted and the curtains were drawn. The noise from their room could have prompted someone to issue a complaint to the main office, so Stephen chose to lie low for a while to avoid drawing more attention to his room. He shut off the lights, pulled his gun, and sat by the door in the dark.

***

Stephen watched Ashley from the back of the coffee shop. She would never recognize him as he looked now. He felt empowered by the anonymity of his new look. His hair was short and much darker than before. With all his spare time, Stephen had hit the weights and bulked up, grown a beard, and gotten additional artwork. He wondered, *What will she think of that?*

Tattoos had become an addiction for him. The pain helped take his mind off losing her. Stephen couldn't wait for her to see the one he had done for her.

Hiding behind his dark sunglasses, he continued to sit and watch. She had changed quite radically. No more soft layers, her extra curves were carved down; she was visibly toned and more muscular. No more blonde hair either, but Stephen had known it was Ashley the minute he saw her.

Stephen had watched her routine the past couple of days. She hit the gym, stopped for a coffee, and then went to work. He did notice she stopped at a different coffee shop each day, trying to break up the pattern. Surprised to see that she had joined a boxing gym, he wanted to investigate and find out what her situation was there.

Ashley, a fighter. He couldn't figure that one out. She was so quiet when she was with him. Ashley never liked the spotlight; blending in was what she wanted. Stephen felt he needed to help her, tell her what to do. She relied on him, needed guidance.

After she left, she faded into black. He had been patiently waiting to find her, waiting for her to trip up and leave a trace. She'd been so careful. She'd covered her tracks well for so long; then, she got sloppy. Time inevitably makes you let your guard down, become careless.

Ashley began competing and then winning fights. She'd become popular in her circuit, and here we are. Of course, she would eat that attention up since she'd been in hiding for so long. Now, she had people looking at her, cheering for her, and wanting her.

It still surprised Stephen that Ashley had become a fighter; she hated to fight. They'd fought a lot. She would cry when he lost his temper, which happened quite a bit toward the end. Maybe too much. *I might have crossed the line,* he thought.

She must have met someone here, and that guy pushed her to do this. That fact infuriated him. Stephen took a deep breath; he needed to control himself and his emotions. That was difficult for him when he was with Ashley. He may have lost his temper a few times—well, many times—but all that was different now. Now, he had control over himself and his emotions, and he needed to show Ashley how much he'd changed.

***

The next day, Stephen checked into the gym and signed up for a free one-week trial. Just to get the routine down, he went in a couple of days in the afternoon when he knew Ashley would not be there.

Then, when he felt it was right, he went at night when he knew Ashley *would* be there and it would be crowded. He made himself blend in; he didn't want to stand out. Stephen wasn't ready for Ashley to see him yet.

He watched her work out, not believing her intensity. Then, there was this guy hanging around her; she followed him around like a puppy dog. Putting it all together, Stephen figured out he was her trainer. He watched him as he spoke to her and put his hands on her to "teach" her the moves. *What a joke. She's probably screwing him. She's probably hooked up with half the guys in this place. How else would she get all this attention? No way this bitch can fight.*

The anger boiled up inside of him, rising in his throat. His left hand started twitching; he needed to get that under control. Squashing the urge to walk over to this asshole and take him down, Stephen concentrated on his breathing.

It was going to take some time, but she would take Stephen back. She would see that he had changed. He would make her see that she didn't need all these other guys or this boxing bullshit. Stephen would save her from herself, and Ashley would realize how lucky she was that he'd found her again and that he was willing to take her back.

CHAPTER 52

"You scared the shit out of me last night." James brushed Ashley's hair away from her shoulder and caressed her back.

"I'm so sorry. My phone died midtext, and I only got the one word out." She rested her hand on his shoulder. "God, that's terrible."

"Yeah. I may need to put a tracking device on you." He laughed. "Just kidding." Then, his expression was serious.

"I won't be satisfied until I wake up next to you every morning." His eyes danced. "I'm not trying to sound like a stalker, either." His hands glided down to her waist and then toward her hips. "You want to… live together?"

Ashley swallowed hard. Sharing her space was a hard concept for her. She wasn't sure she was ready. She wasn't sure she wanted him to see all of her idiosyncrasies.

"I want to be with you, Ashley. We are meant to be together, not apart." He lowered his head and sighed. "There I go, sounding like a stalker again. I am sorry." He buried his head near her belly, then kissed her skin lightly.

Ashley lay frozen a moment, until she felt his warm mouth on her, melting her icy heart. Her hands found his head, and she ran her fingers through his hair. "Don't be sorry," she whispered. She wanted this; she always wanted James. Why was it so hard to take the next step? She and James, together—that is what she dreamt of, imagining his arms around her throughout the night and waking to his beautiful body…

James looked up and broke her runaway train of thought. "Ash?"

"Huh?"

"Did you hear anything I said?"

"Um, yeah." She laughed.

"Liar." He pulled her closer and kissed her belly again.

"I am sorry. I wasn't listening…"

"It's okay. We'll take this slow. I'm not going anywhere." Those eyes of his melted her reserves.

"I know, and I want this. So much…"

"I know, Ash." He lay down on his side, facing her. "I know." He drew her close, putting his arm around her.

Ash scooted in next to him. She had no problem being this close to him. This, with him, was where she felt safe, at home. She breathed him in. She could see herself with him, see their future.

It'll happen in time. That thought made her smile.

He was looking at her, brushing her hair back from her face. "I like that look." He touched her cheek, close to her lips. "That smile for me?"

"Yes." She was breathless. *How does he do that to me?* One touch, one look, and she was jelly.

He closed his eyes and kissed her softly where his fingers had lingered.

He spread warmth throughout her entire body with just a kiss. She brought her hand up to his neck, her fingers tracing circles on his skin. "You are the reason I smile. I'm so happy when I'm with you."

His eyes crinkled as he smiled and hugged her close to him.

Arms and bodies intertwined, they lay, each with the same vision of their future together.

CHAPTER 53

"I'm going to California for the competition next month." James outlined her waist with his hands. "Will you come with me?" He looked hopefully into her deep-green eyes, finding his strength. "You don't have to answer now…just maybe by tomorrow morning." James nervously laughed, searching her eyes.

"Yes! Yes, of course." Ashley sat up and climbed on his lap, taking his face in her hands. "There's nowhere else I'd rather be." She kissed his lips, savoring the taste of him and running her hands through his hair. "This will be amazing. You will be amazing. I can't wait."

James put his arms around her, keeping her close. "It'll be amazing to be away with you. We can stay a few days longer if you can get off from work." He kissed her again, hands roaming.

"Of course, I can take off work." Ashley laughed with delight at the thought of being away with James. "It'll be perfect."

"The fight is on Friday. I figured we could fly in late Wednesday. Then, after the fight, I'm free to do whatever you want."

Daydreaming of James in a hotel bed with her for four glorious days, Ashley absently drew her hands through his hair.

James pulled her close, kissing her, loving her hands on him, loving how she made him feel as if he could do anything. "You're amazing."

"You're not so bad yourself." She trailed her lips along his jaw, down his neck.

He groaned softly.

She moved down his chest and backed off his lap so she could lay him back. She took her time, letting her hands and mouth explore his body.

"Ashley."

She looked up at him and smiled slyly.

James watched her as she kissed down his chest, toward his belly. He ran his hands through her hair as she made her way back up to kiss his neck. He put his arms around her, rolling her onto her back.

As he moved his lips over her jaw, down toward her throat, Ashley shivered, pressing her body against him.

He teased her with his strong hands and soft lips. Touching and kissing lightly—first, slowly; then, pressing in with a sense of urgency.

"You're making me crazy."

"Mission accomplished." She pulled him closer.

Uniting, they moved together as one.

***

He rested his head against her belly, feeling her breath slow and her tremors fade. He loved the feel of her skin, the way her hands moved over him, the warmth of her. He never wanted to let go. He shifted his weight and moved to lay next to her, pulling her into his arms. Her eyes sparkled in the candlelight.

Ashley searched his eyes and saw the heat and the desire for her still there. James's eyes were open doors to her. She wanted to be with him always. By what she saw in the depths of his eyes, she knew in that moment that James felt the same way about her.

Smiling, he touched her cheek. "I love you, Ashley." His voice was low and raspy.

"James, I love you so much." Tears dotted the corners of her eyes.

Both smiled and breathed a sigh.

James hugged her close, kissing her forehead. "I have been waiting for you for so long."

The tears spilled over as Ashley held him, not believing this could be real. "I never thought I could feel this way."

Bodies encircling one another, never breaking hold, they lay together by candlelight until they drifted off to sleep.

***

James woke up; his arm had fallen asleep under Ashley. Carefully, he got out of bed and stood up slowly, then walked to the bathroom to brush his teeth.

Ashley stretched out like a satisfied cat. She heard him banging around in the bathroom and smiled. Getting up, she pulled on a T-shirt and boxers and headed into the bathroom to brush her teeth.

At the same time, James was coming out and almost bumped into her. "Hey, you're up." James put his arms around her hips.

She put her hands on his chest. "Yeah, I missed you."

"Oh yeah?" He kissed her neck.

"I'll be right back in." She kissed his cheek and hurried off so she could get back to bed with James, not wanting to waste a minute. Brushing her teeth, she smiled at her reflection. She looked lighter and happier, and she felt that way, too.

The early morning chill gave her goose bumps. She practically ran to the bed, knowing it was warm in the cocoon with James. She snuggled in, and it felt better than she'd imagined. "You are so warm."

"You are so cold! What, did you open the window in there?"

She laughed, putting her cold feet on his legs. "Oh my God! You're like a corpse." He rubbed her back and arms, creating heat.

She kissed his shoulder, tracing the scar with her fingers. Between them, there were so many untold stories that had left scars. *Some you can see and some you can't,* Ashley thought. Although, James did know most of her dark stories, the one whose scars ran deep. And, still, he'd stayed.

She knew of his battle scars and some of his dark past. He kept his dark side hidden, but she would be there when he needed her to be.

His voice broke the silence. "I meant what I said before. I am in love with you." Rolling on his side, he turned so he could read her face. Her smile told him all he needed to know.

"I meant it, too. I love you. So much. I was going to say it, and you beat me to it."

"Remember that. I said it first." He smirked.

"James!" Ashley pushed into his chest.

Laughing, he hugged her then kissed her mouth.

The kisses gradually became more intense. Ashley felt herself heating up, wanting him again. She wrapped her legs around him.

"You are insatiable," he breathed.

She laughed again. "I blame you." She straddled his legs.

"I take full responsibility and will assist in fulfilling all of your needs in any way that I can." He held his right hand up, swearing his oath.

She leaned down and kissed him. "Perfect."

***

Ashley woke to the bright sunlight coming in from the bathroom. Stretching, once again feeling like that satisfied cat, she rolled over to see James was not beside her; that momentarily decreased her satisfaction.

There was a small Post-it Note on the bedside table:

Getting coffees. Be back soon. Don't move. XO.

Ashley smiled, happy to stay in bed. She glanced at the clock, not believing it read 9:30 a.m. *When was the last time I stayed in bed until 9:30?* This was pure luxury.

She stumbled into the bathroom to freshen up, then happily collapsed back in bed, waiting for James to return. Fading to a dream state, she faintly heard the door unlock and rustling down the hall.

"You awake?" James peered into the dimly lit room with two coffees and a bag in his hands.

"Hey." She rubbed her eyes.

"Hey, sorry, did I wake you?" James sat down beside her, placing the bag and coffees on the side table.

Ashley sat up, running her hand through her tousled hair. "No, I was up. Kind of."

James was wearing a baseball hat and looked amazing to her. As his hand landed on her leg, she felt she must be dreaming.

"I got us coffees and breakfast. Want it in bed, or do you want to get up."

She thought to say, *I want you in bed*, but decided that could wait. She should eat something. Leaning over, she kissed him. "Thank you."

"You're welcome, for whatever it is that I did." James took his hat off.

She tilted her head sideways, taking him in. "Everything. Being you." She kissed him again.

"I'll definitely do more of that." He smiled warmly.

Ashley climbed out of bed and pulled on a hoodie and sweat pants while James carried their breakfast to the kitchen.

"What's your plan for today?" James took breakfast sandwiches out of the paper bag and placed them on napkins.

"Whatever you want to do. It's nice out; we could head out for a walk." She sipped her coffee.

"That sounds great. We should get out for a bit." James smiled at Ashley.

"Yeah, or we could stay in bed all day." She bumped his hip.

"Ha, thought about that, too. We could come back for that."

"Definitely."

Finishing their breakfast, they planned their walk, possibly a trek up Commonwealth Avenue toward Boston Common.

Ashley changed her clothes and fished her sneakers out of her duffel. "Ready?"

"I *am* ready." James threw out the empty cups and bag.

Ashley placed her phone on the entry table before they walked out.

"No phone?" He nodded to her phone.

"No, I'm leaving it behind. No need to check it." She opened the door.

James nodded. "Good idea." He put his phone on the table next to hers. "No need for mine either. You're the only person I'd want to hear from, anyway." He took her hand, and they headed downstairs.

As they walked outside, the sunshine warmed Ashley's face. The heat spread through her, filling her heart until she thought it would burst. She held James's hand with both of hers and smiled up at him.

"Ready, pal?" He smiled down at her.

She nodded, feeling as if she were floating on a cloud; she never wanted to come down.

***

How can this even be real? She laughed to herself. Energy coursed through her; she could hardly stay still. Her face hurt from smiling so much. *People will look at me and think I'm on drugs.* She was, it was the drug called James.

His vibe satisfied her need for a fix. His eyes drew her in and sped up her heart rate. His touch melted her and mellowed her out. He was every wonderful feeling in one dose; it was overwhelming and wonderful, all at the same time.

They stopped at the corner café for coffees and a seat in the sun.

"What are you all smiles about?" James tilted his head sideways and grinned, revealing those beautiful dimples.

I might overdose. "I'm happy." Ashley took his hand.

"Yeah, you look it." He leaned his arms on the table, watching how the sunlight played with the color of her eyes.

"This is a perfect day with you."

"You're perfect."

Blushing, Ashley looked away. "Not me."

"Yes." He placed his other hand on top of hers and leaned across the table. "Come here."

Ashley leaned closer.

"Closer. I want to tell you something."

She leaned in farther, feeling his warm breath on her cheek. His lips brushed her skin. Ashley turned slightly, and their lips were so close. He teased her, being that close to her yet so still. She moved ever so slightly and kissed him.

James melted into her, feeling her warm breath now on him. "I love you, Ashley." He breathed deeply. "You are my dream come true."

Kissing him again, she felt light and warm and never wanted this to end. "I love you, James."

James looked out of the corner of his eye, sensing the people at the table next to them watching. He didn't care. He wanted the whole world to know.

Ashley followed his gaze, and her cheeks turned pink. "We're making quite a spectacle of ourselves." She sat back in her seat and laughed.

As James leaned back in his chair, he didn't take his eyes off her. "Yep. Isn't it great?"

"It is, actually." She raised her coffee to him.

"Cheers." He returned the gesture, smiling.

"To us." Ashley etched this moment in her heart. This perfect day with James. She relished knowing that from this day forward, she was always going to be this happy.

CHAPTER 54

A shley saw the open door to her apartment and had to smile. *He beat me here.*

James had been tied up with clients most of the day, and she didn't get to see him at the gym. She trusted him enough to give him a key. That was big. He texted her while she was at work that he'd come by her place if she was up for a late dinner. She anticipated James surprising her with dinner…and something more.

She rounded the staircase and heard music drifting down the hall. Not able to contain her excitement at seeing him, Ashley felt light on her feet and was a little breathless.

"James?" Ashley pushed the door open, remembering the last time he surprised her. They didn't even get to eat dinner until after they made it out of the bedroom. "James?" The lights were on; music was playing.

She smelled something that took her back to another place—familiar, but not to this space. As she heard footsteps coming down the hall, she smelled smoke, cigarette smoke. Ashley was stuck in a haze… footsteps coming closer…her name being called…but not by James. Not by the voice that melted her heart…but by the voice that froze the blood in her veins.

Dear God, no. She held back tears. *Stephen.*

She heard someone screaming, "No, no, no," and realized it was her own voice. Getting a jolt of adrenaline, she scrambled back down the hall toward the door.

Stephen was at her side in an instant, grabbing hold of her arm and slamming his hand against the door, destroying her chance of escape.

Ashley froze, not able to make herself look at him.

"That's no way to welcome me." Stephen lifted her face to meet his. "Honey, I'm ho-ome." His singsong voice masked the crazy she saw in his eyes. He looked different—his hair dark, the close beard, but those eyes, those crazy ice-blue eyes churned her stomach.

First, making sure the door was locked, Stephen led Ashley by the arm to the living room. "Surely, you're not surprised that I found you."

Eyes darting around, breathing rapid and shallow, Ashley's heart raced as she wondered, *How can I escape?*

"You did surprisingly good keeping me in the dark for a while"—he chuckled—"but not that good!" He pointed a finger at her as if he'd caught her in a childhood game of hide-and-seek.

Shit, think. How can I get away from him?

His grip tightened on her arm.

"Stephen, let go."

He led her to the oversized chair with the matching ottoman in her perfect little living room. "Have a seat, Ashley, and I'll tell you how this is going to go down," he growled.

Ashley felt her body tense. *I need to run; I need to get out of here.*

Stephen pushed her down on the ottoman. "Oh, Ash…" He leaned forward, looking at her intently.

Ashley inwardly cringed. *No way am I letting him see me sweat.*

"You've changed. Look at you. What are you doing?" Sighing, he shook his head. "I got here just in time. You thought you could keep up with this lifestyle?" His smile turned to disgust.

Ashley bit her tongue. *Nope, not giving in to his criticism. Make a plan.* She turned her gaze downward, a sign of submission. *Show him that you're weak; he will loosen that vise grip…then, you can run. But for now, do not fight back.*

"Ash, you see how wrong this is for you, right?" Stephen stooped to eye level with her, his voice quavering slightly. His fingers dug deeper into her arm. "You need to come home."

Those words made her stomach turn. There was no way in hell she would ever get back together with him. She flinched.

His grip tightened. His other hand trailed toward her throat, circling around, pressing harder. "We're going to be together, Ashley," he whispered.

She veered right.

He pushed her down on the ottoman, holding her by the throat. "You're still so stubborn." He gritted his teeth, his hand squeezing ever so slightly.

She froze, not able to breathe for a moment. Panic set in, and she began to thrash. Her control and reasoning were gone. She couldn't budge him or breathe. She couldn't hear the words he was saying; she could only see his evil grin. Ashley's vision was tunneling. She disconnected herself from what was happening. *This is the only way to survive; shut it all down. Stop fighting.*

Stephen's grip loosened on Ashley's throat a little, and she inhaled deeply to fill her lungs. She kept her body relaxed, which allowed her to regain rational thinking. *Wait. Wait for the right moment.*

Stephen shifted his weight; then Ashley shoved the palm of her hand up toward the bridge of his nose, missing and hitting his chin. It threw him off-center, and she kneed him in the stomach. When he bent over, she pushed him to the floor.

"You bitch!" Stephen shouted as he held his stomach.

Ashley scrambled off the ottoman and made a run for the door. Stephen reached around and nearly missed her, but was able to grab her ankle. She tripped, trying to avoid his grasp, and hit the corner of the wall, shoulder first. Pain shot through her bad shoulder, stunning her, but she quickly regained her balance and continued for the door.

Stephen was quick to his feet, determined not to let her escape. Ashley's hand reached for the door; she was almost there. She could yell in the hallway and get the attention of someone who could call the cops. Then, she remembered her phone in her pocket. She could call James; this would all be over soon.

James, she thought as her hand grasped the knob.

424

Ashley felt excruciating pain and a burning sensation on the back of her head. Then, everything faded to black.

***

Stephen knew getting her out of the apartment would be tricky. It was easy getting in. Those girls let him walk right into the building. *I need a story.* He could say she was ill, she passed out, and he was driving her to the emergency room. He could say she drank too much, or took too many pills—*she has that problem, you know…* He could be convincing.

But it was chancy, being seen and remembered. He checked his watch; it was after 8:00 p.m. He had waited around to make sure it was late enough to sneak out of there. However, he would have to carry her down all those stairs.

She couldn't live where there was a fucking elevator? he thought as he began to pace, glancing at Ashley lying on the floor. He hadn't intended to hit her that hard, but he needed to stop her. She was quick. *Bitch kneed me in the stomach, and now she messed up my plan.*

He stopped pacing and thought. He was still in control; he had the upper hand. He would carry her down a couple of flights, rest on the landing, especially if someone came in. He could feign that she was drunk, and he was resting before taking her down the rest of the stairs. Then, when the tenants passed, he could head down the next set of stairs.

If he ran into a nosy landlady, he would tell her he was taking her to a walk-in medical facility, but was keeping it hush-hush; he didn't want to embarrass her because of her alcohol problem… *Yes, this will work.*

He inhaled deeply, straightened himself, and then grabbed her cell phone and keys. "Time to get you out of here, Ashley."

***

Stephen carried her down most of the stairs without any problems; his adrenaline was on high. As he'd predicted, a nosy landlady asked him what he was doing, so he used the story he'd concocted. He impressed himself at how well he pulled off that story. His voice even shook when he hinted at her "problem."

Ms. Nosy bought it, even had a tear in her eye, the situation striking a chord with her. She said it brought back a memory of her former husband, God rest his soul, who'd battled with alcoholism. Secret was safe with her, and she would pray for poor Ashley. God bless him for looking out for her.

Stephen thanked her profusely and hurriedly ushered Ashley to his car, not another person in sight. *Man, I'm good.*

He breathed a sigh of relief as he started the car and pulled away from the curb. Stephen smiled and looked over at Ashley. "I can't wait to get our life put back together again."

***

Light pierced Ashley's eyes as a loud ringing echoed in her ears. A burning, searing pain radiated across the back of her head and down her arm, and extended into the rest of her body. Everything burned.

Ashley tried to move her hands and realized she could not. She tried blinking away the pain and focusing her eyes. There was humming in her head, bright light caused increased pain, and she was uncontrollably shaking. Her body seemed to tremble from deep within.

She couldn't get her bearings in this unfamiliar place. Her mind was slow to register sounds and sights. There was a murmur of voices and banging, but she wasn't sure what it was. *Maybe a radio or TV?*

Then, she saw she was bound and tied to a bed. Straining to break free and feeling the panic start to creep in, Ashley began to remember what happened. Stephen had knocked her out, and he must have taken her somewhere while she was passed out.

But where the hell am I?

"You won't break free, Ashley." His voice cut through the noise in her head like a steel blade, making her freeze. "I tied some rather good knots there. You'll rip your skin before you can make a dent in those." Stephen speaking like that was something he did all the time. "Ashley, I'm happy you're here. You will be, too, if you relax."

426

Ashley cringed, panic seizing her and filling her with dread. *How could I have let this happen?* She'd thought she was careful.

Stephen smiled.

She could see he was a complete psychopath. She needed to focus and get the hell out of there, wherever she was.

CHAPTER 55

*M*y chances were slim, but I couldn't let that stop me.
It was escape or death.
And I wasn't ready to die...

The pain was excruciating. How could she bear another moment? Ropes were searing into the skin at her wrists, where he'd tied her to the bed. Her skin was rubbed raw from her battle to break out of this prison. He'd also tied her ankles to the posts, but she'd kicked free; the skin on her ankles was raw and bloody from straining to get loose.

"Let me go..." Now, her voice was hoarse, but how many times had she yelled this to Stephen? *Why won't he let me go?*

"You are mine, Ashley. Forever," he whispered, his words echoing in her mind, making her shudder. "Give in, and do not fight it. This could be so easy, Ashley. You always make things much more difficult than necessary."

No, I'll never give in. I'll die fighting. She faded into a dream.

***

Pick up your goddamn cell, Ashley.

Brrrrring, brrrrring, brrrrring.

"Hi, it's me!"

James's heart soared. "Ash, thank God—"

"Leave a message after the tone, and I'll call ya back!"

His stomach dropped and tied back into knots. "Damn it!" Slamming the phone down, he covered his face with his hands. "This cannot be happening."

***

He'd texted Ashley after work, saying he was running late and asking her to call him if she still wanted him to come by. When he didn't hear from her, he'd worried. He went by her apartment and found she wasn't there, but her bags were on the floor. The ottoman was knocked over, and James saw drops of blood by the front door.

An awful sense of dread filled him. He texted Lisa. She hadn't heard from Ashley since earlier that afternoon. Panic began to set in.

He called his friend who was a detective with the Boston Police Department. Kevin said he would do whatever he could to help.

James returned to his apartment to wait.

***

In the morning, his phone started ringing; he grabbed it and saw it was Kevin. "Yeah."

"James, it's Kev; how you doing?"

"Not so good, what've you got for me, man?" James tapped the counter.

"I may have found a location. I tracked her phone and called in a favor. Not easy to get the exact address, but I got damn close. Looks like it's in Hyde Park. There's a complex with rows of shitty apartments."

"Got an address? I'll meet you there." James stood, pulling his jacket off the back of his chair.

"Yeah, I'll text it to you. Then, I'll bring back up."

James grabbed his gun, his gear, and flew out of his apartment.

***

The gag was burning Ashley's cheeks. *Fuck.* She needed to lie still and take some deep breaths; then, she could come up with a plan. *Planning is a good thing.*

She couldn't imagine what Stephen was up to, but she knew he had a keen ear and was probably listening in on her. He'd gagged her after she relentlessly yelled for him to let her go, each time raising her voice another level until she was screaming it. Her energy was waning after wasting it on trying to break out of the restraints, but she had to keep fighting the exhaustion that was tempting her to fall asleep.

Whistling.

She hated his whistling. Her stomach turned; that noise was going to drive her insane. She felt anxious and infuriated, yet she was fading fast. *So much for calm breathing. Concentrate…a plan…* She was losing her grip on reality. *Hold on. Hold on for James,* she told herself as she felt her eyes close. *I need to rest…only for a minute…*

***

James floored the gas and drove through the city as if he were in a car chase…until he hit traffic on Beacon Street.

"Goddamn city!" He pounded the steering wheel and made a quick decision to change routes.

As luck would have it, traffic was going the other way, and he sailed through and onto Arbor Way toward Hyde Park. He followed the directions from his GPS to River Street. Coming up on the apartments that Kevin thought Ashley's phone traced activity to, he slowed down, his senses on high alert.

James had his SIG SAUER locked in the center console. He prayed to God Ashley was okay as he fought back images in his head that he was not ready to face.

What if I'm too late? His stomach churned. "No. That cannot happen."

There were too many houses to consider, but he stuck with his hunch that this dirtbag was holed up in the rental apartments. Pulling into a parking spot, he looked around, surveying the building. It was relatively small, about a dozen or so apartments.

"Where are you, Ash?"

His phone buzzed—Kevin again. "Yeah."

"I'm rounding the corner to the apartments. You there?"

"Yeah, pulled in a spot on the side, across the street." James glanced in his rearview mirror.

"All right. I called for backup, but told them to wait three blocks up, then come in silent once we nail down the exact location."

"We need to ask one of these guys hanging around outside who they've seen coming and going. They know who's who."

"Right, see ya in a couple."

James sat for a minute. *This needs to go smoothly; there's no room for error.* He opened the center console and grabbed his SIG SAUER, exhaling a shaky breath as he looked up at the apartments.

"I'm coming for you, Ash."

***

The property was run-down; James doubted there was any type of surveillance. However, Kevin thought he should still check into it; sometimes the slummiest landlords still cared if someone was getting something over on them.

Kevin walked ahead as the official officer, but James was right behind him and ready for whatever came at them. There were three guys hanging around the steps leading up to the main door, but they knew right away Kevin was the police. They eyed James warily with looks that said they were wondering what his role was. Kevin and James kept walking. That didn't look like the group to be asking if they'd seen anything.

They pushed through the door. There was no security, and people were walking in and out of the entry of the apartment building. Kevin stopped a young man around twenty years old who was leaving. "Hey, did you see anyone unusual coming in yesterday, today?"

The guy eyed Kevin then looked at James. "Unusual?"

"Yeah, not the regulars." James blocked the door as Kevin put his hand on his belt, emphasizing the holster.

The guy dropped his gaze, then quickly returned it to Kevin. "Yeah, man. Couple of white people came in during the night. Girl looked to be in rough shape. Didn't look from around here." He was proud of this observation, again flicking his eyes to James.

"Where'd they go?" Kevin wanted to keep this guy focused.

Guy nodded down the hall behind him. "Down there. Last door. He bumped into me as I came out of my apartment. Shoved me into the wall. Asshole."

"What number?"

James's voice startled the guy, and he glanced toward him again. "He's in five. New guy. Seen him yesterday." He wiped the back of his hand across his nose, fidgeting.

"Go on." Kevin stood aside, and James held open the door as he hurriedly left.

"Let's go."

They approached apartment number 5 and stood outside. James felt a surge of panic. "What if it's not them? Then, what?"

Kevin shrugged. "It's our only lead. I'm going in. Ready?"

James nodded and stood back. Kevin drew his gun, stood with his back against the wall, nodded to James, then turned, and kicked the door in.

"Officers! Drop your weapons!"

There was no sign of anyone. Kevin moved into the run-down apartment with his back against the wall, and James followed with his gun drawn.

Kevin approached the main room and drew up short. "Stephen Keene? Drop your weapon! Move away from her, Stephen." He aimed his gun at Stephen.

James slowly rounded the corner, gun drawn and ready to shoot if he had to. *So much for backup.* James tried to keep his focus on Stephen, but his eyes drifted to Ashley. She was visibly beaten and unconscious. Seeing her lying there—tied to a bed, bloody, and lifeless—shook him. *Stay dialed in; do not show him your weakness.*

Then, James saw the flash of metal. A steel blade was pressed against Ashley's throat. *No wonder Kevin hasn't blown this asshole away.* One wrong move, he would thrust that blade through Ashley's jugular.

James felt his knees go weak, his stomach clench, and tunnel vision set in. *Breathe.* Stephen stood on Ashley's left side, pressing the knife blade close to her lifeline, alert to every move James or Kevin made.

I'm completely helpless, even though I hold the gun aimed at his heart. James knew if he made one move, she would be dead. He thought, *If he makes one wrong move, I'll blow his head off.*

Stephen glanced at James for a moment. "Ah, it's the boyfriend. So nice of you to show. Ashley said you'd come." Stephen gave an evil laugh. "You here to finish me off? Going to be her knight in shining armor, are you?"

Those eyes, he has such crazy eyes.

Stephen spoke intellectually, which surprised James, even though he'd never thought that Ashley's ex was an idiot. Stephen's actions were so erratic that, after hearing him speak, James realized Stephen was completely insane. He didn't care about consequences. He did whatever he wanted. And that scared James more than anything.

James's insides shook. He wanted to fall on the ground and give his life for Ashley's freedom.

"Now, my question is, would you do this for all those gym girls you fuck? Or is this show just for Ashley?" He grinned, not breaking eye contact with James.

Hearing him say her name gave James the strength he needed. He wanted to pull that damn trigger.

"You must think she's quite something. I wonder, does she care for you at all? Ya know, she's probably screwing every other guy from that gym. She needs attention. Ya know, Ashley used to do whatever I wanted." He tilted his head, looking James up and down. "I wonder if she does all those things for you?"

James felt his palms sweat and a slight tremor in his hands. He needed to keep his shit together. This guy could smell fear and anger, so James needed to be cool.

"Shut up, asshole," Kevin called out to Stephen while keeping his gun homed in on him. "James, don't let him rattle you. You know he's all talk." Kevin glanced at James briefly, then back at Stephen. "Keep that shit-talking up, and you may seal your fate with these two guns aimed at you."

James's voice was clear when he spoke. "It's over Stephen." *Two can play this game,* he thought. "This is over." His stare bored through Stephen.

Stephen didn't waver. "You're right." He sighed and looked lovingly at Ashley while the blade pressed against her throat. He stared back at James. "It *is* over."

"Move away from her, Stephen. Drop the knife." Kevin clenched his jaw.

Stephen stood perfectly still, his eyes locked on James. "If it's over for me, then it's definitely over for you." In an instant, Stephen slashed the knife down Ashley's forearm before James could run to her fast enough.

Kevin opened fire and shot Stephen in the chest, taking him down.

At that exact moment, James fired his gun, hitting Stephen in the left shoulder. James rushed toward Ashley, blind with fear as blood spilled from the vein Stephen slashed. Blood covered her arm and dripped to the floor.

James ripped part of the sheet that was on the bed and made a tourniquet, swiftly wrapping the wound. Kevin applied pressure as James tried to revive Ashley.

"Ash, wake up! Come on; we are gonna get you fixed up." James could hear sirens approaching and felt his knees giving way under him. *No, Ash is going to be fine.* He couldn't let his mind wander to the dark places. *She will make it.*

The police burst through the doors, and the EMTs followed close behind. Assessing the scene, Kevin shouted orders, and they moved in to work on Ashley.

"Sir, please step aside so we can get in there."

James was frozen at Ashley's side, not wanting to break contact.

"Frankie, it's all right. James can stay with her." Kevin moved in by James, partly to show that he was okay to stay with Ashley, and partly to keep James from getting anywhere near Stephen.

Frankie checked Ashley's vitals. Kevin put his arm around James's shoulder to assist him to the other side of Ashley so the EMTs could do their work. Frankie began applying a clean wrap over Ashley's wrist to stop the bleeding, while Jay, another EMT, checked her vitals.

"Weak pulse." He put an oxygen mask on Ashley and checked her eyes.

"She's losing a lot of blood. We need extra pressure on this." Jay moved over to assist Frankie. "We need to move her." Frankie looked at Jay knowingly. Time was crucial; they needed it to be on their side.

Stephen's body was on the floor behind them. Kevin needed James to keep his focus on Ashley, and not get sidetracked and home in on Stephen. Kevin nodded to the other EMT that there was another body behind him. "Ted, got a gunshot victim over here."

Ted circled around Kevin and kneeled to work on Stephen.

James had his hand on Ashley's shoulder. He looked at Kevin when he heard they were preparing to move Ashley. "I need to go with her."

Kevin knew James could not go in the ambulance with her, and Kevin had to stay on the scene. "Kyle, take James to Boston Medical, all right? The ambulance should be heading out soon."

Kyle nodded. "Yes, sir." He nodded to James. "We'll follow them to the ER."

James tried to focus on what the EMTs were saying, catching pieces of information about Ashley. Things were moving slowly around him. Blood was all over the place—Ashley's blood—and it was all over him. His hands began to shake uncontrollably.

Her arm was bandaged and clean, her face was banged up, but she looked at peace. Then, things sped back up, jerking him back to reality. The noise of the room flooded his ears, and the light stung his eyes. The EMTs moved her to the gurney and carefully carried her out.

James was close behind. *Stay with me, Ashley.*

***

Kyle took full advantage of having the job of getting James to the hospital as fast as possible. Sirens blaring and lights flashing, Kyle expertly maneuvered the police car at high speeds through the crowded Boston streets, getting them to Boston Medical in record time. The EMTs had arrived moments before, whisking Ashley into the ER as James and Kyle pulled in right behind them.

Kyle hopped out of the vehicle with James. "I'll get ya through, no problem. Follow me."

If James had been in the mood, he would have asked this kid where he came from and complimented his straightforward, take-no-shit attitude.

However, James's focus was on one thing only—Ashley.

***

The darkness envelops me. Where am I? Darkness, quiet, nothing…sinking deeper into the abyss. Wanting to cry out, but no strength to find my voice. Spinning away from any source of life and into oblivion.

Seeing his smile, hearing his voice…

"Ashley." His strong hands pull her near; his lips trail down her neck. Warmth, light, and happiness call her back. She tried to tell him she couldn't remember where she was…but he didn't hear her. It must have been a bad dream.

He continued smiling, his breath warm on her body. "Come back, Ashley."

Then, he was gone.

***

Everything was beeping.

"Damn it, Ashley. Pull through this. Don't freaking die on me."

"Mr. Anson, you need to move aside. We need to get in there. She's losing a lot of blood."

James moved to the side as the doctors and the PAs converged. The beeps grew louder, and more alarms started to sound.

"What's happening?" James tried to move closer, but nurses and doctors crowded the area.

"Put pressure on this. She needs clean bandages." They carefully unwrapped the dressing, switching out the bloodied pads.

"Whoa. She's bleeding out."

"Ashley." He was helpless. James wanted desperately to save her, but there was nothing he could do.

Kyle stayed by James's side, trying to hold him back, but knowing he wouldn't be able to stop the guy if he decided to force his way through to Ashley.

"Stand back; we're stabilizing her." They worked quickly to administer clean pads, wrap the wound, and apply pressure to control the bleeding. Once the bandages were on, they elevated her arm.

"Get her in a room."

The nurse escorted James aside as they rushed Ashley to the ER for surgery.

Kyle stood guard by the door.

"Wait out here, Mr. Anson. She'll be all right. I'll be back to let you know."

Nurses and doctors hurried by, caring for patients or running to the next emergency.

James was left alone in the hall. He stood in his own hell…waiting for that ER door to reopen…not sure what he was going to hear when it did.

CHAPTER 56

James held Ashley's cold hand. *Live, Ashley, live. You have so much life left.*

Lying in that cold metal hospital-room bed, looking pale, and hooked up to IVs, tubes, and machines, Ashley didn't look as if she had much life left in her.

Lisa had come to the hospital and waited with James. She couldn't bear the thought of losing her friend. Once she heard Ashley was stable, Lisa left. James promised he would text her when Ashley woke up.

The hospital room, sparse but functional, had a TV mounted from the ceiling across from her bed. Giving a view of the world below, a window was on the wall to the left of the bed. In the corner were two chairs, frayed from wear and tear. James wasn't going anywhere, so he made himself as comfortable as possible in the chair he dragged across the room and sat next to Ashley's bed. Holding her uninjured hand, he sat quietly.

Doctors were able to stabilize Ashley, but she'd lost a lot of blood. After she bled through the first set of sutures, the doctors stitched her left arm a second time. Her arm was secured to the rail of the bed, for fear she would thrash and tear open the stitches. The doctors spoke of nerve damage as she lay unaware, peacefully sedated.

James had brushed her hair away from her face and tied it in an elastic the way she liked to wear it at the gym. *The gym.* He thought of her quick hands and her powerful punches in the ring. The specialist said she would have residual weakness and tremors in that hand because the nerves had been severed.

Things can be taken away in the blink of an eye, James thought.

After the doctors left the room, he leaned his head down and kissed her right hand, praying for Ashley to come back to him. Closing his eyes, flashes of memories replayed in his mind—holding each other in the candlelight…the first time they kissed…training with Ashley…the first time he saw her… He smiled while recalling the look on her face when she stepped into the ring for the first time.

Please, come back to me, James prayed, repeating "The Lord's Prayer" and saying any other prayer he could recall. Finally, exhausted, he drifted off to sleep, dreaming of her face.

***

The nurses and doctors walked in, disturbing James's slumber, and asked him to leave the room while they checked Ashley's vitals. He paced outside her door and talked with the officer stationed outside her room.

After what felt like forever, the doctor and one of the nurses came out. "She is awake, but weak. We gave her medicine for the pain and to help her stay calm. She may ask about what happened, but we are hoping to limit the information we give her at this time." The doctor looked at James pointedly. "You may go in, but, know, if she shows signs of distress, you will be asked to leave."

James knew better than to get into it with the doctor if he wanted to keep the privilege of seeing Ashley while she was under strict watch. "I understand. Thank you."

He opened the door slowly as a nurse was adjusting the IV for the pain medicine. She nodded and told him to press the Nurse button if Ashley or he needed anything.

"Thank you." James pulled a chair up next to Ashley and took hold of her hand. "Ashley, how are you feeling?" He kissed her forehead.

Her voice was barely a whisper—and James had to lean in to hear her—as she said, "I'm okay. Tired." Her eyes were heavy, and she tried for a smile.

"Rest. I'm not going anywhere."

He could see her mind working through the haze of pain meds and exhaustion. "James, how…" She swallowed hard and seemed to be mustering all the energy she had just to speak.

"Ash, don't…" He covered her other hand with his.

"James, I stayed alive for you," she whispered.

His heart melted and ached at the same time. He wasn't there for the trauma, he almost didn't make it in time to save her, yet she had held out hope for him, having faith that he would be there to save her.

"Thank God you did, kid. I couldn't picture it going any other way." James was losing his voice and getting choked up, but he knew he had to say what he had been holding in for so long. "Ashley, I love you. It has always been you…since the first day I saw you."

Tears filled her eyes. The painkillers started taking effect, and Ashley's eyes were getting heavy. But in her haze, she thought, *There is no way I'm losing this moment.*

James held her unbandaged hand with both of his as he spoke, "The minute I saw you after Debra begged me to train you, I knew." He shook his head and a small laugh escaped. "Even though I wanted to run far away from you, you drew me in."

Ashley managed a small smile as she fought to remember that first day, the first time she saw James's face. She remembered she was scared out of her mind the first time she worked with him. He had looked as if he would rather be a hundred other places, but he'd stayed, and that's when it all began. She smiled and closed her eyes.

"It's okay. Rest now. I'll be here when you wake up." He held on to her hand.

She was fighting hard to stay present, not wanting to miss a moment with him, scared of what she couldn't remember and of what would happen if she fell asleep.

James felt her anxiety. "Don't worry. I promise. I'm not going anywhere." Giving her hand a gentle squeeze, he closed his eyes and lifted it to his lips as he pressed a kiss on top of her hand. When he looked back at her, she was asleep. Relieved she didn't start asking questions about what happened, why she was in the hospital, or what happened to Stephen, James glanced at her bandaged arm and shivered at the memory.

The doctors were able to give her enough blood to stabilize her. She was extremely weak and would need more blood and plenty of rest. She was going to be in the hospital for a while, and so was James. He settled back in his chair and watched her sleep. James's heart rate finally slowed, and he realized again just how exhausted he was.

***

"James."

James heard Ashley calling him, but he didn't know where she was. He was at the end of a hallway, the sunlight shining through the windows and a breeze blowing the curtains. They were at the beach cottage.

James walked toward the bedroom, smiling, knowing she was waiting for him in that huge bed.

"James," she called again in a teasing way.

He tried to hurry to get to her. The hallway twisted and turned. Then, suddenly, it became a dark, rat-infested apartment building in Boston. He could hear his name floating on the air as if she were right next to him, but he couldn't find her.

James started to panic, his heart racing. He ran down the dark hall toward an open door, which he knew was Stephen's apartment. His stomach filled with dread, and he suddenly didn't want to see what was waiting inside. But he knew he had to get to Ashley, no matter what he found.

"James," she called louder.

He felt himself run around the corner and into a room as if on rails, with no way of stopping. He tried to force his legs to turn away and run in the opposite direction, but they became as heavy as lead. Entering the dark room, he heard an evil laugh, and a voice called out, "Perfect timing."

Looking down, James saw Ashley's pale, lifeless body lying in a dark pool of blood on the floor, and Stephen was standing over her with a bloody knife hanging from his hand and a sick, evil grin on his face.

***

James jolted awake, covered in sweat, to find himself sitting in the chair at the hospital, next to Ashley's bed. The room was still and quiet, except for the monitor's steady beeps and, now, his thudding heartbeat. He leaned over to hold Ashley's uninjured hand, thankful those horrible images were only a dream.

James bowed his head and took a ragged breath. He needed a walk. Standing and stretching his aching back, he realized he had been in the room for twelve hours straight without a break. Going for a walk and getting a coffee would be ideal, but James didn't want to leave and miss the chance of her waking up.

"James," Ashley breathed in her sleep.

James froze in his tracks and turned to look at her, not believing she'd spoken his name exactly as he'd heard it in his dream. He must have heard her when he was stuck in his nightmare.

He walked back to her side and touched her face. "I'm here."

She didn't move. She lay sleeping, still and peaceful.

If he left, his fear was she would wake up scared and wanting answers. James wanted to be there to give them to her. He decided to talk with the nurse who was always giving him the eye and extra attention. She was working at the nurses' station when he left Ashley's room.

"Hi"—he glanced quickly at her name tag to recall her name—"Sue."

Her face lit up. "Hi, James. You hanging in there? Is there anything you need?" She stood up from her station.

"I'm going for a quick walk and a coffee. Would you be able to contact me if she wakes up?" James leaned on the counter.

"Sure thing." She smiled, leaning in toward him, looking happy that she could help him out.

"Thank you." James walked to the elevators and went down to the cafeteria.

He had to smile to himself, knowing that Ashley was thinking of him while she slept. He couldn't wait to tell her that he knew she had been dreaming about him while she was in her deepest sleep, that she'd been calling his name.

***

"No! Stephen, no!!" Ashley was thrashing in her bed as she jolted awake screaming.

The beeps of the monitors screeched, and nurses surrounded her. "Ashley, you are safe. No one else is here but us."

One nurse held on to her arm and side to make sure she did not start swinging at anyone or pull out any wires or tubes that she was connected to. The other nurse injected the IV with a sedative to calm her down.

Confused, Ashley was breathing heavily, trying to sit up, and looking around the room. "Where... What happened? Where is James?"

The head nurse on Ashley's case, Beverly, was a larger black woman. Bev was holding Ashley's shoulder lightly with one hand and covering her injured hand with the other. "It's all okay, Ashley. We're here, and James will be right back. You rest now."

Ashley felt she could trust this nurse, that she was telling the truth. Her voice was calming, and she had warm, friendly eyes. As her lids got heavy, Ashley lay back down and closed her eyes.

"Rest, baby girl." Bev only had to wait a moment before Ashley was out.

***

Feeling refreshed from getting a coffee and fresh air, James rounded the corner, heading back to Ashley's room. He heard raised voices and saw a nurse run into a room, Ashley's room.

"Damn it!" James ran down the hall and was blocked by a nurse, a doctor, and the officer they had posted at her door.

"Everything is okay. She woke up startled, and we are trying to calm her." The doctor entered the room.

The guard held his arm out, keeping James back.

"Let me in to see her. I can calm her down." James started toward the door.

"Sir, you need to wait outside." The unfriendly nurse put her hand on the door, blocking his way.

The doctor exited Ashley's room and spoke to James. "We need her to settle quickly. She suffered a great trauma to her system, and she cannot have further stress right now. We sedated her so she can sleep."

James winced at that. He hated this was happening to her. Kicking himself for leaving her side, he felt helpless.

The doctor and the nurse turned and entered her room, shutting the door.

The friendly nurse, Sue, approached James. "I'm so sorry I didn't get in touch with you. It all happened so fast, and then you were here already. You can go back in after she's stable." She reassured James that Ashley would be all right and told him to let her know if he needed anything. She stressed the "anything" part.

James sighed and wandered to sit in a quiet part of the waiting area. He put his head back against the wall, closing his eyes. Patience was not one of his best traits, but he would wait. And then, he would never leave her side again.

***

"I don't have much feeling in this hand." Ashley moved her fingers slowly. "I feel tingling and numbness." She looked at James with glistening eyes. "Does that make sense? That I feel the numbness?"

"It does." James reached for her hand, gently placing his on top of it.

"I can feel that." She closed her eyes and smiled; a stray tear rolled down her cheek.

"Hey, it's okay." He wrapped his arms around her as she shook with terror. "It's over now."

444

"No, it's not," she whispered, her voice barely audible. "It will never be over. I must start over; I will lose everything. I almost lost you." She choked up.

"No, you can't lose me. We are together, and nothing can get in the way now."

He could see the way her mind was working, calculating how and where she would run next to start a new life. James weighed his words, remembering the warning from the doctor, but not caring. She remembered details, but she was passed out during the takedown.

"He's gone, Ash."

She blinked, but her haunted eyes still focused on him. "What? Where did he...?"

"No, I mean...Stephen...he's dead."

Her body froze; then her shoulders dropped as she looked at him in disbelief. "What?" Her voice was barely audible.

"I wasn't supposed to tell you yet. The doctors wanted to limit your stress, but you looked so upset. You don't have to run anymore." James held her hand and held his breath. He thought he would surely get kicked out of here for this if she started freaking out.

Staring at James, Ashley leaned her head back on the pillow. Tears filled her eyes, and she looked as if the weight of the world had been lifted from her. "Oh my God." She swallowed hard. "Thank God. I'm free."

CHAPTER 57

The modest cape house overlooked a small private beach and the ocean in a small town tucked away in the North Shore of Boston. There was a private sandy path that led to the shore from the house. Wide spans of grassy dunes separated the house from the beach. The waves' energy constantly changed, alternating between calm waters and wild waves that sculpted into crested shapes and crashed onto the rocky ledges.

Ashley rolled over, reaching across the empty space in their bed. Stretching and smiling to herself, she guessed James was standing down by the water with his coffee. Just as she found him that first morning at his client's beach cottage. *This house—a little smaller in scale from the Marblehead house…well, a lot smaller…but no matter—this is our little paradise,* Ashley reflected.

Slowly, she rolled out of bed and stood, making her way over to the window. She peeked down to see James standing in the golden sunlight, facing the ocean, just as she'd pictured him. Placing her hand on the glass, she felt the heat from the sun and the heat from their connection.

She remembered, not too long ago, feeling so scared, afraid to experience all the intense emotions she felt with James. But now he was a part of her. There was no question or fear.

Freedom and peace.

James turned and glanced up to the window, smiling from his eyes, as if he had known she was standing there watching him.

She laughed to herself. *He always catches me watching him.*

Nodding toward the beach, he waved Ashley down.

She gave a thumbs-up then quickly brushed her teeth, pulled on jeans and a sweater, and made her way down to the kitchen.

The open-air kitchen let in the glorious rays of sunlight in the mornings, the warmth of the sun comforting the entire area, whether the weather was chilly or warm. Her mug was set on the counter. She filled it with coffee and walked toward the sliders and out to the beach path to meet James.

Walking down the path and feeling the warm sand under her feet was surreal. Ashley felt a sense of déjà vu, reminding her of their moments at his client's beach cottage, which seemed like a lifetime ago. *So much has happened since then.*

Warmth spread through her. They'd come full circle. She found James, he found her, they'd gone through so much already in their short time together, and it had made them stronger. Nothing could break their bond, their love. It sounded like an old, corny cliché of a love story; living through it had been anything but. So much had been stacked against them, but they'd endured.

It wasn't an insane love or an obsessive love. No one abused their power. It was a love neither wanted to live without. It was pure, happy, and could stand up to any test.

She smiled as she approached James. He was throwing a stick to Charlie, their chocolate Lab, as he ran like crazy to fetch it.

James turned and encircled Ashley in his arms. "Morning."

She leaned into him, inhaling deeply, capturing the faint scent of his cologne mixed with his own essence. "Morning. I missed you up there." She leaned back to catch a glimpse of his smile.

"I didn't have the heart to disturb you. You were in such a deep sleep." He brushed her hair away from her eyes. "Although, I tried nudging you a few times." He smiled deviously. "We could head back up there." He caught her smiling up at him.

Charlie came racing back with the stick in his mouth and dropped it at their feet.

"Hey, Charlie." Ashley petted him as he panted at her side. She handed her mug to James, threw the stick with her right hand, and off he went.

James handed her coffee back, searching her expression. "Are you happy?"

Ashley nodded, her smile broadening. "Yes. Beyond words." She pulled him closer. "You?"

"Absolutely." The sun danced in the tiny specks of color in his eyes. He held her hand and kissed her.

Then, they both looked down at her left hand, smiling and ignoring the slight tremor. Leaning their foreheads together, James touched her ring finger. The diamond shone and sparkled, catching the sunlight and refracting it into hundreds of glittering reflections against their skin. Reflecting all the moments, the crossroads, the bumps, and the detours that led them to this point.

Everything came full circle. They were destined to be together. They were now bound by fate, by their promises to each other, and by this ring. A ring without end.

Not The End—
The Beginning…

ACKNOWLEDGMENTS

T hank you to my husband, Vaughan, for being an unending source of encouragement, strength, and love. Thank you to my three children for always giving me hope. Thank you to God for showing me light in the darkest times. Thank you to my family and friends for their encouragement on my writing journey. Thank you to Lisa Umina at Halo Publishing and her editing staff for bringing this book to life.

Thank you to Michael Golden for introducing me to Muay Thai kickboxing and teaching me how to become strong again. Thank you to Kyoshi Darin Reisler and everyone I've met through Plus One Defense Systems for their knowledge, respect, and friendship. Thank you to Elias Morales, Shane Tidrick and Jonathan Colon for the inside look at a fighter's life. Thank you to Kendra Tidrick for her cover design, artwork, and friendship. Thank you to Joanne and Maria for your valuable input.

I'm grateful for the positive role models in my life, and for those who were not. You taught me how to be resilient.

Other books by Gina Marecki

Fifty Scattered Pieces

Transformation 2020

GINA MARECKI

Gina Marecki helps people grow and transform themselves both with her personal-training business and as an author whose stories are often about overcoming trauma. As owner of G Fitness, she conducts private and group sessions, focusing on women's fitness and on using past experiences to help both women and men feel empowered.

Gina conquered her battle with depression, anxiety, and haunting triggers as a result of childhood sexual abuse and young-adult domestic abuse. She found healing through exercise. This motivated her to become a personal trainer, earning her NASM certified personal trainer certification and continuing her education in how movement heals the body and mind, eventually adding high intensity training, weight lifting, and Muay Thai kickboxing to her arsenal. Gina also found healing through writing. She shares her journey from victim to victor through her poetry and real-life stories.

Gina earned her bachelor's degree in business at Boston College and lived in Boston for several years, working at John Hancock in marketing as an event planner. There she met her husband, Vaughan, and moved to Connecticut to raise a family. Gina loves fitness, writing, cooking, painting, and spending time with her family. Gina is a wife, a mother of three grown children, and has two cats.

CPSIA information can be obtained
at www.ICGtesting.com
Printed in the USA
BVHW051300220821
614415BV00003B/6